PASSION'S FLOURISH

Sorrel heard Mathew's approaching gait, and with each footfall her heart beat more erratically. She felt his blue eyes upon her, and her breathing came in short, tiny gasps.

Taking her small, delicate hand into his larger one, Mathew forced Sorrel's gaze upward. For a moment he felt a driving desire to grab her from the chair and to grasp her in his arms until he could force a confession from those tempting, teasing lips. But this was not the way to win her. He would have to be careful, gentle, and coaxing. Slowly, he tried to say the words that would lead him to the truth. "I cannot be away from you, and I cannot stay here alone with you." Mathew's words were torn from him as he took the small lovely beauty in his arms. Sorrel's eyes rose, and she found herself clinging to his strong, sturdy frame—until, at last, his lips descended upon hers. . . .

HISTORICAL ROMANCE AT ITS BEST!

by KATHLEEN DRYMON

TEXAS BLOSSOM (1305, $3.75)
When Sorrel's luscious curves silhouetted the firelight, Mathew felt lust and desire like he never felt before. Soon, he was enmeshed in her silvery web of love—their passion flowering like a wild TEXAS BLOSSOM!

WILD DESIRES (1103, $3.50)
The tempestuous saga of three generations of women, set in the back streets of London, glamorous New Orleans and the sultry tropics—where each finds passion in a stranger's arms!

TENDER PASSIONS (1032, $3.50)
While countless men professed their adoration for Katherine, she tossed her head in rejection. But when she's pirated away by a man whose object is lust, she finds herself willing!

by CAROL FINCH

RAPTURE'S DREAM (1037, $3.50)
By day Gabrielle is the insufferable waif who tests Dane Hampton's patience; by night she is the phantom lover who brings him to the heights of ecstasy!

ENDLESS PASSION (1155, $3.50)
Brianna was a sensuous temptress who longed for the fires of everlasting love. But Seth Donovan's heart was as cold as ice . . . until her lips burned his with the flames of desire!

DAWN'S DESIRE (1340, $3.50)
Kathryn never dreamed that the tall handsome stranger was wise to her trickery and would steal her innocence—and her heart. And when he captured her lips in one long, luscious kiss, he knew he'd make her his forever . . . in the light of DAWN'S DESIRE.

Available wherever paperbacks are sold, or order direct from the Publisher. Send cover price plus 50¢ per copy for mailing and handling to Zebra Books, 475 Park Avenue South, New York, N.Y. 10016. DO NOT SEND CASH.

Texas Blossom

BY
KATHLEEN DRYMON

ZEBRA BOOKS
KENSINGTON PUBLISHING CORP.

ZEBRA BOOKS

are published by

KENSINGTON PUBLISHING CORP.
475 Park Avenue South
New York, N.Y. 10016

Copyright © 1984 by Kathleen Drymon

All rights reserved. No part of this book may be reproduced in any form or by any means without the prior written consent of the Publisher, excepting brief quotes used in reviews.

First printing: January 1984

Printed in the United States of America

With my deepest love to Rodger and Judy Meadows. Though you are miles away, you are ever in my heart.

Prologue

Texas, 1746

A huge, burning orange sun was setting to the west, dropping lower and lower behind the long, flat-roofed house. On the outside the house seemed complacent and at peace. The bunkhouse off to the right was all quiet, the corral, a little distance off and full of horses, was also still. But a bit further on, a small, bent-over figure huddled over the wooden fence that enclosed the large animals.

"Hush now, my beauties," the bearded figure soothed and whispered to the horses. "It can't be much longer now."

A large tan stallion nuzzled the man nervously, as though trying to convey a message of some sort. And then, as though the beast had sensed something that had escaped the man, a chilling and resounding scream came from the main house and echoed amidst the surrounding grounds and buildings.

The horses quivered and whinnied as though the sound was cruelly affecting them in some way. The man himself seemed to shrink as he sat there on the rail. The sounds coming from the big house were sounds of pain, and sounds that had been filling the air since the day before. He wondered for a fleeting minute how much a body could take before giving in.

The horrible scream from the big house came from a room in which a roaring fire was burning hotly upon the hearth and the heavy drapes were closed, making the room an inferno on this summer afternoon. In the middle of the room stood a large bed, and in the folds of the deep, soft coverlet lay, panting from her latest pains, a small, blond woman whose features, though beautiful and fragile, were now drawn and pale.

In the corner of the room sat a small woman, who crossed herself before standing and going to the woman lying on the overlarge four-poster bed. She wiped the beads of sweat from her brow. Knowing the room had to be shut up and a fire roaring so as to keep out germs, she put the thought of heat from her mind. With tender hands she took a cloth from the bowl of water sitting on a small table and wrung the water from it. She laid it upon the head of the young woman who lay writhing upon the bed. She had been doing this continually since the day before.

"It is time once more to try, Mrs. Morgan. Bear down with all your strength. Do not give up now. Push!" The elder woman stood over the younger one, her dark brown eyes filled with worry for the woman moaning and panting with her pain.

This was now the second evening and still the babe had not made its way out of its mother's womb. Once again the older woman crossed herself and silently she mumbled a prayer to the Lord above to help the woman on the bed.

As the young woman fell back and stilled from sheer exhaustion, the older woman patted her hand lightly and tried to soothe her as best she could.

If something did not happen soon to help the woman and the babe, the midwife knew that there would be no hope. She had been helping to deliver children ever since she herself had reached her womanhood and she had seen this same thing happen before. For some reason the babe seemed to refuse to be born, and all she could do was what she had done in the past, which was to watch helplessly as the woman weakened from the loss of blood, and then as the woman and the babe within her would pass from this life and go on to another.

For a second, a slight shudder went through the elder woman, and fear for herself at the prospect of this woman's death touched her. She had been most anxious to help with the birthing of this babe. The owner of this ranch was quite wealthy, and she had anticipated a large, fat purse for her efforts on behalf of his wife. She was in dire need of a new coat for the coming winter, but now, as she looked down at the pale, beautiful face which for the moment was still of all movement, she saw her new coat vanish from her future, and she wondered what would be her fate after this woman's death.

Her husband had come into the room several times now since yesterday morning. He would enter the room silently and go to his wife's side. Not uttering a word, he would reach down and take her hand and watch her in her pain. Then, as silently, and as though he could not bear to watch any longer, he would leave, with never a word for his wife or the woman who tended her. But there was something in his ice-blue eyes that told the midwife that the man cared a great deal about the outcome of the events unfolding in this room.

Once more a long, drawn-out scream filled the room, bringing the woman at once back to her duties. "There love, there," she tried soothing the woman, but this time nothing could stop her writhing and gasping with her racking pain.

The midwife herself gasped as she saw that at last the birth was to take place. Quickly she murmured a prayer of thanks and reached down to help the young woman.

Time passed slowly for the occupants of the room, as, in between pains and screams from her torture, the woman upon the bed bore her child. The midwife smiled grimly as she took the tiny infant from its mother's body. With barely a thought for the child other than to make sure that it was breathing, she placed it in a basket set up near the bed. Then she quickly turned back to the woman. She knew that she would have to work fast if she were to have a chance of saving her, and silently and quickly she tried to stop the flow of blood coming from her body. After seeing the vast flow of the blood she quickly began to pack the woman with cloth that she had been soaking in medicinal herbs, which she prayed would cause a clot to form that would eventually stop the flowing redness.

But her prayers were not to be answered, for though she did all that she knew how, still a trickling stream of the woman's life substance flowed from her body.

Heavily the midwife sighed, and, looking down once more at the lovely woman upon the spotless sheets, she slowly walked to the door and opened it. The woman's husband was pacing back and forth outside in the hallway awaiting word.

As the large man saw the midwife open his wife's bedchamber door he stilled. From the look upon her aging face he knew that all had not gone as it should have. Quickly, brushing past the woman, he went to his wife's side and lowered his frame into the chair next to the bed. He saw the slight rise and fall of her chest and knew that she still might have a chance. As her light green eyes opened a lone tear slipped down his cheek.

"Do not be sad Graylin," her soft, velvety words came to him. "We have made a child from our love."

He had not noticed a child as he came into the room—his thoughts had been too busy upon his wife—but now he looked up and saw the midwife tending to a tiny form in the basket. "Aye, my love, you have done fine." His words came out from the depths of his soul.

"Nay, Graylin, I know that I have only a small time left to me. But you shall have our babe." A soft sigh came from her pale lips, but now that the birth was finished she seemed not to bear any pain.

"You are wrong Leona, you shall not leave me."

The young woman smiled at her husband and tenderly traced her small hand across his worn, hard features. "Bring the babe to me this one time."

Graylin looked to the midwife who had heard every word. As the tiny bundle was placed next to its mother's side the older woman whispered, "'Tis a girl child."

Leona smiled into her husband's blue eyes. "She is beautiful." And for a moment her thoughts were of more than the pain she had just borne. She would not be here to watch her daughter grow into a young woman, she would not be there for support and to help her make the right decisions. She had hoped that she would give birth to a girl, but she had also thought that she would be there to care for her, and now the thought struck her that it would have been better if the child had been a son; then Graylin would have been able to raise him and the child would become a man like her husband. She would know her daughter's future before she left this life, she thought to herself as she looked down at the tiny features surrounded by the blanket.

Graylin Morgan knew none of what his wife was thinking. His own mind was full of what was going to happen to him after she was taken from him. How could he go on without her at his side? They had planned so much, his hopes had been so high for himself and his Leona. Now what was he going to do?

"Graylin, what will happen to the child?" Her words caught him unaware.

"What do you mean, love?" he questioned, not being able to admit aloud that he would be left in this world with nothing of her but this small bundle lying next to her.

"I would know, Graylin." Her soft voice was weaker now, and her husband could see that she was pushing herself into asking these questions.

"The child is a girl. I imagine that she will grow up here on the ranch, and when she is of an age she will marry well. Perhaps an arrangement could be made with the Sumters; their son Clifford is a boy of twelve now, and if the two married, our ranches one day would be joined." His words were said absently, with barely any real thought of what he would actually do when left with a daughter to raise by himself.

Leona Morgan heard his words and a cold chill coursed over her body. She herself had been raised in the way he described. She had been betrothed to this man Graylin Morgan at a young age by their two families, and as soon as she was of a proper age her mother had married her off. Leona thanked her lucky fortune that the man she had married was this strong, loving man, for she had known many other girls who had not been so lucky, girls who had been trusted into a loveless marriage, and who were little more than slaves to the men they had married.

"Nay, Graylin." Her words came out in a strong gasp. "You must not do our daughter in this manner."

Her husband looked to her as though not understanding. Things were always done in this way, parents took care of their daughters' futures.

"I would wish for our child to have more than I. Perhaps she could go to some school and learn things that most women have not been given the opportunity to learn. I would also wish for her not to be forced into an early marriage." At his look of wonder she went on. "Ah, Graylin, I know what you are thinking, that I was made to marry at an early age.

But our marriage was different than most. You and I have something special, something that often takes people all their lives to find, and even then most do not ever know the kind of happiness that we have known. I only wish that our daughter be given more time than usual, and the chance to find for herself the love that I found with you."

Graylin's eyes once more misted as he bent down and lightly kissed his wife's forehead. He could feel the coldness of her brow and he knew as he saw her color turn paler that she would not live much longer. "Whatever you wish for the child, it shall be as you say," he promised her. "Do not worry, Leona, I promise our daughter shall be taken care of."

As though this was all that had kept Leona Morgan hanging on, the blond-haired woman upon the bed sighed as though she had no more worries.

Tears ran down the large man's face as he sat and saw his wife's gentle green eyes close for the last time. Picking the child up from her side he stood up, left the bedchamber, and made his way to the front of the house. He opened the door, wishing to view another sight, a sight that had always brought him pleasure. He stood, holding his daughter, and watched as the sun lowered over his ranch.

"I am sorry, Mr. Morgan. I did my best for your lady." The old midwife came up behind him on silent feet.

"Aye, you did, and she went in peace." His words were a whisper, touching lightly upon the old woman's ears. "I'll send payment to you tomorrow with my foreman."

The old woman knew when she was dismissed and

as she started through the door she glanced once more to the babe in the large man's arms. "She be needing a name. Without a mother the poor little mite at least should be having a name." And so saying, she started down the path leading down from the front porch.

Graylin Morgan looked down at the babe in his arms. He would have to name her. He should have thought and asked Leona what she would have the child be called. He had no idea what to call a baby girl.

At this same time Less, Graylin's foreman, brought out of the corral the sleek, reddish-colored mare that had been Leona's favorite. Graylin watched as the mare was haltered and taken to the barn. Leona had loved the horse well, and Graylin remembered now how much he had enjoyed watching her ride the trim beast.

As he looked from the horse to his child, the name Sorrel came to his mind. He would name their child Sorrel, and he would always remember when he looked upon her his Leona, as she had looked while riding her horse.

Chapter One

Kentucky, 1764

As Mathew Danner reclined against the cushion of the wing chair his face reflected some of the pain that was seeming at this moment to be consuming his very soul. This room—he looked about at the white, frilly bedchamber in which he seemed so out of place—had now seen his presence for the last past week; or was it longer, he wondered, bringing his large hand up before his closed eyes and laying it across his forehead. It seemed to him that he had spent most of his life in this chamber. Each moment seemed to be drawn out into hours.

"When will she awake?" he questioned aloud to the empty room, taking his hand away, his dark blue eyes going to the large brass bed.

In the folds of this bed lay a creature who, even in her sleep, was the most beautiful woman this large man had ever seen before in his life. Her soft, blond, almost white, curls fanned across the pillow. Her small, heart-shaped face drew his attention. He could see in his mind her light china-blue eyes looking up into his face. Her soft, pliant lips, which in the past he had never been able to fully enjoy, always so pink and beckoning, were now silent and pale.

A soft moan escaped him, and once again he bent his dark head in prayer. He prayed to the Lord to save this woman lying so still upon her bed, this woman who was to be his wife and one day the mother of his children could not be taken from him.

His thoughts went to the last day he had seen his Elizabeth vibrant and so full of life. She had been out riding and he had come upon her by accident as he cut across her father's back fields, trying to save time in his quest to find her at home.

He had been surprised and quite pleased to see her blond head, those soft, shiny curls bound together tightly at the nape of her head in a small ball held together by pins and ribbons, as she rode at a gallop in his direction.

His heart had thumped wildly as she drew near and his flashing white smile showed his unashamed joy at just viewing this beauty who had consented to be his wife.

"Why Mathew," she had smiled lightly, pulling her mount to a stop before him.

"I was on my way to visit you, Elizabeth." His voice was a soft caress, but then, in a bit of a sterner tone, he reprimanded her softly. "You should not be riding about by yourself at the back of your father's property, and you should not be riding your horse at such a dangerous pace."

For a second Mathew had thought he viewed anger in the depths of those china-blue eyes, but as quickly Elizabeth's head lowered and in a contrite voice she said silkly, "Whatever you say Mathew. I shall not do such a foolish thing again."

She was so beautiful, he remembered thinking, and the two of them had ridden on to the Strickland plantation and enjoyed an afternoon of light talk and plans for their coming marriage.

That had been the last time he had seen Elizabeth as he had known her these past two years. That same evening a young black boy from the Strickland plantation had come at a run to Mathew's father's plantation, Crescent Mist, with the news of Elizabeth's having been thrown from her horse that very afternoon shortly after he had left her side. The doctor had been called and should be arriving at any moment.

Without any delay Mathew had raced to the barn and had one of the black boys saddle his horse. Mathew had been shown into Elizabeth's bedchamber for the first time ever by her older sister Penny, and from that day to this Mathew Danner had not left the young woman's room.

Mathew Danner was more than just the son of a wealthy plantation owner. He was also a man who loved his God and had served him these past six years with all of his heart and strength. Mathew's mother had taken her son to church with her each Sabbath, and as the boy grew he had found a love that ran deep and true in between the pages of the black book from which the preacher read at each Sunday service.

It had been hard for Mathew as he had grown into manhood and after his mother had passed away to remain true to this deep-seated love. His father had stormed and ranted at him and then finally he had sent his son to France in the hopes that he would put away his nonsense and come to his senses.

Justin Danner had gone to church occasionally with his wife and son, but he kept all things in their proper place, or so he thought. His son was one day to be the master of Crescent Mist, and to his way of thinking there was no room in a plantation owner's life for any thoughts other than those concerned with caring for the land and for the people who ran his plantation.

He had realized finally, though with some distress, upon his son's return from Europe that he was wasting his time trying to turn the boy's head. If he had any further desires to change his son's mind he quickly put them from him when Mathew, twenty-one years old and a large, unbending man, explained to his father that he would either stay on at Crescent Mist and become the man he thought the Lord wished for him to be or he would leave his father's house and the only home he had ever known and find the place that would accept him.

Of course, Justin Danner had no choice in the matter. Mathew was his only heir and there was no one else, so, swallowing his pride, he had shaken his head but finally given his consent.

Soon after Mathew had become the preacher in the same small Kentucky church that he had been brought up in as a child. He found no greater love than walking into that whitewashed building and looking out from the pulpit at the anxious faces turned his way. And then one fine Sunday morning he had looked about and seen a new face, and his world had seemed to shine even brighter.

Terrance Strickland and his family had moved from a small plantation in West Virginia to the vast plantation in Kentucky that adjoined Crescent Mist, and as Mathew Danner looked at Terrance Strickland's family he had felt his heart beginning to race. From the first moment his dark blue eyes had met those of Elizabeth Strickland he had known that she would be the only woman for him.

It had taken him some time in his pursuit of this lovely young woman before she had seemed to find him of any interest. She had appeared cold and evasive on their first meeting, and during the following almost two years he had eventually almost given up any hope of finding any favor with her. But then finally one Sunday Terrance Strickland had asked Mathew to dinner, and from that day on Elizabeth had seemed to change. She was no longer cold and unresponsive, and she seemed to welcome his conversation and courtship.

And then when she finally had consented to become his bride, his joy knew no bounds. It seemed to Mathew that his world would finally be complete, he loved the Lord and served him well, he would one day own the home that had belonged to his family for over fifty years, and he would be the husband of Elizabeth Strickland.

As the door to the bedchamber was opened Mathew was pulled from his thoughts and sat up straighter in his chair.

"I have brought you something to eat, Mathew. You must not make yourself ill also." Dorothy Strickland placed a covered tray on the table next to his chair.

"Thank you, Mrs. Strickland." Mathew rose from the chair and went to the window and pulled back the lacy French pleated panels that hid his view of the outside world. "Has the doctor arrived yet?" He asked this question, knowing that the doctor had made a visit each afternoon for the past week, but had been unable to tell the worried family anything about their daughter that might encourage them. She had fallen off her horse while riding him hard and trying to jump him over an overgrown hedge. Her head had been badly hit near the temple by a log that had been lying off to the side of the hedge, and an ugly gash in her scalp was all that was known of her ailment.

"Yes, Mathew, Dr. Martin is downstairs talking to Terrance now. Do you not think that you would be more comfortable in another room?" She questioned kindly, knowing that he had slept nowhere but in the chair by her daughter's bed since the first day of her accident.

Mathew dropped the curtains back into place and walked about the room. How pale and soft everything in this room was, he thought. Just like Elizabeth. "No, no thank you, Mrs. Strickland," he brought himself to answer the question put to him. He had already made arrangements for another man to pastor his church while he was here beside Elizabeth, and with her mother's question he knew that he could not bear to be pulled from her side.

"All right Mathew, I shall send the doctor up in a moment. Try to eat a few bites from the tray." Dorothy Strickland started to the door with a worried look at the young man who was to become her son-in-law. It had been a long and harrowing ordeal for Terrance to convince Elizabeth to let Mathew Danner court her and then again to convince her to accept his proposal. But now Dorothy Strickland knew that for Mathew there was more than just lands and money in the arrangement. She knew now as she had all week that Mathew Danner loved her daughter beyond all human reason.

Once again, as he had done so many times in the past days, Mathew began to pray. "Oh Lord, please let her wake. Do not take her from me. After giving me this woman to love and after she has filled my heart so, do not take her from me now." He knelt beside the bed, his face covered by his hands as he called aloud in the silent room.

And as though in answer to the many prayers that he had called aloud to the one above, the form upon the bed stirred.

Mathew felt the slight movement of the bed, and, with tears shining in his dark blue eyes he looked to the china-blue eyes that were staring at him full of questions.

"Mathew—what on earth?" Her voice seemed chilled as she saw the man kneeling at her bedside.

Mathew Danner did not notice the coldness of her voice. All that he could comprehend was that his Elizabeth was awake, she was speaking, his prayers were answered. Without answering her question he rushed to the door and shouted aloud down the stairs to the front parlor, "She is awake. Come quickly, she has finally come back to us!"

Footsteps could be heard rushing from all corners of the large, wood house, and within seconds

Elizabeth's large chambers were filled with family and servants.

Terrance shouted for one of the blacks to help the old doctor up the stairs, and Dorothy Strickland, with tears running down her cheeks, rushed to her daughter and gathered her up into her arms.

Elizabeth at first did not know what had happened, but finally she was made to understand the full consequences of her daring ride that afternoon after Mathew had left her.

Her first thoughts when she had heard that she had hit her head were of her appearance, and at once she called to Penny to bring her her gold-framed hand mirror.

With the mirror in her hand she looked at herself from all angles, trying to see the disfigurement on her head.

Her family laughed fondly, thinking it like their Elizabeth, to care for nothing else but her looks. They were so glad that she was once again amongst them that they overlooked this selfish flaw in her as they had time and again in the past.

Mathew also gave little thought to his future wife's vanity. His eyes were filled with the sight of her and he could not take them away. His thoughts were only of his thanks to God for sparing her and giving him another chance with this woman who he loved.

In a short time Dr. Martin came into the chamber, a small black man supporting his arm. "Well, young lady, at last you have found your way back to us." He grinned down into her face, placing his small black bag upon the table next to the bed and taking out an odd assortment of instruments.

To Elizabeth all seemed to be in confusion. She felt fine, except for a slight headache, and all this fuss over her was, to her way of thinking, more than a bit overplayed. Her family knew that she did not take to being fawned over, and though Mathew did not know her well enough yet, he would after they were married. "Yes, doctor, I guess one could say from what I have been told that I am indeed back." Her tone was still cold.

Dr. Martin made his examination without further conversation, and after chasing everyone out into the hall so that he would be able to examine his patient alone, he proceeded in a quiet and intense mood.

The doctor seemed to be much longer than necessary to Mathew's way of thinking, and he walked back and forth impatiently through the hallway. He cared for nothing but to fill his eyes with the woman that he loved. He had almost lost her, he thought over and over to himself. He would not let anything else happen to her, they would be married sooner than planned, he decided. He could not chance such an incident's happening again while he was not about to protect her.

Dr. Martin came through the portal with a dour look upon his face. Closing the door behind him quietly he looked to Terrance Strickland. His look was for the young lady's manners as much as for the nasty gash upon her head. "I hope that she will be fine, Terrance, but it is still too early to tell," he said to Mr. Strickland.

Both Terrance and Mathew started to speak at the same time, but their questions were waved away by the doctor's beefy hand.

"She received quite a bump on the side of her head, gentlemen, and I am afraid I still do not like the look in her eyes; they seem a bit fuzzy and unresponsive, I'm afraid, for my taste."

All were quiet as the doctor said these compelling words. "Do you think that she could lapse into unconsciousness again?" It was Dorothy Strickland who dared to voice what was on all of their minds.

"Truthfully, Mrs. Strickland, I have no idea," Dr. Martin answered softly.

For a few minutes the hall remained quiet, and then Mathew spoke. "The Lord has answered our prayers, and Elizabeth will be fine. After a few days' rest and care she will be her old self once again." He had to say these words, he thought, as he looked about at the faces turned his way. He needed as much convincing as the others, but to him, now, all had been taken care of by the Lord.

Dorothy was the first to speak after Mathew. "I agree with Mathew. Elizabeth has been all but dead to us this past week, but now that she has come to her senses, we must believe that she will be fine." She turned and started back into her daughter's chambers.

Mathew stood near the door and watched as mother hovered over daughter for a few minutes.

"You had best go on over to Crescent Mist now, Mathew. I imagine that your father has been mighty upset not having you home this past week." Terrance Strickland came up to the younger man and placed his hand lightly upon his shoulder as he also watched his wife and daughter.

"I guess you are right, sir," Mathew answered, not

wishing to leave the woman he loved but knowing that it would be for the best. With short steps he made his way to his betrothed's side and stood waiting for a chance to speak a few words to her.

Dorothy noticed Mathew first and quickly realized his wish to speak to her daughter and silently she made her way to her husband.

"I had better leave now, Elizabeth." Mathew gently picked up her small, white hand and brought it to his lips. "I'm afraid that I have let everything go in order to be here at your side this week, and I am sure that my father will wish to hear of your recovery." He wished fervently that she was already his wife and that he would never have to leave her side.

Elizabeth smiled weakly toward the man she had promised to wed. "Thank you, Mathew, for your concern."

"You had best get your rest. I shall come tomorrow to visit with you." He thought already that her voice seemed weaker.

"You are right," was her reply, and with no more ado she laid her head back down upon her pillow and slowly shut her eyes.

Being harshly jerked to a stop atop his mount, Mathew realized that he was sitting outside the large barn at Crescent Mist. He had been so wrapped up in his own thoughts that he had not noticed how close to home he was.

Before he dismounted one of the boys who worked in the barn was reaching up to take hold of his horse's reins.

From the front veranda of the large, two-story brick house, his father called out a loud greeting. "How is the lass, Mathew? I am glad to see you finally getting on back home."

"Fine, Father," came his reply. "She came to her senses only a short time ago, and I thought it best to get back here and get some rest and a clean change of clothes." Mathew realized now how truly tired he was as he walked up the front steps leading to the large, airy veranda.

"So the lass pulled through, did she?"

Mathew noticed the difference in his father's voice whenever he spoke of Elizabeth Strickland, and this day was no different. He knew his father did not approve of his future bride, but to Mathew's way of thinking his father did not approve of any of his decisions.

"Yes, Father, the Lord was merciful and brought her back to us." He did not feel like arguing with this strong-willed older man and stepped around him and entered the front door. "I am going to get some rest before dinner," he threw over his back.

This huge house at Crescent Mist was one of the largest in the community and the inside was even more impressive than the vast, sprawling outside. Mathew had never stopped before and looked about him, having been brought up surrounded by all of this magnificence and being used to it, but now, after his stay at the Strickland home, he took a better view. This old house had a warmth and friendliness that the Strickland home had somehow left out. His future bride's home was furnished in pale, light colors, while here at Crescent Mist everything was warm and vibrant in color, proclaiming to all that within this massive mansion life thrived and was fully enjoyed.

He could hear noises coming from the back of the house, and with slow, halting steps he went out into the kitchen. He grinned widely as the old black woman with her back turned to him spun around as she heard the kitchen door swing to.

"Why you finally did come on home. I been a'telling your pa that you'd be back, but he done fretted half of his years away this here past week." The old woman was as black as mahogany and sometimes seemed as large and enduring as the house itself. Without second thought she brought her large girth over to Mathew and wrapped her arms about him. "I sure did miss you, boy. Now you tells old Mally how that young lady be a'doing."

Mathew was pushed into a strong wood chair near a small table before Mally went back to her cooking. Mathew smiled fondly at the large black woman and breathed in the scents all about him from her cooking. She had always been here, and he loved her as if she were his own mother. "She seems to be better, Mally."

"That be a good boy." Mally turned from stirring a pot on the stove and looked Mathew in the eye. "You sho do need to be getting youself back to your church, Master Mat."

Mathew looked at her with some concern. "Has something happened, Mally? Have you heard word from someone?"

"Why no, honey child. I just know that the Lord be

a'wanting for you to preach his word." She set a plate of cold meat down in front of him and poured him a large glass of cider.

Mathew's mother had died when he was in his early teens, and, other than making sure that her son went to church on the Sabbath, she had left most of his raising to the servants. And Mally was the one to whom he brought all of his troubles and woes. The two seemed to have a special bond, and Mathew knew that nothing would ever come between them. He smiled inwardly as he thought of all the endearing names she had called him since he had been young. To this day she reminded him that she had brought him up, and that to her he was still nothing more than the dirty-faced child she had scolded so many times in the past for being in her kitchen and underfoot.

He ate only a small bit of the repast she had set before him, and to her questioning look he answered that he wished only for a bath and to rest for a time.

Mally smiled understandingly and called in one of the girls who had been sitting on the back porch and snapping peas. "You, gal, you start the young master some hot water and get that shifless Nan to be helping you to get his bath ready." To Mathew she said, "You be going on up the stairs and I have everything ready for you."

Mathew smiled his thanks, and before leaving the kitchen he enfolded the large black woman in his embrace. "I sure did miss you, Mally." And then with a bit of humor he playfully pinched her cheeks and sallied, "I also missed your good cooking. That cook at the Stricklands' sure can't hold a candle to you."

Mally laughed with pride ringing loud and clear. "That be a-teaching you to run off from this here old house." Her loud voice followed him up the stairs.

In his room Mathew sat back in a velvet-cushioned chair and propped his feet up, awaiting his bath. His chambers, he reflected, were extremely different from those of his intended bride. Where hers were light and womanish, his were quite the opposite. Dark, rich paneling graced the walls, and an even darker brown carpet covered the floor. On the right stood a massive bed with dark brown netting draped over it, gathered together at the large wood posts. On one wall books of all descriptions lined numerous shelves, and on the opposite wall a large oak desk was cluttered with various papers and books.

Mathew did most of his work and study in this room, leaving the library downstairs to his father, and now, for the first time, he thought about what changes would have to be made when he married. He hoped that Elizabeth would not insist on changing this room beyond removing the desk, but he knew that his working habits would have to change and that he would have to impose on his father's privacy. He did not mind this, but what he would not care for at all would be to have the rich warm colors changed to lighter ones. "Ah, well," he sighed aloud. He would not worry over such unimportant matters now.

The two girls brought in buckets of steaming water and in between giggles and shy looks at their young master they set about to make his bath ready.

Mathew watched the two light-cocoa-colored girls with some amusement. They must be sisters, he thought, and Mally must just be breaking them in to being housegirls. Mathew Danner was not a man to truly care for slavery, but here on Crescent Mist the people were treated well, and Mathew knew that if he chose to live in the South he would have to tolerate the life style. The only thing he would not tolerate was the mistreatment of another human being.

So often did Mathew voice his opinion when he saw a white man doing some harm to his black slave that Justin Danner had cautioned him on more than one occasion to watch what he said. "The blacks aren't human, boy," he would reprimand his son. "They're like animals, and put here to tend to the needs of others."

These lectures may have stayed in young Mathew's mind, but as he grew older he knew that these statements of his father were not true. He had argued this over and over with his father, but no good had come from his explaining to him that before the Lord all men are the same. There was no changing Justin Danner's mind, as there was no changing the minds of half of the South. So Mathew lived in this world of royal splendor at Crescent Mist, where any desire of his was immediately gratified. But he made sure that the people on his land were treated fairly, and he even thought at times of how things would be different when he became the sole master of the plantation. He had ideas of teaching his people how to read and to write and of how they could cope with their everyday lives more easily.

His bath completed, Mathew lay down on the rich

brown satin coverlet that was thrown over the bed, and within minutes his blue eyes were shut and he was sleeping soundly.

Justin Danner slowly left the coolness of the wide front veranda to find his way to the sanctuary of his study. His once handsome but now aged face was lined with worry as he sat his large bulk down upon the leather-cushioned chair behind his long, dark wood desk. He tried for some minutes to go over his ledgers and to make some sense of the scrawled numerals, but finally, after finding that no matter how long he sat and faced the pages he was not going to make any headway, he slammed the book closed.

Throwing the book off to the side of his desk, he sat and looked about him, trying to take from his mind the angry thoughts that were plaguing him. But even the usual peacefulness that he felt within these walls forsook him. His son was all that had ever mattered to him. Even the plantation that he had lived on since his own boyhood and that at one time he had thought that he loved more than anything else was no longer important to him. All that truly mattered now was the happiness of his only child.

His faded blue eyes shut for a minute and he thought back to happier days, when Mathew had been a boy. He and Margret, his wife, and Mally, had, all three of them, done a fine job of raising the lad. Now, as a man, Mathew was strong and unbendable in his beliefs, and, though at times Justin did not agree with his son, he did not begrudge him what he felt.

He and Mathew had had many ups and downs in the past, but things had always been worked out. Justin Danner had been used, all of his life, to having things to his own liking. So, he had reasoned over the years, his son's being so much like himself was the cause of their tempers' clashing so violently at times. He had always proven the victor in these combats, until the day when the boy had come back from Europe a man and had boldly put before his father his wish to become a preacher.

Justin had known for years that he would one day have to have this subject out with his son. For had he not sent the lad to France hoping that he would find some other interest in his studies? But Justin Danner had not been prepared for the strong, determined young man who stood before him and told him that he would preach with or without his father's permission.

Justin had felt the years slip away from him that afternoon. And though he did not agree with Mathew, he had had no choice but to conform to his wishes.

He had found in this case, though, that he had no need for worry. His boy was a fine man and he did all that he believed and did not let any that cared for him down. He preached the word (as Mathew so aptly put it) and he did his share here at Crescent Mist—actually, if Justin were truthful he would have to admit that his son did more than his share. He himself tended most of the blacks when they came down sick, and he worked the fields from daybreak until dusk right beside the strongest men when the need arose. He also helped with Justin Danner's horses, these being the main income of Crescent Mist.

Yes, Justin Danner had to admit that his son was a cut above most young men of this time, and now all that Mathew did his father approved of—except when it came to the subject of Elizabeth Strickland.

Justin ran his fingers through his thick silver waves as he sat there thinking about his son's future wife and the future mistress of Crescent Mist. In this case of the Strickland girl, Justin Danner knew—as he had not known in other matters of conflict with his son—what would be the final outcome.

Indeed, for years now, he had wanted his son to take a bride and to begin a family. Time was seeming to gain upon the elder Danner more swiftly with each day that passed, and he wished to know the grandchildren who would one day be masters over this land he loved so well. But he knew that no daughter of Terrance Strickland would be a fit match for Mathew.

It was now almost three years ago that Terrance Strickland had moved to Kentucky and onto his dead cousin's plantation. From his first meeting with the other man Justin Danner had felt himself put off and was made uneasy by the other's manners and his treatment of people. At first Justin had reasoned that the man had been a small plantation holder in West Virginia and that perhaps it would take him some time to be able to get used to dealing with the huge estate his cousin had left to him. But as time had passed Terrance Strickland had seemed to grow worse instead of improving, and when the rumors of his foul treatment of his servants had started to spread about the neighboring plantations, Justin had been reinforced in his first impressions of his neighbor.

And then one day as Justin had been riding in from his southern fields Terrance Strickland had pulled him up before he reached the house and had started making conversation as though on a friendly visit. Justin had been on his guard, for the other man had never before made a visit to Crescent Mist without wishing to buy something—horses, for instance, and on one of his visits he had even offered to purchase Mally to replace the cook at his own house. Justin had at once, of course, explained in a gentlemanly fashion that there was no amount of money that could buy the woman who had lived so long on Crescent Mist. He had avoided speaking what was truly on his mind—that no black person from Crescent Mist would ever be turned over to Terrance Strickland. The people on Crescent Mist were treated well and fed adequately, each family having a small section of land behind their cabin to grow their own vegetables, and each man allowed Sundays to roam the thick forest on the outskirts of the property to snare rabbits or to gather herbs. All this Justin did for his people, so that his plantation should thrive. But he could not see that Terrance Strickland maintained any kind of conscience where his people were concerned.

That afternoon, though, Justin Danner had sensed something else in his neighbor's manner, and, as he slid from the side of his mount and started to walk the short distance toward the barn, the man beside him did the same.

Only pleasantries were spoken until Justin invited his unwanted guest into his house and from there into his study, for a glass of brandy.

Terrance Strickland seemed well relaxed once he was inside the other's private room, and, sitting in a well-cushioned chair, he stretched out his long legs and started to come to the point. "Well, Justin, I must say I am more impressed each time I come to Crescent Mist." He looked about him boldly, as though appraising each item in the room.

Justin did not comment. Only a small grunt came from his lips as he poured the drinks and placed one beside his guest and then sat behind his massive desk. His blue eyes, which had at one time been as bright and searing as his son's, probed the man before him.

Terrance Strickland began to feel the quiet of the room, and, not showing his uncomfortableness, he started once more. "I know, Justin, that you are a man who does not take to beating around the bush, so I shall come right to the point."

"Please do." Justin's tone was already bored.

Terrance cleared his throat, knowing how hard this man could be. From the sound of his voice he was not going to make it easy on him. "As I am sure you know, for some time now my family have been going to your son's church." With Justin's nod of his head he continued. "Well, my wife and I both find Mathew to be a sound young man, and, as you know, we have two daughters."

Justin did not say a word but remained stone still, his light blue eyes showing his only response.

"Well, I can see that you are not going to make this easy for me, so I might as well just say it and have an end to it. If we were to wed my oldest girl Penny with your Mathew and combine the two plantations we would have one of the richest properties in all of the South." He sat back upon his chair awaiting the other's reaction. He had said what he had come to say and now wished only for Justin's consent.

Justin, for some reason, had never quite been able to tell this man just what he thought of him, but now the words flew across his mind. His rich laughter filled the small book-lined room, turning Terrance Strickland's face a bright pink.

"I find no humor in my suggestions, sir." He stood to his feet.

"Ah, but I indeed do. My son, sir, is not one to take orders from his father, he is his own man and makes his own decisions. And I myself find the idea of my son marrying into your family one of some hilarity." At the time of this meeting Justin Danner had no idea of his son's already being half in love with Terrance Strickland's youngest daughter. How could he when the boy had never told him how he felt, and he was always so busy here on Crescent Mist that he would not know such a thing unless told. So without second thoughts he continued. "My plantation will never be joined with yours. I have sweated to make her what she is and I shall not have her life's blood drained and my people suffering by the likes of you." Justin's voice had risen loud enough for the whole of the downstairs to hear his words.

Terrance Strickland had not been spoken to in such a disrespectful manner since moving to Kentucky. He knew what most of the neighboring plantation owners thought of him but he also knew that no one would dare to face him with these thoughts. He owned one of the largest pieces of land around and no one wished to be on the wrong side of a man as wealthy as he. But he found now that this man before him would indeed dare such a thing. He knew that Justin Danner had only tolerated him before, but now he was openly insulting him. "I shall not stand here and listen to your slurs upon my name, sir. I came in good faith to put a proposition to you, but if your answer is to be no, than I shall no longer detain you." He turned about swiftly and started to the door. For a moment he thought to tell the smug old man about his son and his hot pursuit of his youngest daughter but as quickly this thought passed. He would use the boy for his own ends.

Justin's laughter followed the man out the front door and down the steps of the veranda.

It was only a few months later that Mathew had come to him and told him of his intentions of marrying the youngest Strickland girl. Of course, Justin had been crushed, but Mathew had been steadfast in his decision. He had already asked the girl to wife, and she and her father had accepted. So, with only the hope that his son would wake up to the truth about the family he was getting involved with, Justin had silently watched the situation until the day he heard that the girl had been thrown from her horse.

He shook his silver head as though in fierce denial. He had wished for the girl's death, though he hated himself for it. He had hoped to free his son, but now that Mathew had returned home he could see that his hopes were not to be realized. He had scolded himself harshly more than once in the past week for wishing that Elizabeth Strickland not awaken from her deep sleep. He knew that it was wrong of him, but over the past months he had seen how she coldly calculated her movements around Mathew. She was a fine, cold actress, he had to admit. He knew that his son would one day wake up, but his fear was that this one day would be too late for Mathew and Crescent Mist.

Justin knew that Mathew was expecting his wife to act in the manner that his own mother had, but the Strickland girl was, Justin knew, cut from a different cloth than Mathew's mother had been. Margret Danner had been a quiet, reserved woman who had spent her time reading her bible and tending to her husband, even going so far as to let Mathew be taken care of by the servants so she would not have to be called away from her husband's side.

A loud knocking at the large front door pulled Justin from his dark thoughts. "Mally!" he shouted, wishing for someone to let in the intruder. Raising to his feet Justin decided that he would have to be the receiver of this noisy knocker. None of the servants seemed to be in the front portion of the house.

Pulling the portal open he confronted a thin, almost bony black man. "What you doing beating my door in this manner?" Justin shouted at the black man, angry that he had not used the back kitchen door.

"My master sent me, sir, for Master Mat, sir. I's sorry to beat on you door but Master Strickland said I was to hurry." The man's head bowed and his feet kept up a rapid shuffle.

"Why you just get on back and tell your master

that my son is sleeping. I think he has spent enough time at that house." Justin was truly beginning to get angry now. What did that girl want? Mathew to sit beside her day and night? It would be like that Terrance Strickland to send one of his servants to fetch Mathew back to his home just to pacify his daughter.

"But, sir, I do what you be telling me. Yes, sir, I be getting on back right away to Master Strickland, but he sent me because of the missy. She done gone again."

"What you be meaning boy, gone where?" Justin looked with more interest now at the boy before him.

"I ain't be too sure master, sir, but I be hearing one of the girls from at the big house saying that the missy this time done gone and died."

The words rang hollowly in Justin's ears. "My God, man, why did you not say so? Run back to your master and tell him that Mathew will be there soon." Knowing that his orders would be carried out Justin turned his back on the black man and shut the door. Leaning his broad frame against the portal, he let out his breath. He had wished for this news, but now that it had come to pass he felt somehow deflated. How was he to tell his son that the woman he wished to marry, even though she was not good enough for him, was dead?

With halting steps Justin walked up the stairs and stood before his son's chamber door. Without knocking he entered. Everything was how it should be, he told himself as he looked about the room, and then he let his eyes rest on his son.

For a moment he stood over him and let his vision

silently fill with his son's lean, handsome face. In his slumber he looked little different from the lad who used to fall alseep upon his lap while he read him bedtime stories. If the girl were truly dead he knew that it would be some time before he saw Mathew in this same peaceful condition again. Slowly reaching down he shook him by the shoulder.

Mathew awoke on the instant and looked at his father. "Is dinner ready?" he questioned, rising on an elbow and wondering why Mally or one of the girls had not come to wake him.

"You had better rise, Mathew. One of the Strickland servants just arrived and left word that you are needed." At his son's worried look, he added, "It's the girl."

It took only a few minutes for Mathew to be dressed and riding from Crescent Mist at a hurried pace. All of his fears had been realized with his father's look. The older man did not have to say the words for him to know before he ever reached the Strickland house that Elizabeth would be gone from him.

The funeral was held two days later on a gray, drizzly morning, with only the Strickland family and a handful of neighbors coming to mourn for the young woman who had died.

Mathew stood to the back of the small group, off to himself, still not believing that the wooden coffin held his Elizabeth. How could God above be so cruel? he questioned over and over. When asked to say the sermon over the grave he had sternly said no, and no one had thought too much of it, putting it down to his closeness to the girl and to the fact that he was very upset. But something within Mathew had died with the girl he loved. He no longer felt as he had only a week ago. He was no longer so sure of all those words he had spoken about his loving and good God, behind the pulpit all those Sunday mornings.

That same God had taken the only thing that he had cared about. He had taken the most beautiful and kind woman that he had ever created. How could the Lord do this cruel thing to him, after he had given all he had unto him, spreading his word and devoting all that he could to further his goodness?

"It's not fair," he had shouted to the skies as he left the Strickland house that horrible afternoon after viewing his love cold and still upon her bed. It was not fair, and it was a waste, and as Mathew stood watching as a group of black slaves lowered the coffin into the hole in the earth and covered it with dirt, the Lord was gone from his heart.

Long after the dirt covered the grave and all that was in its place was a small mound, and long after family and friends were gone, Mathew stood vigil over the woman he had wanted for his own.

It was almost dark and the rain had still not let up when Mathew finally made his way back to Crescent Mist. He had no words to speak to the servants, who greeted him as he opened the door and entered the front foyer, nor did he have words for his father, who came out of his study as he heard the door swing shut.

Without looking about him Mathew made his way up the stairs. Very shortly he was back downstairs again. He had changed his clothes; instead of the dark pants, vest and jacket and white shirt he had worn earlier that day he now wore the darker-colored shirt and tight-fitting breeches that he usually used for hunting or working. A pack was slung over his back. In his hand he clutched a leather-fringed jacket, and as he headed straight for the study he pulled a rifle down from the wall and took shot and powder from a side table, and started back to the door.

"Where do you think you are going?" Justin entered the room, seeing him cramming the implements for the rifle into his pack.

"I'm going away for a while," came the only answer Mathew would volunteer.

"What do you mean you're leaving? You cannot just up and leave like this, son. I know it is hard for you right now, but, boy, you know that you have responsibilities," Justin tried to reason.

But his son's bright blue eyes had gone dead with a chilling, biting coldness. "I have no longer anything keeping me here. You can run Crescent Mist without me."

"But your church, boy? You cannot just leave all those people to their own means." Justin was trying anything to keep Mathew from this hasty decision. Given time Mathew would come to his senses. Any man faced with the death of the woman that he loved would be feeling this same defeat.

"The church will have to do without me. I am no longer the man who I thought the Lord wanted." Mathew started past his father and through the door.

"You are no different, son," Justin shouted, trying

to make him stop and listen. "It is only your grief that is making you talk like this. Do not run off, Mathew, at least wait and take some rest for a few days. Things may turn out different from what you now think."

"And if in that time, Father, I find that I am no different than at this very moment, will you then admit that I have been living a lie?" Before Justin could answer he started again. "I know my answer now. All has been in vain, I cannot stay here." Mathew started out the front door and down the front veranda steps as though a thousand devils were on his tail.

Going to the barn he saddled his own stallion. Hearing the barking of the dogs in the pens out back he stopped for a moment and went in their direction. Coming to the pen of a huge mastiff, he unlatched the door and called the beast by name. "Come Lancer, it has been a season since last we have done any hunting."

The dog, as though knowing what his master was saying, seemed to pull back his lips in a huge grin, and speedily his tail brushed back and forth, showing his pleasure. It had been weeks since Mathew had taken him anywhere, and he was more than ready to follow wherever he was led.

So, with the sky an ominous black and rain pelting down, master and beast rode off from the direction of Crescent Mist and all that they had known and loved.

Chapter Two

Texas, 1765

"No, no, no, I shall not see him this afternoon!" The fiery words spewed forth from the mouth of a young woman, and her rage was punctuated at each word by the loud tapping of her tiny foot on the marble tile floor.

"You, young lady, can no longer go on in this fashion. I will not stand for it any longer, and neither will your father," an older, plump, red-haired woman calmly said as she gathered the dresses lying in a large pile on the satin chair. With some exasperation she went to the wall-length wardrobe and began to hang the dresses in their place. "I would also dearly appreciate it, miss, if you would try to keep yourself clothed, so that the servants are not running about and whispering behind every door." The girl, as usual on hot days, had been in the courtyard lying in the sun and trying to roast her body. To Corrine Borden this was the most preposterous thing that anyone could ever do to try to turn lovely white skin to a dark brown. She did admit that on this young lady, with her golden curls, the color was quite becoming, the only real offense to her sense of decency was the fact that the girl insisted on lying in the sun without a stitch of clothing upon her body, and, though Corrine Borden had spoken to her numerous times before, she did not seem to care, for she still did as she pleased.

Something in the older woman's words had caught in the younger one's mind, and she quickly stilled and watched her as she finished with the dresses. "You have heard from Papa? Is he to be here soon?"

The elder woman noticed the light that came to the green eyes and she sighed. "Yes, love, I have heard from your papa, and what good will that do me? I am afraid that he lets you by with even more than I."

"When shall he be here, Aunt Corry?" The girl's small, bow-shaped lips formed a cheerful smile now.

"Soon child, soon. And one would think that you would care about his viewing your chambers in this scrambled state." Corrine Borden looked about in distaste. It seemed the older this young woman-girl became, the messier she became. "Have a care, Sorrel, the maids have plenty to do without having to pick up after you all of the day."

Sorrel Morgan was jubilant. Ignoring her aunt's words of caution she swung about in the satin robe she had hastily donned when she entered her chambers after her afternoon sunning. "It has been ages since Papa has come for a visit. Oh, I do hope he has not forgotten the present I asked for the last time he was here."

Corrine Borden looked up with shocked eyes, but truly she had to admit that nothing this young lady did anymore shocked her. She had seen it all since she had taken charge of her brother's daughter. "You are an ungrateful child, Sorrel Morgan, I hope the Lord above forgives you for your behavior."

"Oh, pooh, Aunt Corry." Going to the dressing table the young beauty started to brush out the long, honey-gold curls that ran down the length of her straight back. She viewed her reflection in the mirror and smiled softly, allowing the one tiny dimple to show before putting the brush back to its place and turning back to her aunt. "Well, since Papa might be here today, Aunt Corry, you can please tell Mr. Ryan that I cannot possibly see him this afternoon."

Her aunt sternly watched her as she turned about, thinking how easily Sorrel had put the matter of the young man from her, but Corrine Borden had not been duped that easily. "You shall indeed receive young Mr. Ryan, Sorrel. You, my dear, are the one who parades about town, swishing your skirts right and left and entertaining all manner of gentlemen at the parties you attend. I shall not any longer be the one who stands between them and you. You must begin to have a care for the outcome of your behavior."

"Oh, fiddle, Aunt Corry, why should I have a care for the outcome of what I do. Papa has already said that I shall marry Clifford Sumter." With this name she made a sour face, causing a smile to come to her aunt's lips. "Why should I not enjoy myself during what time is left me?"

Corrine knew that her niece was right, but still there was no reason for her to do the young men as she did. Also, she was but nineteen years old now, and she still had two years of being her own woman before the marriage contract that Graylin had made up for his only daughter would become effective. "You must act the lady, Sorrel. I have told you this often enough without having to repeat myself. Young ladies do not invite guests to tea and then for no reason other than their ill mood refuse to entertain them."

"I feel a headache coming on, you may tell him this." Sorrel was used to her aunt's speeches and did not pay any notice to this one. Her thoughts were on her father's visit.

"No!" Corrine Borden shouted loudly, making her niece sit up at her small pearl-colored desk and take notice. "I shall not be a party to your schemes again. You shall dress and be downstairs waiting for Mr. Ryan when he arrives. I shall not hear any more on this subject, Sorrel."

Sorrel was surprised by her aunt's vehemence and nodded her head in assent. For a second she was contrite, but she put the matter from her mind as soon as her aunt left her chambers. Her father would be coming from the ranch, and she could hardly contain the excitement she felt each time he made a visit to see her. Graylin Morgan, in the mind of his nineteen-year-old daughter, was the most wonderful man in the world.

She had not seen her father much in her nineteen years. She had lived with his sister since she had been an infant and had spent most of her girlhood being taught and trained by the nuns in a nearby parish. Sorrel smiled broadly as she thought back to those years. She had been quite a handful, and by the time she was twelve her aunt had been called to take her ward home, the good nuns no longer being able to keep a close enough hand on the wayward young girl. She had not been exactly bad, but she was a disturbance to the devoted women, and they were truly afraid that Sorrel Morgan would sooner or later bring one of their other good girls down with her. Sorrel as a young girl had loved nothing more than to provoke the good sisters, and no matter what the discipline, she could not be changed. Remembering back now, Sorrel thought of the night when, after the candles had been extinguished, she and two other girls had craftily tied sheets together until they made a long sheet-rope that they threw out of the upstairs window to the ground. They had silently climbed down it, their intentions being to go into town and return before morning when they would be missed. Their one mistake was that the sheet-rope hung directly in front of the Mother Superior's study, and as the girls slipped down the knotted sheets each one was watched by stern eyes.

All three girls had been severely punished for this conduct. The other two girls had wept and pleaded with the Mother Superior not to call their parents in and had promised not to do such a thing again. But Sorrel Morgan had made no such promises. The only time she had ever been punished was here with the nuns, so to her way of thinking if they were to call her father in and expel her she would be better off in the long run. She had always wanted to live with her father on the Morgan ranch, so she had thought this a good opportunity. But she had once more been fooled; oh yes, she had been sent away from the parish, but she had been sent to her Aunt Corry, her father claiming that the life on the ranch was too rough for a girl and that her aunt could tend her and teach her to become a proper lady.

Well, so much for being a proper lady, Sorrel thought as she began to prepare herself for her afternoon gentleman caller. Her Aunt Corry had had worse luck than the nuns with her niece. Sorrel had remained stubborn and willful, thinking only of her own wants and needs. Actually she had to admit to herself that she loved her aunt, and that truly her aunt had let her get by with far too much.

Pulling a forest-green satin gown over her petticoats Sorrel sighed loudly. "Drat." She hated getting dressed up in the middle of the day. Why on earth she had consented to let young Mr. Ryan visit was a mystery to her. But, in fact, it was no mystery. The young man was simply the rage now, having been gone to Europe and only recently returned. Most of the girls in town were all agog over the well-dressed young man, and when, at Mary Tyner's party two days ago, the young man had requested the pleasure of calling on Sorrel, she had told him with a lovely smile that she would be more than pleased to have him do so, for tea. She had done so only to show the other girls that she knew how she attracted men and that she had the power to get any man she wished. But now she regretted her hasty decision.

Pulling on her hose and her tiny green slippers she impatiently went to her dressing table and started to brush out her hair. She gazed at the mirror and smiled at the image that she saw before her. Young Mr. Ryan would be impressed, and more than likely become a nuisance, as others had been in the past. Perhaps she would this time be able to persuade her father to allow her to move to the ranch.

Sorrel had more luck with her young suitor than she had with her father and her wish to move out to the ranch. Graylin Morgan had arrived shortly after Sorrel's visitor had taken his leave. His young daughter was told of her father's arrival, and she rushed into the parlor and propelled herself into his arms, and with a huge grin Graylin smiled with his approval.

Corrine had already filled him in on his daughter's willfulness, but all that Graylin saw in his arms was the lovely daughter whom he and the woman he had loved years ago, and whose memory still lingered as though he had seen her the day before, had created.

With tender movements he set her from his grasp and helped her to be seated upon the satin settee. She was indeed beautiful, he thought to himself as he sat across from her and took one of her hands within his own. She had a bit of Leona in her and also a bit of him, and the combination was miraculous to him.

Her eyes were a light emerald, almost a soft turquoise, and, being slanted just a touch, they were slightly exotic. Her lashes were thick and long, as Leona's had been, and when she shut her eyes they delicately brushed her smooth peach skin. She seemed to radiate a kind of vibrant exhilaration. Even her skin color and the texture of her hair seemed to glow with the sun and good health. Aye, Graylin Morgan was proud of this young woman who sat before him, though she was a bit spoiled, as his sister had informed him often enough, still she was a beauty. If only Leona could see her daughter, Graylin had thought as he sat there and let himself drink her in. This was exactly how his Leona would have wished her child to be, not exactly like all other young women, but a woman with a mind of her own. And this did not upset Graylin Morgan in the least. He wanted his only child to enjoy life while she could, for one day she would have to conform to the rigidity and hardship of living on a ranch, and start a family of her own.

"Oh, Papa, I am so glad to see you," Sorrel cried, squeezing her father's large hand between her own. "You cannot imagine how boring and meaningless life here in this town is." She was preparing her father for her request, one that each time she had seen him she had put to him. So far he had denied her desire to leave her aunt's house. But this time Sorrel was determined that she would not be lightly put off. Was she not nineteen years old? Why, most girls she knew of at this age were already married and the mother of one or more children. How could her father keep treating her as though she were a child?

Graylin seemed to know what she wanted before she got the words out. His eyes looked at her with a bit of pity, for he himself understood her feelings well, but his lips remained firm as he answered, "You look to be doing well, daughter. And Corrine told me of your visitor this afternoon. You cannot be too bored with half the gentlemen of this town beating a pathway to your door."

"Oh, fiddle, Papa, I care nothing for the likes of

Mr. Ryan. I only let young men visit so I may have some entertainment." She thought that if she shocked her father with her behavior, perhaps he would relent.

Laughter filled the room. "Entertain all you care, my pet. For soon enough you will be living the life of an old married woman." Saying these words Graylin could not in the least imagine his daughter as she sat now in any way resembling an old married matron.

"But, Papa, I do not wish to live here in town." Sorrel threw her arms about, indicating the lavish parlor that they sat in. "I want to be with you on the ranch. I want to be able to ride and to roam about without worrying about what Aunt Corry will be thinking."

Graylin looked again with some pity at his child. It was too bad the girl had not been born a boy. But this was neither here nor there and could not now be changed, he thought. Perhaps his news would help her to adjust herself somewhat. "I am afraid that this cannot be, Sorrel." As she started to protest he held up a hand. "Let me explain. I am not returning to the ranch right away. I am leaving Texas and going to Virginia."

Sorrel's surprise was written on her features. Her father had never before left Texas, he loved his ranch too much to leave it for any greath length of time. "What on earth for?" was all she could get out.

"Do not look so upset." Graylin reached over and lightly caressed her golden cheek. "I shall not be gone long. I am going to look at some horses. We need some fresh-blooded mares on the ranch, and I have been informed that there may be what I am looking for in Virginia."

Some of her concern left Sorrel's face, and within seconds she was forming an idea. "Let me go with you, Papa." She stood up from the settee, not being able to sit long with her thoughts flying from every angle. What an adventure, all the way to Virginia! Why, she had been nowhere, except here in Texas. She just had to go, she told herself.

Her father, though, was of a different mind. "Do not be so thoughtless child. You cannot go with me."

"But why?" Her voice rose almost to pleading, something Sorrel Morgan never did.

"Why, your aunt needs you right here," was the only reason that Graylin could think of. If he had thought that the chit would have wished to go with him, he would never have mentioned his plans.

"Aunt Corry does not need me, Papa. I am afraid if the truth were out she would indeed be most pleased to see me gone and giving her a much needed rest," Sorrel shot back, not wanting to be put off. The longer she thought about the trip her father was going to make the more she longed to go. Just she and her father, after all of this time of her having been sent away from him—why the idea was sheer heaven to her!

But Graylin would not hear of it. He did not know how to take care of a young girl. He was a rancher and had lived a life of bachelorhood for many years now. What would he do with the willful young woman who stood before him now, her eyes pleading with him to let her have her way? Shaking his head he answered, "It is out of the question, Sorrel. Let us talk of different matters."

Sorrel felt like throwing herself upon his chest and weeping like a small child who could not have her own way, but her pride was stronger than her wish to show him how much he affected her, and, slowly, with some grace, she sat back down upon the settee and went through another hour of conversation with the man who was her father.

Later, alone in her room, Sorrel tried to form a plan that would see her going with her father to Virginia. She was possessed with the thought, to be able to leave her aunt's care and to go to unknown places with the man she had always loved and admired would be wonderful.

After hours of trying to come up with some kind of act that would sway his stubborn mind, the only decision that Sorrel could come up with was that of going to her Aunt Corry and expressing her wishes. She knew that if her Aunt Corry were to be on her side her father would have little choice but to relent. But how best to approach her aunt on this subject, she wondered as she strutted across her marble floor.

She was hardly ever the young woman that her aunt wished her to be, so to go to her as though she was requesting this because of her good behavior over the years would certainly be a farce. Her aunt knew her well, and now, after their small exchange of words over the way Sorrel flaunted gentlemen, she doubted that her aunt would even listen to her wish to go along with her father.

Coming to a fast decision Sorrel left her chambers and started down the vast hallway. It was suddenly as though nothing else mattered except going on this trip with her father. It was even more than just to be free of the things she had grown up around, Sorrel realized. After this afternoon of thinking and planning ways to sway her father she knew there was more; she felt in her depths a need far stronger than any she had ever known before, to be able to go to this faraway place called Virginia. She could not be denied.

She stood quietly in front of the closed door that led to her aunt's private chambers. Knocking lightly, she closed her eyes, then entered in response to her aunt's voice.

"Why, Sorrel, dear is something the matter?" Corrine Borden rose from her chair where she had been reading a French romantic novel. The child looked completely drained as she came through the door. Quickly Corrine went to her and felt her forehead. No matter how the girl acted, Corrine Borden loved her as though she were her own daughter, and she could not stand by and watch her being ill.

Sorrel smiled and shook her head as her aunt lowered her hand from her brow and looked questioningly toward her. "I am not ill, Aunt Corry. I was wondering if we may perhaps talk for a few minutes?"

Corrine was mystified. The child had never looked more serious in her life. "Why certainly, Sorrel. We have not long before dinner, but I suppose that we can take a few minutes. Come and sit over here." She led the way toward a small loveseat facing a delicately engraved French marble fireplace.

Sorrel, now that she was facing her aunt, found that for the first time in her life she was at a loss for words.

Corrine watched the girl silently for a few minutes and then tried to coax her into talking. "You saw your father this afternoon?" She had a good idea that whatever was bothering the girl was caused by something that Graylin had said.

Nodding her head Sorrel began. "I did indeed speak to Papa, Aunt Corry, and that is why I am here now."

Corrine looked questioningly at her niece. "What is it child? Did you ask again to go to the ranch?" Shaking her red head Corrine continued. "You know that Graylin does not wish you to be out there in the wilderness with no other women about you. It is a hard life on a ranch, and child, you will be out there soon enough, but with a husband."

Tiny tears started to form for no reason in the depths of Sorrel's green eyes, bringing the quick attention of her aunt. The girl had never before cried for no reason, Corrine thought to herself. There must be more here than she knew about. "Tell me, Sorrel, what is bothering you? Do not keep anything from me."

The woman before her had been the only mother Sorrel had ever known, and her words sounded like those she had heard as a young child. "Oh Aunt Corry," she sobbed, tears now flowing in earnest. Sorrel herself was at a loss to know why she was so upset about this trip her father was to make. "I did ask father about going to the ranch and he did tell me no, but that is not what is bothering me," she finally got out.

"Why, child, then what is it?" Corrine sat spellbound watching the tears falling from her niece's eyes.

"Papa is not going back to the ranch. He is leaving Texas and going to Virginia." There she had gotten it out. Sorrel sat back against the seat and wept openly.

"Going to Virginia?" Corrine whispered, not knowing what to make of this disclosure by her niece. "But why on earth would he be going to Virginia?" Was there something going on here that her brother had not told her about? Was he perhaps seeking a bride? She herself had suggested this idea on more than one occasion but he had remained steadfast in his decision to remain a bachelor. But he must have told this child some terrible news, she thought, as she went to her and took her in her arms. "There, there, love, it will be all right. Did Graylin mention what he was to do in Virginia?"

In between sobs Sorrel tried to tell her aunt what her father had told her.

"But Sorrel, why are you so upset?" Corrine pushed the girl from her and looked into her face. "I see nothing to cry about in the fact that your father wishes to obtain more horses. That is his main business on the ranch, raising horses."

Sorrel tried to explain. "I asked Papa if I could go, and he told me no, Aunt Corry. I wish to go so badly."

Corrine Borden watched the girl silently for a few minutes, thinking over in her mind all that she had heard. At first she agreed with her brother. Why should Sorrel leave the shelter of a beautiful home to travel about in ships and who knows what other kinds of conveyances? But as she reasoned with herself she began to identify somewhat what the girl must feel. Sorrel had not known any maternal love other than what she herself had given her. Corrine had been glad to take over the raising of her brother's child. She had loved the child passionately from the first time she had seen her asleep in her small baby blankets. But now, she thought, it was about time that her brother took some responsibility for the child of his flesh. She had agreed with him on Sorrel's not moving to the ranch until her marriage, for she could not envision any young woman roaming about with nothing but men, and rough men at that, at every turn. But if Graylin was going on a trip where his daughter could be taken care of in the fashion that she was accustomed to, Corrine could see no reason why she should not be allowed to go. After all, the child would be married in only two years, and then she would more than likely be buried out in the wilderness for the rest of her life. She would talk to her brother and tell him her thoughts on the matter.

"There, there, child." She pulled a handkerchief from the pocket of her gown and handed it to Sorrel. "I shall talk to Graylin myself about your going with him."

Sorrel looked up, her tears forgotten at her aunt's words. "You will?"

"But of course. Why else did you come in here but for me to plead your cause? And honey," her aunt's plump hand patted her own, "I see no reason you should not go along. Perhaps it would even benefit your behavior if you had to do without some of the things that you take for granted."

Not believing her ears Sorrel flung her arms about her aunt and hugged her tightly to her. "Oh, I love you Aunt Corry, I love you."

Dinner that evening was a delight. Course after course of mouth-savoring, delicious-smelling food was brought into the formal dining room by servants and served to the three people seated about the large table.

After leaving her aunt's room Sorrel had gone directly to her own chambers. She had had a maid bring cool water and cloths to her room, and she had applied these to her swollen eyes and rested for a time before she prepared for the evening repast.

She dressed in one of her loveliest gowns, a flowing blue satin trimmed with creamy French lace. The bodice of the gown was cut low and pushed gently against Sorrel's bosom making her breasts appear fuller, and her waist, which was tiny indeed, now looked even trimmer. She coiled her honey-gold curls about her head, making a crown of the shining ringlets, and within each she stuck a tiny, glittering diamond hair pin. She swung about in front of her full-length mirror and laughed gaily at the image that was reflected therein.

Her father would be pleased with her dress, she told herself. She would do her part in putting him in a good mood, for after dinner her aunt had told her to take to her room with the excuse of being tired and that she would then find the time to talk to her father about her going to Virginia with him.

Now, as the food was being set before them, Sorrel smiled lovingly at her father and easily made pleasant small talk as though his telling her no this afternoon had never occurred.

Graylin was much relieved when he took his place at the head of the table and saw that his daughter was dressed beautifully and that she was in a most pleasant mood. He had thought today that the remainder of his stay in his sister's house might be a bit chilly if left up to Sorrel, but now he could see that this was not to be the case. Even Corrine was in a gracious mood, complimenting him on the cut of his clothes and questioning him about his ranch. He knew that this latter she did out of curiosity, for she cared not a wit for his ranch, but for her charming manners he smiled fondly at this woman who was his only sister.

Dinner was completed. Sorrel had barely been able to eat any of the good food served her, so anxious was she about the outcome of her aunt's talk with her father. She hurriedly excused herself, claiming that she felt weary and wished to retire.

Corrine fondly watched Sorrel leave the room and then smiled toward her brother. "Can you remember being that young and alive, Graylin?"

"Aye, Corry, I remember well. But I know now as I feel the aches and pains of my old body that youth is to be lived to its fullest."

"I agree completely, brother. Let us take our wine in the parlor, Graylin." Corrine rose with her glass and started to the parlor. "I think that we have done a fine job with your daughter. Tell me what you think." She sat down upon the settee, spreading her full skirts about herself.

"I am afraid that I owe you all of the credit, Corry." Graylin also sat back upon the settee. "I have not been much of a father to the child, have I?"

"Nonsense." Corrine scolded, sipping at her wine. "Sorrel loves you as much as any young girl should love her father. She understands that she must stay with me, since there is no woman to tend to her needs at the ranch."

"You are kind, sister." Graylin smiled fondly at his sister, knowing that he owed this woman more than he could ever repay. "Sorrel is what I think Leona would have wished her to be, and I owe that all to you."

"You know that I loved Leona also, Graylin, and I would wish to do as she would have wanted. But as I said, I think that the pair of us have raised the girl well. Tell me of your plans, Graylin?" Corrine changed the subject.

Graylin Morgan was used to his sister's brusque manner. Sipping his wine he thought reflectively over what he would tell her. He knew that she was not interested in his ranch or the life he led by himself. "I have plans to take a trip, Corry," he said, thinking that perhaps she would find this of some interest.

At her questioning look he continued, "Aye, at the end of the week I am to sail on the *Seafare Lady* to Virginia."

Corrine waited for only a second before she spoke.

"A trip, but how wonderful! You could not have found a better time."

Graylin looked at his sister, not understanding.

"You will of course wish to take Sorrel with you? Unless of course, this is to be a trip where a daughter is not welcomed? Is it to be your honeymoon, Graylin?" Corrine felt like smiling, but she kept her face impassive.

"A honeymoon?" Graylin sputtered. "Of course not. You know me better than that."

"Well, fine, fine. I can at last go on a vacation myself. And one that I shall confess to you I have been most anxious for."

"Vacation—you? Why did you not mention this to me before? I had no idea that you wished to go away."

"Well, dear, before I had your daughter to care for, but now that you will not be on the ranch but going on a vacation yourself, I see no reason that I should not be able to enjoy myself also."

"Well, Corry, I am not exactly going on a pleasure cruise. I am going to purchase horses for the ranch. I do not see how Sorrel can possibly . . ."

Before he could finish his sister cut him off. "Oh, I think this is wonderful. This is just what the two of you have been needing, a trip alone. You can both get to know each other better. You mustn't forget, Graylin, that Sorrel will marry in only two years, and then you will not have such a chance again."

Graylin Morgan knew when he had been bested. Corry could always do this to him, he stormed to himself. But he could not in all fairness tell her no. She had done more than enough with the raising of his daughter. Perhaps she was right, and it was time for him to take a hand with her. "All right Corry, I concede. I shall take Sorrel with me and you can go on your vacation."

Corrine Borden smiled with her pleasure. "Do you know how long this trip will last, Graylin?" She would miss Sorrel more than she would admit even to herself, and she hoped that the time would not be too long.

"I am not certain, Corry. I shall have to find the horses I want, and then I am not sure on the course back. Perhaps I shall travel overland. I am realizing a little late in life that I have missed seeing quite a bit of this large country that we live in."

That same evening Corrine went to her niece's chambers and knocked lightly on her door.

Sorrel was trying to read, not being able to sleep in her anxiety over the outcome of the meeting between her aunt and her father. But as her aunt came into her room and she saw the broad smile on her face she felt the breath leave her body. She was to go. She jumped up and grabbed her aunt about the waist. "He said yes? Papa did say yes?" she asked, not believing the answer was yes.

"He said exactly that, my pet." Corrine answered, smiling down at Sorrel.

"I shall truly go? I cannot believe it!" Sorrel swung about, laughing and shouting with her happiness.

"I promise you can believe it, love, but for now you had better get some rest, for your father plans to leave at the end of the week, so that only leaves us a few days to have your wardrobe ready and everything prepared." Corrine kissed her niece fondly on the cheek and started to the door.

"I love you, Aunt Corry." Sorrel said, going to her bed and slipping between the cool sheets.

"I love you also, my little princess." Her aunt's words barely reached her as she shut the door.

Chapter Three

The next few days were busy, indeed, for Sorrel Morgan. With her head high in the clouds she went from seamstress to bootmaker, and then back again, at the prodding of her Aunt Corry, to the seamstress. Not a thing was wanting, no article of her wardrobe went without a critical glance of her aunt's eye. She would see that her niece left with nothing but the best. The thought of the young girl she had raised going such a distance without her at her side filled her with worry, but she was determined that none would find any fault, at least, with her niece's attire.

Sorrel went through all of the motions without complaint. This in itself her aunt found quite unusual, for always in the past Sorrel had complained and stalled, not wishing to be bothered with the ordeal of having to be hemmed in, pinched, and turned by the seamstress. So, with such a willing niece now in hand, Corrine Borden dismissed her usual daily headaches and smiled sweetly at everyone who passed along the wood plank sidewalks, as she pulled Sorrel along after her.

To the young girl's thinking the daily trips to the

dressmaker were nothing compared to the afternoon teas that her Aunt Corry insisted on attending after each of these trips. She followed meekly though, knowing how much this small thing meant to her aunt.

Corrine Borden was indeed proud of her niece, thinking that no other in their town could compare to the girl, and with this fact ever present in her thoughts she held her head high as she entered a friend's home, Sorrel following close on her heels. She wished for this last chance to show the girl off and to tell the story over one more time to anyone who would listen, of how her brother was to take a trip and of how his daughter was to accompany him. Little had affected Corrine Borden's life but the activities of her niece, so she boasted with relish to her elderly lady friends of all news that pertained to Sorrel.

Sorrel nodded her head in the affirmative once again as the woman sitting across from her directed her beaklike features in her direction.

"Did I hear you correctly, child?" The voice directed toward Sorrel was almost a shout. "Speak up, girl. I wish to know if this trip is to your liking? Would you not rather stay here with Corrine and all of your comforts? What on earth was your father thinking to make plans for you to accompany him so far away? Why, once some time ago my own darling niece Emmy—you know who I am speaking of?" The birdlike features once more bobbed in Sorrel's direction, but this time she waited for the girl to nod her head.

"Of course, you know Emmy. She married that

nice Mr. Langston, and today she is expecting her third child." The elderly thin woman seemed to puff up with this bit of information she was passing along.

Sorrel indeed knew of the Emily whom Mrs. Kendall, her aunt's oldest friend, was speaking of, but, biting her tongue, she glanced down at her folded hands. She had seen Emily Langston only a few days before walking down the sidewalk, each hand holding on to a squirming child, her shape announcing to all that she was to have another shortly. She could remember Emily in her younger years, and, though the girl had never had what one called beautiful features—was, in fact, rather plain— she had had a dignified bearing. But now after being married to Harry Langston for only three years and having had two babies, she looked old beyond her years, and little was left of any bearing of refinement.

"As I was saying, child. Emmy went to New Orleans when she and Mr. Langston first married, he claiming that he could make a better life for his young bride away from Texas, but you see where they are now, do you not?" With each word the gray head bobbed in Sorrel's direction, reminding the girl of a huge bird ready to attack and devour its prey.

"Yes ma'am," Sorrel murmured, her emerald eyes going once again to her aunt at the other side of the parlor enjoying the company of another one of the ladies at the tea. If this woman thought to discourage her from going with her father, she would be surprised to know her thoughts. Instead of scaring her about the trip ahead, she was more than encouraging her. She would be glad to be away from the pomp and finery of all of these houses she was dragged to. This woman exemplified the falseness that was all around them. Her talking about poor Emily as though she was so well off here in Texas—could she have been any worse off in New Orleans? Was the poor girl doing what was expected of her by having baby after baby and living with a man who drank and could hardly support his small family? Was this all that these women thought another woman's life was for?

"Is it not time yet for you and Clifford to marry?" Again the stern visage was turned toward her. "I cannot understand why your father has agreed to such a long betrothal. You should be doing as my Emmy is, raising a family and making a man happy."

Sorrel could stand no more. She rose to her feet, looked down at the woman before her, and politely excused herself, leaving a gaping Mrs. Kendall following her across the room with her eyes.

Corrine Borden looked up from her cup of tea as she saw Sorrel making her way toward her. She had intended some time ago to go to her niece and rescue her from Ellen Kendall. She had not realized so much time had passed. Ellen Kendall was Corrine's oldest friend, but the years had not been kind to Ellen. She had turned from a most pleasant young woman into an old, picking snob.

"Are you ready dear?" Corrine smiled at her niece as she stood before her, reading the answer to her question on the young girl's face.

"I am rather weary Aunt Corry, it has been a long day and the evening is still ahead. Have you forgotten that father mentioned that Clifford Sumter would be coming by to pick me up at seven?"

"I have not forgotten, child." Corrine rose from the soft chair. "I was about to come to get you."

"I wish that you had," was the murmured reply that barely reached Corrine Borden's ears.

Small gulps of laughter came from Corrine's mouth as she imagined what Ellen had had to say to the girl on the matter of her leaving Texas. Over the years Ellen had come to the decision that no other place on earth was as deserving as her precious Texas.

Corrine had to admit that she also loved this country, but Ellen seemed to think it a crime that anyone would wish to leave her beloved state even for a short time. Corrine remembered when Ellen's poor niece had left Texas and gone somewhere to begin a new life. She could still feel her ears ringing with the slurs that Ellen had cast upon her niece's head for leaving Texas. Corrine smiled thinly as she ushered her niece toward the door of the stately house. She could also remember the day when Ellen had called on her with the news that she had been right all along and that her dear Emmy had finally come to her senses and had wired her aunt for the funds for her and her husband to return to Texas.

Ellen had been smug that day, and that was the day that Corrine had first taken a good look at her oldest friend and seen what kind of woman she had become.

"I did not mean to leave you so long alone with Ellen, dear." Corrine took hold of Sorrel's hand as they left the front door and started down the steps. Humor was evident in her voice as she looked at the young girl at her side.

With the fresh air hitting her full in the face Sorrel smiled at her aunt. "Do not worry yourself about it, Aunt Corry."

"Was she worse today than usual, dear?" Corrine looked for a moment at Sorrel with a worried frown, thinking that perhaps Ellen had said things that she should not have to her niece. She would go along with much, but if anyone were really to try and harm Sorrel she would quickly bare her own thoughts to them, no matter if they were Ellen Kendall or any other.

"No, indeed, Aunt Corry. She was no worse than usual. She seems to think that I would do well to conduct myself like her niece Emily."

Corrine laughed aloud at this, bringing a full smile to Sorrel's lovely features.

"And I am sure that you agreed wholeheartedly with her opinion?"

"You know me better than that, Aunt Corry. Her poor niece Emily is hardly better off than one of your servants. A new baby every year, bah!" Sorrel slowed her walking and turned to her aunt, a serious turn to her golden features. "Emily's life will not be mine. My destiny must hold more than babies every year and caring for a man who does not care whether I become old and haggard before my time."

"Aye child," Corrine smiled toward her. "Your life will be better than most. You would never be satisfied with events going against you."

"You know me well, Aunt Corry. I wish to have a hand in my future, and I wish to know ahead of time what will happen."

"You are satisfied with your future husband, then?" Once again the couple walked at a steady pace toward Corrine's home.

For a second Sorrel did not speak as she thought of how best to phrase her answer. Then she said, "Though I know little of Clifford, since I only see him on rare occasions, I agree with the betrothal to bring the two families together. I do not think that Clifford Sumter will be one to try to bind me down to a woman's place. If he does, Father will be close at hand and will stand fast in my favor."

"You have it all planned out?" Corrine was saddened by the fact that her niece could be so cold and deliberate about her life.

"There have been plenty of years for all this to be arranged in my mind, and I see no reason now for things to have a turnabout."

"Are you not anxious to be alone with your betrothed?" Corrine questioned as they entered the front foyer of her house. She could never truly read Sorrel and upon occasion had to be forward with her questions to the girl if she wished to know her feelings on a subject.

"My, no, Aunt Corry." Sorrel laughed aloud, throwing her purse and parasol down upon the chair before going into the parlor. "Why would I be anxious about Clifford Sumter? One day he shall be my husband and that day will be soon enough to become anxious."

Corrine laughed along with the girl, but an underlying tension in Sorrel disturbed her.

Sorrel soon excused herself to her own chambers to rest and freshen up before dinner. Her aunt's words had brought thoughts to the surface of her mind that she usually tried to put from her.

She had, of course, like any other young girl, had thoughts of what was to happen upon her wedding bed, and, too, as she had been held in the arms of a handsome young man and twirled around the dance floor at some affair, of what it would be like to feel this young man's lips upon her own and his hands claiming her and letting her know what had always been hidden from her.

This evening would be the first that she had ever had alone with Clifford Sumter, and the thoughts could not help but come in her mind of his tall, thin form standing before her. Always in past meetings he had seemed cold and distant. His silver-light eyes and sand-colored hair making him appear a bit far away from everything about him. It had been some time since last she had seen him though, and perhaps he was not really what she had always thought him.

Perhaps he would take her in his arms this very night and leave her breathless with his kisses. She envisioned in her mind her shaking limbs and panting breath. Would this be the way of things, she wondered as she lay down and tried to shut her eyes.

But sleep would not come to her now that the floodgates of her deepest thoughts had been opened. Would Clifford declare his hidden love for her this very night? Would he even beg her not to leave with her father but to stay instead and to marry him sooner than had been planned? Was this perhaps the reason for his visit to town and his request of her father to escort her to the Shatners' ball? If she acted reluctant would he perhaps seduce her into agreeing?

Her blood seemed to pound in her veins with these thoughts. Never before had these feelings for the unknown dark secrets of her body's yearnings seemed so overpowering. She seemed not to be able to still her fevered pulse, and, finding no rest on her soft bed, she pulled herself up and strode about her chambers.

Forcing herself to still she stood at the end of her bed. She would have to pull herself together. If not, she would be a fumbling mess of nerves this evening at dinner and then there would be questions, both from her aunt and her father.

Taking a deep breath of air she once more forced herself to lie down upon her bed and try to take a small rest. It took some time before her body could relent and relax, but even as she lay in a hazy form of dreaming sleep she felt her mind at work, thinking beyond to this evening when she would be alone with the man she was to marry.

Sorrel awoke refreshed and much more herself as a maid came into her chambers to help her to dress for dinner. Pushing all thoughts from her mind of Clifford Sumter and the ball that she was to attend this evening she set about making herself presentable. Sitting before her dressing table mirror in only a white, sheer chemise the girl began to take her golden strands of hair and mold them into ringlets atop her head. Within each of these fashionable curls she placed a tiny snow-white pearl hairpin, holding the coiffure tightly in place.

"You will be wishing to wear the pearls, ma'am?" The maid looked into the mirror at the girl-woman before her before reaching about and taking up the strand of pearls and matching ear bobs lying upon the dressing table.

At the nodding of the golden head the girl proceeded to place the pearls about Sorrel's neck. "You are a vision as you are, ma'am," she sighed aloud as she stepped back and viewed her handwork. "Only a slight touch of rouge to the cheeks and lips to bring a bit of color, and you will be ready for your dress."

Sorrel sat patiently letting the girl work with deft fingers to bring out the fullness of her beauty. Little seemed to affect Sorrel Morgan about the woman in the mirror. She had seen this same sight time and again before leaving for a party given by one of her aunt's friends or a ball such as this evening's given by the parents of one of her own friends.

As the girl went to the wardrobe to fetch the dress that Sorrel was to wear she pulled on her silk stockings and put on her white slippers.

"Here is your dress, Miss Sorrel." The girl lovingly laid out the white taffeta dress and softly let her hands slide over the delicate material.

Sorrel's eyes also went to the creation as it lay across the bed, her eyes lighting up somewhat with the sight. Her Aunt Corry had insisted that she not pack this dress but keep it for this night, and now Sorrel knew the reason for her insistence. Never before had she had a gown of such beauty, sewn with such perfect workmanship. The material was taffeta, but it seemed to glitter with the snow-whiteness of its color. The bodice was cut low and bordered with tiny white seed pearls, the sleeves puffed to the elbows and then tightly gathered to the wrists. So much material had been used to make the dress that it covered one end of Sorrel's bed, and the girl could well imagine the feel of the flowing softness all about her.

"If you would stand, ma'am, I will help you on with the gown," the small maid said.

Sorrel stood and the maid hurriedly went about her work, pulling the gown over Sorrel's head and straightening the material in every direction. It was only a short time before the girl stood back and admired her mistress. "You are quite beautiful, ma'am," the girl breathed in admiration of the woman standing before her, her brown, laughing eyes telling Sorrel the truth of her words as they went over Sorrel's form from head to toe.

Sorrel went to the mirror to see for herself, and what she saw made her gasp with surprise. She had never considered white to be too flattering a color on her somewhat cream and golden form, but as her emerald eyes went from the tips of her tiny white satin slippers, which peeked out from beneath the hem of the gown, to the top of her golden curls glittering with the tiny white pearl hairpins, she knew that she was looking her loveliest. The green of her eyes and the honey-gold of her hair brought just the right amount of color to the whiteness of the gown.

The small maid stood behind her and watched the view in the mirror of her mistress admiring herself and a large smile came over her lips. "'Tis beautiful you are, Miss Sorrel. Mrs. Borden shall be quite pleased with the sight of you when you go down to dinner."

At the girl's words Sorrel was once more reminded

of the evening before her, and now the eyes that had been traveling over her form gazed consideringly toward the mirror. Would Clifford Sumter find her appearance appealing? Would she sweep him off his feet, as the saying went, and bring him to his knees this very night?

"There is only a few more minutes until dinner shall be served, miss." The girl brought Sorrel from her thoughts of Clifford Sumter as she turned and started from the room.

With only a last glance over her shoulder at the mirror Sorrel also started to the door. She did not wish to be late and keep her father and aunt waiting at the dinner table. Perhaps Clifford had even arrived early and was this minute also awaiting her appearance.

With this thought in mind she went out of the room and started down the staircase, voices coming from the main parlor drawing her attention.

With excited anticipation Sorrel entered the parlor, but as her eyes went about the room she quickly realized that Clifford had as yet not arrived.

"Why, my dear," Corrine rose from the settee, "the gown is simply stunning!" She rushed toward the door and took Sorrel by the arm.

"Thank you, Aunt Corry," Sorrel smiled, accepting the arm and let herself be led toward the settee and sat down across from her father.

Graylin Morgan's eyes came alight with the entrance of his daughter into the parlor. He did not rise as Corrine beat him to the girl and escorted her to the settee opposite him. "Indeed, quite stunning, indeed," he murmured loud enough for all to hear. "I think that perhaps it will be a mistake, your going on this trip with me."

Sorrel looked with some concern at her father, thinking that he had changed his mind about taking her with him.

A soft smile came to Graylin's face. "I shall have to watch you quite closely. And also, there is the matter of taking you away from Houston and from all of the eligible young men here that your aunt has been telling me about."

"Not a one means a thing to me, Papa. You know that I am but passing the time until I can marry and have a home of my own." Sorrel thought that perhaps he was angry with her aunt's report of her flirtatious behavior with the young men in Houston.

Graylin's guffs of laughter filled the parlor. "I was teasing, child. I would in no way wish to bind you until the time of your marriage. You have not forgotten that Clifford should be arriving at any time?" He watched for her reaction to his words.

A slight blush came over her creamy features with the mention of Clifford Sumter's name, her thoughts of the young man throughout the day having made her vulnerable.

Instantly Graylin noticed the color coming to his daughter's face, and, thinking it only a womanly shyness at the boldness of his tone, he went on, "It has been some time since last you saw the Sumter boy. Actually, he is no longer a boy," Graylin murmured, more to himself. "If you find that you have any doubts about the match—"

Sorrel did not let him finish. "I am sure that it will all be fine. I wish for no more than what the Sumters can offer. The two ranches will be joined, and then also I shall be able to leave town and live on the ranch." This was truly about all her betrothal meant to Sorrel, and she spoke truthfully to her father.

"I would wish for you to want more," Graylin said, but before any more could be added one of the servants entered the parlor and announced that dinner would be served as soon as they were ready.

Ushering both women toward the dining room, Graylin was pulled up short by the sound of voices coming from the front foyer. "Perhaps this is the young man now. I shall only be a moment, if you will excuse me?" His look was directed toward his sister before he left the two of them. They proceeded without him to the dining room.

Sorrel sat nervously before her plate waiting for the gentlemen to come into the dining room, her hands fidgeting upon her lap as her emerald eyes strayed toward the door.

"What is it, child? Is the meal not to your liking?" Corrine questioned, though she knew the reason for her niece's distress. She rather enjoyed watching the girl as she sat watching for her father and the young man to enter the room. It was a rare scene indeed for her to witness Sorrel in any kind of discomfort.

"No, no Aunt Corry, the food is fine. I guess that the thought of the ball ahead of me this evening is leaving me with the wish not to eat too much. I would hate to dance across the ballroom with a full stomach." She tried some humor to regain her composure.

Graylin was the only one to enter the dining room.

He sat and took a bite of food before his blue eyes rose to meet Sorrel's. He could see the question in her eyes before he spoke up. "Clifford will await you in the parlor. Finish your meal."

From the tone of Graylin's voice Sorrel did not prompt him to find out why he had left Clifford alone in the parlor. Perhaps he had eaten and did not wish to disturb them at their mealtime, she reasoned, as she finished picking at the food upon her plate.

The rest of the meal was eaten in silence. Sorrel, when she dared a look at her father, found that his visage was somewhat piqued, and she could not help wonder what words had been said between the two men.

Pushing his chair away from the table Graylin stood to his feet and looked from his sister to his daughter. Would you care to join me in the parlor? I think that we have left the young man long enough."

Clifford stood near the hearth, his tall, thin frame seeming to stand out starkly in the small room.

Graylin cleared his throat. The young man seemed absorbed in his own thoughts as he leaned with one hand on the mantel and looked down into the hearth.

Clifford spun on his heels as he heard the noise from the door.

The look upon his face was the one that Sorrel had remembered from past visits from this young man: always serious. The icy gray eyes regarded the other three penetratingly.

"Miss Morgan, I hope that you are ready to be leaving?" One light brow arched in Sorrel's direction.

Sorrel nodded her head, realizing that all her

thoughts of romance earlier that day had been for naught. She had forgotten how coldly arrogant this young man could be. Actually, she had to admit to herself that she found him rather distasteful. He seemed bent only on his own desires, no warmth evident in his face as he directed his gaze toward her.

"Then if you will excuse us, Mr. Morgan? I have a carriage waiting." Without answer he went to Sorrel's side and took a firm hold of her elbow. "I shall not keep Sorrel too late."

"Aye, I would wish for her to be home early," Graylin responded to Clifford Sumter. "She has a busy day ahead of her tomorrow."

Sorrel's disappointment was monumental in the dismally quiet interior of the carriage and extended their arrival at the Shatners' front door.

She had hoped that since last she had seen Clifford he would have changed in some way, but it was clear that this had not happened. She had wished to attract him with her gown but as of yet he had in no way indicated that he even noticed that she wore anything other than her everyday clothes. Not by the slightest glance had he shown that he was attracted to her in any fashion.

Sorrel sighed loudly as she leaned her head back against the cushioned seat of the vehicle, her day's dreaming and romantic notions leaving her with the cold frustration of reality. This was the real Clifford Sumter, the man whom she would one day wed and live with. This cold, unresponsive gentleman sitting across from her, his eyes now seeming a bit sharper with her sigh.

"Is there something the matter, Miss Morgan?"

She wished to shout out her misery with his question. How could he ask such a thing of her? Not even allowing himself the right to use her given name. How bland and withdrawn a man he seemed to her. Not daring to answer him, for fear that her voice would in some way give way to her emotions, she shook her head in the negative, and once more he turned his head toward the window and seemed lost to her presence.

The ride to the Shatners was longer than Sorrel would have wished, the driver seeming to take an unusual amount of time to reach the end of the slightly bumpy ride. But when he did finally pull down the long drive and up to the front of the huge, stylish mansion, a soft sigh escaped her once more.

The driver jumped from the top of the vehicle and placed the small steps on the ground in front of the door. After helping Clifford from the interior he helped the lovely young lady who was his employer's guest, as Clifford Sumter stood to the side and watched with his gray-chilled glare.

With no words spoken he once more took hold of Sorrel's elbow and proceeded to steer her toward the main entrance, where loud music, talk, and laughter could quite plainly be heard.

As Sorrel looked at the gaiety and the brilliant colors of the ball swirling about her she lost herself for a short time to the happy affair.

Clifford seemed to take little notice of anyone about him as he handed the butler his hat and cane. "Be sure to take good care my man," he cautioned the servant, not seeming to notice the resentful glare that came from the butler at his distrustful words.

Sorrel was not one to be mildly led about, so with Clifford's being busy with the worry of his belongings she went with little thought toward the ballroom, and there she found couples already gliding across the floor, beautiful multicolored gowns sparkling with jewels and spangles adorning the forms of the most elegant women of Houston as they in turn were swept about the dance floor by gentlemen in the most dashing and distinguished dress.

Only a short moment went by before Sorrel was spotted standing within the doorway unescorted. No young man with any understanding of beauty was willing to let Sorrel Morgan stay long as a wallflower, and as soon as eyes were cast her way a score of young men were at her side for their names to be placed on her dance card.

Sorrel, as always in the company of young men, became the gracious, flirting young woman whom all of Houston knew and loved. And, peering sweetly at one young man and then the next, she wrote their names on the small dance card that was kept in the white taffeta purse secured about her wrist. She seemed in her element here in the ballroom with the sparkling lights, the music filling her ears, and the young adoring eyes watching her every movement. Even thoughts of the one who was one day to become her husband fled her mind as she replied with witty charm to questions posed in her direction.

Clifford seemed in no way upset at the sight of his betrothed laughing and responding so willingly to the men all about her. To his mind she already belonged to him, and anything that was his was in no way in jeopardy. He had been informed that the girl never dared any more than to invite a gentleman to tea. Though she was well known in Houston for her flirtatious ways, he knew that she had never invited a man more than once to her aunt's home and that she was always chaperoned. He reasoned with himself that she was much like him. Their future was all that mattered, and in the end, with their two ranches joined, they would one day be reckoned with in Texas.

He smiled thoughtfully as he watched one of the men from the group about Sorrel take her hand and lead her out onto the dance floor. He could understand the reason for the others' enthusiasm over the young woman. She was somewhat of a beauty, that is, he thought, if one liked the type. She was a bit too perfect for his taste. He leaned to the dark and sultry; the earthy type woman always seemed to attract him. For a moment black, flashing eyes came to his mind, and he thought of the night past. His pulses raced for a second as he relived the excitement of standing before the woman as victor, her eyes pleading for pity as he again reached out to her.

Clifford Sumter's delight was in not easily being given what he wished. To him the excitement was in force and in taking what he wanted. A cry of pain on lush red lips and pleading cries had always brought a ready response in him. As he came back to reality and the room about him he looked about the swirling couples until he found the one he sought. She was indeed different than any woman in his past. White and golden and light emerald eyes. He was sure that he would, within a very short time after their marriage, be bored to death with the girl. He was glad that she was so like him and cared for the finer things in life. Of course he was not one to share what was his, but he would let her have her way about the ranch, and perhaps she would even prefer to stay here in Houston most of the time with her aunt. Her father was a man of some means here in Texas, and Clifford knew that he would never easily take to his only daughter's being deliberately mistreated. And with their marriage only a short two years away, Clifford now had begun to make some small plans.

Sorrel had no awareness of the thoughts of her betrothed as she was swung about the ballroom floor, her head floating with the lively music and sharp steps of her partner. "Oh, Mr. Channing, I fear that I am completely breathless," she gasped as the tune came to a halt and the couples across the floor all took a break to fan themselves.

"Would you care for something to drink, Miss Morgan?" Tom Channing questioned, wishing to please this young woman in any way possible. "It will only take a short moment." He had already started from her side to fetch the desired object.

"Lemonade would do quite nicely," Sorrel laughed aloud, finding the young man's hurried manner a bit amusing.

Without another word he was hurrying across the room to the punchbowl, not realizing that with the leaving of Sorrel's side he was leaving her free game to any other young man within sight. And within a few seconds she was once more being swept across the floor, all thoughts of her tired feet and the lemonade that Mr. Channing had gone to fetch long gone from her mind.

"Why, Mr. Fleming, I am afraid that that would be quite impossible. You see, I did come escorted. In fact, I am here this evening with Clifford Sumter." And with her eyes downcast and her long golden lashes delicately fanning over the emerald orbs she added, "He is also my betrothed."

The gentleman had been questioning Sorrel about how she was to get back to her aunt's. He had seen her come into the ballroom earlier this evening with no escort and had dared to hope that somehow he could be lucky enough to get this beautiful creature alone in his carriage. But now as her words were spoken his face became most crestfallen. "You do wound me Miss Morgan, with these words. I had had the slight hope that you and I could find but a moment to be alone and to enjoy each other's company."

Sorrel knew his thoughts well and laughed gaily as she was swung around the young man in a flowing sweep. "You must indeed be jesting, Mr. Fleming. Why, you have met my aunt." She stood before him now, cheek to cheek. "My Aunt Corry would never allow me to attend an affair such as this without proper escort. Why Mr. Fleming, if not for Mr. Sumter's being here at the Shatners' ball, my aunt herself would be here now at my side."

At the young man's doubtful look Sorrel watched him fully for a moment. "I had heard some talk a while back about Clifford Sumter being engaged to you, but I thought at the time that this could hardly be the truth." The words were out before Dale Fleming really thought of what he was saying.

"Why would you doubt it?" Sorrel questioned with interest.

Dale Fleming caught himself in time before he said much more. "I only meant, I mean—nothing really. I had heard that you and Clifford Sumter were to marry, that is all." He would not be the one to tell this young woman what kind of man she was to marry. Perhaps she knew already for herself and did not mind his arrogant ways and his harsh treatment of people who were not quite his equal.

"Is there something you would like to add, Mr. Fleming?" Sorrel looked to him as the music stopped and they stood in the middle of the dance floor.

"No, no, Miss Morgan," he hurriedly replied, also noticing the closing of the dance. "I see that there are others awaiting the pleasure of your company." He looked toward a small group of men who stood looking in their direction.

Sorrel would have detained him to try and find out more about the man she was to marry but he took her arm and rushed her off the dance floor. Within seconds she was in another man's arms, dancing across the room. She would have liked to find out more about Clifford Sumter. For the first time she realized that no one she knew really knew much about the man, and that she, in fact, knew almost nothing about him. All her information about him came from her father, and even Graylin had said little. Most of his remarks had been about the Sumter ranch, not Clifford himself. Dale Fleming's voice had sounded dubious when he was talking about Clifford and the fact that she was engaged to him. There had to be a reason for his reaction and now she really wanted to know what it was. But she was not to find out any more about her betrothed that evening than she had learned in the past. Dance after dance she was swept across the floor, until she thought herself about to fall from exhaustion.

It was with some relief after the ending of the music that she happened to glimpse Clifford. He stood casually near the french windows talking to a plump, elderly man with graying hair. They seemed to be quite deep in their conversation, but with hardly a thought Sorrel directed her partner to escort her to their corner.

"I am afraid that I have been quite delinquent as far as Mr. Sumter is concerned," she told the young man at her arm. "Why I came to the ball with him, but, in fact, I have as yet not even danced a turn with him."

The young man seemed to understand perfectly and without another word brought her before the two men.

Clifford's words stopped in midair as he saw Sorrel coming toward him. What was the chit up to, he wondered idly as he glanced at her weary smile. Was she ready to leave and go back to her aunt's house? As he awaited her approach he pulled out his gold pocket watch, flipped the case open, and he studied the time.

The elderly man noticed the approaching of the couple and the irritated manner of Clifford Sumter. He excused himself and left to seek out another gentleman whom he had been watching for during the evening.

"Why, Mr. Sumter, I have been looking for you

and am glad to finally find you here near the windows. I am afraid that the time is growing late, and I have not allowed you one dance." Sorrel smiled from the young man at her arm to the stern visage of the man standing next to the windows and watching her so intently.

For a moment no one said another word. Then Clifford took hold of her elbow and with a light nod of his head he excused the young man from their small party and led Sorrel out into the gardens and through the french doors.

"I am afraid, Sorrel, that I do not dance." His pace was leisurely as he walked along the marble court.

Sorrel sighed with relief, glad that she would not once again have to be swung about the dance floor. She took a deep breath of the fresh air, in which mingled the delicious scents of blossoming flowers. These Texas nights seemed to blossom with a heady fragrance that filled her senses with sheer delight. Her aunt's gardens were much like these, and she enjoyed nothing more than to walk in them at the close of the evening and let her mind fill with their pleasure.

Clifford looked down into her face at her sigh. He had thought her serious about his leading her about the dance floor, but now he realized that she had used him only as a ruse to be away from the young man at her side and a reason to have a short respite from the ballroom. A small, tight grin came over his features. He rather liked her spirit. Perhaps he would not grow bored so quickly with her. After all, there were still two years before their marriage, and in that time she could still change quite a bit.

Sorrel spotted a small bench in front of them. She took charge of their direction, and, spreading out her gown, she sat back against the bench. Enjoying the gardens, she could almost imagine herself alone. She shut her emerald eyes for a slight moment and listened to the small night sounds all about her.

Clifford stood above her and looked down into her face, seeing the beauty that everyone in Houston saw in her features. She still did not appeal to him as many others in his past had. But he had to admit that she would be a fine mate, and that together they could produce fine sons to carry on his ranch. Without preamble he bent down and hastily took the petal-pink lips below his own, his first reaction delight at the surprise and then the frantic struggle of her young, firm body.

Sorrel was surprised by his actions. She had all but forgotten his presence, and, at the feel of those cool, almost lifeless lips upon her own, she felt herself captured, like a bird in a cage, and her first impulse was to fight for her freedom.

Nothing could please Clifford Sumter more than this small fight that Sorrel was presenting to him. With her pushing against him and trying to draw her mouth away he grasped his arms tightly about her and pulled her to her feet and up against his chest, his lips now descending relentlessly.

Sorrel felt breathless, as though smothering under the torture of those thin, hard lips. It was not at all as she had dreamed that afternoon. She had envisioned herself half swooning from the sheer pleasure of being held in this man's arms, but she was now in no way about to collapse with delight; on the contrary, she was about to buckle under from the pressure of his hard body and twisted mouth. Anger began to rise in her and she began to push harder. With no other option open to her, she brought her tiny slipper up and kicked out, feeling the foot making contact with his shin.

Clifford felt the small pain in his leg from her outburst and some of his senses came back to him. He was here in the Shatners' gardens holding Graylin Morgan's only daughter in his arms and attacking her as though she was no better than any common woman of the street. With some restraint he pulled himself away, but in the gray eyes was the promise that soon he would see an end to his waiting. Without a word of apology or a declaration of love or admiration such as Sorrel had heard in the past from overeager young men, Clifford began to straighten out his clothes.

"If you are about ready, I think it is time that I had you back to your aunt's house."

Sorrel looked him in the face, trying to read what was in his mind. How unfeeling and cruel was this man that she was to marry. Did he think he had the right to treat her in such a foul manner? She also tried pulling her gown into some order before she could force her voice from her throat. "I agree, Mr. Sumter."

"I would have you call me Clifford."

His tone was still cold and unyielding, Sorrel thought. Perhaps she was not giving him a fair chance, she thought as he led her through a side door of the Shatners' house and toward the front foyer to receive his hat and cane. Perhaps he was not as hard as he made out and with time he would mellow toward her somewhat. She knew that she would marry him, for it had been planned since she had been a child, and she more than anyone knew wished to live out and away from the hustle and activity of Houston. She wished for the two ranches to be combined so that she would be a part of her father's destiny. She had grown into a woman with these plans always before her, and in her thoughts had always been the wish for the days to hurry by.

The ride home was in silence. Their leaving of the Shatners' ball was much like their arrival, with Clifford looking stonily out the window and Sorrel reclining on the opposite seat with her hands folded primly in her lap.

The next day Sorrel spent mostly in her bed, telling her aunt that she wished to rest before the trip the following day. Mostly, though, her thoughts were of the night before. She would in no way change her marriage plans, but she could not for a moment forget those piercing gray eyes upon her and the feel of those slanted, hard lips brutally descending upon her own.

No relief came to her, though, so finally, with the finishing of the afternoon, she scolded herself sternly and determined within her own mind that she would set thoughts of Clifford Sumter from her. She had two years before the marriage agreement was to be consummated, and within that time perhaps he would change.

With some determination she brushed out her long golden curls, put on her dressing robe, and went downstairs to take dinner with her father and Aunt Corry.

Chapter Four

It was an early, warm morning, the sun not yet rising, when the sleek ship the *Seafare Lady* left her port in Houston, Texas. Her passengers had all boarded the evening before, and Captain Spencer with his crew at the ready pulled up anchor and began his trip to sea.

Sorrel had been delighted with her accommodations aboard ship. She had not known what to expect and had thought that, with so little notice of her accompanying her father, she would have to make do with whatever was afforded her. But as the first mate showed her and her father to their cabins she smiled with her delight at the two adjoining rooms, one her bedchamber and the other a small sitting room. Whatever she had expected it had not been what was before her now. The wood floor was carpeted, and, though the furniture was sparse, it was very tasteful.

Her father made no mention of the rooms as he was also shown to his quarters. He had paid well for what they were receiving and he would have been disappointed with anything less.

That first night, after a tray of light dinner was sent

to Sorrel's cabin, her father made a late visit to his daughter. They sat in the small sitting room and Graylin Morgan tried to get a bit closer to the woman-girl who was his daughter. He had missed a lot in her growing up and had decided that this trip would be one where the two of them could make up for the time they had lost. Perhaps, he thought as he questioned her about her life at her aunt's, they would become good friends on this voyage.

Sorrel was pleased with everything about her and when her father left her to her sleep she swung her arms wide and turned about wildly. She was truly leaving Houston and going with her father! It had all seemed like some strange dream these past few days, packing and having gowns readied and leaving messages with her few close friends that she would be leaving. But now here she was, Sorrel Morgan, the girl who had thought only a week ago that she would be forever living with her aunt until the day of her marriage (and that was a subject that she did not want to dwell on)—here she was on this huge ship and in the morning she would be far out to sea.

She threw herself upon the soft mattress of the bed and sighed with pleasure. It was as though the hand of destiny was directing her path. The thought fleetingly went through her mind: Was there something waiting for her in this unknown place that she would be visiting? Was that the reason for that fear she had felt that day that her father had told her that she would not be able to make this trip with him? That same desperation for a second again stole over her as she lay looking up at the wood ceiling of the ship. Aye, for some reason she could not grasp, she had felt a desperate need grip at her vitals at the thought of not accompanying her father, and now, as she felt that bit of desperation, she also felt the same surging exhilaration that she had the night her aunt had come to her chambers and told her that she would be going to Virginia.

What was there about this trip? she questioned herself. What was she to find at the journey's end? Her green eyes softly shut with these thoughts and a peaceful slumber induced by the slight rolling motion of the *Seafare Lady* overtook her body.

Early the next morning Sorrel awoke to the creaking and dipping movement of the ship. No light came through the porthole in her chambers, so she knew as she glanced about that it was indeed quite early, and, before rolling over and once more shutting her eyes, she said softly to the vacant room, "Good-bye sweet aunt, good-bye Texas."

The days aboard the *Seafare Lady* were calm and peaceful for the passengers as the large ship sailed for her destination.

Sorrel found, as her father did not, that life aboard a ship agreed with her. She loved the rocking motion of the waves hitting the hull of the *Seafare Lady* and she delighted in the salt spray hitting against her face and the wind blowing her hair out from her as she stood along the deck looking out to the vast, blue-green sea.

Graylin, though, was of a different constitution. After two days of the rolling of the ship he took to his cabin and to his bed. Sorrel offered to stay with him and tend him but he would not hear of her having to stay shut up because he could not handle the rocking sea as well as he could a galloping horse. He had laughed aloud when he told his concerned daughter this sallie. He was not really too ill, he explained, just a bit off his feed. He assured Sorrel that the ship's doctor had checked with him and left him some pills, which the good man had assured him would put him back to his old self in no time at all, and that though he was lying abed, he was not all that sick.

Sorrel had watched her father with a keen eye, noticing the greenish tint to his usually tanned and healthy complexion and also seeing the way his eyes would widen with each motion of the ship. She would never have thought that such a healthy man as her father would so easily get seasick, but the ship's doctor had assured her that he had seen the same thing happen before and that usually it did not last but a few days. "He only needs a few days to be finding his sea legs." The words of the rotund, gray-haired doctor came back to Sorrel now as she sat and read a while to her ailing father.

When Sorrel was not trying to bring some small bit of comfort to her father she was either visiting with another passenger along the deck or exploring the vast ship. Everyone aboard the *Seafare Lady* found the beautiful, golden-haired girl delightful. Even the captain, who was well known for his bad temper, seemed to mellow and smile whenever the Morgan girl was about.

The first mate, Nate Palmer, was younger than the captain, and, hoping that the girl would find some favor with him, would find different excuses that would put him near Sorrel. He knew that her father had been taken ill, so he thought that there was nothing in the way, that was, if the girl agreed. So, with careful and calculating mind, he went after what he wanted.

Sorrel, though, was no greenhorn when it came to young men, and she had fended off many unwelcome advances for the last several years. So, with a mind to having some pleasure aboard this voyage, she let the young Mr. Palmer bring her tray himself to her cabin, and, when he invited her for a stroll along the deck one fair evening, she told him without second thought to meet her outside of her father's cabin. She would have to make sure that he was well before she could leave him for the night.

Nate Palmer was in heaven as he strutted along the deck with Sorrel Morgan on his arm. Never before had he seen, let alone escorted, a young lady as beautiful as this one. He could smell the light lemon scent that clung to her honey curls, and with each smile that she bestowed upon him he thought himself to be melting from within. This Miss Morgan was a vision from an unreal dream, he told himself over and over that night.

As the pair walked about they passed by another couple strolling around the deck. "Good evening, Mrs. Willows," Sorrel greeted the elder woman who looked as she always did, dressed in black with a dark bonnet pulled over her head and casting a shadow over her large features. Adell Willows nodded her head curtly and then turned back to her husband Sherman. Sherman Willows seemed to have been cut in much the same mold as his wife, he also wore all black and was tall and quite large, his dark eyes darting about him constantly. He too greeted the young woman who approached them on the arm of the first mate.

Sorrel stopped for a second before the elder pair, her peach satin dress shimmering noticeably in the moonlight. She smiled softly. "Is it not just a glorious evening?" Her green eyes looked above her at the stars and the other couple followed her movement.

"Aye 'tis a fine evening, Miss Morgan," Sherman Willows replied, looking to his wife for her agreement.

Adell Willows was a stern and domineering woman who disliked any frivolity in others, especially her husband, and with a hard look at the man at her side she took hold of his hand and stated, "'Tis late. We must be getting our rest. Excuse us please, Miss Morgan." And with these words she turned, pulling her husband by the arm behind her.

Sorrel laughed lightly when the pair were out of sight and Nate Palmer watched her with glowing eyes. Any other woman would have been insulted by Mrs. Willows' nasty behavior, but not this Sorrel Morgan. She was a wonder.

Sorrel walked to the rail and looked out to sea, her emerald eyes gazing dreamily over the churning waves caused by the *Seafare Lady*. Aloud she sighed her pleasure, and for a moment she forgot about her companion standing at her side.

"You love her, too," the first mate said softly.

Coming back to reality Sorrel looked at the young man next to her. Nate Palmer was barely inches taller than she, and his build was rather slight. His only truly appealing features were his mouth, which was always smiling, and his brown, cheerful eyes. Now she looked into those dark brown eyes with her own questioning.

"I mean the sea. You love her also," the first mate tried to explain himself.

Sorrel laughed lightly, her tinkling voice touching softly upon her companion's ears. "Aye, I guess I do love her."

"I thought as much by the way you watch her. Only someone who truly cares for her great beauty and courage could watch her so." Nate Palmer's tone was gentle as his own eyes looked over the sea. Hardly ever did he express himself in this line, and now, if a light were to be put near his face, one would see that his words had brought a dark pink flush over his features.

"Why, how beautiful, Mr. Palmer. You should have been a writer instead of a ship's first mate, then you could have put to paper all of these feelings that you have about the sea."

Nate Palmer flushed even a deeper shade of red. "Nay, ma'am, that is why I am a first mate. One day I hope to have my own ship, as my father and his before him did. It is a long and passionate love in my family line, this love of the sea, and the only way to share that love is to stay near her."

"Oh, I see, Mr. Palmer. And I agree you should captain a ship and stay near the one that holds your heart so," Sorrel replied.

At that moment Nate Palmer wished that he had the courage to hold this beautiful young girl and tell her how he felt about her, but though he may have had the courage to talk of his love of the sea, he knew that he did not dare to say the things that were going through his mind about the woman at his side. Instead, he took Sorrel by the arm and steered her about the rest of the deck, and then finally they were once again at her cabin door.

"Thank you for a lovely walk, Mr. Palmer." Sorrel started through her open door.

"Miss Morgan," the first mate stopped her hand as she held the doorknob, "could you find it permissible to call me Nate?" he dared.

Sorrel stood for a moment, and then with a tiny laugh she answered, "Why Mr. Palmer, I am afraid that I should not dare such a thing such as that. You see how people like the Willows notice what goes on about them on the ship. I am afraid that my father would be shocked if word made its way to him that I was using a gentleman's given name." Sorrel's emerald eyes sparkled with her humor. She loved this game of flirting with young men.

"Oh, I am sorry for even suggesting such a thing, Miss Morgan. Do forgive me." Nate Palmer was disappointed, but he did not want Sorrel to become angry with his brash manner and refuse to see him again. He thought that, given the chance, he could win her over to him, and then who knew what could happen. This was to be a long voyage and the nights grew longer with each passing day.

"I do forgive you," Sorrel laughed, calling over her shoulder as she entered her cabin and shut the door tightly behind herself.

But Nate Palmer was not to gain another chance of

winning Sorrel. The following day Graylin Morgan regained his health, and, true to the doctor's predictions, he was hale and hearty once again, and now, wherever the daughter was, there also was the father.

The pair spent their days and evenings together, either walking and visiting about the ship with the other passengers, or sitting and talking with only each other in the confines of Sorrel's small sitting room.

Graylin found himself more than intrigued with this daughter of his and found that he enjoyed her company tremendously. When they were apart he missed her immensely. She was like a bursting bubble of joy, her spirits always at a high and her humor never far away. She seemed to find the best in any situation and always delighted him with her smiles of pleasure. And as the trip neared its end Graylin found himself glad to have his daughter along. He could not imagine himself now without her. He had to confess that he would have been bored to distraction with only the other passengers aboard for company.

Sorrel herself was overjoyed at her father's recovery. She loved the special care that he gave her and the way his eyes filled with a tender love when they watched her move about her cabin. After all the years of being without her father, she seemed to glow with the attention that he now paid her.

By the time Richmond, Virginia was sighted the first mate, Mr. Palmer, was fit to be tied. He had tried on several occasions to find Sorrel Morgan alone, but all had been to no avail, and with the thought that the following day would bring them to dock in Richmond his mind became panicked. Perhaps this night he would be able to find a moment alone with her, he thought to himself as he went to find the captain and tell him that land had been sighted. If he could find no time before dinner, perhaps this evening on his watch he could find a moment to go to her cabin.

Dinner that evening was a gay affair, the passengers and the captain of the *Seafare Lady* all knowing that this would be their last night together. Captain Spencer had ordered his first mate to go to each of the passengers personally and to invite them all to his cabin for the evening meal. His ship's galley was rather small, so usually on his trips his passengers were served their meals in their own cabins, but for this night he had had several of his men working the day through with moving furniture about and setting up tables to accommodate his guests.

Sorrel looked anxiously toward the evening ahead, it being the only gay affair aboard the *Seafare Lady* since they had boarded her in Houston. She dressed with special care, wanting to impress the company that would be in the captain's cabin and also to make her father proud of her. She did not want him to regret for a moment that he had brought her along.

Her gown was of a silver satin, the bodice low cut and the sleeves tight fitting to show the shape of her arms. The material clung softly to the contours of her young body, and as Sorrel looked in the mirror her green eyes twinkled brightly. Her Aunt Corry had been ecstatic when she had found this satin material and had exclaimed her delight when the dressmaker had finished with the gown. Sorrel had not worn the creation until this evening and now she viewed what her aunt must have envisioned in her mind. The gown was beautiful, and Sorrel, with her golden-streaked hair piled high atop her head in curl after curl with tiny glittering hairpins within each of the circles, was beyond the mere, simple idea of beauty. She was breathtaking, and she knew as her slanted, emerald eyes looked at her reflection in the glass that none aboard the *Seafare Lady* would compare with her this evening.

Graylin Morgan arrived at his daughter's cabin an hour before the appointed time for dinner, and with his entrance into her room he felt his heart skip a tremendous beat. The woman who stood before him, her silver gown glistening in the candlelight, her skin a golden satin and her beautiful eyes glowing, belonged to him. How could he have made anything this perfect, he thought as he came to himself and quickly walked to her side and gathered her hand in his own. "Sorrel, you are a vision." He brought her dainty hand to his lips and kissed the tips of her pearl-shaped fingers. "If only your mother could see you now." His last words came out in a sigh of longing.

A sadness came over Sorrel that she was not used to, her life always having been carefree and without worry. She had never had time even to miss her mother with her Aunt Corry always with her and acting as though she was her mother. But now, as she heard the longing and sadness of her father's voice, she knew there was something she had missed. "What was she like, Papa?" She had never before asked this question, and no one in her family had told her very much about Leona Morgan.

Graylin looked deep into the green eyes before him. "Much like you, I would wish to think, if she had been free to live her own life, that is."

Sorrel looked at him not quite knowing what his words meant. "Free, Papa? Was she not free as your wife?"

"Your mother was a very rare woman, Sorrel. She loved life and all that was about her." Graylin let go his daughter's hand and went to the sideboard and poured himself a glass of wine. "I never knew until the last minute her true feelings about her life. Oh, I do not mean that she was dissatisfied, I only mean that she had been pushed into marrying me at a young age, and, though I know that she loved me, I still think at times that perhaps if things had been different she perhaps would still be alive today." Graylin shook himself as though he had said too much. He was not the type of man to bare his soul and now he felt the discomfort of the quiet room.

Sorrel found as she looked at her handsome but aging father that her eyes had filled with tears. "I am sure that you are wrong, Papa. My mother must have loved you very much, and for that love she would not have wished her life any different."

"Those are similar words to those that she used before she was taken from me," he absently said and his mind went back to that day, "but our love was different from most. 'You and I have something special, something that often takes people all their lives to find, and even then most do not ever know the kind of happiness that we have known.' Aye, your mother and I loved with a rare love, and that is why she told me of her hopes for you before she died."

Sorrel looked with interest at her father. She had never before heard this story of her mother's being concerned for her infant daughter. "What was it she wished, Papa?" Her words were softly spoken so as to not break the mood of her father's telling her what lay on his heart.

"She wished to be sure that you were not treated as she had been. She wanted for you to go to school and live a bit before you were married." Graylin raised his head from his hand and looked to his daughter. "She would be quite proud of you now, Sorrel."

"Oh Papa," Sorrel's arms encircled his neck. She thought back over the trouble she had caused him and her aunt in the past and tears of shame came to her eyes. "I am afraid that I have not been the most obedient child."

Graylin kissed her smooth forehead and smiled fondly down at his daughter. "You have been perfect. I only hope that you find the happiness that you deserve."

The tears vanished with his words and Sorrel smiled. "I am sure that I shall find a great deal of happiness. When I marry, the Sumters' ranch and ours shall be joined, and though Clifford and I do not know each other well, I am sure that we shall be happy."

"You are happy with the match I made for you then?" He wished to know her true feelings. If she did not wish Clifford Sumter for her husband he would tear the marriage contract up. He himself was not too sure about the match he had made. He liked the idea of having Sorrel close to him, and with the joining of the ranches they could visit often, but sometimes when he was around Clifford he felt uncomfortable. He could not quite find a reason, other than that the young man had some growing up to do and that his arrogant ways could get rather boring, but if for some reason Sorrel did not want him he would not push her into a marriage she did not wish.

Sorrel did not directly answer her father but let her emerald eyes roam about the cabin that had been her home for these past days. She had had a lot of time to think in these past leisurely days aboard the *Seafare Lady* and she had realized that her blood was more her father's than anyone knew. After some serious reflection she decided she did not mind the match he had made for her future. Though her last meeting with Clifford Sumter had not been the hot, passionate one she would have wished for with the man who was to be her husband, and though Clifford did indeed have a great many faults, she still had every intention of going through with the planned arrangements.

The major fact to settle her mind about the cool, pale Clifford Sumter was that sooner or later she would have to marry anyway, and she had reasoned that it would be to the best advantage of her family for her to marry Clifford Sumter. With the Sumter ranch adjoining her father's this would be the best match that she or her father could come up with. "I do not mind at all the match you have made for me,

Papa. I will have to marry one day anyway, so it might as well be to our advantage." With the saying of these words Sorrel felt a slight shiver of distaste course through her body.

Graylin looked deep into his daughter's face. It was clear that this young woman had never been in love. For a moment he thought that it would be a shame for her to go through her life without ever loving fully. The love he had shared with her mother had been strong and binding and he would wish the same for his daughter. But something deep within him stirred, and he knew as he looked at his beautiful daughter that Clifford Sumter was not the man to bring her this unquenchable feeling of love.

Rising from the settee Graylin set his glass down, pulled Sorrel to her feet, and smiled. "Enough of this serious talk, we have a party to attend," he said, and taking her hand he swung her about in a circle and laughed, "and I shall have the prettiest young woman at the affair on my arm."

Sorrel laughed gaily as her father swung her about. Nothing mattered but this moment, not the fact that she would marry a man she did not care for or the fact that her father was sad and lonely. "Let us hurry, Papa, so we are not late." She smoothed down her gown and made one more check in the mirror to assure herself that her hair was in order.

Most of Captain Spencer's guests were already in his cabin by the time Graylin escorted his daughter into the room. Both father and daughter looked about with large smiles as they greeted the calls and cheers and greetings that came from the other passengers. The cabin had been decorated gaily with

Chinese lanterns and colored streamers.

Within minutes after Sorrel entered the room the first mate of the *Seafare Lady* made his way to her side. His dark eyes burned greedily as they roamed over Sorrel from her tiny silver slippers to the glittering hairpins in her curls. Never had he seen a more beautiful woman, he thought to himself as he bowed low over her head and then greeted her father.

Sorrel smiled sweetly at the young man. She had enjoyed his company that one night when the two of them had walked about the ship, but now as she viewed him in his dark blue shipman's suit she was even more impressed.

"You look wonderful, Miss Morgan," he breathed as her father turned his attention to the captain.

"Why thank you, Mr. Palmer," Sorrel smiled. "You are very kind with your compliments, sir."

"Not at all. I only speak the truth. Could I perhaps bring you something to drink?" He tried to steer her somewhat away from the protection of her father.

"Why yes, that would be nice." Sorrel followed him over to a small side table laden with an assortment of drinks.

He started to pour her a glass of wine but at the shake of her head he looked questioningly toward her.

"I would prefer something less strong. I have never been able to abide strong drink." She looked toward the small pitcher of lemonade.

"Whatever you wish, Miss Morgan." Nate had wished her to drink a stronger brew in order to further his plans for the night ahead. So a bit reluctantly he poured her the glass of lemonade.

There were at least seven other couples in the captain's cabin, and with the few members of the crew whom he had invited the little room was packed and the party was gay.

Nate Palmer did his best to stay at Sorrel's side throughout the evening. And though he often caught Captain Spencer's scowl directed at him he could not force himself to relinquish his position next to this beautiful woman.

Graylin Morgan had, once in the captain's cabin, left his daughter to the younger gentlemen. He delighted in her beauty and each time he looked in her direction and found her flirting or smiling gaily toward a young man he would feel his chest swell with pride. He wished only her happiness.

The dinner consisted of far better fare than the passengers had seen since leaving Texas. Almost everyone at the table eyed the captain somewhat suspiciously.

Captain Spencer felt the eyes upon him and the accusations. He began to explain expansively from the far end of the long table. "You must forgive my cook for the somewhat hasty meals that he has prepared in the past. I also have had to endure the man's frugal meals. But when I have confronted him in the past his answer is always the same—he fears that the ship will not make its way to port safely and that we shall all starve aboard the *Seafare Lady*, so he prepares skimpy meals. But this evening he knows that the Richmond port is in sight, and the good man has outdone himself with I believe half of what must have been in his larder." The captain's laughter sailed about the room and shortly all at the table were joining him in his merriment.

Sorrel was shown to her seat by the first mate, and, as though he had planned the table seating arrangements beforehand, he took the seat next to her. On her other side was a space for her father.

Sorrel listened avidly to the talk about her of the Virginia colonies. Her excitement grew with each word that was uttered by the passengers and crew about the unknown land that they would be docking at tomorrow morning. There were only one couple aboard the *Seafare Lady* who had a home in Richmond. The rest were either visiting or moving. When the Langston couple spoke of their homeland there was a feeling of pride and longing in their voices.

Wishing to know all that she could find out, Sorrel fired question after question at the friendly couple. She wanted to know about the town itself and the country around it, and the Langstons were the people to ask.

Graylin also was interested, and though he had on occasion talked to this couple before he now found himself listening to his daughter's questions and the answers she was receiving and also venturing to ask a few of his own. His questions were more in the line of the business that had brought him to this land in the beginning. He wished to know where he could find the best horses. The Langstons, though, were not country people. They lived in town in a fine house, and Mr. Langston owned several warehouses bulging with cotton, and they did not know too much about horses. Mr. Langston did say, though, that he had some very good connections and that if Graylin

114

would visit his office in a few days he would find him the information that he needed or he would find someone who could direct him to the finest horses that were to be found in the state or out of it.

Graylin Morgan was beyond pleased. He had not thought that he would be lucky enough to find someone in Mr. Langston's position who would help him so quickly. He had thought to make inquiries on his own and then perhaps hire someone to help him with his search. He boldly reached across the table and extended his hand to the man across from him. "I certainly will welcome any help you can give me, Mr. Langston." He pumped the hand reaching out to his own vigorously.

The other man smiled broadly. "Call me Leroy. All my friends do."

"It will be a pleasure, Leroy. And you call me Graylin." For the rest of the evening the two gentlemen were deep in conversation, about Virginia or about Graylin's ranch and his love for Texas.

With the father thus occupied Nate Palmer found his way easier to entertain the daughter. He set out with all of his charm and manners to win her to him. Whenever another member of the crew came near to speak with the lovely Morgan girl he would receive a fierce glare from the first mate, and, all of them being lower in rank than Palmer, they quickly were gone and Nate was left alone once again with this vision of beauty. She was to him a sparkling silver creation made solely for his enjoyment, and he wished no one else to glimpse her beauty but himself. And the longer the evening lasted the more he was into his cups. The heady wine, though not showing its effects upon his person, was indeed doing its damage on the inside of his mind and body. His thoughts were clouded with only one desire, and that was to find time alone with Sorrel Morgan.

At the close of the evening the captain lifted his glass and toasted all of his passengers and wished them well. Graylin made his way to his daughter's side. "Are you ready, Sorrel? We have a big day tomorrow, so I think it is time for us to be retiring." He pulled his gold pocket watch from his breast pocket and opened the lid. Tinkling music hit Sorrel's ears from the opening of the watch and she smiled softly. "It is already past the midnight hour." He took hold of her arm.

"I have only to tell the nice Mr. Palmer good night, Papa." Sorrel placed her tiny hand upon his jacket sleeve. "I am afraid that you have neglected me shamefully, and the first mate did me the honor of not leaving me to be a wallflower in the captain's cabin." Her gay laughter filled her father's ears.

"For shame upon me, daughter. I did not realize that I was neglecting you. I was so busy talking to Leroy Langston. But I am sure that the good Mr. Palmer will have no regrets over my actions." Her father also laughed loudly and even more so when he looked up and saw the young man they had been talking about looking with wounded eyes, with room in them only for Sorrel, in their direction. "Go and say your good nights, child. I shall tell the captain what a delight this evening has been."

Sorrel hurried across the room and smiled toward Nate Palmer. "I wish to thank you for your kindness this evening, Mr. Palmer. I do not know what I would have done without your company this evening."

The first mate took Sorrel's tiny hand within his own and looked boldly into those slanted emerald eyes that to him were tempting invitations of promises unfulfilled. He slowly brought his hand up with hers encased in it, his dark eyes never leaving her own as his lips brushed the back of her hand.

Sorrel giggled nervously as she glimpsed for a moment the fierceness of the man's passion.

As she pulled her hand from his tight grasp soft words came to her ear. "May I come to your cabin later, Sorrel?"

Shock was evident on her features, but Nate Palmer was wound up in his thoughts and his mind was really not functioning too well from all the drink, so that he never noticed her stiffened manner or the changing look on her face. "I am afraid that you are outstepping yourself, sir." She began to turn about and leave this rude young man, but as quickly he took hold of her arm in a tight grip, and, not wishing to cause a scene, she stood still and looked back at him.

"I did not mean to offend you, Miss Morgan. I only thought that if you were not too tired we could talk for a while. I would leave whenever you wished." Nate tried to coax her, knowing that he had scared her with his bold manner.

"I am afraid, Mr. Palmer, that I am indeed quite tired, so if you will let loose of my arm before my father comes to see what is keeping me, I shall be on my way." Sorrel was not so forgiving, nor did she dare to do as this young man wished. She had seen something for a moment in his eyes that told her that she could not trust him, and she was not one to go back on her feelings.

Nate Palmer looked down at his hand encircled over her forearm and then dropped his arm to his side. "I am sorry Miss Morgan, I did not . . ."

Sorrel did not give him the chance he wished to promote his apology. She swung about without another word, her silver gown shining brilliantly with each move she made as she reached her father's side. She took deep breaths of air once she and father were out of the captain's cabin, in order to control the anger she was feeling. Who did this Nate Palmer think he was? Did he think that any woman that he spent some small measure of time with would willingly fall at his feet? Well, the young man would soon learn if he already had not that Sorrel Morgan was not like most women, she was a woman made to think and to make her own decisions and one of those decisions was that she would not let any man take advantage of her. She did not have to depend on any man and she had been taught well by her aunt to read a man's mind. She had fended well for herself throughout her young life and men like this Mr. Palmer had learnt a well-deserved lesson from her hands on more than one occasion in Houston.

Graylin watched his daughter's agitated steps and ventured to question her, "Is all not well, Sorrel? Are you taken ill?"

As they reached her door he took her by the arm and Sorrel, feeling her temper leave her, smiled fondly at the elder man and kissed him gently on the cheek. "All is fine, Papa. I must be tired." She opened her door and as she entered her room her father called good night and turned to his own cabin.

Sorrel began to undress. She pulled the silver material from her body, then the striped chemise and petticoats and then her silk stockings, until she stood naked before her mirror. She critically viewed her golden skin and then with a sigh she pulled her red-wine dressing gown around her abundant curves. The several weeks aboard ship had taken some of the color from her skin. She had always loved the way the sun made her body and hair a rich gold, and now for a fraction of a moment as she looked at the mirror and started to pull the tiny pins from her hair she wished she were home with her aunt and her privacy.

But soon that thought was gone. She had begged to come with her father and she knew deep within her that nothing could have prevented her from coming along on this trip. She brushed the golden strands of hair until they lay soft and clinging down her back to her waist. As she turned from her mirror and started to her bed she heard something from the front room.

It sounded like a soft knock and as she entered the small sitting room she realized that there was indeed someone outside her door. Her first thoughts were that her father wished to say something to her before he retired for the night, so without a second thought she turned the knob and opened the door wide.

To her surprise though it was not her father who stood there but the first mate of the *Seafare Lady*, Nate Palmer.

Sorrel could not at first believe the nerve of the young man and she stood as though paralyzed, her hand still resting on the doorknob.

Nate Palmer, however, was far from paralyzed as his dark eyes roamed over the length of the woman whom he had wanted for the past several weeks. His eyes lingered at the folds of her gown. The golden tresses hanging freely down her back and about her shoulders were tempting him beyond control. He took one step toward her, his eyes dark points of desire, consuming her with their heat.

He was brought up short, though, when his dark eyes rose and correctly read the anger that was brewing in the emerald eyes before him. They were storming, fierce eyes, and for a moment Nate was reminded of a story he had heard years ago in Ireland of a she-cat-woman (half-woman, half-cat) living in a swamp. If any young man ventured into her lair he was never heard from again. The thought struck him that that she-cat must have had eyes like the ones before him now.

"What do you want?" The words were an angry hiss, unsettling him even more. He had not thought to be met with such anger, instead he had imagined in his drunken mind that his reception would be quite the opposite.

"I thought that we could talk for a minute," was all that he could get out.

"I told you in the captain's cabin that the answer was no, and it is no different now. I do not entertain gentlemen in my room, sir." Sorrel stepped back into the room and began to shut the door.

Regaining some of his earlier courage Nate Palmer also stepped closer and with his hand he prevented her from shutting the wood portal. "Do not be hasty Sorrel. There is only this one night left aboard ship, and there are things that I would wish for you to hear."

Pushing with all her strength Sorrel tried to bar him from entering her room. But it was quickly evident who was the stronger as Nate Palmer entered the front sitting room and slammed the door behind him.

So angry was Sorrel that words would not come to her. This man was insane. He was a madman, entering her room in this fashion. She finally got out, "Leave my room at once Mr. Palmer."

The first mate barely heard her words. His mind was on his own desires as he stood and watched Sorrel become even more lovelier with her anger. Without a word he was in front of her and grabbing her boldly to his chest, his harsh lips descending upon the petal-soft mouth that had so tempted him all through the evening.

Shock kept Sorrel still for the briefest of seconds, but then her mind registered what was happening and her nostrils filled with the stale, alcohol breath of the man as he held her tightly and daringly assailed her lips, and she came to life.

Nate Palmer had been right in comparing Sorrel to a she-cat. No cat could have inflicted such a barrage of wounds and pain upon a person as this young woman now proceeded to do.

Sorrel bit at his tongue as he tried to force it between her lips, and as he pulled back yelling with his pain her hands reached up to leave their mark upon his cheeks and her tiny slippered feet struck out, kicking at any part of him that she could come in contact with.

Trying to protect himself, Nate Palmer stood defenseless against the woman before him. He had never expected this response to his advances, and as the wine began to clear from his brain he realized that he had indeed made a dangerous mistake. He felt the deep rivulets left on his face from her nails and the thought struck him that his face would be a bloody mess if he did not do something. But when he felt her foot making contact with his groin he fell to his knees and moaned aloud with his pain.

"How dare you!" Sorrel screamed, stepping back and seeing her handiwork. "Who do you think you are coming into my room and accosting me in this manner?" Her hands hurriedly reached a table and brought up a large brass candlestick.

Nate had never hit a woman in his life and for a moment the sensation of wishing to hit this one came to his mind, but as he viewed her standing above him with candlestick held high, the wish left him as he saw the sheer terror on her face. Slowly rising, he became fully aware of his actions. He could well lose his job over this affair, and he could not blame Captain Spencer in the least for dismissing him if this deed became known to him. Also, this young woman's father was a man to be reckoned with—he could well call him out or publicize his behavior and disgrace him for the rest of his life. "I am sorry, Miss Morgan." He stood to his full height, his cheeks burning from the scratches left by her hands.

Sorrel looked at him as though he was insane. "Sorry?" The one word came from her lips.

Nate Palmer saw the full impact of his assault upon her. Her delicate pink lips were swollen and bruised from his hungry kiss and one shoulder of her robe was torn. The alcohol was completely gone now from his mind and all that was left for him to do was to face his dastardly deeds. "I can only say I was not fully aware of what I was doing. I do not deny, though, that I have wanted to be alone with you, but you must believe me when I say that I never intended for things to become this out of hand."

Sorrel was truly not the forgiving type and she still stood with arm outraised, ready to fight him with the candlestick if necessary. Her eyes were slanted green orbs screaming out their loathing as she watched his every move. "Take yourself out of my cabin."

"Miss Morgan, I wish us to still be friends. Perhaps my actions call for more and I should talk to your father. That mayhap would be the most gentlemanly thing to do."

"What are you talking about? Don't you dare to go to my father with your foul actions. He would kill you." Sorrel was truly outraged. What was wrong with this young man? First he assaulted her and then he wished to tell his black, disgusting actions to her father.

"Perhaps you do not understand me, Miss Morgan, I wish to ask your father for the honor of your hand in marriage. If anyone finds out what has occurred this night your reputation could be ruined."

"Marry you?" Laughter rose from the depths of Sorrel's throat. "Do not waste your time with my father, for all you will find in that corner would be a bullet for your behavior. I would never marry you." Her green eyes scanned him from head to toe and she once more had to hold back her laughter. "Besides which, I am already betrothed to a man in Texas, and as for my reputation do not concern yourself, that is wholely my affair. Now leave." She pointed the candlestick toward the door.

Nothing else needed to be said. Nate Palmer was through the door and glad to be still able to walk on his own. He had not before noticed what a hard woman Sorrel Morgan was, but now that he had found out, he could forever ease his conscience with thoughts of her callousness.

Chapter Five

Richmond, Virginia looked large and clear, her streets bustling with activity, her docks crowded with sailors rushing back and forth loading and unloading ships and crates. The *Seafare Lady* pulled into dock and tied her ropes securely.

All the passengers aboard the ship stood expectantly along the long decks waiting to disembark. The Langstons stood close to Graylin and his daughter, once more reminding them to pay a visit and giving them instructions on how to find their house and Leroy's office.

The weather was cool and crisp, so Sorrel had dressed in a forest-green gown with matching cape and a fox fur hat and hand muff. She looked her best, and as her emerald eyes looked at the town before them Graylin smiled with pleasure. She was so beautiful to watch, he thought to himself.

The first mate of the *Seafare Lady* had not been seen this morning and Sorrel had overheard one of the crew members talking about the young man's sending word to Captain Spencer before daylight this morning that he was very ill and would not be up and about until later that day. Sorrel had smiled to herself. It was obvious that the young Mr. Palmer could not face her after making such a fool of himself the previous evening. It was just as well, she thought, for she was still angry. She, for one, would not have any kind words for the first mate of the *Seafare Lady*.

Captain Spencer stood to the side of the gangplank and bid each of his passengers a personal farewell. He always paid his passengers this simple courtesy. Most of his fortune had been made over the years from passengers' fees, and he wanted these people to use his ship again or to suggest her to a friend.

Sorrel smiled and shook the captain's hand, already anticipating the feel of good, hard ground under her slippers.

Graylin felt as she did, and as he led her down the gangplank and onto the dock he sighed aloud.

Looking at her father with some concern Sorrel asked him, "Is anything amiss, Papa?"

Graylin smiled at her concern. "Nay, I but am glad to feel the hardness beneath my feet. I hope that it will be a long time before I have to cross the seas again."

Tinkling laughter filled his ears as his daughter remembered how sick the voyage had made this large, strong man for the first part of their trip. "I too welcome land, Papa."

Graylin steered her onto one of the streets leading away from the dock. "We shall first find an inn to stay in, and then we shall walk about and see some of the town."

The first inn that appeared was large and crowded.

The main room was filled to capacity, with men ranged all along the room-length bar and most of the tables occupied by customers awaiting their noonday meal.

Graylin and Sorrel were both surprised at the sight of the crowded room. It took some time to find the portly proprietor of the large establishment.

In only a few short moments they were assured that there would be a room for each of them. The proprietor explained proudly that at each mealtime his inn was crowded because it was famous throughout all of Richmond for its delicious meals.

Standing at her father's side and watching as the serving girls brought large trays of every kind of food to the tables, Sorrel felt her mouth beginning to water. She had barely been able to touch the tray that had been brought to her cabin this morning with all of the excitement she had felt at having finally arrived in Richmond. "Papa," she asked her father, "do you think that we could get us something to eat before we see our rooms?"

Seeing the way his daughter's eyes followed a girl carrying a tray laden with food high over her head Graylin smiled fondly down toward her. "Of course, child. I shall just pay this good man for our rooms and instruct him about our luggage. Why do you not find a table and order for the both of us?" Graylin followed the proprietor over to the bar and pulled out his wallet, leaving his daughter to find the table as he had instructed her.

Left to her own devices, Sorrel made her way nearer to the hearth. Pulling off her cape, she got a chair. But before she could seat herself a man in a dark brown suit was helping to place her in the chair and pushing her to the table.

"Why thank you, sir," she murmured, not truly interested in starting a conversation with this well-dressed, handsome man whom she did not know.

"The pleasure is mine, madam." The man's light blue eyes roamed over the young woman's form, noting the unusual beauty of her features and the richness of her dress. The eyes of half the gentlemen in the inn were on this young woman, and he had no desires to be second place. He started to pull a chair out from the same table and to place his bulk upon it.

"I beg your pardon, sir, but I am afraid . . ."

The man's light brown brow rose and he interrupted Sorrel boldly. "I could not stand the thought of a beautiful young lady such as yourself dining alone." He snapped his fingers loudly and a plump, short, blond-haired girl came quickly to their table and asked to take their order.

The man smiled with all too confident an expression and began to order for himself and the young lady sitting next to him. A bottle of wine was the first thing to be ordered, next a leg of mutton and vegetables, and for dessert the man ordered apple cobbler. When he was finished he looked at Sorrel and grinned broadly, but as the serving girl started to leave the table Sorrel cleared her throat and clearly said words that obviously did not please the gentleman.

"I would like to order now for myself and the gentleman over there standing at the bar and talking to the proprietor." Sorrel deliberately looked at the man across the table and then pointed to her father for the girl. "We do not require wine with our meal, but would rather have cool water, and I think beef would be pleasant," she went on, deliberately ordering differently from the man sitting next to her. "And perhaps potatoes. I do not think either of us would care for dessert; if we do we will order later." For a split second Sorrel felt some sympathy for the man as the girl looked at him and a small giggle escaped her.

"Bring my meal over there," he ordered the girl, pulling himself up and glaring down at Sorrel.

"If you had not been so overconfident sir, I would have been able to explain the situation to you earlier." Sorrel did not really feel that she owed this man any apology, but something made her try to explain.

Graylin approached the table as the younger man was moving away, and at the dark look that was directed toward him by the young man he looked to his daughter with some concern.

Sorrel smiled fondly toward her father, putting the young man from her mind. "I have already ordered, Papa. Did you have any trouble securing our rooms?"

"No, no, child. In fact, we were lucky enough to get rooms really close to each other. There is something about this place that makes me wish to keep an eye on you at all times." His light blue eyes went to the man who had just left theirs, he also noticed a number of other pairs of male eyes looking in Sorrel's direction. He had not thought that her beauty would cause him any trouble, but now he was not so sure. He would not let her out of his sight, he told himself sternly. He would never forgive himself if something were to happen to his precious child.

The proprietor had given her father the keys to their rooms, so, after lingering over their dinner, they went slowly up the stairs and found the rooms. Their rooms were a few doors apart, and Sorrel felt safer at the thought that her father was only down the hall.

Graylin did not linger in his daughter's room but made sure that all was satisfactory and then left to seek out his own room. He said over his shoulder that he would return shortly and that they would venture out and see the sights of the town.

Sorrel looked about herself with some distaste. She hoped that they would not be staying here at this inn for too long a time, for by the looks of this room she knew that the longer she was in it the more she would find fault with it. The room was small with only one chair, a bed pushed against the far wall under a dirty window, and, on the opposite wall, an old but well-used armoire. Her luggage had already been carried from the ship and now it all sat at the foot of the bed. There being little else to do, she set about hanging gowns up and straightening out her clothing.

A soft knock at the door pulled Sorrel from her work, and with some surprise she was greeted by a large black girl who, without preamble, entered her chambers and took hold of the gown that Sorrel had thrown over her arm as she had walked to the door.

"You shouldn't be a'doing this here work, missy. You just sit youself down and rest for a few minutes."

The girl must have been only sixteen, but she acted the part of a much older, more experienced woman as she ordered Sorrel about and pointed to the solitary chair in the room for her to rest upon.

"My master, he own this here inn, he be telling me to come on up here and to help you with your unpacking and such," the girl explained to the dumbfounded Sorrel. "My name be Sis, that what they call me, so if you be a'needing anything you just call for me."

Sorrel did not know what to say. She had seen black slaves before, but she had never had one to wait on her let alone to talk with her. At home most of the servants were Mexican women, not of Indian origin. "Why, I am pleased to meet you, Sis," she stammered softly.

The black girl grinned from ear to ear, her pearl-white teeth gleaming in her ebony face. "I'll have the kitchen girls press these here gowns for you, missy," Sis said as she placed several gowns across the bed that had been badly crushed in the travel bags. The others she shook and hung on hangers, judging that the wrinkles would shortly disappear.

Sorrel sat back in the chair, finding herself rather tired after the large lunch and all of the excitement of that morning.

"You be wishing to take a nap?" Sis questioned, taking the gowns off the bed and smoothing down the covers.

"No, thank you. My father is to come soon and we are to walk about your town for a while." Sorrel stifled a yawn with the palm of her hand.

Sis giggled loudly as she viewed this young girl trying to hold back her sleepiness. "You be needing to change, then, if you plan to go out with your pappy. Why don't you stand up and I will help you out of that old gown. And you lie down upon that bed and I won't be gone but a minute and run downstairs and get some ointment to massage into your tired bones. That will make you as good as new."

The idea of a massage more than appealed to Sorrel. She had not had such luxury since leaving her aunt's house. Without a second thought she stood and Sis helped her to undress.

When the black girl left the room Sorrel fell into a soft, drifting slumber, but as she felt her skin being rubbed and soothed she came back unwillingly to the room about her. Sis was more than talented with her hands and soon Sorrel felt her blood flowing vigorously once again through her veins. By the time her father knocked outside of her door she was smiling brightly, her hair combed out and held back with a pink velvet ribbon and her body encased in a matching pink day dress.

They spent the rest of the afternoon walking about and viewing the different sights of Richmond. It was a small but lively town and wherever one looked something exciting was happening. From a fist fight in front of an inn to a small, frail-looking woman chasing a young black boy with a broom down the sidewalk, this town throbbed with life and living.

As they rounded a street corner they were pulled to a halt by the sight of a large, imposing sign hanging above a monstrous building stating in bold lettering Langston's Warehouse and Trade.

A large grin came upon Graylin's features as he took hold of Sorrel's arm. "Come, Sorrel let us see what Leroy's establishment looks like. I doubt that the good man himself is there, but we can take a quick look about."

Sorrel was gladly led into the cool interior of the large building, her emerald eyes going hurriedly in all directions. Never had she seen such a display of goods of every description. There were barrels of dry goods with their lids set aside, displaying their contents to the numerous shoppers strolling about. Beans of every variety, flour, sugar, meal, coffee, and tea were lined against one wall, and along another were barrels of dried meat, so many, in fact, that Sorrel could not even name them.

She turned toward the opposite area and was astounded at the bolts and piles of material. With a soft sigh she left her father's side and approached the cloth. Her mind could barely comprehend the vast supply of such luxurious wealth. Her fingers, with a will of their own, reached out and softly touched a piece of Irish lace.

Graylin watched his daughter with some amusement. She had never been in such an establishment before, and he himself had rarely been in one of such magnitude and wealth. Leroy Langston was indeed quite a wealthy man, he surmised as he watched people buying and trading and took in all the barrels filled with supplies.

"Graylin Morgan." The shout came from above, drawing Graylin's blue eyes to the stairway leading to a floor overhead.

Graylin grinned broadly as he saw Leroy Langston waving him up the stairs. Nodding his head in agreement, he hurriedly went to his daughter and told her that Leroy was there and that he had invited him up to his office.

Sorrel was too enthralled with what was offered below to go up the stairs with her father. "I will browse for a while, Papa. Go ahead and talk with Mr. Langston, I am sure that I can keep myself busy."

Graylin agreed, knowing that the talk of business would only bore her and that she would be much more entertained here among the different sights. "I shall not be long if you are sure, Sorrel." He started to turn, and then with an afterthought he looked back in her direction. "Do not leave the building. If you tire ask one of Leroy's assistants to come and fetch me. I would not wish for you to become lost the first day in Richmond."

Smiling in agreement Sorrel watched her father walk toward the staircase. Her thoughts swiftly left him as she walked about the emporium, her eyes taking it all in. She watched as a small blond-haired child pulled and tugged at his mother's skirts until she finally gave him her attention. The child began to beg for a candy stick in one of the candy jars that were lined neatly upon a high shelf. Sorrel smiled to herself, knowing full well the reason for these treasures being placed so high and out of reach. She watched for a full moment longer, enjoying the delight that came over the youngster's features as the mother handed a young man in a white apron the penny for the candy. The boy attacked the candy without delay, and with a smile of pure heaven he followed his mother about the store.

At the farthest end of the building Sorrel could see huge piles of cotton and tables stacked with hides of different shades and varieties. She edged her way nearer to this side of the building, noticing as she did that mostly men were standing about there and talking companionably. Their laughter was loud and boisterous as they bantered back and forth about the hides that they had to offer for sale. Mr. Langston's employee good-naturedly felt the furs and then nodded his head in agreement about their worth, but still, as a good trader, he delved into the art of dickering down the price before giving his hand as a contract.

Sorrel stood fascinated with this corner of the emporium, her eyes going from the luxurious furs of every different texture and shade to the collection of different men who, with hands lightly resting upon the piles, indicated to all that they were the ones who had brought all this wealth to Langston's warehouse.

One man in particular stood out in Sorrel's vision as she stood off to the side and watched. As yet she had not seen his face, but from the rearside view that she was afforded she thought the man to be quite unique. He stood a head above those about him, and plainly coming to her ears were the words of both the clerk as he responded to the richness of the furs before him and of the large man as he told the young man his opinion of their worth and the price that he would take for them.

There was no dickering with this man, and the clerk, as though knowing this fact in advance, shook the gentleman's hand, and, agreeing with a nod of his head, he answered, "Yes sir, Mr. Danner I quite agree. As always, your furs are the finest that come to

Langston's emporium. If you will go to the cashier before you leave you will be given the full price."

Turning without an answer, the large man started toward the same area in which Sorrel was idly fingering fine silks and trying to act as though she was interested in making a purchase. But as his face filled her vision a call from across the way turned his back once again toward her.

"Mathew, is that ye, boy?" the caller shouted, rushing to the younger man with an arm ready to throw about the tall frame.

"Well, I'll be," the tall man greeted the other older, grizzled-looking trapper, and he threw an arm about his shoulder. "I would have thought for sure that by this time the Indians or bears would have gotten you." Rich laughter filled the ears within hearing distance of the two men.

"Na, Mathew, old Sammy ain't about to lose none of his hair." The unkempt man pulled his fur cap from his head, exposing a bald, shining pate.

The young man called Mathew laughed loudly in agreement, pulling Sorrel's eyes again in his direction.

She had only glimpsed his features for a split moment, but in her mind were imprinted forever the deep blue eyes and the handsomest face that she had ever in her life seen. She seemed to be entranced as she stood there listening to his rich voice but now only seeing his back, her eyes lingering at the nape of his neck, where, over the collar of his shirt, dark black curls sprang unattended. In that short time that she had been allowed a view of his face she had been impressed by the strength and ability starkly written on his tanned, chiseled features. A dark, neatly trimmed beard covered the lower portion of his chin. Usually Sorrel disliked hair on a man's face, but to this man it only added a touch of dashing appeal.

She had been so intent on watching the man that she had not been listening to the pair's conversation. Now, with an easy turn of his large body, the blue eyes were once more looking in her direction. Sorrel felt her own face turning a deep, warm color, but as she lowered her head to the material near her hand the man passed by her side without a look in her direction.

Sorrel's breath caught in her throat as she felt the nearness of his body as it passed her own. A scent of maleness seemed to touch her senses, leaving her hands and even her knees trembling.

She clasped her hands tightly to the folds of her gown and as though without a will of her own she turned when he was a few steps away from her and watched his tall frame as he went toward the front of the building. With halting steps she began to follow, her thoughts only of keeping him within her vision. There was something about this man that drew her as though he was a magnet, her brain telling her not to let him from her sight, that to do so would be to destroy this feeling welling up within her, this feeling that seemed to be growing from the very depths of her being and seemed to be choking her with the magnitude of its power. There was something within her now that she had never before experienced, a deep, burning desire to know this man and for him to know her.

He had been called Mathew by the elderly trapper

and Mr. Danner by the clerk, she remembered as she stood still and watched while he went to the cashier and handed him a piece of paper, receiving a large number of bills in return.

For a moment he turned and looked about the emporium, his eyes seeming to settle upon her as she hurriedly began to study some pots hanging from a shelf. Then as quickly the blue eyes were gone as he started out of the door.

Sorrel watched with a short gasp of breath and then with slow steps she continued on, halting before going through the doorway, her father's words coming to mind about her becoming lost in this strange town. For a few moments longer she watched until she could no longer see the tall frame in its leather jacket and pants on the sidewalks. And as she lost sight of him she felt a great weight in her chest. A feeling of something dying within her grew as she stood in the same spot near the door and looked out at the side streets of Richmond.

"Were you awaiting me here, Sorrel?" Graylin took hold of her arm and questioned her as he found her standing next to the door of the emporium. There seemed something strange about her as she stood thus, her face turned to the outside, as though she cared nothing about the goings on inside. "Is something wrong? Has something gone amiss?" Graylin questioned her as an afterthought. Her whole attitude seemed out of character. As he had taken hold of her arm she had barely seemed to notice him, and now she acted as though she barely even recognized him.

For a moment Sorrel felt lost to all around her. She

had no idea how long she had stood in this same spot staring out at the busy street. All her senses were tuned to but one thing, the man who had unexpectedly come into her life and just as quickly had left it. Never had she been so drawn by just the merest sight of a man before. "What, Papa?" She seemed at a loss.

"Are you all right, Sorrel?" Had someone offended her in some way or was it something else that was wrong with her?

Sorrel shook herself, trying to clear her mind and concentrate on what her father was saying to her. "I am fine, Papa. A bit tired is all." She brought her lace handkerchief to her lips as though to cover a yawn.

Still Graylin was not too sure of her reply and stood for a small time longer watching her. Finally he cleared his throat and taking hold of her arm once again he began to steer her out of the building. "It was quite fortunate that I came today. Leroy already has been in touch with someone about helping me to find the horses that I shall be needing. I'll come back this evening to find out more."

"That is fine, Papa," Sorrel responded, her interest not on her father but still on the man in her thoughts.

"I shall take you back to the inn and let you get your rest, child." This outing so soon off the *Seafare Lady* must have been too much for her, he thought as he heard the lack of enthusiasm in her tone.

It was only a short time later that Graylin smiled his understanding as he took her to her door, assuring her that he would have his dinner and for her not to worry. He would have the innkeeper send his servant girl to his daughter's room to help her with her long-desired bath.

Only moments passed before Sis burst through the door, a large grin on her face and each hand carrying a bucket of water. "I done seen you and yer pa coming in the front of the inn and just that soon I put kettles of water on the hearth for your bath," she smiled at Sorrel.

Sorrel smiled her own pleasure in return and began to pull her clothes from her body as the large black girl dragged a brass tub into the room and began to pour the buckets of steaming water into it. Hurrying back down the stairs, she was only gone a short time before she returned with more water.

It had been some time since Sorrel had been able to sit herself down in a large tub of water. She sighed aloud when she was finally able to sink her body up to her neck into the silky, lemon-scented water. On board the *Seafare Lady* she had mostly sponge bathed, and now she delighted in the water all about her.

Sis stood over the young woman whose care she had been charged with and smiled largely. The girl, her hair piled atop her head and held securely with ribbons, her skin glowing with pinkness from the hot water, looked quite satisfied at this moment. Reaching down, Sis began to scrub the delicate back, and then, with tender ministrations, she lathered soap over Sorrel's arms and upper portion, neglecting not a spot until finally she stood back and said to a relaxed Sorrel, whose emerald eyes were now practically shut from her exhaustion, "You just sit here and rest for a few minutes, missy. I'll go on downstairs and get you a tray of food."

Sorrel did not answer. Her thoughts were already far from the black girl. She lay her golden head back against the rim of the tub, and with the sensuous feel of the satiny water enveloping her and the dim light of the tallow candle sitting on a small stool next to the tub, she let her thoughts, as though seeking out the perfect dream to go along with this most desirable spot, go to the tall, handsome man of that afternoon.

In her deepest thoughts, where she alone could direct the action, the man stood before her, his blue eyes glowing with desire, as his slanted, sensuous lips began to lower to her own. Even in her dreams she could feel the breath catch in her throat and the erratic beating of her pulse. His large hands seemed to tenderly reach out and gently caress her face, and soft, unintelligible words floated through her mind as his lips made a path from her fragile jaw line to her small, perfect ears. With a soft sigh of pleasure Sorrel lost herself even more deeply within the realms of fantasy. The man before her became bolder, pulling her more firmly into his grasp, and with soft, fleeting motions his hands now slowly, with a touch as gentle as that of a butterfly, stroked and petted.

So lost in this place of dreamlike reality was Sorrel that she failed to hear the soft opening of the door, nor did she hear the steps that approached the tub. But some impression of noise did penetrate through her hazy mind as she heard a ragged sigh fall upon her ears. Slowly, as though fighting to do so, her eyes opened and she looked before her.

She had supposed the noise to be Sis and it took her some time to adjust her eyes to the dimness in the room and then to finally make out the tall shadow of a figure standing before her.

With a loud thumping of her heart she thought for a second that the figure belonged to the man of her dreams. But with the clearing of her brain and the adjustment of her eyes to the candlelight she realized that this certainly was not the large man to whom she had been so drawn that day. And with a sudden realization she knew who this intruder was.

The man though needed no adjustment for his eyes. Never had he seen such a creation of beauty before. The glow of the candle against the sparkling water added a sheen to her skin that left him breathless and though he could not see her breasts the fullness was evident from the top of the water gently lying against her skin. "I am sorry, I must have made a mistake and taken your room for my own." After a few silent moments he began to apologize, feeling the heat of her beauty all but scorching him at the same time as he felt the need to explain his bad manners in entering a lady's room unannounced.

Sorrel sank her body even lower into the silky warm water. She had at first been dull-witted from her tiredness and from the effects of her dreaming, but now she was fully awake and seeing who this man was her green eyes began to flash with their intense anger. How dare this man stand here in her chambers as though an everyday event were taking place?

"I see that you remember me." His voice reached her in a deep, throaty caress. "I could only wish that those dreams that you were having were of me." He had stood watching her for a short moment before he had made the noise that had drawn her attention, and from her expression as she lay against the rim of the tub with her eyes shut he had known that her thoughts were deep in another world, and with a daring hope he ventured to question her about what they consisted of.

"I do indeed remember you quite well, sir, and I can see by your presence that your manners have still not improved." She could not believe her eyes—this was the same man who had daringly sat down and tried to have dinner with her earlier that day, and now here he was in her chambers questioning her about her thoughts.

"Ah, yes, I see now that you do remember me quite well." The man backed up a few steps and leaned against the door jamb casually watching Sorrel's distress. "I also see that you have not lost any of your venom." A large, toothy smile caressed his face with these words.

"Get out of my room!" Sorrel was beginning to become furious now and the man's arrogance only furthered her rage. "Get out or I shall scream these walls down."

The man grinned at her as though she would not dare to cause such a disturbance, but he did not know his opponent well for in the next breath Sorrel was filling her lungs with air and letting it all out in a mighty scream that filled his ears and had to reach at least down the hall and more than likely down the stairs.

"I see that you do not jest, my lady." He opened the door and began to back out. "I do apologize though for my rudeness," and, sweeping his hat wide and bowing at the waist in a mock salute, he was gone.

Sorrel was furious. What a blackguard the man was, and where on earth was Sis? She should not have been gone this long. Rising from the cooled water Sorrel wrapped a large, fleecy towel about her body, then set to pacing angrily across the carpet. If only she had not been naked and in the tub, she thought. She would have shown that arrogant madman a thing or two. She was no prim lady, she was Sorrel Morgan and she would not be insulted! She raged angrily about the room.

What infuriated her more than anything else was the fact that the insufferable man had associated himself with her dreams. He had dirtied her fantasies by his intrusion. How dare he ask if she were dreaming about him? Once again the features of the large man she had seen that day came to her mind, but this time they did not calm her angry thoughts. She was infuriated by this other man's ability to so anger her.

When Sis finally did make her way back to Sorrel's room the girl's anger was still visible. The gall of the man, thinking that he could so easily tamper with her!

"I be sorry, missy that I be so long, but the common room was filled to the brim with people wanting their dinner, and the master he done be giving me extra chores to help out," Sis hurriedly explained, seeing the distress on the young woman's face. She hoped that the girl was not angry because she had not come right back and had had to help herself from the tub and tend to her own needs, but upon reflection Sis decided that this young woman was not that selfish and petty.

Sorrel could not be mad at the friendly black girl, and as she set a tray of cold meat, fruit, and bread upon a table near the bed she pulled herself together and showed her a kinder disposition. Was it the girl's fault that she had been ordered to help out downstairs and it so happened that while she was away that horrible man had dared to enter her room? "Thank you, Sis," she smiled to the girl as she took up an apple and bit into the delicious sweetness. She would act as though nothing had ever gone amiss; she did not want Sis to think that she was in any way responsible for the man's entering her chambers.

Sis also smiled, but her smile rather a thoughtful twist to her large lips. There seemed to be something bothering this young girl that had not been there before. "Is everything all right, missy?" Sis ventured softly as she went to the wardrobe and pulled a sheer, light blue nightgown from the clothes rack.

Sorrel did indeed feel much better now that Sis was here in the room with her, and to answer the black girl's question she only smiled and shook her head, pulling the towel from her body so that she could dress for the night. "I guess that I am tired. That is all."

Sis nodded her head in understanding as she helped Sorrel to dress and brush out her long, beautiful curls.

"Did you see my father downstairs Sis?" Sorrel questioned the girl, wondering if her father had eaten and had already gone to his room.

"Yes missy, yer pa done ate and I see him heading up the stairs when I was still down helping out with the dishes."

Sorrel had grown accustomed to tending to her father aboard the *Seafare Lady* when he had been ill and she was still concerned about his eating and taking care of himself. "Thank you, Sis. I suppose that he already has gone to bed." She had thought for a moment to go next door and wish him a good night. For some reason she thought that she would feel more secure if she could see his strong, caring face, but she rebuked herself for her silliness as she thought of him already asleep in his bed and how thoughtless it would be for her to wake him.

"I suppose that you be right, missy. It done already be late, and yer pa he gone upstairs some time ago." Sis did not know her thoughts or her need to feel safe in this strange land, and after pulling her hair back and tying a blue velvet ribbon around it she hurriedly tidied up the room, telling Sorrel that her master had told her to hurry for she still had to help out in the kitchen with the cleaning of the evening's dishes.

Sorrel did not try to keep the girl for she knew that she had a hard life and did not wish her to get into any trouble because of her. So without comment she went to the large bed and climbed in between the cool sheets. She felt herself yawning with the feel of the softness of the mattress and she missed Sis's grin from the door as she observed the tiredness of the young woman upon the bed.

"I be seeing you tomorrow, missy," she called and went through the door, leaving Sorrel to her sleep.

Sorrel lay awake for only a short time before her emerald eyes were pulled shut by her need for rest. And with the closing of those green orbs a light smile came over her features. Her mind seemed only to want this quiet time of relaxing to bring forth dark, fathomless blue eyes and black wavy hair set upon a darkly tanned and all too handsome face.

Being pulled from the dark recess of her dreams, Sorrel bolted upright in her bed, her mind fighting frantically for answers. What had awakened her? she looked in fright about her chambers, trying to find in the dark corners of the room some form that would explain her terror.

It had been a loud noise, like that of a door slamming, she remembered as she sat still, trying to adjust to the darkness about her. She would have lit a candle but she was too frightened to remember where Sis had left the matches.

With the thought of her father she slowly slipped her feet to the side of the bed, still breathing hard as she was not sure that the door that she had heard slamming had not been her own. She sat still for another moment before she slipped her feet into her slippers.

Her eyes frantically searched about her as she stood and pulled on the matching wrapper to her gown and then slowly her steps sought out the door. Her father had the room only a few doors down from her own.

With a thumping heart she opened her chamber door, and in the soft lighting from the hallway she was able to see that no intruder had ventured into her room while she was asleep. It must have been another room, she told herself, and for a moment she debated whether to turn and climb back into her bed. But she knew that she would find no sleep now. She needed her father.

With slow, halting steps she started down the hall, debating at each door whether this could be the one that stood between her and her father. She was only three doors down from her own when she heard voices from down the hall. They were loud and rough sounding to her ears, the jovial laughter and hearty shouts reminding Sorrel once again of the man intruding into her chamber as she was bathing earlier that very evening. It could be the same man and one of his friends, she thought in panic, and with no more thoughts her small hand went to the knob on the door and she softly pushed it open, hoping as she was doing so that this would be the room that her father was in.

This should be the chamber, she told herself, stepping inside and softly shutting the wood door behind her. This room like her own was in total darkness, but now, it was only a few moments before she could make out the shape of the large bed in the center of the room and also the figure of chairs placed near the hearth. The thought entered Sorrel's mind as she looked about that her father had been given a larger and much more comfortable chamber than her own.

With halting steps she began to approach the large bed. "Papa," she called softly as she stood at the foot. But there was no reaction. Remembering from the past how sound a sleeper her father was, Sorrel walked around the bed and gently reached out a hand to the shoulder of the bed's occupant. "Papa, are you awake?" she ventured again. Her father seemed to be sleeping with the covers pulled tightly to his chin and a pillow half covering his face. Sorrel tried as well as she was able to see him, but in the darkness of the room the only thing she had to identify him by was the softness of his breathing.

For a second Sorrel's hand stilled as the thought came to her that perhaps this was not, in fact, her father's chamber, and that some strange man was sleeping here in this bed.

This was her last thought before her hand was captured and held in a viselike grip. With a gasp of dismay Sorrel was pulled into the softness of the bed and grasped up tightly to a large, steellike chest. Her worst fears were realized as the blankets were pulled away and the form of a huge man came dimly to her eyes. This certainly was not her father. Her instinct to fight and flee seemed to be paralyzed as the man took hold of her chin and with dark blue, penetrating eyes glared into her own.

Before Sorrel could cry for release his mouth descended upon hers, and with a fiery-burning desire of passion she was totally consumed by that one kiss. With a soft moan, Sorrel knew who it was that held her in his arms, and though she fought within her mind against the reality of the situation her body did not seem able to move or to fight for her release. She seemed to have been born for this one moment. Her whole being was tuned for this night, seeming from the beginning of creation to have been set for this moment in this man's arms, as his mouth and tongue devoured all that she was capable of giving.

It was he who pulled back, and, shaking his head, he sat up upon the bed.

In this short space of time Sorrel pulled her senses somewhat together, and with a gasp at her own willingness to be handled by a man she had only seen from a distance she jumped from the bed, pulled her wrapper more tightly about her body, and twirling upon her slippered heels, she rushed to the door. But before she could gain her objective strong hands were holding her still, their hardness going through the thin material of her gown and to the very bone of her being.

"Does my beautiful night blossom wish to flee so quickly?" His words were hushed in a deep-throated whisper as they touched upon her ears.

Sorrel could not speak but shook her head from side to side, knowing that if not for the support of his arms holding on to her arms she would collapse at his feet in a crumpled heap. So powerful was his hold upon her with only the merest glimpse of his blue eyes looking into her face that she felt her will leave her and she knew that whatever he wished of her she would not be able to deny.

With the strong shaking of his hands upon her shoulders he now firmly questioned her, "What are you about here in my chambers?" Something within the panic-stricken eyes touched him deeply and he went on in a more gentle tone. "Were you looking for someone? Did you lose your way?"

Without an answer the man was helpless to understand her plight, but finally Sorrel got out, "I—I thought this to be my father's chamber. I am sorry."

The large man smiled down tenderly at the wisp of a woman, and she was certainly a woman, he thought, as he once again went over the feel of her in his arms upon his bed. He would not have so treated her, he thought now as he looked into her frightened face, but upon waking and seeing the hand and the form outlined so clearly by the sheerness of her gown and wrapper he had, without a will of his own, pulled her to him. But now, with reality staring him so full in the face, he only wished for her to be gone and to leave him to his own tormented thoughts. "I am afraid that you made a mistake, madam. This is my chamber, not your father's." He could not fully see the beauty of her features, but he knew that there was a fineness here that was quite unusual in the outline of her face.

Sorrel gulped and then started. "I am sorry, if you will but let me go, I shall go to my own chamber. I would not have come in here without knocking in the first place if not for the fact that I heard voices down the hall and did not wish to be seen dressed as I am." Thus she tried to explain her presence in his chambers.

Relaxing now that he knew it had all been a mistake, the large man smiled down at the girl-woman. Opening the door a bit he spoke softly. "I shall watch that you make your way back to your own room." Without another word he let her go, and Sorrel did not take any more time but fled down the hall.

The large man stood watching the form as though some rare dream were rushing down the long hall. The soft lighting of the candles along the hall lit her hair with a golden gleam. But as he watched her turn the knob at her door and disappear into the room, another form came to his mind, and with its presence he shut his own door and went back to his bed, hoping that with some luck the night had not been ruined and that he would be able to fall back to sleep without the dreams that so often plagued him.

Sorrel had hurried across the floor of her chamber and buried herself deep within the folds of her covers, trying without result to find a way in which to block out the happenings of the night. She would not dare again to look for her father's room. She shivered slightly at what had happened and what could have taken place if it had been another's room she had entered.

Wrapping her arms about herself she forced herself to relax, and with the easing of the tension of her body she let her thoughts go over what had only moments ago happened in the stranger's chamber. She brought her hand up and softly brushed her fingertips across her pink, slightly quivering lips. It had been as she had dreamed this evening in the tub. There had been an enraptured arousal of her senses that she had never before known. This had been the first time in her life that she had been willing to be led by a man, willing to be led and not care about the outcome. If the truth were fully known she would have to admit that within those few seconds that she had been in his arms she had been completely vulnerable, completely at his mercy, and willing to do anything that he might have wanted.

This fact came as a shock to Sorrel and for a few moments she thought deeply of her feelings. What was it about this man to whom she had not even been properly introduced that so affected her? When she had gone to the ball with Clifford no such reaction had quickened her body and thoughts, nor had any other young man that she had met. Why did this man have such a power over her? she wondered, seeing his dark blue eyes looking deep within her face as he tried to see who had disturbed his sleep and broken into his chamber unannounced.

In that moment of the searching of his eyes she had known who it was who held her so tightly against his chest. She had realized, she remembered with a drastic thumping of her heart, that this bed that she had been pulled into was the bed of the man she had so admired in Langston's emporium that very afternoon. And with this fast-dawning realization she had become numb, her body unwilling to break his grip upon her and the deepest recesses of her mind taking a special delight in the lips that sought out her own and seemed to draw out her secret being and lay bare all her inner thoughts.

She felt a deep flush cover her face at the memory. She had not wished for him to release her. She had wanted—but with a cautious dawning she realized that she had no idea of what she had wanted. It was the first time that she had been alone with a man who drew her as this one did. She had never been kissed and held as she had in this stranger's bed. All thoughts of any other man were totally swept from her mind leaving room only for this tall, handsome stranger.

It was some time before sleep finally overtook Sorrel's troubled thoughts, but with her slumber a soft, pleasurable smile came to her lips, indicating that her dreams were much to her liking.

It was late in the morning the following day when Graylin Morgan knocked lightly upon his daughter's door and awaited her call to enter.

It was Sis who bid her young charge's father into the room as she patted the last piece of golden hair into place and with one last tuck at Sorrel's gown pronounced the girl fit for the day ahead.

Graylin greeted his only child with a kiss upon her forehead and then thanked Sis for the care that she had lavished upon his daughter. "Would you care to break the fast with me Sorrel? I know that the hour is rather late, but I am afraid that I slept late. I have just now awakened and dressed." He seemed in a fine humor this morning, having slept well and feeling hopeful of success in his ventures because of the help of Leroy Langston.

"That will be fine, Papa. I am afraid that I also overslept." She smiled at her parent but the smile was rather thin and was visibly strained.

Graylin looked at her with some concern now. After Sis left the room he questioned Sorrel. "Are you feeling all right, dear? Did you not sleep well?" He could not fathom what could be the matter with her except that she had not gotten the rest that she needed. She was usually so full of life and high spirits, but today, like yesterday afternoon after they had left Langston's, she seemed somehow quiet and pensive.

"I'm fine, Papa. I guess that I did not sleep too

well, perhaps because of the change from ship to land." She did not wish to worry him with the events of the night before. He would want answers and she herself was not sure of what had happened and why. She would keep this secret to herself and mayhap she would be able to sort out this feeling that overcame her each time she thought of the tall, dashing stranger. There had to be an explanation for her actions, she reasoned to herself as her father watched her intently trying to decide whether she was really just tired or if there was more to this look of weariness on her face.

"If you're sure, child?" Graylin's brow rose as his eyes looked deep into her own. "Let's go down to the common room and have our meal. Perhaps the food will do you some good and revive your spirits."

Sorrel did not answer but followed her father from her chamber and down the stairs.

As Graylin ordered the meal Sorrel sat and watched him, noticing as she did that his mood was more than jovial. He was acting as though he was hoarding a great surprise, from which he would burst if he did not tell it soon. Each time he looked at his daughter his eyes gleamed with excitement, and as soon as the maid took their order and left, Sorrel ventured to find out what he was holding back from her.

"Papa, what on earth have you been up to? You are as jittery as a newborn pup."

Graylin laughed lightly and bent over and placed a small kiss on his daughter's creased forehead. "Nothing to concern yourself with, child. I have only been making arrangements for us to travel a bit and look for some good horseflesh."

"But I thought that Mr. Langston was to help you in this matter? Why do you have to make such arrangements?" Sorrel's mind was not really on the horses that her father had made this trip for. In fact, this was the first time in several days that the matter of the horses had been mentioned, and Sorrel, with more important things to concern herself about, such as the man she had met last night, had forgotten about her father's plans.

"Let me explain, my dear." Graylin's excitement was infectious and Sorrel now smiled fondly across the table at her father. "Leroy met me for dinner here at the inn last night and we talked more about my venture. And, as luck would have it, after our visit to his warehouse yesterday he had gotten in touch with a gentleman who he thought would be willing to help me find the animals I want and also get them back to Texas."

"Well, that was luck Papa." Sorrel put her spoon to her creamed cereal and made a small face before drinking her tea. The only real interest in horseflesh that she had was to make sure that when she rode she was astride a fine, spirited beast. She was not going to try and fool her father or herself at playing at an interest in his dealings.

Graylin saw that his daughter was not truly interested in his business, but he felt no great letdown. She was young, and the young thought not of the future but of today and of life. "There is more news, Sorrel." He waited until he had caught her full attention. "We shall be leaving the first thing tomorrow morning and going to Kentucky."

Sorrel's attention had indeed been grabbed by this

bit of information. This was what she had wished for, travel and excitement.

"The gentleman who will be helping us—I shall call him our guide—told me he is also staying at this inn, and last night he shared the meal with me and Leroy. He informed me that the better-bred horses are mostly found in Kentucky, and he even has had dealings with some of the horse farms in that area."

"Well, this indeed is good news, Papa, and it was fortunate for you that you met this guide." Sorrel was feeling some excitement beginning to grow within her now. She would have plenty to do in order to be ready to travel by the morning. The hurry and rushing would be an aid, she suddenly realized, in overcoming her feelings and bringing her thoughts back under the submission of her own will.

As they sat thus talking and eating Sorrel's green eyes kept roaming about the common room. Though she wished to have total control over her feelings, something within her retained a deep hunger to at least view from afar the man whom she had been held close to the night before. But as her wandering eyes went about the large room she glimpsed from the corner of her eye the man who had twice, in the one day that they had been in Richmond, done his best to insult her, and now, to her utter horror, he seemed to be heading in their direction.

"Ah, there is the good man now, Sorrel." Graylin rose from his chair and clasped hands with the tall, handsome man, who had strode boldly across the room and now stood directly in front of their table.

"Alexander Gentry, madam, at your service." As he clasped her father's hand the words fell on Sorrel and the dark eyes took in her flushed composure and the sparks of anger beginning to grow in the depths of her emerald eyes.

"Indeed," Sorrel sniffed, her look toward this intruder one of pure disdain and loathing.

"How wonderful for us that you came along, Alex," Graylin started, not noticing the undercurrent between the younger pair. "I was only just now telling my daughter about our plans to go to Kentucky. Perhaps now that you are joining us you can elaborate somewhat where I have left off." Graylin was smiling broadly, feeling comfortable and completely at his ease with this man he had only met the night before.

"Of course, anything I can tell your daughter I would find a pleasure." The man called Alex took his eyes from the father and turned them toward the daughter. "What would you wish to know, Miss Morgan?"

Sorrel wished to know nothing from this blackguard who dared to look upon her as his dark eyes had the night before when he had barged without invitation into her chamber while she bathed—they were eyes that told her and anyone else who bothered to look at them that he found her desirable and beautiful. How dare he look at her in this manner, she fumed, with her father sitting right next to him. "Whatever my father wishes will suffice, sir." Her voice was haughty and chilled, not letting the smallest trace of warmth come from her.

Graylin laughed loudly. "I told you Alex, my daughter will be no trouble at all. She will not complain and she is well able to ride a horse as well as any man, so you have no worry on that account, either."

"Far be it from me to be concerned with your daughter's abilities, sir. I am sure that she will be able to care for herself." His mind was wandering back to the evening before when this lovely creature had been sitting in her bath, and as the vision of her beauty began to clear her loud screams came back to mind. His handsome face broke out into a grin as he watched the girl. She was a spirited thing, he would say this much for Miss Morgan.

Sorrel knew somehow what he was thinking and her face began to turn a bright red. She also could envision the scene of her in her bath, trying to shrink her body into the tub of water as this man stood before her and his eyes rudely sought out her privacy. "Papa, if you will excuse me." She began to rise from the table, the only thought in her mind to flee from this man who so arrogantly thought he could plague her thoughts.

Graylin and Alex rose, and Graylin looked at his daughter with some concern. He had noticed the deep flush on her cheeks and not understanding her reasons took her look for a malady of some sort. It seemed to him that since arriving here his daughter had not looked well. "Are you ill, Sorrel?" Before she could answer he was reaching a hand up and feeling her forehead.

"No, Papa, do not concern yourself. I feel a slight headache. Perhaps it has to do with my rest of last evening." She pointedly looked at the man called Alex Gentry, hoping that he would take her reason for her headache as his fault.

If she had wished him to know that he had upset her she was in for somewhat of a surprise. He had hoped to upset her and even more, so all she received from him was another one of his toothy grins.

"Well, if you are sure Sorrel," Graylin said, none too sure himself about his daughter's health. "You had best lie down and rest when you reach your chamber. I shall come up as soon as I have finished my breakfast and check on you myself. I do not want you traveling if you are ill. Perhaps I should call a doctor." Graylin was worried. Perhaps he should have left the girl with her aunt. Corrine would know how to treat her ups and downs. He had no idea of what to do, except to seek out help.

"Oh, Papa, I am fine." Sorrel smiled at her father, but she was beginning to feel some real anger at this intruder who dared to flaunt himself before her. How dare he be the cause of her father's distress? She did not think that this was the first time that she had caused her father concern about her health, but the mood of quietness that had come over her from her thoughts of the man she had met yesterday did not enter her mind. Right now she could only think of this Alex Gentry who stood before her as the cause of her father's distress. Rising up on tiptoes she placed a light kiss upon her father's chin. "Do not worry over me, Papa. A little rest and I shall be as good as new." With no word to her father's guest she turned about and with a swish of her skirts she started across the room and up the stairs.

Graylin watched his daughter's progress with a thoughtful look.

"Your daughter is quite lovely, Mr. Morgan," Alex

Gentry commented as he sipped his strong coffee.

Graylin's eyes were pulled from his daughter to the man sitting next to him. For a moment he did not speak but watched the other's eyes also following Sorrel up the stairs. But after a moment he smiled as though to himself. Sorrel could well take care of herself, and if this man thought to win her, well let him try. He almost welcomed these thoughts. Though the man did not appear to have any wealth, perhaps he would still be a better match than the man she was betrothed to. Perhaps the weeks ahead would prove even more interesting than he had at first thought.

Sorrel had no thoughts of taking to her bed. Her life was much too active for anything like that. Her only reason for leaving the downstairs was the young man who seemed to presume too much. As she started down the hall to her chambers she had to pass by the door through which she had boldly entered the night before, thinking it to be her father's. Her steps seemed to slow as she came near it, but pushing herself she went on. With some will she opened her door and entered her own room.

Sis had already straightened up so there was nothing for Sorrel to do but occupy her time with her thoughts. She quickly put the infamous Alex Gentry out of her mind, and, throwing herself upon the coverlet spread across the bed, she shut her eyes and once more went over the night before in the stranger's room.

As she felt in her mind the sensuous pressure of his

mouth upon her own she jerked herself upright and jumped from the bed. For a few moments she paced across the carpet. She felt the true strain of her imprisonment here in this room, her thoughts wondering once more to the hallway beyond her door. Could she dare be so bold as to step out and go down that path that would lead her to the stranger's door?

She felt her body beginning to break out into a cold sweat with the feelings welling within her. But she knew that she, Sorrel Morgan, could not dare such an action. Last night had been a mistake, an accident that should never have happened. If she were to boldly go to this man there would be a difference. She had never in the past taken such a deliberate action where a man was concerned, and she knew that she could not change, no matter how much she wanted to.

It was not long before Sorrel heard a knock on her own door and finding her father with his face all concern she invited him in, assuring him that she felt much better and that her rest had taken her headache completely away.

Graylin was much gratified to hear this. After she had left the common room he had had thoughts of postponing his trip. But now with her reassurances he could see for himself from her smiling face that she was telling the truth, and he left her with his wish that she spend the rest of the day in her room while he was about town seeking out what would be needed for the trip.

Sorrel agreed willingly, having no wish to be around Alex Gentry, and she thought that more than likely he would be along with her father that day. Her only real desire was to see once more the man of yesterday. Perhaps somehow she would be able to at least get one more glimpse of him before she left Richmond.

Sis brought Sorrel a tray for lunch. Sorrel ate hardly anything, and Sis, looking at her sternly with hands upon her hips, questioned her, "You going to mope about all the day girl? What is the matter with you? You can tell Sis anything."

For a moment Sorrel said nothing, her emerald eyes going to the girl and looking at the black face, and then, as though she had no other way to turn, she slowly began. "Do you know the man who has the room down the hallway, Sis?"

"The man down the hallway? Why honey, there be all manner of men in this inn with rooms down this here hall. What man you be a'meaning?" Sis thought she knew the one the girl was questioning her about and now a slow dawning of knowledge came to her. The young girl was not really sick, she was only mooning over a young man. Sis had seen the young man down in the common room sitting with her father and she had even glimpsed that young Mr. Gentry with her eating breakfast this very morning. She could not blame the girl for her mood, she thought with a gleam of delight coming to her black eyes, she had even thought the man to be quite attractive.

Sorrel hated that she had to try and explain further, but now that she had started this affair she was determined to have an ending to it. "I saw him yesterday, Sis, while I was with Papa at Mr.

Langston's emporium." She left out the telling of her adventure during the night. She wished for no one to know this one secret, not even this smiling, kind girl before her. "I think I also saw him a few doors down the hall. He is rather large with dark black hair."

Sis knew now that she was not talking about the one she had thought. She realized exactly who Sorrel meant, and with a large grin she looked at her. "You sure got some good taste, missy. I be knowing who you meaning, and that man is sure an eyeful, yes, indeed."

Sorrel's eyes came alight with the prospect of finding out something about the man who seemed to possess her very thoughts.

"You be out of luck, though, missy, for this man he done left the first thing this morning." Sis hated to disappoint the young girl but she knew no other way to tell her.

"He left?" was all that Sorrel could get out.

"Yes, ma'am, he done left the first thing. I don't be knowing if he coming back, I only seen him one other time here at this inn and that was some time ago."

Sorrel felt a great letdown within her. He had left this morning, while she was probably fast asleep. He had come into her life and turned her insides all about and now he was gone. With nothing else to say to the black girl and her disappointment apparent on her face, Sorrel hung her head over her plate and acted as though she wished to hear no more but wanted only to finish her meal.

Sis took her quiet as a wish to be alone with her thoughts, and quickly she left the girl's chamber.

With plenty to do downstairs she hurried down to the kitchen, thoughts of the girl's problems quickly leaving her mind.

Sorrel had the rest of the afternoon to determine her feelings for the strange man whom she had met. This was the first time that she had let herself feel anything for a man. In fact, no other man had ever provoked more than a second glance from the girl until now. But as the hours went by, and with nothing else to do but to think over the matter, she tried to force him from her mind, telling herself over and over that he did not matter. It had been just a small thing in her life and she would see that in the future many more men would affect her and some perhaps even more strongly. Perhaps she had read more into this than had truly been there, mayhap she had only wished for some strong emotion and had jumped at the chance with this complete stranger. These thoughts came to her, but deep within her she knew that they were not the truth; there had been something that she had never before felt, and a small doubt came to her that she would ever again feel this sweet desire that she had tasted for such a brief moment.

But with her strong will Sorrel set her face and determined in her own mind to put this adventure to the back of her mind. She would place it there, she told herself, and only think of it when she wished to. It would be the first of many adventures in this new land.

As she readied herself for the night she was even able to smile softly into the mirror. In the future, when she was home in Texas, she would be able to pull from her memory that her very first day in Richmond she had started a new adventure and had experienced a completely new feeling, one that she did not know if she would ever feel again. But she had thought the matter over carefully and had decided that at least she had had the feeling—and if her life were to be lacking in the future she would be able to think back on this one night in a stranger's arms.

Chapter Six

The next morning Sorrel was pulled from her sleep by a loud knocking outside of her chamber door. "Sorrel, are you wakening?" her father called.

"Yes, Papa," she yawned as she rose up on her elbows. "I shall be down shortly."

"All right, child, but try to hurry. I shall have a cup of hot tea and some breakfast ready when you come down."

Sorrel had been told the evening before by her father that they would be leaving the inn and hiring a carriage to start them on their way to Kentucky. But she had never guessed that they would be leaving this early, she thought as she looked about the dark room.

Lighting the small wick candle she began to dress in the dark blue woolen gown that she had left over the back of the chair the night before. Sis had been wonderful the day before, helping her to pack all of her gowns and making sure that all was in order for their trip this morning. If not for Sis, Sorrel knew that she would have been up most of the night doing things that the girl's capable hands did in a short time.

She reminded herself once again as she started down the stairs to mention to her father to tell the proprietor of the black girl's special care and attention and to leave her a generous tip.

Sorrel was relieved to see that the infamous Mr. Alex Gentry was nowhere to be seen in the common room. Her father was sitting at a table and sipping a mug of coffee. Large plates of food were set in front of him.

It was much earlier than Sorrel was used to rising, and at first she doubted her appetite. But as she sat and tasted the savory breakfast she ate all that her father had placed upon her plate.

She enjoyed this quiet time with her father, but all too quickly he rose and told her that they would have to be on their way. Sorrel was to find that the future would not hold too many of these desired quiet moments alone with her father.

The next several days were not what Sorrel had expected at all. She had imagined cool hours during the day riding in the carriage and visiting towns and the countryside, but, in fact, she found herself weary and dusty each evening from the long day's bumpy carriage ride over rough and sometimes overgrown roads. They stopped only for short lunches, and in the evening they would find an inn. After eating a hurried supper her father would rush her off to her room and seemingly only minutes later he would once again be knocking at her door and calling to her that it was time for her to wake and come down to breakfast.

Sorrel had not talked to Alex Gentry since that morning in Richmond, and now, with each passing day, she ranted at the man in her mind, calling him every manner of a scoundrel, for she knew that he was to blame for this uncomfortable travel and hurried pace that they had been pushed into.

She had several times asked her father while she was being thrown to one side of the carriage or having to cling to her hat in order for it not to sail from her head, why they were traveling in such a manner. And his answer was always the same. Though his eyes showed sympathy for his daughter's condition, he told her that this hurried trip was necessary. For if they were to find the animals that he wished they would need to be through the Cumberlands before the winter snows caught them. He had no intention of going back to his ranch by way of the sea. They would hire more men in Kentucky and a couple of wagons and take the horses overland.

Sorrel thought the idea of going overland a fine one and she also knew that she would be much better off whenever they did obtain horses and she could ride one instead of sitting in a bumpy carriage, but still she seethed each time she thought of the arrogant Mr. Alex Gentry. Thank God, she thought, that the man did not share their carriage but instead rode ahead on his horse.

The days, though they passed slowly, did pass, and soon the carriage was pulling down long drives and heading up to fine plantation houses and her father was inspecting horses and deciding on which ones he wished to purchase.

Kentucky was beautiful, and though the weather

was now chilly Sorrel knew that in the spring and summer the land would have been the most beautiful that she ever could have wished to see. Her father also was impressed with the land around him and even more so with the fine animal flesh that was brought before his eyes by the plantation owners of this wonderful Kentucky. On more than one occasion Sorrel heard her father telling Mr. Gentry of his appreciation for the man's knowledge of the area, though she hated to admit it, she had to agree. If not for Alex Gentry they would more than likely still be in Richmond, but now here they were, and each day they were acquiring more horses to take back to her father's ranch.

Finally, one morning over breakfast in a town called Lexington, her father told her that they had only one more stop to see horses and they would start their trip home. Sorrel was truly glad that his buying was nearing its end. She doubted that she would be able to endure much more of the carriage, and though it meant that they would return to Texas, still she would be able to ride a horse instead of being cramped up and thrown about in a tiny vehicle. She smiled happily at her father and told him that she was more than ready to be going home.

He agreed with her, but before they could say anything Alex Gentry walked up to their table and pulled himself up a chair without being asked. "I hope I am not disturbing you?" His bold eyes went to Sorrel.

"Why, of course not, lad, have a cup of coffee." Graylin poured the young man a cup from the pot that the serving girl had left at their table.

"Thank you, sir. I came in to tell you that I have gotten all the supplies that we shall be needing and the exra men, too. Though I am afraid that I had to offer a bit more money to the men than we had planned on. They think that the trip may be a bit harder through the passes with the weather already starting to get bad. It might not be too long before it begins to snow."

"Pay them what they want, lad. Do you think it will be too risky to try to go through the mountains?" Graylin looked worried as he watched the other man's face, trying to read by his look the answer that he wished to see. He would not be the cause of any harm coming to anyone, especially not to his own daughter.

"No sir, I think we'll be fine." Alex noticed his worry and smiled at the older man. He had become quite fond of Graylin Morgan and he hoped over the next weeks to become on better terms with his daughter. He had not spoken much to the young lady during their travel, but he had decided that first morning in Richmond at the breakfast table that he would have her for his own. The first thing to do, he had reasoned with himself, was to give her a cooling-down period, so he had left her and her father to their carriage, but as soon as she was on horseback and they were heading toward Texas he would begin to play his cards in a different style. "I think we shall make it in good time to Texas," he added with a slow, lazy grin.

The last horses were bought from a plantation called Crescent Mist, and as Sorrel was retiring for the night she went over once more in her mind the afternoon she had just spent out at the vast plantation.

What a warm and beautiful brick house it had been, she mused as she brushed out her rich honey-gold curls. Again the man named Justin Danner came before her emerald eyes. He must certainly have been a dashing young man in his youth, she thought, setting the hairbrush aside. But now he was gray and something deep in his eyes spoke of a great sorrow.

She did not know why this one particular plantation was sticking in her mind as it was. After all, they had visited a dozen since being in Kentucky and no other had affected her in this way. But from the moment they had started down the long drive lined with large, overhanging oaks she had known something was different about this place. She had watched expectantly from the carriage window as her father and Mr. Gentry had gone up the front veranda and knocked on the front door. But not knowing what it was she had expected, she sighed a deep sigh as an elderly man, tall and well built with a fawn-colored suit and lacy white shirt, had greeted them at the door. The men had conversed for only a few short moments before all heads turned toward the carriage and three pairs of eyes focused upon her face at the window. Her father had immediately left the front door and come to the door of the vehicle.

"Sorrel, Mr. Danner would like for you to come up to the veranda in the shade and perhaps have a drink of something cool while you wait."

"Why, of course Papa," she answered, starting to step through the door as he opened it for her. She had at almost all of the other plantation homes been extended this same courtesy. She would either sit on the front veranda or be invited into the house and entertained by the women of the house.

A large black woman with a bright red scarf tied about her head met Sorrel on the front veranda with a large glass of lemonade in her hand.

"Here is that drink you be calling for, Master Justin," the woman said, stepping around her master in order to gain a better view of the guests who had arrived at Crescent Mist.

"Set it down on that table, Mally, and see if the young lady would care for anything else," Justin Danner told the woman. Turning to the men he added, "If you will follow me, gentlemen, I shall go as far as the back barn with you. I have a man there who will go along with you to view my stock."

Graylin was surprised by this. Most of the other plantation owners whom he had met here in Kentucky took a great deal of pride in their horses and would not have thought to let him view them without their presence. "Whatever you say, Mr. Danner," he said, though, not wishing to offend the good man.

Sorrel sat down upon a large, comfortable wicker chair and sipped the cool drink the black woman had brought her. "Ah," she sighed as she tasted the drink. It had a different taste to it, she thought. They must have put something special in it, perhaps some sweet herb.

Mally saw her smile and heard her sigh and her chest swelled with pride. She was no ordinary cook, and she prided herself on serving food and drinks that tasted in no way like anyone else's. "I'm mighty glad you be liking that there drink, missy," she ventured.

"Oh, it is quite good." Sorrel took another long drink. "What on earth gives it that sweet, tangy flavor?"

"It just be something I be learning over the years, missy. Can I be getting you something else? Perhaps some cookies or cake?"

Sorrel laughed aloud. This woman was friendly and truly seemed willing to please. "No, thank you, I am really not hungry. But thank you for your kind concern."

Mally grinned at the young woman as she stood near the front door. "You sure is a pretty little thing, missy. It sure be a wonder that some young handsome man ain't already snapped you on up." Mally had always spoken her mind here at Crescent Mist and she had noticed that the girl was here with her father and he had been the one to see to her needs, so she had spoken the first thoughts aloud that had come to her mind.

Gay, tinkling laughter filled the veranda and settled about the large brick house, and this was the sound that greeted Justin Danner's ears as he rounded the corner. "I must admit—is it Mally?" Sorrel made sure that she was saying the name correctly. She thought that was the name that Mr. Danner had called the large black woman. With her head shaking up and down she continued. "Yes, I do admit that plenty of young men have tried to—as you put it—snap me up, but I have not been an easy prey, I am afraid."

"You don't be a'sorry for that, young missy. It

sometimes best to be a'waiting. If'in my young master had a'waited he wouldn't be in the bad fix he be in now."

Before Sorrel could respond to the black woman's comment Justin Danner started up the steps. "I see that Mally has been entertaining you, Miss Morgan." His features seemed gentler now with his smile. "Thank you, Mally, that will be all for now." With these words directed to the black woman he dismissed her.

The large woman winked fondly at Sorrel and left the front porch with a swish of her calico skirts.

"Perhaps you would care to view the inside of my home, Miss Morgan?" It had been some time since Justin had heard female laughter, and something within him stirred when he looked at this woman's young and beautiful face.

"That would be wonderful, Mr. Danner. I must admit that since we first started up your drive and I saw the magnificence of your house I have been curious." Sorrel rose to her feet and taking the arm that was extended to her walked through the front door.

The foyer was of a black and white marble, having the desired effect of making one cool and comfortable on first entering. Justin steered Sorrel into the front parlor and disengaged her arm. "Make yourself comfortable, Miss Morgan. I shall tell Mally to bring us some tea and cakes in here." He left her to herself, knowing that most women, though they did not say so, would rather walk about and view things on their own.

And Sorrel did exactly that. She looked about her

at first and then slowly walked about, taking in all that the room had to offer. The furniture was of a dark, rich wood and solid rose material, the draperies being only a slight shade lighter and matching the oriental carpeting under her feet. One whole length of a wall was a huge fireplace, the hearth standing even higher than her own height, and what caught her eyes were the portraits that hung over the mantel. There were two and both were of young men. But what captured Sorrel's attention was the fact that they both looked to be a younger version of Mr. Danner. Why he would wish two such pictures of himself hung in the same room was a mystery to her, but something about them kept her attention from wandering. Then, as she looked up at them she noticed that though they looked to be the same person the eyes in each were different. The eyes of one were light, almost silver-colored, and the other's were so blue they were almost startling.

Either the artist had made a drastic mistake or the two portraits were not of the same person, she realized, and standing before them her eyes kept going over and over the painting of the man with the darker eyes. There was something about the portrait, she thought. It was as though she knew the man, and then for a moment the features of a handsome man with a trimmed beard came to her mind. She had tried for the past weeks to shun all thoughts of him. This man in the painting did resemble the man that she had seen in Richmond but now that night in the handsome stranger's arms, feeling his kiss upon her lips and his hands boldly on her body, seemed like ages ago.

And as she stood thus, totally wrapped up in the portraits before her, Justin Danner entered the room. He made no noise as he made his way to her side and softly spoke. "My son and myself."

"Oh." Sorrel said, for little else to say. And as she looked at her host she saw that his were the eyes that were a light, gray-blue. She wondered for a moment if she should question him about his son and perhaps tell this kind man that mayhap she had met him in Richmond. But something held her back. Perhaps she was mistaken, she thought. After all, it had been some time ago and she had only seen the gentleman that short time while she was in the emporium. She had not gotten a good look at him while she was in his room. "You both look so much alike," was all that she got out.

"Aye, we do at that. And I think that perhaps we both act too much alike. That could perhaps be the cause of so much of our discontent with one another."

Sorrel turned about the room, not wishing to impose on this man's personal problems, and at the same time Mally entered the room with a large tea tray.

For the rest of the time that Sorrel spent with this kindly man her emerald eyes kept, as though without a will of their own, rising and going over the portraits placed over the hearth. A strong pull seemed to come from the one with the dark blue eyes, as though beckoning her to look at him again and again.

It was not for much longer, though, that Sorrel was left to Justin Danner's company, for her father and

Alex returned. Leaving the grand house and its gracious host, she felt a deep loss as the carriage started its ride back to town.

Now as Sorrel lay down to sleep for the night, she saw once more before her eyes shut Justin Danner's face. What a kind man he had been, she thought. But with her mind on the gentleman she had met that day, she also found herself thinking of the man she had met in Richmond. Vibrant, lapis-blue eyes came to her as she shut her own green ones. She had tried to keep from thinking of the man but for this one night she let herself go over every second that she had spent in his chamber.

It was some time before Sorrel Morgan found rest that evening, but with her sleep a deep, hazy, dreamlike sphere surrounded her and brought the peace to her mind that her own will could not find. The stranger filled her thoughts, and with their own will her dreams led her where they were wont.

The next morning Sorrel was left to sleep later than usual, but in midmorning when Graylin could wait no longer he woke his daughter, had her bags carried downstairs and loaded aboard one of the wagons he had purchased, and then joined her for a light meal.

They were on their way shortly after lunch. Three wagons, twelve hired men, over forty horses, and Sorrel, Graylin, and Alex Gentry, beginning the long journey that would take them to the Morgan ranch.

On this first day Sorrel found some relief on the back of a spirited mare her father had purchased for her for the trip, but by the end of the long day she was more than glad when the wagons were halted and the horses were tied and watchers were set up to make sure that no animals came around them to disturb them. Sorrel, like the animals that had been driven that day, found herself exhausted, and shortly after eating her meal near the fire that had been built she went into one of the wagons and fell immediately to sleep.

The next day, though, she felt fine when she awoke and stretched her limbs. The day before she had thought that she would surely awake with all manner of cramps and aches, but to her relief she felt fit and ready for the day ahead. She decided that the jostling of the carriage must have been what had kept her in such good shape.

Before leaving the wagon she donned a pair of tight men's breeches that she had purchased in Lexington and a white satin long-sleeved shirt. She had also bought a pair of boots that fit snugly and went well with her outfit, she thought, as she tried without a mirror to turn this way and that to view herself. She pulled her hair on top of her head and placed a hat over the golden mass, drawing the strings securely under her chin.

If Graylin Morgan was surprised with his daughter's attire he did not show the slightest traces of it as she left the back of the wagon. "Ah, Sorrel, I was just on my way to see if you were oversleeping. You must have your breakfast, for it will be some time before we break for lunch." His eyes went over her form from head to toe, and there glowed in their depths admiration and praise for this lovely young creature who was his daughter.

The men who had come along on this venture with Graylin Morgan were not of the same mind, however, as Sorrel's father. As she walked along with her father from behind the wagon and the pair made their way to the fire, several loud grunts and even some low whistles could be heard following Sorrel's tight-fitted walk and the sway of her hips.

Alex Gentry was the only one, though, to actually voice his opinion as Sorrel and her father came into his line of vision. His mouth opened visibly as she approached him where he sat near the fire sipping his last cup of coffee before he started his men moving about their business. "What do you think you are about?" he asked incredulously, not believing his eyes even though this creature standing before him with her proud breasts pushing enticingly against the soft satin material of her shirt and her form outlined perfectly within her tight-fitting jeans was easily only a few feet from his reach.

"What?" was the only word Sorrel glared at him before accepting a cup of the strong coffee, which had been perking all the morning on the fire, from the cook.

Even Graylin looked at the young man with a stern expression at the tone he was using with his daughter. It was clear to see, he thought, that this young man was not used to being around a woman with a mind of her own.

"Mr. Morgan, sir," Alex tried the father knowing that he would get nowhere with the daughter. He could not stand for what was going on here. There was no way he would allow Sorrel Morgan to dress in that manner with all of his men staring at her agape. He would constantly have to be on the watch in order to protect her. His thoughts flew wildly across his mind.

Graylin shook his head at the young man, and he too accepted a cup of the coffee. "My daughter is a woman with a mind and thoughts of her own, lad. Leave it be."

"Why yes, sir. I did not mean to tell you how to handle your own daughter, I only thought that you would see the dangers of her being dressed in such a manner. I doubt that I will be able to get any of my men to keep their minds on their work with her riding about in those tight breeches." Alex felt his face sweating as he once more looked at Sorrel and saw the swelling of her breasts with each breath of air she took. He was the one he was worried about, he admitted to himself, not his men but himself.

"Mr. Gentry," Sorrel addressed the young man for the first time since they had started out on this trip. "You will do well to remember that you are only hired by my father and that your opinion is of no importance to me whatsoever. I shall dress in any fashion that *I* think fit, not you!" Anger was now shooting out of the depths of her emerald eyes and with a swish she turned about and headed toward her horse.

Graylin chuckled loudly, causing Alex to fume with anger, and he too stomped off but in the other direction, shouting and yelling at his men.

The weather was growing colder now as the group started their endless daily ride across the country. As they began their climb over mountains and through thick forest it was even colder, but Sorrel didn't mind, she loved this land around her, and each day held new adventures for her.

From that morning when she had stepped out of her wagon in her new outfit, she and Alex Gentry had not spoken a word. There seemed to be a silent feud between the two of them. Everyone was aware of it, but no one spoke about it.

Sorrel helped with the horses as much as possible, either leading a line of the mounts behind her own or following close behind in order to make sure that none broke away and got free. This latter she enjoyed the most, for while she was supposed to be helping she would dream and watch the land about her, delighting in the huge trees and the winter greenery that abounded in this fresh, new land.

Alex Gentry seemed to know the land and trails well, and during their second week on the trail he announced one night that they would be reaching the Cumberlands the following day. He wore a huge grin as he said this to Graylin, proud of the short time that they had made so much progress in. They would be well clear of the passes before the first snows set in. And by the way the dark clouds were beginning to build up, he knew that they truly had only just made it in time.

Even Sorrel smiled that night at the younger man, also thankful that all was going as well as could be.

Her smile was not lost either on her father or the young man for whom it was intended. This night was a night made for the young, black and moonless, but with a million stars shining to light the earth as though by candlelight.

As the evening progressed most of the men made their way one by one to their sleeping mats, and the fire that was usually stoked and tended by the cook began to die down. But still Sorrel had not gone to seek the shelter of her wagon and her bed, and neither had Alex Gentry.

"Do you miss your home much?" Alex's voice came softly across the space of the fire to Sorrel's ears.

She did not answer quickly but thought the question over carefully. "I guess I do somewhat, but not like one would expect. I am afraid that I have never really had a home of my own, so there is simply not too much to miss." She tried to explain her feelings to this man she had sworn to be her enemy.

Alex was curious about her answer, but he did not wish to push her. He had been bold in the inn when first he had met this proud, beautiful woman, but he saw that he had made a mistake in his pursuit of her. He now thought that to win her he must go in another direction. She was a woman who would need gentle breaking, but break her he would, of that he had no doubt. There was not a woman alive who would stand still under his planned attack, he thought to himself. "I thought that you lived with your father on his ranch?" Still his voice was soft, not disturbing the quiet of the camp or sending any panic over Sorrel.

Graylin had only a short time ago himself retired for the night and with the mention of her father Sorrel looked in the direction of his sleeping pallet. "Nay, I have lived since a babe with my aunt in Houston." She did not elaborate.

Alex thought this answer over carefully. He would

have thought, from the closeness of daughter and father and the independent manner in which Sorrel went about her everyday life, that the two had never been separated. He smiled in a sly, anticipating manner, his white teeth hidden by the darkness of the evening. At least she was finally opening up somewhat to him, and if things went on in this manner by the time they reached Texas he would have her bending to his will. Again the smile flashed boldly across his handsome face. Perhaps he would even have her once again wearing dresses instead of those insufferable jeans she insisted on.

Sorrel knew none of the thoughts that were raging through the young man's mind. Her own thoughts were far from the campsite as she sat staring into the burning coals of the fire. At the start of this trip she had had high hopes that something of great importance was going to occur, but now, sitting here before a campfire in the middle of the wilderness and heading back to Texas, she knew that nothing was to change for her. She would return to her aunt's home and be the belle of the ball at all of the parties and affairs that she felt forced to attend. And her father would go back to his ranch, not knowing how his daughter hated the life of a pampered pretty miss who could not go along with him for fear of some great harm's befalling her. For a moment she felt like weeping out her despair, but in that instant she once again remembered where she was and looked across the fire at the man who had been talking only moments ago to her. At least she did have that to look forward to, she reasoned with herself. She would eventually marry and be able to move from town—

but what enjoyment would she find then? Tied down to a man who seemed insufferable and overbearing. Would he not try to change her and tie her spirit? Would she not be better off with her aunt? She absently rubbed her forehead with the back of her hand as she felt herself slipping into a state of total and black despair. Nothing would change for her in the future, her life would stay an empty void.

Alex saw within the fire's dim glow the sadness upon the lovely features before him and as she rubbed her forehead he ventured softly, "Is something wrong, Miss Morgan?"

"No," Sorrel said quickly, rising to her feet. "I am tired is all. I think I shall say good night now, Mr. Gentry." With these words she turned from the campfire and strode to the wagon that she had been sleeping in since the beginning of the trip.

But tonight she felt herself hemmed in as she climbed up into the back of the large wagon. The canvas covering felt suffocating as it shut off the fresh air. As suffocating as her own laid-out life, she idly thought as she looked at the small cot that she usually slept in.

Grabbing up a couple of blankets she left the wagon's confines and climbed underneath the large vehicle. Spreading out her blankets she snuggled into them, her last thought being that she must be insane to be sleeping out here in the cold, before her eyes shut and she fell asleep.

Chapter Seven

Sorrel awoke before daylight, taking a moment to accustom her emerald eyes to her surroundings as she lay still. She slowly stretched out her cramped muscles, her senses alert as though expecting something to happen. But seeing that all was quiet she lay where she was enjoying the pleasure of this feeling of anticipation that had come over her.

She had not felt this feeling in some time. It was as though she was awaiting a great revelation of some sort, she thought, feeling her breathing beginning to quicken and her pulse to race. There was a vast difference between this feeling that was now stirring her and the ones that she had tried to put from her mind as she had lain down under the wagon only a few short hours before.

She knew now with a certainty that somehow something was going to happen to change her life and she found with growing excitement that she was ready. Ready for any kind of change that would rescue her from the boring, dull future that loomed ahead of her. Her thoughts were those of most romantic young girls: something like a gallant knight in shining armor coming riding through the camp on a giant white stallion and scooping her up into his arms and riding off with her into the wilderness. Pictures such as these were all that her limited imagination could conjure up. She did not reason that there were no shining knights in armor here in the Cumberland mountains. Here in this dense wilderness there were only wild beasts, both animal and human.

For the rest of the morning Sorrel held on to this anticipation of something about to happen. And even after the camp came awake and began to stir and they began their never-ending steady pace through the Cumberlands, Sorrel kept constant watch all around her at the foliage and the rocks and boulders.

About midday, as the men were looking for a spot to stop for lunch and to give the animals a chance to rest for a bit, Sorrel, being at the back of the long procession of travelers, spotted a small ravine of water and followed it for a little way, hoping that she would come across a larger pool.

Not far off of the path she did indeed get her wish. Before her rose up a portion of a mountain and from its side gushed forth a glistening waterfall, showering its rain down upon a small pond.

She sat atop her horse for the briefest of minutes before jumping down and hurriedly pulling her boots from her feet. She looked around before she proceeded to pull her breeches and shirt from her body. It had been so long since she had been in the inn in Lexington and had a bath that she did not consider the possible consequences of her headstrong act. All the could think about was immersing her whole body in the water.

She had been hoping for the last few days for just such a chance as was now before her. She was tired of sponge baths in the wagon at nights, she wished to scrub her whole body until it glowed with cleanliness. She pulled a bar of lemon-scented soap from her saddle bag and dove smiling into the icy depths of the pond.

She came up shivering, her teeth rattling so hard in her head that she thought they would break, but this still did not dim her pleasure. She first washed her long, thick hair with the soapy lather and then, diving once again below the service, she came up gulping and began the attack on her body. Quickly, because the cold water was beginning to turn her body blue, she began to lather each arm and the upper portion of her body, and then, her skin glowing pink now instead of blue from her scrubbing, she began to do the same to her lower half.

After one more dive into the water she made her climb back to shore and taking the blanket from the back of her saddle she dried herself off. Spreading the blanket upon a boulder near the edge of the pond, she lay back and let the rays of the sun touch her body.

She delighted in the heat pouring down upon her. It had been a long time since she had been able to find enough privacy to lie naked beneath the sun. She shut her eyes, barely feeling the cool wind blowing from the north, all of her concentration upon the rays of the sun.

And here in the warmth beating down upon her she was lulled into a soft slumber where she could dream at her will and imagine herself far away and in the arms of a man whom she had only viewed from afar until she had stumbled into the wrong room. It all seemed eons ago now.

The sun touched down upon her like the gentle, stroking hands of a lover, and she could with little effort imagine the stranger's hands once again upon her, and with the light shuddering of her senses she could again feel the pressure of his slanted, seeking lips, his searching, branding tongue delving out all of her secrets and leaving all bare before his gaze, and in the throes of her dreams she wished for even more, for something that she could not name but knew was there just beyond her vision.

It was some time before Sorrel jerked herself awake, her dreams now put away in a distant section of her mind from where she could easily pull them to the fore when the occasion called for it. She had not meant to sleep, she thought as she sat up on the blanket, and, with some regret at having to leave the pleasure of her deepest thoughts, she looked about herself. She was alert, her body stiffening as she for no apparent reason felt a presence near her. What had awakened her, she wondered, looking now more deeply into the trees about the pond. But try as she might she could not see anything out of the ordinary. Still, though, the feeling persisted. It was as though eyes were watching her, and she could feel the fine hairs on the back of her neck sticking straight up.

It must be an animal, she tried to reassure herself. Of course, any number of different animals must come to this very spot to drink. But why did her horse not sense the presence of another animal if she did? The view of her mount standing and munching quietly upon the green grass along the pond's edge somehow frightened her.

Rising from the boulder and wrapping the blanket around her naked body Sorrel started toward her clothes and her horse. But before she could reach her mare's side a horse and rider emerged boldly from the trees and watched her with silent intent.

Sorrel's mind became panicked as she saw who was quietly sitting upon his horse near the line of trees. It was an Indian. She wanted to run, to scream, to cry. But some inner voice warned her that to do so would only bring disaster down upon her.

The Indian sat proud and only his coal-black eyes moved as they followed Sorrel as she now slowly finished her attempt to reach her clothes and her horse. The horse the Indian rode was white with only a few brown spots lightly speckled upon his sides, but on both sides of the stallion's buttocks were paintings that his master had undoubtedly painted there himself.

As Sorrel reached her clothes she began to pull them on under the protection that the blanket offered her, her emerald eyes never leaving the intruder who sat and stared at her every movement. The man was large, tall, and muscular. He wore leather pants that were opened down each thigh, a leather shirt that was open in the front, and leather boots that rose to each knee. No wonder she had not been able to discern him from the trees, Sorrel thought fleetingly. There was no telling how long this savage had been sitting in the safety of the trees and watching her. Anger rose up in her chest as she thought of this man's watching her bath and her lying in the sun. How dare he do such a thing? She jerked her feet into her boots and now openly glaring her anger she marched to her horse and jumped onto its back.

The Indian sat stock still, as though he was an animal watching its prey's every move.

As she swung her horse back into the direction of the path she had come from earlier, Sorrel's green eyes caught and held the Indian's for the briefest of seconds. And there, for that short amount of time, she thought she saw something in those black depths that she had never seen before. Was it admiration? Or a challenge? she wondered about it briefly as she started down the path and back to her father's camp.

The Indian did not follow but sat immobile as she passed him by. Why had he not said something to her? she wondered. Why had he only sat there and watched her in that hawkish manner? She had little time, though, to ponder these thoughts for she was almost at camp and Alex Gentry was riding up to her.

He pulled his horse's reins tightly, causing the beast to rise up on his hind legs. His light blue eyes blazed at the woman before him. "Where the blazes have you been?" he hissed between clenched teeth.

Sorrel looked with some irritation at the young man before her. She had only a few minutes ago been with a heathen Indian with more manners than this man. "That, Mr. Gentry, is absolutely none of your buisness." She kicked her mare's side and tried to get around Alex.

His long arm shot out and took hold of her reins before she could make good her escape. "One day I shall take that fine temper from you, Sorrel Morgan." His words were a soft, threatening promise.

"And you will enjoy every moment of it, I promise." He grinned down at her.

Bright, sparkling points of anger consumed Sorrel's green eyes as she glared at the man before her. "You will not be the man to tame my spirit, Mr. Gentry. And another thing, sir, when addressing me you have not my leave to call me by my given name. Miss Morgan will be sufficient." With her small hand whip she lightly struck out at the hand that held her reins and smiled as he let out an oath at the pain she had inflicted. Once again she kicked her horse's sides and rode on to camp.

Graylin also had been concerned about his daughter and, in fact, if Alex had not volunteered to look for her he himself would have been off searching this moment. But Sorrel did not view her father's concern in the same irrational way she did Alex Gentry's. She described in detail the pond she had found and told her father that she had taken a bath and lain in the sun for a time. For some reason, though, she did not tell him about the Indian. She would keep this a secret for a time, she thought, and when she wished she would be able to pull the scene of the Indian sitting so proud and erect upon his horse from her mind and go over it again and again without anyone's knowing about it. She had another secret.

To her surprise Sorrel found that she had been gone much longer than she had at first thought. Her father had ordered the camp set up for the night when he had first realized that she was not following behind them. But Graylin was not too worried until some time later. He had imagined his daughter doing something similar to what she had done, and he had no wish to disturb her privacy. As the time went by, though, he had become somewhat edgy. That was why he had finally consented to Alex Gentry's request that he allow him to go and look for Sorrel.

Graylin had been somewhat surprised at the young man's concern, but as Alex came back to camp with a black scowl upon his features and no kind words for anyone who asked him a question, Graylin surmised that his daughter had not taken kindly to the young man's worry over her well-being. Graylin chuckled to himself as Alex jumped from his mount and angrily strutted about the camp before finally walking off into the trees. This young man had a lot to learn if he wished to win his daughter. "Yes," Graylin laughed aloud, a lot indeed.

That evening Sorrel sat quietly off to herself as the camp set itself up for the night. Some of the men walked out to the edge of camp and set up their lookouts, to watch over the animals and make sure that no predators snuck in among them while other men set up their sleeping mats with the intentions of catching a few hours of sleep before they were awakened to take their turns at the night watch.

Graylin sat near the fire smoking a cigar and watching his daughter from the corner of his eyes. She had been unusually quiet since her return this afternoon and something in her manner kept his attention solely upon her. There was something in her eyes that spoke of deep and stirring feelings. Perhaps Alex Gentry had upset her, he mused as he took a deep pull upon the fragrant tobacco.

But as Alex joined him near the fire and lit up an

offered cigar Sorrel still seemed to be a million miles away. She did not even seem to notice the men around her, her father thought. She seemed to be locked in a world of her own.

Suddenly she jumped, startled by a noise from behind her, and Graylin furrowed his brow with worry. He wondered for the slightest of moments if something could have happened to her on her adventure this afternoon that she had not told him of. But no, she would have said. Unless it was something that this young man had said to scare her. For a moment his black look caressed the younger man. Had he told Sorrel of hidden dangers that could be lying in wait for her in this vast wilderness? If he were to find out that Alex had scared his daughter he would without a qualm straighten the young man out. He did not wish his daughter to be a frightened, whimpering miss. He admired her strength and courage.

It was not long after this that Sorrel rose to her feet and stepped over to her father. Kissing his forehead, she turned and made her way toward her wagon.

Again, like the night before, she felt herself stifled within the confines of the canvas, and again she took her blankets and made a pallet under the body of the large wagon. Only this time she found herself awake long into the darkness of the night. Her thoughts of the afternoon plagued her deeply.

Her meeting with the Indian seemed to Sorrel to be some kind of turning point in her life. She knew with a certainty that she would see the man again and that from their next meeting her world would be turned upside down.

Finally sleep did come, and with it dreams. Light, timeless dreams wherein Sorrel found herself slipping into an airless distance in space. She was floating as though upon a cloud, peace filling her and leaving her smiling with pleasure.

She awoke once and sighed aloud, dimly taking in the quietness of the camp and that the fire had burned down and all of the men had either taken to their pallets or were on watch. Perhaps their leaving the fireside was what had awakened her, she thought, snuggling a bit deeper into her covers, once more closing her green eyes and finding that peaceful slumber.

A black quiet enveloped the camp and once more Sorrel's dreams came to her. As she felt herself being lifted she smiled and sighed softly. She felt weightless, as though she was surrounded by water as she had been that very afternoon as she lay afloat upon her back in the chilled water of the mountain pond, and, in front of her, dark blue eyes swam in and out of her vision.

Suddenly, though, Sorrel felt herself being pulled down, held by an invisible, relentless hand. She began to push herself away from this intrusion as the lapis-blue eyes disappeared and she found herself more deeply enmeshed. It was as though a thousand hands were pulling her from every angle. She felt her breath come in quick, hurried gasps, and, with a desperation born of a frantic need and a part of her brain's warning her that something was not as it should be, her slanted green eyes slowly were pulled open, as though they too were fighting reality, and to her utter horror she found that not only was she not in water as she had been dreaming, but she was no longer under the protection of the wagon. She was far from the blue eyes of the man of her dreams, but with the dawning of reality she soon realized that she was in the arms of another man.

She came fully awake as this realization hit her brain, and panic of such a frightening magnitude came over her that she was at first powerless to respond. But within seconds she became a fighting tigress. She began to pummel her abductor with her fists, hitting out where she knew his head was, trying to scratch, kick, bite, anything to earn herself her release, but she found that all that she gained was a large hand over her mouth and her body more tightly clutched.

The night was so black that Sorrel could not make out who held her. Her first reaction was that either Alex or one of the other men working for her father had dared such an affront but now, as the man quickly trotted through the forest with her held in his arms as though she were no more than a sack of flour or sugar she reasoned with herself that no man that was in their company had this kind of strength. Her abductor seemed to be made of steel, and with each jolt given to her body from his hurried pace she became more and more aware of his powerful muscles.

As his hand slipped for a second from her lips she screamed, "Let me go! What do you think . . ." But her words were silenced once again by his hand and her abductor paid little attention to her pleas as he pushed on at a faster pace.

Sorrel lashed out again and again with all her

strength, but not a grunt or a whimper did she bring from her captor. He seemed not to notice her feeble attempts, the only acknowledgment he made was the tightening of his grip about her body.

It seemed as though hours had passed at this never-ending pace, and Sorrel felt her body's complete exhaustion. She had no more strength to try to gain her release, though her mind screamed over and over that she must not give up.

Only a short time before dawn Sorrel felt her abductor slowing his pace and with the pale lightening of the night she tried once more to see into the face of her abductor and make some sense of this whole affair.

What met her eyes brought a fear over Sorrel that she had never before felt in her life. Her captor was not one of her father's men, but instead was the Indian who had watched her from the trees as she had taken her bath at the pond.

As though sensing her realization, the Indian looked down and his black eyes probed deeply into her green depths. Then quickly he pulled his eyes from hers and once more started off, this time not going far before he stilled again and gave a shrilling whistle.

Sorrel, watching in terror for the unknown, first heard the sound of hoofbeats and then from the depths of the thick trees the same white horse that she had seen the Indian riding during the day appeared as though from out of nowhere.

Not wasting any time, the Indian threw Sorrel upon the animal's back and with an easy grace he swung himself up behind her. The only words Sorrel had thus far heard from her abductor were those he now softly crooned to his animal as he patted his long, sleek neck.

Everything seemed to be going by at an unreal pace. How could this be happening to her? Where were her father and his men? Were they not going to try to rescue her? Could this be her, Sorrel Morgan, upon this painted horse with the arms of an Indian circling her and taking her to only the Lord knew where?

The Indian pushed the horse as hard as he had pushed himself all through the night, never slackening his hurried pace.

Once Sorrel thought that she would fall as she shut her eyes and immediately fell asleep, but she was quickly jerked awake as she fell to the side and then felt her attacker's arms hold her back upright.

She had tried several times during the night to try and talk to her captor but it had all been to no avail. When she had not known who he was it had been easier to beg him to release her, but now that she knew that her abductor was a savage red man each time she tried to get the words out to beg for her release they seemed to freeze in her throat, coming out in moaning pleas.

Time passed in a blur of motion of moving trees and the never-ending thudding of the horse's hoofs upon the soft ground. Sorrel felt aching in her limbs, and with the sagging of her head she tried to find relief in shutting her eyes and trying to block out what was happening to her.

It was well into the afternoon when the Indian slowed his pace and slowly walked his horse into a large thicket, stopping altogether at the edge of a small stream. Without preamble he jumped from his mount's back and without a word spoken took hold of Sorrel and tried to pull her down.

With this contact of their hands Sorrel seemed to go wild, all of her anger and physical pain coming to the surface. Pulling back and trying to get out of this red man's reach she at the same time kicked out at the horse's side to try and make him move. But her ploy was all in vain. The horse and the master were of one mind and neither took much notice of the fighting woman. The Indian only grabbed her harder and the horse stood as though she had never kicked his side.

Sorrel cried out her frustration as her feet hit the earth. "Who do you think you are treating me in this manner?" she screamed, running toward the Indian as though she were crazed and beating upon his broad chest.

Taking both her hands within one of his own the Indian pushed her from him and toward the stream of water as though she were of no more concern than a pesty insect.

Sorrel, though, would not so easily be put off. Her hair now tangled and falling down about her waist, her green eyes glazed from fear and exhaustion, she once again attacked her abductor. "Let me go! Let me go!" she tried desperately to rake her nails across his devilishly handsome face.

Catching her hands once more the Indian brought his captive closely up against his chest and for a moment Sorrel knew true fear as she saw a deep, throbbing anger beginning to boil in the depths of those indigo eyes. Without a word, as though he knew now that she understood him, the Indian pushed her once more toward the water. He followed and went down upon his knees and began to cup the water in the palms of his hands and bring it to his lips.

Feeling herself beginning to break, for the moment Sorrel also kneeled down to the stream and began to drink. The cold, chilling water brought some sense back to her mind. "Where are you taking me?" she questioned, as her head rose and she saw again those piercing black orbs watching her deeply.

No answer was to come and bring her peace. Turning his head once again to the water the Indian drank a bit more and then rose and went to his horse.

Sorrel was confused and dazed. The Indian seemed to be leaving her to her privacy for the moment so she made good of the time allotted her. Splashing water on her face and arms she thought to try and calm herself so she could think properly. So far she had gained nothing with her panic. Could this man really not speak English? she wondered as she went over what so far had occurred since the night before. Was this the reason why he would not answer her? Perhaps she could try again, and this time she would try to use her hands as she talked.

Rising from the stream she went to where the Indian stood rubbing down and crooning unintelligible words to his animal. His back was to her and to Sorrel's tormented mind this man was the fiercest, most towering creature she had ever seen. "Sir," she ventured timidly, her words barely a whisper in the quiet wood.

Her captor's ears, though, were trained since

boyhood to hear the slightest noise, and he turned and looked directly into her frightened face. Not a sound came from him, and, as before, he stood and seemed to penetrate her mind with his sharp, ebony eyes.

Swallowing deeply and clasping her hands together in order to stay their trembling Sorrel once more began. "I think you have made some terrible mistake. You must return me to my father." She pointed to herself and then toward the direction from which they had been traveling for the past many hours. He had to understand, she thought as he only quietly stood and watched her. "You cannot keep me. You must return me to my father." Great diamondlike tears slowly appeared from her emerald eyes and silently flowed over her smooth, clear cheeks. What more could she do? she wondered. How could she make him see reason and understand that what he was doing was wrong? Her body slowly began to slip to the ground, exhaustion and a total shattering of her bravado combining to render her completely helpless and unresisting.

The Indian, sensing her feelings, reached down with tender hands and lifted her into his arms. His eyes no longer were piercing coals trying to see into her mind but now, as he held her to him, she saw mirrored in their depths something she had not seen in him until this moment, a compassion and a tenderness that she knew at once was rare for this man. It was as though she was seeing a vision, almost as though she were seeing into his very soul.

Sorrel's tears quieted as she looked up into his face. This man was an Indian, and from the stories that she had heard about the wild Indians in this area she knew that he could and would kill without showing any mercy. But now, for some unknown reason, she felt that she would not be harmed by this fierce warrior. She relaxed suddenly, letting him pick her up and place her once again upon the horse's back.

It was late in the afternoon, and the sun just was beginning to lower when Sorrel pulled herself unwillingly from sleep. At first she began to fight the arms wrapped about her that seemed to imprison her cruelly, but then her eyes opened and she slowly remembered what had happened the night before and that she was still at the mercy of this strange Indian. She stilled somewhat and tried to take in her surroundings.

The Indian sat quietly upon his horse, his back straight as his dark eyes took in the valley laid out before them. And as Sorrel strained her eyes downward she thought for a moment that she glimpsed a cabin at the floor of the valley practically hidden by the surrounding huge trees. She felt her heart flutter as she strained her eyes harder in the direction where she thought she had seen the cabin. If there were a cabin then there should be people! Her hopes soared. And as the Indian gently kicked his horse's sides and began the climb down toward the valley and in the direction of the trees that hid from view what she wished to see, she felt her excitement growing by the minute.

Holding her breath as the Indian halted his horse outside of the small wooden cabin, Sorrel looked about her for any movement that would indicate that people were about and that help would be forthcoming.

As no movement appeared and as the Indian jumped from the back of his horse Sorrel began to realize that something was wrong. Surely this was not this Indian's home, she frantically worried. Indians did not live in wooden buildings such as this, but in structures made of animal hides and lodge poles. She had learned this from the nuns at school. Never had she heard of an Indian living in a cabin, not even from any of the stories that she had heard since starting this journey with her father.

Her green, slanted eyes told all as the Indian reached up and lifted her down to his side. And deep within his chest a slight rumbling barely reached Sorrel's ears. She knew it was his laughter.

How dare he laugh at her, she thought angrily, pulling herself quickly away from his side and glaring her hatred at him.

Ignoring her outburst the Indian strode past her and opened the cabin door. He quickly entered, and after a few minutes he came through the door once more, took hold of her arm and pulled her inside.

Standing still for a moment Sorrel adjusted her eyes to the dimly lit room. And as she stood near the door the Indian went to the hearth and piled it high with logs, starting a fire that quickly sent its warming heat about the small single room.

Sorrel had never before been in such a cabin, so for a time she stood and looked about herself. There was no indication whatsoever that an Indian lived in this room. There was a small table to one side of the hearth, under which two handmade chairs were placed, and on the opposite wall from the hearth was the only other furniture, a large, soft, inviting-looking bed, piled with luxuriant, beautiful furs. The wood floor was also adorned with the furs, and Sorrel wondered for a moment at their beauty.

The Indian left the room for a moment and Sorrel imagined him to be tending his horse. So it was with some surprise that she saw him bring in a pail of water some minutes later and place this upon the table along with a small leather packet that he held in his other hand.

Her eyes widened at his actions. It seemed strange to her that this man would kidnap her and then casually set about such tasks when alone with her in his house.

"Do not try to escape here," came the first words from his mouth that Sorrel could understand. "There is no place for you to go and I shall only find you again if you try." He strode to the door and then swung about once again. "There is meat in the pack. I shall bring you more tomorrow."

As he opened the door Sorrel regained some of her senses. "Wait," she called running after him as he shut the door behind him. "If you can speak English tell me why you have taken me from my father." She ran the short distance and shouted up to him as he jumped upon his horse's back.

Her only answer though was, as in the past, black piercing eyes searing her for a short moment before he kicked his mount's sides and rode away from the cabin.

Feeling paralyzed for a moment Sorrel stood watching his broad back through the trees until finally the chilly wind drove her back into the warmth of the cabin.

Sitting in one of the chairs near the table she tried to figure out what was happening to her. Why had he left her here in this cabin? Was he coming back? But of course he was, she scolded herself. Why would he abduct her and then take her to this desolate cabin and leave her and not return? It did not make sense. She brought her hand up and pushed the sides of her temples where her head seemed to be throbbing insanely.

What was she going to do? Should she try and escape? She rose to her feet and began to pace the floor. How long would he be gone? Would she have time to get far enough away before he caught up with her? Her mind was in a frenzied rush, trying to sort out what she should do. If she left the cabin he would surely find her before she could get far. She remembered his words. And what of the cold? All that she now owned was upon her back, a shirt and pair of men's pants. There was not even a pair of shoes on her feet, only the warm socks that she had left on that night the Indian had taken her from her father's camp. She tried to remember now how long ago that had happened. Was it last night or the night before? She was so tired, she could barely think straight.

She would rest for a few minutes, she told herself, lying down on the bed, on the very edge so that she would be fully alert if he were to come back to the cabin. She shut her eyes and within seconds she was fast asleep.

Burrowing deeply beneath the furs and then stretching contentedly Sorrel awoke, at first with no remembrance of the past few days, thinking herself once more in her aunt's house in Houston. But with only one small glimpse around her she jerked up into a sitting position and was fully alert.

The sun was streaming through the windows indicating that she had slept the night through, and as she looked about she realized that the Indian had not returned.

Rising from the bed she went to the hearth and threw a few more logs upon the glowing coals. A shiver coursed over her body and quickly she went back to the bed and under the furs, waiting for the room to warm before she ventured out again.

She felt somewhat better this morning, and as she realized that more than likely the Indian would not return she sighed aloud. For some reason he had abducted her and then left her on her own. Perhaps someone would be coming by soon and she could seek help, she thought hopefully. Her father must be frantic with worry and out even now looking for her. Perhaps he would even find her this very day. She did not let enter her mind how silent and cautious the Indian had been in his abduction, carrying her for miles before getting on his horse's back. She would pray as the good nuns had taught her, she decided, her eyes falling on the packet that the Indian had left for her the day before, and with the growling of her belly she rose from the bed and quickly went to the table.

Finding a small cupboard next to the table Sorrel took out pans and a bit of meal and without a second thought she tried her hand at cooking.

And to the inexperienced girl her first lesson in the culinary arts was a huge success. She wolfed down the meal cakes and venison she had cooked with the gusto of one who is near to starving.

Smiling to herself with some small bit of satisfaction she put away the remainder of the food, knowing that she would have to ration herself on the meat the Indian had left, so as to have enough for the remainder of the day and perhaps tomorrow.

She would go and search around the cabin, she decided as she was cleaning up after her breakfast. She would wait for the sun to rise more and then venture outside. Perhaps she would be able to find something that would help her in her predicament.

The weather seemed to be growing colder with each passing hour, but by the early afternoon she could no longer stand being cooped up in the tiny cabin. Throwing a large fur about her shoulders she went out in search of some extra food or anything that would help her to protect herself from the animals that surely were about, or, with any luck, something that would protect her from any other Indians that might wander near the cabin.

The journey about the cabin was a brief one. Sorrel, in only her stocking feet, was soon racing back to the cabin's warmth. Huge, menacing gray clouds raced overhead and an icy, drizzling rain lightly pelted her during her attempts to search the area around her. As she slammed the cabin door she sighed with relief, and after taking a deep breath she went over to the blazing fire and set down a large sack that she had found hanging by a cord from the back roof, filled with potatoes and in the very bottom a few onions.

After she had found the bag of vegetables she had only lingered a short time more in the hopes of finding some kind of weapon. The only thing that she could find was a heavy stick that fit her hand nicely, in a way that would be beneficial if she were to need to try and defend herself.

Hanging the dampened fur over the back of a chair she once more threw more wood upon the fire, and deciding that now, with the finding of the extra food, she could dare to fix herself another meal, she peeled some of the potatoes and put them on to cook along with a bit more of the venison that the Indian had left.

By late afternoon Sorrel had grown accustomed to being alone. She had decided without a doubt that the Indian would not return and that her only hope was to stay in the cabin until help came to her.

So, as the room began to grow darker with the lowering of the sun and she had put away all of the supplies that she had used for her meal, she was more than surprised when the cabin door swung open and the Indian once more stood filling the doorway.

He took in Sorrel's startled appearance as she swung about in the direction of the door and the way in which her slanted green eyes enlarged with recognition. "You did not think I would come back?"

Her honey-gold hair shook slowly as she stood

staring at him as fear once again filled her every pore.

Shutting the door he walked to the table and put down another leather sack. "I brought more meat." With this he turned and left the cabin once again, but he was only gone a few minutes and returned with his strong, muscular arms laden with wood.

Sorrel sat back in the chair and as he set the wood next to the hearth she swallowed and tried to question her prisoner. "Why did you take me from my father? Please let me go."

He seemed to have reverted back to when she had thought him not able to understand her. He stacked the wood neatly but not by the slightest movement did he indicate that he had heard a word she had said.

"You must take me back to my father." She jumped to her feet, throwing caution to the wind as her anger mounted at his quietness. "What right have you to keep me here? Answer me." She was screaming now and she found herself standing directly in front of the dark-skinned warrior with her fists raised as though ready to strike out at him.

"You have much spirit for a white woman, little dove." His voice was soft but something in his eyes held Sorrel's hands in midair. "You ask for answers but a strong brave does not have to talk to a woman's wild rantings. I, Red Hawk, do as I please."

With the hardening of his voice with this last sentence Sorrel's hands fell to her sides, but her green eyes flashed with an unrelenting anger that seemed to be filling her with fire with each passing second. How dare this barbarian, this wild savage, tell her that she was only a woman and that he did not have to answer her? How dare he? She could not believe his utter conceit.

Pulling his piercing black eyes from her own he turned with a tight smile and took hold of the water buckets and started to the door.

As he left Sorrel reached out and took up a piece of the firewood and threw it out in his direction. An unreasonable fury seemed to be possessing her and she began to shout out her anger and hate, stomping about the small cabin in her fury until her green eyes fell on the large stick she had found outside that day. She had laid it against the wall near the bed in case she would be needing it during the night hours, but now her mind filled with another thought. She would stand near the door and as he entered with his hands filled with the water buckets she would bring it down upon his head, and then, her thoughts flew, she would get his horse and try to find her father or some of his men who were, she was sure, searching for her at this very minute.

Without any further delay or thought she stood behind the door and waited, her stick over her head at the ready. She could not fail, she told herself over and over as her heart raced at a maddening pace within her chest.

Her wait was short-lived as she heard the handle of the latch on the door being lifted, and then the door itself opened.

As she saw dark, bronzed skin enter through the doorway she shut her green eyes tightly and struck down with all of her might.

Deep-throated laughter filled her ears and forced her eyes wide open. The Indian stood laughing at her. He had easily side-stepped her swing and now he filled his lungs with air again and again and let it out in loud guffaws of laughter. His laughter grated on Sorrel's ears and reminded her over and over that she had tried and failed. Tears filled her eyes and rolled down her cheeks.

"How dare you!" She brought the stick up over her head once again. "You savage!" She rushed at him but he, even though he saw her raise the stick once again, did not quiet his loud gails of glee.

His laughter did quickly die though as he felt the weight of the stick hitting him across the shoulders. Within seconds after swinging her arm down at him Sorrel felt herself imprisoned in his grasp. His dark, piercing eyes glared his anger into her own, which now were very frightened. As suddenly as his laughter had come moments ago it now returned. "You have a fine spirit. I wonder how Mathew will handle the pleasure of taming you into a docile squaw?" His words were spoken softly, barely reaching Sorrel's ears, but as he had begun to smile once more she had in turn begun to find her anger returning, so, pushing at his muscular chest, she had failed to comprehend what he had said.

"Take your filthy hands off of me!" she screamed now, kicking and scratching at his face.

The Indian looked down with an ugly grimace at his hand, which was now bleeding from her teeth. He pushed her across the room. "Do not try to leave this cabin," he shouted as he started to leave through the door.

"And just how do you think I could get anywhere without my shoes?" Her anger now was beyond anything she had ever felt before as she found herself flung on the furs of the bed.

With only a grunt the Indian left once again, and with his departure Sorrel burst into tears. Great sobbing wails filled the cabin. What was going to happen to her? Was this to be her fate? The fate that she had traveled thousands of miles to find? Was this bronzed Indian to be her imprisoner and was her life now in his hands? Was she to wait until he was ready to use her at his whim?

Her sobs filled the tiny room even as the fire upon the hearth burnt down to glowing embers and echoed there long after her green eyes had shut.

Chapter Eight

Time seemed to crawl by at a snail's pace, each day slowly turning into the next, and with each sunrise more snow showered down upon the valley where Sorrel was held prisoner.

Sitting before the fire and trying to reflect back over the past days was how Sorrel spent most of her time. As far as she could calculate she must have been living here at this cabin for the past two weeks. She had all but given up any hope that she was to be rescued. Even if her father or Alex Gentry knew where to find her the snow now was so thick that she doubted they would be able to make it through the valley. The Lord above only knew how the Indian was able to make his daily visits, bringing meat and being sure that she had a vast supply of water and dry wood.

The Indian she now viewed as she would a total stranger, never saying a word to him, and he, in return, only repeated his warning before shutting the door and leaving her to herself. This warning now rang in Sorrel's ears: "Do not leave this cabin, for I shall be watching."

What kind of insane fool did he take her for? she wondered. With no shoes she was not about to venture far in this weather. She had only left the warmth of the cabin one time, that being the day following the first one, when she had tried to hit the Indian with her stick. She had left with the hopes of discovering where the Indian was finding the water that he was filling the buckets with each day. She felt the stench of her own body and wished for nothing more than to find a pond or a lake to bathe quickly in.

To her surprise she struck upon her first bit of luck since becoming the Indian's captive. A few feet from the back of the cabin and hidden somewhat by bushes she spied a large wooden tub. On her first glimpse of it she had not thought over the possibilities that this tub could offer so she had gone on further through the rough foliage, trying to find the water. But as she found a sparkling, rushing stream toward the right of the cabin her mind began to work furiously. Testing the water with her hand she discovered that it was freezing.

As she slowly and without any relish for the task at hand began to unbutton her shirt, she thought with a stroke of brilliance about the large wooden tub. Of course, the tub had been used to water animals or something, but the idea came to Sorrel that with a small bit of scrubbing she might be able to have the tub clean and be able to use it for her bathing.

She ran back to the cabin, her feet now freezing from the cold, and hurriedly began to drag the tub around to the front of the building. With any luck at all she would find the wood not too full of holes and able to hold water.

It took her several hours to get the tub sparkling and clean enough that she thought it would be able to hold her body, but that evening after the Indian had left and after she had talked him into carrying several more buckets of water from the stream and she had heated these upon the hearth, she sighed with her first true pleasure. She had found a bar of soap in the small cupboard that held the pots and food staples, along with a couple of men's shirts and a few other articles of men's clothing on the bottom shelf. Taking one of the shirts, she laid it upon the chair near the hearth to use as a towel, and another shirt she set out to wear.

After washing herself and lingering in her warm bath, Sorrel took her pants and shirt and washed them well and hung them up to dry in front of the hearth.

Now, after two weeks of living in this cabin, she found that the only bit of enjoyment that she had was her nightly ritual of bathing.

Huddling closer to the warmth of the fire, Sorrel felt her spirits sinking to their lowest depths. She was sure now that she would be held prisoner at least through the rest of the winter, and though she did not know what the Indian's intentions were toward her and she had to admit that she had not thus far been treated badly, still she was frightened of what tomorrow would bring.

She threw a few more logs on the warm fire and left the chair, going to the bed and snuggling deep down amongst the furs. Softly she said the prayers that she remembered from her childhood from the kindly nuns at the school and then, finishing, she added her own pleas to God and shut her eyes.

She had found that for some reason she was never frightened at being left alone here at the cabin and she slept through the nights without a thought for her own safety. She reasoned that the Indian was more than likely somewhere close enough to watch out for her. Why else would he tell her not to leave the cabin, and that he would be watching over her. Sleep began to cloud her mind, and slowly the hazy nonreality of peaceful dreams took the place of her tormented thoughts.

Pulling herself from the bottom of the pits of darkness that were enveloping her senses Sorrel sat up upon the furs, a loud resounding crash bringing a paralyzing fright to her mind. Even in her deepest sleep she had sensed that she was no longer alone in the cabin.

A low, trembling growl came from across the room, and through the opening of the door in the moonlight that was softly glowing across the wood floor Sorrel made out the shape of a furry animal. Her first thoughts were for her stick and that the intruder must be a hungry timber wolf.

She could see the yellow glint now of shining eyes as they went over the room and then rested upon her form upon the bed. Slowly, with barely discernible movements, she tried to find the large stick that she kept at the head of the bed. She was sure that the animal could hear the loud beating of her heart and with a will that she did not know she possessed she tried to quiet herself and her emotions. At the same moment she felt the wood beneath her fingertips and slowly brought the stick to her chest, her own green eyes never leaving those of the animal.

The fire upon the hearth had burnt down and the animal sniffed loudly, walking slowly toward the middle of the room, each step cautious and dangerous, his body at the ready to leap and attack at the slightest provocation.

Sorrel had no idea what to do as she saw the animal slowly come toward the bed. Some inbred sense born of her own wish to save herself told her not to move.

As the animal came within a few feet of the handmade structure that served as a bed it once more began to make the awful growling noise from its chest that had first alerted Sorrel that she was no longer alone in the cabin.

With the sound of the deep, low growling Sorrel knew that all hope was lost. Her stick was no defense to ward off the huge teeth of an angry and hungry wolf. She would not last long under its assault. For a fleeting second the Indian came to her mind, and she wondered if he would feel any regret tomorrow at having taken her from her father only to be the meal for a depraved animal. She shut her eyes, no longer wishing to see those yellow glowing ones coming ever nearer. She would take what was to be, but she could no longer be tormented by those eyes.

From outside of the cabin something brought Sorrel's eyes flying open. A noise, she thought. Like a loud whistle. The animal had heard it also and was now looking toward the door. The Indian, Sorrel's mind worked furiously. It was the Indian come to save her.

Again she heard the loud, piercing sound coming closer now, and with one last glance at the form upon the bed the animal turned and ran to the door and as quietly slipped through it.

Quickly jumping from the safety of the bed Sorrel hurried to the door, pushing it shut and throwing the small weight of her body against its bulk to insure that the animal would not once again be able to push it aside and enter the room.

She stood thus, her heart beating at a tremendous rate as she waited for the Indian or the wolf to make a sound on the other side of the protection of the door.

There was no lock on the door so after a few minutes of standing in the same position Sorrel looked about and her eyes fell on the chair. She would prop it against the latch—this should afford some protection from an intruder while she put more wood upon the hearth and brought some light to the room. She felt her body quivering as she stood there in only a shirt and barefoot.

Sorrel was squatting down and building up the fire when she swung about, the chair flying across the room as the door flew open. Her green eyes registered her fright as she viewed the man and animal standing in the doorway. Her hand froze as she held a piece of wood, her whole body trembling from this new terror.

The man looked to be a giant standing there, his head reaching almost to the top of the door and his girth covering almost completely the view of the moonlight outside.

Sorrel quickly noticed that the dog was the same

animal that had earlier been in the cabin, but now with the light from the fire she could see that he was not a wolf but some other kind of fierce, furry dog, and reason told her that this animal was even more dangerous than she had at first thought.

Slowly looking around, the man entered the cabin and shut the door. He ordered the dog to silence, and its low growls quietly settled deep in its chest.

With some caution but also with some small hope rising in her, Sorrel got up from her position near the fire and stood before the large man's forceful gaze. As her green eyes looked into his bearded face trying to discover what manner of man he was, a small spark of recognition ignited within her chest. With pumping heart she focused all of her attention upon the dark blue eyes.

"Who are you and what the blazes are you doing here in my cabin?" The voice seemed to echo across the room in an angry, forceful timbre, almost as frightening as the sounds his animal had made. Sorrel thought back to the day at the Langston's emporium and then to the night at the inn. The voice of the stranger had in no way been like the one that came to her ears now. There had been a tender warmth that had settled about her heart with the merest remembrance of that day and night in Richmond. Always in her thoughts the man's voice had sounded gently and softly.

The man took a step closer toward her, his visage dark with anger, making Sorrel cringe with fear.

"I—I am Sorrel Morgan," was all she could get out. Her whole body was atremble, even her lips could not stop their trembling. She was not so sure now that this was the same man. It had been so long ago now, she realized, and all that she had to remind her of that day and night were her dreams and they were always as she wished them to be. This man before her was a stranger—a fierce, dominating figure standing threateningly before her.

"Speak up. What are you doing here, Sorrel Morgan?" The man's own composure had been quite shattered when he had opened the door to his cabin. It was not often that he came home after a few weeks of hunting and trapping and found a beautiful woman in his home with nothing on. Then as he looked at her closely he noticed that one of his white shirts adorned her small, well-formed figure. Why would this girl be all the way here in his valley and staying in his cabin? He needed answers, and he was going to get them, and now.

His angry glare set Sorrel's trembling even more visibly, and seeing her state he pointed toward the remaining chair near the hearth. "Sit down while I build up the fire and you can try to explain what in tarnation you are doing here miles away from anything and all alone." Without answer he went to the fire and started to stoke up the wood already burning and then added more fuel to the ignited greedy sparks.

Sorrel sat upon the chair and clasped her hands tightly in her lap, trying to quiet their shaking. Her eyes watched every movement the large man made, her mind telling her that she had been wrong, that this was not the man of her dreams. The only resemblance had been in his eyes, and there was no telling how many other men had the same dark blue eyes.

Looking up from the fire the man scowled darkly as he viewed Sorrel's naked, long golden legs, and rising back to his full height he went to the bed and brought her back a fur, which he draped across her lap. "Perhaps this will help to warm you, madam."

"Thank you," Sorrel said softly, the fur and the fire now indeed bringing some warmth to her body and leaving her cheeks a rosy flushed color that softened her features.

Without saying another word the man pulled off his fur jacket. Picking up the chair that had earlier sailed across the room he brought it to the hearth and now sat his huge bulk upon it and watched the woman across from him. "Are you warm enough now, madam?" He knew that he had frightened her, and her sorrowful, frightened look caused his insides to begin to melt toward her somewhat and he wished to put her more at ease.

"This is your cabin, then?" Sorrel asked, looking up from her hands and gazing into the bearded face before her. This man's size and apparent strength truly frightened her. She had never in her life met a man who had sent this chilling fright through her body. Even the Indian did not stoke this fear within her. It was as though this man held unleashed powers within his body that were being held in check by a will much stronger than she would ever know.

"Aye, 'tis my home." His dark blue eyes now studied her as she had earlier studied him. He took in her honey-gold curls that were flowing loose and free down to her waist, tangled from her sleep and also from not having had a comb put through them for the past two weeks, only her fingers running through the mass to keep it in order. His eyes went lower, to her face, and as she sat looking up at him with a defiant tilt to her chin and her emerald eyes held up to his own with a most captivating slant to them, he was rendered all but speechless. She was indeed a beauty, he thought. Even her lips, petal shaped and pink, seemed to beckon to him. He shook himself and waited for her to speak once again.

"Sir, I must beg you to take me to my father." Her fright seemed to leave her as the thought finally entered her head that here at last was her freedom. This man was a white man and would not let an Indian take her from him; he would return her to her own people. She smiled at her discovery, wondering now why she had been so frightened earlier. She was finally saved.

The man watched her face change from solemn to almost ecstatic, and his own features seemed to soften somewhat with her calmness. "Let us start at the beginning. How did you find your way to my cabin and where is this father of yours? How could any man with a daughter such as yourself let her loose from his protection?" For some unreasonable moments his mind clouded with anger. Why was this young woman's father not here at this moment looking after her and making sure that she did not come to harm?

"I was abducted, sir." She paused here for a slight moment and let the full meaning of her statement fill the man's mind, and as she saw that it had from the set look upon his face she continued. "An Indian came to my father's camp one evening and took me by force and brought me here to your cabin."

"An Indian brought you here?" The man's face became red and he rose to his feet. "What did this Indian look like? Or by some chance did he tell you his name?" The man prowled about the cabin as though it were too small to contain him. Even the dog in the corner looked toward his master and a soft growl came from his throat. "Settle, Lancer," he rebuked the animal and once again the dog laid his head upon his front paws and shut his eyes.

Sorrel did not know what could have caused the man's irritation but she began to answer his questions. "He was a large, fierce-looking bronzed Indian and he did indeed tell me his name one day. I believe he called himself something like Red Hawk."

At the man's stony look in her direction she continued, "Do you know of this Indian?"

As he nodded his head a small shiver of fear started up her back and silently made its way about her heart. "You would not let that Indian take me again?" Tears started to squeeze from her eyes and silently flow down her cheeks. She could not bear this, she had thought that she would be safe and now she was finding that this man knew the Indian who had abducted her and perhaps he would even turn her over to him. "Oh, please, help me to get back to my father. He will pay you any amount of money that you ask, only return me to him." She fell completely to pieces saying this and seemed visibly to shrink in her chair.

Another woman from a long ago dead past sprang up in the man's mind but quickly he shunned the vision. "Here, here," he gently tried to console the girl. "Of course I will not let Red Hawk take you again." He patted her softly on the shoulder, not truly knowing how to handle a woman's tears.

At his words Sorrel's crying seemed to quieten.

But as her face rose to his he once again began to speak. "I am afraid, though, that it will be impossible to return you to your father at this time. You see the passes are all snowed in."

"There has to be some way." Sorrel was swiftly realizing that she would not be gaining the freedom that she had wished for, at least not right away.

His shoulder-length dark hair shook slowly. "I am afraid the answer is no, Miss Morgan. There is no way out but through the pass, and as I said it is snowed in, and even if your father had been in the area I am sure that by now he has left and sought the safety of the other side of the pass."

"Then I am snowed in in this valley? But this is impossible. There has to be some way out." From the shaking of his head she knew that it was futile, but she kept on anyway. "I cannot stay here in this cabin. You must help me," she cried softly. Once more tears came to her, tears that were brought on because this was the only recourse now open to her. She was helpless and though her tears did no good they were all she had left.

Bending down to her chair the man took her up in his arms and sat back down in the chair with her in his lap. She was like a small lost child and he only wished to comfort her. He softly whispered words of comfort to her and tenderly his hand traced the form of her curls. "Do not weep so, little one," he said softly over and over again, and then finally as he looked down into her face as her sobbing ceased he saw that she was sleeping. He realized that this small slip of a girl had stirred something deep within him. He also felt pity in his heart for the girl's father, the man must be frantic with worry over her. His large, sun-browned hand softly traced the softness of her cheek. He felt within him what her father must feel, a wish to protect her and not let harm befall her in any form.

After holding this woman in his arms for a short time longer he rose to his feet and went to the bed and placed her down upon the furs. She was even more lovely in her sleep, he thought, as he tenderly brought a fur up beneath her chin.

With a sigh he turned about and after letting his dog outside for a quick run about the cabin he made himself up a pallet near the hearth and tried to sleep.

But sleep was the farthest thing from his mind as he lay there and tried to get comfortable on the hard wood floor. Why would Red Hawk bring this girl here to his cabin? What could have been going through the Indian's mind when he had taken this girl from her father? And the girl herself, what was he to do with her? Of course he would not let Red Hawk have her, if that was the Indian's plan, but to him this seemed almost impossible. What would Red Hawk want of the girl when he already had himself a wife? Tossing over and over on his makeshift bed he told himself that his answers would just have to wait until morning when he could talk to Red Hawk for himself.

* * *

Before her eyes opened the next morning the delicious smells of coffee perking and bacon frying hit Sorrel's nostrils and for a moment she stretched and softly smiled, thinking herself once again in her father's camp and that at any moment Graylin himself would put his head in the back of the wagon and tell her it was time for her to rise. But these thoughts only lasted a short time, for as a strange whistling tune came to her ears she remembered where she was and what had strangely occurred the night before. Rising on her elbows she looked about the cabin, finding nothing changed except for the man bent down at the hearth with his back facing her, and the large, dark-furred dog who, looking up from where he lay, noticed that she was awake and slowly made his way to her side of the bed.

The man turned, greeting Sorrel and calling for his dog not to bother her. "Breakfast will be ready in a moment," he said and then turned his back to tend to his cooking and also to give her some privacy, which she took advantage of to hurriedly pull on her breeches and socks.

The dog sat down next to the bed and this morning instead of his fierce growling his lips seemed to be pulled back in some form of lopsided smile. Sorrel was not one easily to be misled, so even though he seemed willing enough this morning to be on friendly terms she still stayed her distance, his long, sharp teeth of the night before coming quickly to her mind.

"I think Lancer wishes to apologize for his rudeness of last night," the man said as he placed food upon the table. As he looked in her direction, though, surprise was written on his features and his hands stopped in midair as he turned about. Never before had he seen a woman in men's breeches, let alone one so lovely. She stood with her hair in disarray, his shirt tucked into her breeches, making the whole outfit mold tightly against her body.

Sorrel felt his eyes going over her and lowered her head, for the first time feeling some embarrassment over her clothing.

Clearing his throat he called her to the table. "If you are ready, madam." He pulled out a chair for her and waited for her to place herself upon the seat.

Quiet filled the cabin as the pair ate the food in front of them. Sorrel was the first to speak. "Thank you, sir. The meal is delicious." After the days of her own cooking anything cooked by someone else would have tasted delicious to her.

"My name is Mathew, Sorrel." He sipped at his cup of coffee and sat back and watched her as he finished with the last of the food on his plate.

Sorrel's face reddened somewhat from his close perusal of her.

"I must admit, Miss Morgan, that I spent a very restless night last evening trying to best think of a way out of your predicament."

Sorrel looked at him as though he had the answers to all of her problems. With the light of the morning he did not look as large and angry as he had the night before. His features seemed softened, his blue eyes filled with a kindness that she had not noticed before.

Sensing her thoughts, Mathew went on, "I still do not know how to get you out of this situation. The only option that I can come up with is that you will have to stay here until the snows thaw."

Sorrel's green eyes opened with shock. "I cannot stay here in this cabin with only you." She had not meant to sound ungrateful or harsh but her words came out sounding rather hard.

Mathew rose from his seat. "The only other side to the coin would be for you to go to Red Hawk's village and stay there throughout the rest of the winter."

Not only Sorrel's eyes but also her mouth opened wide at his words. For her to stay in the Indian village for the next coming months was impossible for her to envision. She could not imagine what it would be like to live like an Indian, but from what she had heard she knew that she had no desire to do so. "That is impossible. I would rather be dead!"

Mathew looked sharply toward her as he began to clear the table. "You have your choice." He picked up the water bucket and started to the door. "I am afraid though the choices are not to your liking they are all that are at hand." He shut the door behind him, leaving Sorrel to the quiet of the room.

As Mathew started through the thick snow toward the stream he felt his body shivering from the cold and hurried his pace. He had forgotten his jacket and the icy fingers of the bitter weather were trying his body to its limits.

Pulling up the bucket from the stream he spun around as he heard a movement behind him. There standing directly in his path stood Red Hawk.

The Indian was dressed now in warm, fur-lined clothing, and he stood at his ease and faced this man that he had befriended with a huge grin upon his bronzed face. "It is good to see you once more,

Mathew Danner." He held out his hand and waited for Mathew to take it in his grasp.

Mathew's own face broke out into a large smile for this man whom he had grown to love as though he were his own brother. Setting the bucket on the ground he extended his own hand, and the two walked up to each other and threw their arms about each other's shoulders.

"I hope your hunting was worthy of your trip, Mathew Danner. Did you bring home plenty of meat and furs on this long trip that you have been on?"

Mathew sensed some amusement in his friend's voice as he said this and he drew away from him and with a solemn face watched the Indian. "Aye, Red Hawk, the hunting was good, but I can see that you yourself were also busy hunting."

Mathew's words were not lost on Red Hawk and loud guffaws of laughter came from him. "As you say, Mathew, the hunting was good." His laughter rippled from his mouth.

"What were you thinking, Red Hawk, when you took the girl from her father? You know that you cannot keep her?" For a fleeting minute Mathew was not sure if his friend knew what the situation truly was.

"I do not wish to keep the girl, Mathew."

"Then why? Why would you kidnap her and bring her here to my cabin?" Even as he said the words he knew the answer but he dared not voice it until the Indian did; it was too insane.

"She is my gift to you, Mathew." The words came with warmth, from a friend giving another a gift of great value, but to Mathew they hit against his chest as though they were mighty rocks.

"You cannot think that I could keep her?" Mathew's voice was incredulous at the Indian's confession.

"She does not please you, Mathew Danner?" Red Hawk's expression was serious now. He had not thought that his friend would not wish this woman.

"Of course she pleases me, Red Hawk. She would please any man, but one does not take a woman and keep her against her will."

"My people do. Many women in our village are taken from different tribes, and even from old Fleeing Buck from the time that I was a boy I heard the stories of the white woman that he had captured and brought back as his wife from a raid against the white man. She had sired him five strong young bucks before the fever took her life one winter."

"But my people do not do this, nor would they tolerate my keeping her against her will," Mathew tried to reason with Red Hawk, knowing that it would do no good. The Indian had grown with such customs, and he saw no wrong in taking Sorrel from her people and bringing her here.

"If she does not please you, Mathew Danner, I shall take her for myself. She is quite pleasant to look upon and she will give me many strong sons. Perhaps even more than Fleeing Buck's white woman gave him before dying. She also has a fiery temper when tried, Mathew. I find this most pleasing to my nature, to have a woman who will not bend easily."

Mathew looked doubtfully at his friend. "What about your own wife, Tame Elk, would she not have something to say about your bringing home another wife?"

Red Hawk smiled again. "She would be pleased to make me happy, Mathew. She would welcome the woman as a sister. She would not go without, if that is what worries you. I am a fine hunter and can care for many women, not only one."

Mathew now laughed at his friend's seriousness. "Nay Red Hawk, I cannot let you take her from my cabin. I have already promised her that I would take care of her and not let you take her."

Red Hawk seemed well pleased with the answer, and taking the bucket from the ground he stated, "You will freeze if you do not get near a fire soon. Your lips are already turning blue in color."

Mathew had forgotten that he was standing in only his shirt sleeves but now with the reminder he felt the full extent of the cold. "Come in and have a cup of coffee to warm yourself old friend, and I shall tell you of my trip."

Sorrel swung about in the direction of the door as she heard it open and heard the loud laughter of male voices. She was taken aback when she saw Mathew enter followed by the Indian. She saw immediately that they were more than just mere acquaintants. They seemed to be on the best of terms.

The Indian smiled his appreciation of her as he entered the room and glanced in her direction. She was indeed quite beautiful, he thought, and for a moment he felt some resentment toward this friend of his. He secretly wished that Mathew had told him to take the woman. He was sure that she would have filled his pallet with a warmth that he had never known before.

The two men warmed themselves as the coffee heated over on the hearth, sitting companionably together as they talked about the trip that Mathew had just taken. The conversation excluded Sorrel, so with nothing else to do she sat upon the bed and tried to occupy her mind with the happenings of the past day and night.

As she sat there the large dog that Mathew had called Lancer came to her feet and sat down and with a mournful face placed his huge head in her lap.

At first she was afraid but as he looked up to her, his yellow eyes soft and trusting, she slowly brought her hand down and lightly ventured to smooth back the fur on his forehead.

Lancer showed his appreciation by licking her hand and wagging his long tail.

Mathew watched his dog and the girl from the corner of his eye. This was the first time that he had ever seen Lancer take to another person besides himself. Even Red Hawk still did not trust the large animal and Mathew knew that the dog had no trust of the Indian either, nor had he in the past favored any other person with a licking by his tongue. A small smile filled Mathew's face as he pulled his gaze from the scene across the room and answered the question that his friend had put to him.

Red Hawk himself saw the smile and knew that it was directed toward the woman and for a moment he felt a twinge of jealousy, but then he harshly told himself as he listened to Mathew talk about his journey that this woman now belonged to his friend. He could not go back on a gift given in friendship.

Shortly the Indian rose and Mathew walked him to the door, asking him to hurry his journey and to return before dark. Sorrel watched the two men at the door. She had thought that the Indian was a large man, but Mathew Danner stood at least a half a head taller than the dark man and probably outweighed him by some small amount. For a moment longer her green eyes lingered on the expanse of his back, marveling at the muscles that strained with his every movement through the fabric of his shirt.

As Mathew turned in her direction she felt her face color at being caught in her perusal of him. The man, who Sorrel now thought of in her mind as a mountain man, scowled darkly as he viewed her on the bed with his dog's head in her lap.

"Lancer, come boy," he called, opening the door to let the animal out to roam.

Sorrel wondered as she had while the two men were near the hearth talking in low tones what was going to be the decision that they would make about her fate. Surely they must have decided that it was impossible to keep her here. They would have to return her to civilization. She only wondered who would be the one to take her back to her father, the Indian or this mountain man. She secretly hoped that this tall, rugged man would be the one to ride behind her on the back of a horse and take her out of this valley.

Mathew still did not speak but instead went to the hearth and resumed the seat that he had been sitting on earlier.

Not being able to stand the suspense of not knowing what was to happen any longer, Sorrel jumped to the wood floor and started toward the man. "Did your friend tell you the reason that he brought me here?"

"Aye, Red Hawk spoke freely of his actions," Mathew mumbled, seeming not to wish to talk to the girl.

"Well?" Sorrel pushed, not able to leave this man to his thoughts when her own mind was in such a frantic state. "What on earth did he say?"

Mathew looked up with some irritation. He did not know what to tell this woman who was looking at him as though he could settle all of her troubles with one simple word. "He brought you here as a gift for me." With her look of incredulity he continued, "He did add that if I was not pleased with you he would be more than willing to take you himself to wife."

His words were like doom to Sorrel and she sank into the opposite chair. "To wife?" She could not believe that she had heard right.

"Aye. It seems that my friend Red Hawk is quite taken with you, Miss Morgan."

"But surely you could talk some reason to him? You did explain that this situation was impossible and that I must be returned to my father at once?"

"An Indian is not brought up in the same way as whites. He does not feel that it was wrong to kidnap you. I did tell him, though, that I was well pleased with you and that he could not take you, and for the last time, Miss Morgan, I shall explain that it is quite impossible for myself or for Red Hawk or for anyone to take you through the pass while it has snow up to one's neck on its trails." Mathew rose and began to pace angrily about the small cabin.

"Then what do you suppose that I should do?" Her own anger was now equaling his own.

"Why, I would suppose that you should spend the winter here in my cabin, Miss Morgan, unless I told Red Hawk too hastily that you would not be going with him?" Mathew glared at her, helpless in this situation that he could see no way out of.

"How dare you!" Sorrel rose to her feet, her face bright red as she stood and glared right back at this angry, large man.

"I dare what I please, miss. And the sooner that you realize that you have few options the better off you and I shall both be. As soon as the weather permits I shall be more than glad to see you to the nearest town, but until that time I suggest that you try and make the best of it here in my cabin."

Sorrel slipped back to the chair as though stunned. For the first time she was beginning to realize that she really did not have any other recourse except that of spending the winter here in this valley far from her father and all that she loved.

Each time she thought of her father she could envision his face stretched in pain at the loss of his daughter. And by now had he sent word to her Aunt Corry? Was she too frantic with grief? Tears began to make a slow path down Sorrel's face. Would she ever again know the love and security that she had known in the past?

Mathew looked down at her as he slowed his pacing and a helpless fury overtook him. How could Red Hawk have done this to this girl and also put him in such a predicament? Without another word he turned on his heels and stomped from the room, slamming the door in his wake.

Sorrel took Mathew's departure as a sign of his not caring about her plight. Jumping up from the chair and knocking it down she flounced about the room, her tears still flowing from her green eyes. She felt like screaming out her anger, raving at the walls and shouting her rage. How could this be happening to her, Sorrel Morgan? She had known nothing but love and protection all of her life, and now here she was thrown on her own and this man, this Mathew Danner, was to be her jailer instead of the Indian. What was to become of her, she wept aloud, was she to survive or to perish?

Mathew left the girl to herself. Hearing her stomp about the cabin and shouting out her fury, he decided to give her time to vent all her frustration. For a second again his own anger seemed to possess him. Why had Red Hawk started this whole business to begin with? He had fled his home and everything he had ever wanted in the hopes that he could purge from his mind the memory of another woman, and now here he was in this vast wilderness and again his thoughts were being tormented by a female.

He began to chop wood, his axe coming down in a tremendous attack upon the pile of fire logs. Long into the afternoon and with the sinking of the sun the dull, heavy thud of steal hitting wood could be heard resounding throughout the valley and the encircling forest.

Before the last of the light disappeared completely from the sky Red Hawk once again appeared at the small cabin. This time as he jumped from the back of his horse his arms were laden with a large packet.

His black eyes took in the pile of wood that Mathew had chopped all of that day and his face broke out in a small, tight smile. "Does my brother wish to harm his body with so much work?" Never had he seen so much wood being split in half in one day. Perhaps he and the woman were not getting along. Red Hawk's lips formed a larger smile at this thought. Mathew always seemed lost to some inner hurt that kept him solemn and hard. That was the real reason why the Indian had brought the girl here for his friend, in the hopes that she could bring him out of his glumness and bring him some happiness. He himself had known no greater happiness in all of his years than the hours that he had spent alone in his lodge with his woman. And even if Mathew and the girl were at odds, he reasoned, they had all of the winter to come to know each other.

Mathew slammed the axe into a large log and glared for a small second at his friend, then turned his back and started off to the stream. Even though the temperature was below freezing Mathew felt his body sweating profusely. Pulling off his clothes quickly he dove into the icy depths of the stream, coming up quickly with teeth chattering and his skin within moments turning a light blue.

Red Hawk stood at the bank and watched the white man, who seemed to have completely taken leave of his senses. Finally though, as Mathew scrambled back into his breeches and shirt, he burst out laughing. "I have brought the clothes for your woman as you have asked, Mathew Danner." He had never known a man like this one who he now claimed as brother, but he had always thought the white men to be strange and the more that he was around this one the more he was sure of being right in his estimation.

"She is not my woman, Red Hawk." Mathew threw his dark head back, showering droplets of water in all directions. "But I thank you for the clothes, anyway."

"Why do you say that the white woman is not yours? I give her to you, for you are like a brother to me." Red Hawk was confused by Mathew's words and looked at his friend for his meaning.

"I simply mean," Mathew took the package from Red Hawk's hands and started to the cabin, feeling chilled after his swim, "that as soon as the snows clear I shall be taking Miss Morgan back to her father. You cannot take someone by force and expect them to be happy."

"But I brought her for you as your woman."

Mathew turned and looked at his friend. "I know you meant well, but she is not my woman. The white men first court and woo their women before they marry. You cannot expect Miss Morgan to stay here any longer than she must, Red Hawk."

Some of what Mathew was saying must have made sense to Red Hawk for his face seemed to clear of his confusion as he regarded the other man. "Then you shall do this thing, what do you call it? This thing that you call court and woo?"

They had just arrived outside of the cabin door and Mathew, his face reddening from Red Hawk's question, seemed to explode with his anger. He did not wish any woman, the only woman he could ever have loved had been taken from him, and his irritation mounted by the moment at the red man's stupidity. "I don't want the woman. She will return to her own as soon as the snow thaws." With this he opened the door and stomped into the cabin.

Red Hawk followed quietly, not really knowing what he had said to cause his friend's anger but knowing for sure that he had more of a devil in him than anyone could see from the outside. He would need time to settle his wounds and hurts, the Indian decided. "I shall leave these here for the woman, Mathew." He started to the door, his ebony eyes going to where Sorrel was starting to prepare supper. He smiled softly as he watched her before turning the latch to the door. A woman was the finest comforter that he could think of and with the passage of time he was sure that Mathew Danner would come to grips with whatever had happened in his past. If this woman could not help him to find himself then perhaps the man was truly lost. She seemed to be as bright as the morning sun, her hair a golden array about her body and her features as soft as the morning dew to look upon. He silently left the cabin and mounted his horse.

Sorrel glanced at the packet that Red Hawk had thrown carelessly upon the table for the briefest of moments before going back to her cooking. She had heard Mathew's angry shouts outside of the door, and though she had not been able to make out his words she had known without being told that they were in some way connected with her.

She stirred the potatoes gently in the pan with a spoon and dared a glance in Mathew's direction. He seemed in a black, noncommunicative mood, and Sorrel, like the night before, felt a quiver of fear run up her back. He seemed well able to shatter anyone who got in his way, and his penetrating glaring into the fire only lent him the look of a man who would easily and without second thoughts put down anyone who stood before him and tried to challenge him. She felt her hands begin to shake and quickly clasped them together. How was she to share this small cabin with this man who sent such fright over her? She felt that with the slightest provocation he would turn on her, and then what? He had so far acted the gentleman, but there seemed to be a thin veneer covering his black anger. What would happen if he let slip his mood of concern and stopped playing the gentleman?

She was not to think her problem through, for Mathew disturbed her thoughts by opening the package that Red Hawk had brought and holding up a pair of leather moccasins. He tossed them toward Sorrel's feet. "I think these will provide more warmth than your thin stockings, madam."

Some of Sorrel's worry left her face as she held up the treasure that had been thrown her way. The moccasins were of a dark hide and trying them on she found them to fit snugly, reaching up to above the calves of her legs. "Thank you. They are fine, indeed," she replied, admiring the fine stitching that had sewed the skins together.

"Red Hawk also brought you this," Mathew smiled as he held up a dress sewn in the same Indian fashion as the footwear. "I did not tell him to bring this but you may find it more comfortable than men's breeches."

Sorrel's face reddened at his remark but she quickly took the dress and held it up to her. She was tired of wearing the same shirt and pants and the dress, like the moccasins, was beautifully made. "I shall have to thank Red Hawk for his kind thoughts," she smiled, and she saw Mathew's face glower once again, but this time it was from her words, and she smiled even more.

He had tried to taunt her about her clothing, but somehow she had turned the tables on him. An unreasonable anger filled him at her words, but for the life of him he had no idea why.

Sorrel placed the dress upon the bed and quickly finished her cooking. They ate the meal in silence, the only noise in the small room being that of Lancer's tail beating a rapid tattoo against the wood floor as he happily anticipated the meal he would have after the table was cleared.

It was a house in which two people sat, ate, and slept in constant sight of one another, but no sounds were heard. The only communication was in the daring glances they each threw at the other in unexpected moments. The atmosphere in the cabin seemed more ice-chilled than outside of it, where tiny white flakes fell without let-up from the gray sky and covered the outer world in a downy blanket of white. The tension that filled the small cabin and circled about the hidden valley was thick enough to cut into slices.

Sorrel had awakened that morning after receiving

the presents from Red Hawk to a cold room. The fire had died down in the hearth and the room itself was empty. The pallet in front of the hearth was unoccupied and Lancer was not in sight.

Rising from the soft comfort of the bed of furs Sorrel donned the dress and moccasins before stoking the fire to a blazing warmth. For a moment she lingered before the heat, rubbing her hands together and idly wondering where the man called Mathew could have gone to so early in the morning.

Shaking her head and trying to push this strange, giantlike man to the back of her mind she slowly roused herself and began to prepare breakfast.

She had no recourse except to stay within these walls and she told herself sternly that she was not going to starve while she did so. She was built of strong stuff that allowed of no self-destruction. She would wait out her term of imprisonment and seek her release when the first chance appeared, and with any luck she would also win a small victory for herself. Perhaps the Indian would also be punished for her abduction, and with the wrath that had built up in her for the past few days she hoped that the mountain man with his angry face would also be punished. Though right now she could think of no reason for his punishment, she was sure that by the time she obtained her freedom she would have some complaints against him.

It was late in the afternoon when Mathew returned to his cabin. He had left early with only his gun and Lancer and had roamed the forest close about the cabin. His intentions had been to try and shake from his mind the woman who had been thrust upon him.

But with every turn his thoughts were brought back to his cabin. Sorrel Morgan was beginning to plauge him night and day. He reasoned with himself that the only reason he saw her beautiful face so clearly in his thoughts no matter what he was doing was because he so desperately wished to be alone. And all this day, as he trudged through the thick snow and watched for any sign of a deer, he would push those emerald eyes from his mind and force himself to concentrate only on the vision of the woman he had loved.

By the time he arrived back at the cabin his mind was pulsating in an unbearable turmoil. He was not the type of man to love easily, and he thought that Elizabeth would always, even after her death, be the only woman to hold his heart. But something of his baser nature was beginning to take control of him, and this woman who was under his roof and completely in his power was becoming an obsession with him, ever tantalizing his mind and thoughts.

Throwing the cabin door open he scowled darkly as Sorrel jumped from the chair she had been sitting on and stood to her feet.

She had not thought that he would come back to the cabin so silently, and this afternoon with nothing to do she had daringly glanced into his leather saddle bags that he had thrown into the cupboard that first night of his arrival. To her surprise she had glimpsed a leather-bound book of poetry, and besides some other articles she had found a comb.

The comb being more temptation than she could bear, she took it up almost with loving fingers. One did not truly appreciate the value of an item until one was forced to do without it. She quickly combed out her long, honey-gold tresses and then plaited the shining mass into one long braid down her back.

She had put the comb back, silently hoping that the mountain man, who seemed able with the slightest look to fill her with an unreasoning fear, would not suspect that she had so boldly trespassed on his property.

But as the moments ticked by she was constantly plagued by thoughts of the book that was so close at hand. She had loved reading and when she had lived with her Aunt Corry she had read as much as possible. Early during her schooling she had learned that if she could read well she could lose herself in the realm of fantasy. So the fact that there was a book so close at hand and yet was forbidden to her was more of a torment than any that Sorrel could at the moment imagine.

Pulling herself up quickly she went to the cupboard and before she could change her mind or the fear of getting caught could overpower her once again, she pulled the book from the bag and went back to her seat.

And this is how Mathew found Sorrel as he opened the door, standing red-faced and clutching the book close to her chest.

Lancer ran with tongue lolling and tail wagging toward the woman he was fast coming to trust. But he found neither a pat upon the head nor a soft word in this quarter as Sorrel barely noticed him near her side, her full attention was directed to the man coming through the open door.

Mathew did not at first notice the book clutched

tightly in Sorrel's hand nor did he at first see the flaming guilt written over her features. His mood was rather stormy from his day of black thoughts so as he stamped the snow from his boots and began to pull his buckskin jacket from his back he only afforded the woman standing next to the hearth a fleeting glare before tending to his own needs.

Sorrel's guilt at having been caught redhanded with another's property was monumental. With shaking lips she tried to explain her actions. "I—I did not mean to pry into your things."

Mathew now looked more closely at the woman standing across the room, noticing as he did so the gleaming soft tresses pulled back neatly into a braid lying down her back. For a second his blue eyes softened as they lingered on her delicate face where tiny curls had escaped her braid and gently hugged her temples and forehead. As his eyes lowered he noticed the book clutched to her breast and he began to realize what her words of apology were for. He felt his lips begin to quiver with mirth for a moment at her thinking that he would become angry over a simple thing like her reading his book, but then as quickly and for a reason he could barely fathom the dark scowl returned over his bearded features. Deep within himself he was cautioning himself to keep a cold distance between himself and this beauty.

"Well, madam, since you have taken it upon yourself to pry into my personal belongings, I guess it is only fair that you should be able to enjoy the spoils of your venture."

His stilted words left no doubt in Sorrel's mind that he was indeed angry with her intrusion, and though for a fleeting second she felt an anger building swiftly within her, she squelched it quickly as the words came to her mouth to rebuke him. This man more than frightened her, she was left quivering at his merest look. For a second a thought of the past came to her mind, a past where she boldly put down a suitor, not caring about the outcome of her words or actions. But something told her that this man who lived alone here in the mountains was not of the same ilk as the men in her past. He would not take kindly to any verbal abuse, so she held her tongue and rushed quickly to the cupboard and put the book back where it had come from.

Mathew walked to the hearth and warmed his hands, his blue eyes following the slim back and the swish of her trim hips as she walked away from him. Aye, he cautioned himself, he would be in need of keeping an overtight rein upon himself around this woman. She was beginning to wreak havoc upon his senses with her smallest movement.

Sorrel did not venture another word or look in the mountain man's direction. She prepared dinner, and after eating with her head bowed over her plate she swiftly cleaned up. Then as the dark descended and Mathew went outside with Lancer at his side, she hurriedly pulled her dress from her body and donned her shirt and then snuggled deeply into the furs of the bed, her body turned against the wall in a stiffened manner. It was better to find sleep than to see again the man's furious glare.

Mathew returned after a short time and as he entered the room his eyes went about the small cabin until they fell upon the form on the bed. Her unyielding back was stiff to his gaze and for a moment longer he stood, a fleeting regret filling him as he viewed the softness of his bed yielding to her small frame. The pallet on the wood floor had little to like about it, its hardness making itself felt with each turn of his body.

And so for the next few days the small cabin followed the same routine. Mathew would leave early each morning, before Sorrel woke, and on his return no words were spoken between the two. They each went about their business with only stolen glances at the other.

Then one evening after finishing dinner Mathew announced to the quiet room that he would be leaving to check on his traps upstream the following day.

Sorrel did not answer, but her eyes could not hide her trepidation at the thought of once again being left alone here at this isolated cabin.

Mathew sensed her worry, and quelling the wish to be cold and hurting, he spoke in a voice that was not unkind and even expressed a bit of tenderness. "There is nothing to fear, Sorrel. I would not leave you completely to yourself. Lancer will stay and watch over you."

Sorrel felt some of her worry leave her, for though she had never seen the huge dog angry except for that first night, she could well imagine his brutal fury if provoked. "Thank you, sir," she murmured softly, as she finished drying and putting away the last of the supper dishes.

"My name is Mathew. I see no reason why you should not use it." Mathew's words were still spoken softly, surprising Sorrel as she turned in his direction, and himself, as well, as he rose from his chair and took Lancer outside the cabin for his nightly run.

Sorrel pondered his words while she undressed for bed. This was the first time that their conversation had not ended in angry words, and deep down she felt a peacefulness settling over her.

The following day and the next seemed to pass by at a pace that a turtle would have enjoyed. With no one but Lancer for company Sorrel began to feel the weight of the mountain man's absence. She had even fleetingly hoped that the Indian would pay a visit. Any company was better than none, she had reasoned. But the Indian had not returned to the cabin since the afternoon he had brought her the clothing, so after the first lonesome day she gave up this hope.

She pondered her feelings as she sat alone each evening. She really missed the presence of Mathew. Though they seemed to constantly provoke each other and spent most of their time not talking, there was still some unnamed force that seemed to be pushing his darkly bearded, handsome face into the forefront of her mind at every turn of the hour.

Throwing the book down upon the chair she began to pace in an agitated manner. That was another thing, why had he left his book of poetry on the table for her that day when he had left? If he had truly been angry with her prying into his saddle bag and taking the book, why now would he leave it for her?

Everything about the man seemed to pull her in opposite directions. Never before had she felt this way. Always in the past men had been fairly simple to set straight and to ban from her mind, but now here she was in absolute torment.

Lancer rose as her pacing continued and worriedly watched after her steps.

Seeing the animal's agitation mount Sorrel relented and with a soft laugh at her own folly for worrying over a strange man who meant nothing to her, she bent down and rubbed the dog behind his ears. "There Lancer, I am sorry, boy. Your master seems to be ever present in my thoughts of late, and these thoughts for some reason are vexing me greatly." She murmured softly to the great beast and for her kindness she was rewarded with his great lopping tongue on her hand.

Each morning Sorrel would wake and after fixing a meal for herself and the dog she would venture outside of the warm cabin into the snow-laden world. She would first bring inside enough firewood for that day and then she would carry the buckets to the stream and bring back enough water for the cabin's use and also for her bath.

She loved this time of the day, when she could let Lancer outside and then relax back against the rim of the wooden tub and let the heat of the water soothe her body and mind. She had begun this custom of an early toilet while Mathew was still at the cabin and would leave early each day and not return until the afternoon.

Her thoughts seemed gentler now as she shut her

eyes and willed her mind to try and forget the reasons for her being in this cabin. She let the warmth of the water surrounding her body relax her tired limbs and gently lull her into a dreamlike mood.

For the past few nights her dreams had been filled with Mathew. She had determined that this man could not possibly be the same one she had met in Richmond and had dreamed about for so many weeks, but now with the passage of the days this man who shared his cabin with her seemed to take on a gentler aspect, reminding her of that other man with the same deep, fathomless blue eyes. Within these hazy realms of unreality she envisioned the same tender lips smiling at her with a gentleness that she had never known, except in the depths of her deepest secret thoughts. Even his towering form in her dreams did not fill her with fear as it did when she was awake.

As Sorrel let her mind go and she leaned back against the rim of the tub and enjoyed the lulling of the warm, sensuous water, a tender smile filled her flushed face. These past nights her dreaming had taken on the same delight as she had known other nights when she had thought of another man. For now the mountain man was the one taking her up in his strong arms and those lips that could scowl so fiercely at her were descending upon her own with the softness and gentleness that she had experienced on that night long ago when she had stumbled into the wrong room while seeking her father.

She could feel the tender ministrations of his hands as they encircled her and gently stroked the length of her arms, bringing shivers of delight coursing over her inexperienced body. Even though it all was but a delusion conjured up in the depths of her mind, Sorrel could even while lying here in the tub imagine the manly smell of the person who was holding her and placing small, delicate kisses along her face and neck. With a sweet daring that swept over Sorrel's body she could envision the mountain man's lips lowering from her neck and descending toward her breast. She was completely lost to her surroundings, not hearing the quiet closing of the door or the harsh intake of breath coming from only a few feet away.

Something brought some small sound to her ears, and with a small fluttering of her lashes she fairly collapsed in the now barely warm water when her green, shining orbs fell on the tall, intimidating frame of the mountain man standing only a few steps away from the tub.

Mathew had come back to the cabin earlier than he had planned, but from the moment of his leaving he had been plagued with thoughts of Sorrel Morgan. So after finishing with the last of his traps yesterday afternoon he had started back to his cabin, deciding that since he could not seem to be able to do anything without wondering how the girl was faring, he might as well call a halt to his hunting.

Upon opening the cabin door Mathew's blue eyes had been automatically drawn to the round tub near the hearth containing Sorrel Morgan. He had been all but rendered senseless, his eyes being hungrily drawn, as though he was a man starving, to the delectable beauty before him. Her eyes were shut, her golden head leaning back against the rim of the tub. Her curls had been swept up into a small knot atop her head and small, damp, dangling ringlets delicately brushed against her face. She seemed to be in a dreamlike state, and he was touched for a moment with a feeling of total unreality, all of his energy numbed as he watched her. But after a moment he gently reached out and shut the door behind him, not being able for a second to pull his eyes from the softly flushed face before him. He felt his breathing coming in harsh, ragged breaths, and, as though without a will of his own, Mathew's feet began slowly to move toward the woman.

He was not sure of what he was about, but as his vision filled with the upper portion of her body glistening with droplets of crystal water and seeming to be bathed in a creamy, intoxicating glow, he was drawn—knowing only that he had to get closer—as a moth to a licking flame. He slowly approached the tub, but, standing back as though he might get burned, he let his blue eyes feast on what was before him.

As Sorrel's eyes flew wide, some of Mathew's senses did return and he saw her fright. In the days past he had relished this look of fear, knowing that it was a wedge between them, but now as he saw this same fright in those emerald depths he knew a moment of deep regret. Her look stayed in his mind as she hurriedly lowered her body into the cool water, submerging to her chin.

The moment of tranquility and desire had been thoroughly broken, and Mathew felt a deep, penetrating loss.

"You—but what are you doing here?" Sorrel squirmed in the confines of the water, not knowing what to do next and feeling the scarlet of her face. It was clear that he had been watching her, perhaps reading her thoughts. Again she thought about her dreams and could see his lips showering tiny kisses upon her face and neck. She wished only that she could somehow drown herself in this small amount of water as she felt the heat of her body's betrayal.

Mathew's smile was that of an indulgent father. "Perhaps you have tarried overly long at your bath, madam, and your mind has been slightly affected. This is my cabin." His words were meant to be not harsh but chiding, but to Sorrel they sounded cold and taunting.

"I did not mean . . ." Sorrel started, her face now flaming from her embarrassment.

Mathew felt her embarrassment as though it was his own and swiftly waved her words aside. "You have no need to apologize, it is I who have that need. I am sorry to have intruded on your privacy." Even as he said these words his eyes lingered on the form in the water.

Harshly pulling himself away he turned about and left Sorrel to the empty room, and with a pounding heart she hurried from the water and into her clothes. She felt her heart beating rapidly. She had been caught in the middle of her dreaming by the very man about whom she dreamed. How long had he been standing there? she wondered as she began to plait her hair. Had he somehow read into her thoughts and seen the wishes of her soul? When she had first opened her eyes there had been a strange look in the turn of his face, a tender, almost longing look, and that very look, if nothing else, had frightened her more than any other look of his in the past.

Mathew made his way back inside the cabin and for the remainder of the day he sat in a chair and brooded, his eyes ever traveling about the small room and resting on the slim form of Sorrel Morgan. He followed her about as she set to cleaning the cabin, finding that with every turn he seemed to be watching her, she busied herself with one task after another.

By the time dinner was placed upon the table the cabin fairly sparkled and Sorrel felt the weariness of the day.

After the meal was cleared away she sat before the hearth and took her hair from the confines of its leather strap. Holding it down her back, she shook it out thick and long about her shoulders, waiting for Mathew to leave the cabin for his usual walk outside with Lancer.

But things did not seem to be going as she wished this evening. Mathew sat back relaxing in his chair, not showing any inclination for his usual routine, and Sorrel sat chafing at his delay. She was bone weary and wished for no more than to rest her head upon the bed. For a moment her emerald eyes lingered on it.

Mathew watched for a moment as Sorrel's gaze turned from the fire to the bed and then back once more to the burning log, which crackled loudly in the hearth. Stretching his long legs out before him Mathew softly spoke, making Sorrel jump in her seat. "You are welcome to the comb in my bags, Sorrel." He had been admiring her as she had set her hair free and for a second he could envision his own strong fingers running through those inviting curls.

Sorrel did not move but sat with hands primly clasped in her lap. Did he know that she had used his comb already? Was that the reason for his mentioning of it now? Her guilt at having used another's possession left her red-faced and hanging her head.

Mathew watched her for a moment, and seeing the redness of her face and her apparent wish not to look in his direction, he put her attitude down to her still heated embarrassment. Smiling softly he rose and reaching his saddle bags pulled the comb out and brought it to her.

Sorrel was forced to raise her eyes as he stood there holding out the comb. "Thank you," she murmured, her voice barely reaching his ears, her shaky hand reaching out for the object.

Mathew's smile never left his face as he once more took his seat and anticipated the sight of this woman brushing out her long golden curls.

She was wearing the Indian dress and the moccasins that Red Hawk had brought for her and while she sat before the hearth and took long strokes through her hair, he thought that never before had he seen a woman quite as beautiful as this one now sitting before him. As this thought struck him another image of pale blond features and china-blue eyes fleetingly crossed his mind, but with a stronger will he pushed this image from him, his eyes resting once more on the woman before him.

Sorrel felt those bold blue eyes upon her every move and her flush increased with each passing moment. There was a physical tension as strong as an electrical current in the small space of the tiny cabin.

Each of them was more than aware of the other's physical presence.

It was some time before they were distracted from thoughts of each other by the sound of Lancer's whining and scratching at the door, wanting to get to the outside.

Mathew rose, though reluctantly, and went to the animal, for the first time wishing that his dog was not there. With one last glance over his shoulder at Sorrel he opened the door and stepped through that barrier and out into the ice-chilled air.

Quickly rising to her feet Sorrel took advantage of the solitude of the room. Going to the bed she sat upon the furs and hurriedly pulled off her moccasins, then stood and began to pull her dress over her head.

As she stood thus with hands raised over her head, tightly grasping and pulling the dress off of her body, she heard the door open. Not hearing the sounds of Mathew's footsteps on the wooden floor, she knew that he was standing and watching her. She clutched the deerskin dress tightly to her chest, covering the front portion of her body and slowly turned around to stare into the fathomless blue eyes.

Mathew visibly shook himself as he tried to pull his eyes from the sight before him. Never had he seen such beauty as now was displayed to him. He felt his own body's growing passion as he cleared his throat and tried lightly to put Sorrel at her ease. "It would seem, madam, that I do have the most dad-blasted luck for entering into this cabin at the wrong time." Acting as though nothing more was unusual and no more apology was required, he strode casually over to the hearth and presented his back to the bed and to

Sorrel as he began to warm his hands.

Sorrel rushed with the pulling of her shirt around her body, still holding her dress up by the support of her chin. She was quickly finished with her change and buried deep under the safety of her covers. She shut her eyes, praying for the oblivion of sleep to hurry to her and to keep the thoughts of the mountain man from creeping into her mind. But with each second that passed her mind filled with deep blue eyes and a dark, handsome face slowly descending toward her, an enraptured glaze of desire in his every look.

Mathew felt his insides twisting as though a sharp knife blade was finding its mark. This long day had been far too much for him—first his happening upon this beautiful woman at her leisure in her bath and now, as he turned about and sat his large frame in the chair by the hearth, he was presented with the full, ripe beauty of the curve through the furs of her back and buttocks. He felt his heart accelerating to a drastic speed and the palms of his large hands began to sweat from his torture.

Forcefully he tried to put an iron band of control upon his overstimulated instincts, for he was sure that if he let up on his vigilance on himself his animal desires would overpower him and then for certain the girl upon the bed, who was solely at his mercy, would be anything but safe alone with him in this cabin.

He scolded himself harshly under his breath for his foul thoughts. Then, as he kept his gaze directed toward the bed, he began to feel some irritation at being presented with her back. With great will he pulled himself from the chair, and like a stalking panther he went to the table and picked up the book. Wishing for anything to distract his mind, he went back to the chair and tried to concentrate on reading.

He soon found, though, that this was not the type of book to take his mind off a woman. The poet had been blessed with a gift for words, and he seemed also to have been blessed with an overabundant supply of lovely women to write about. Glowing phrases of love sang with the fulfilled desires of both men and women, their passions at the very highest plateau. With each line Mathew's eyes were pulled from the pages and roamed to the beauty buried in the soft, downy folds of the furs.

Throwing down the book Mathew rose, noticing that the fire had dimmed and that the room was now lightly dosed with a dim and tranquil light. Starting from his chair and going toward the door, Mathew was pulled up short as he glanced over to the bed of furs. The woman was now rolled over facing the room, her eyes closed. Studying her from afar Mathew wondered what could be inside that golden head. What thoughts and dreams did that beautiful mind think while asleep? Did she dream of him, as he now often did of her?

Mathew's feet as though with a will of their own covered the small distance that brought him up to the bed. He had no idea of what he was doing, but he tried to rationalize that he only wished to see her more closely as she slept. Perhaps seeing her thus he would be able to put her from his tormented mind for the remainder of the night. The thought reminded him that he had to make his pallet once again before the hearth and to stretch out full length upon the floor. He knew that he would never be able to go to sleep, she would be ever present in his thoughts.

His plans were abruptly squelched as his blue eyes went over her form. She had thrown the furs back and her gentle curves were plainly visible through the thin cotton of the shirt she wore. Her woman's body seemed to hold tempting, hidden secrets, drawing his blue eyes from that beautiful form to her face. Long, thick copper curls cascaded about her shoulders and lightly draped over her pillow, appearing to be liquid gold as the moonlight shone through the window and fell lightly upon the bed. Soft, creamy cheeks rested lightly upon that pillow that seemed to glow with a shining fire, and even in her sleep her features became lightly flushed as though she knew of the eyes looking down so critically upon her. Below these cheeks tiny petal-pink lips rose up softly, invitingly. They seemed to beckon Mathew, and with no more than a light butterfly's touch he bent and traced those tempting lips with his own.

Sorrel, thinking herself still in the hazy, pleasant depths of her dream world, felt the slight pressure upon her mouth, and instead of pulling away she drew up her sleek arms and wrapped them about Mathew's neck, her own lips now slanting across his and seeking out the pleasure that was before her. It was as though she was once again in that room in the inn, where a stranger's arms had tightly clasped her to him and his lips had swept boldly across her own and sought out all that she possessed. She felt at this moment that same desperate desire to become a part of him, to belong completely to him.

Mathew was more than surprised at her reaction, and knowing that she was still in her sleep he did not pull himself away as he knew he should, instead his arms encircled her, capturing her to him as though he thought she would fly at any moment, and his tongue drove between her teeth, tasting and searching the sweet ambrosia that was hers alone and awaiting this moment of total delight.

From some place far within her, Sorrel slowly became aware of what was happening to her, and she slowly opened her eyes, with the realization that she was no longer sleeping and that all that was happening was indeed no longer a dream but was truly happening, as it had on another night. And with this realization came a tiny spark of fear, which within seconds became a real fright. To dream of this thing happening between her and this man was one thing, but to awake to the reality of it was something else. Trying now to pull her mouth away she began to push at Mathew's broad chest with all the strength she could possibly muster. But this show of her strength was hardly discernible as his large arms pulled her more tightly against him.

Mathew felt her frightened response at the same moment that she awoke, but his will now seemed to be beyond his own control, all of rational thoughts flying from him as his grip tightened about her body.

"No," she gasped as for a second his lips left hers as his bold, desire-filled eyes looked deeply down into her face, seeking for the response that would ease his mind. Though Sorrel had desired this moment and had craved these same hands touching her body in its most secret places, something in her heart told her not to so easily give herself.

Pushing her pleas to the back of his mind, Mathew's lips once more descended. He was a man obsessed, not caring about the outcome of his actions, only knowing that his need for her was such that every pore of his body seemed to be throbbing with his want for her.

With his mouth once more upon hers, Sorrel's own mind was confused. She had been dreaming that this very thing had happened to her for the past two nights, but even in her wildest imaginings she had not thought that the pressure and pleasure could be as sweet as this. She fought off the feeling of desire that was beginning to course through her. Never had a man kissed her in this manner before, always she had been in control, but now, without this control, she found herself beginning to respond to his embraces.

Mathew sensed her resistance wearing thin and doubled his attack, bringing soft moans of pleasure from the woman in his arms. He found himself full length now upon the bed, his body pressed tightly against her. His broad chest, thickly matted with crisp black hair, lightly pushed against her swelling breasts, the thin shirt she wore as her nightclothes leaving little protection for her modesty.

As his hands began boldly to caress her face and shoulders Sorrel thought that she had never felt as desirable and womanly. But as his hands began to roam lower she once more felt a nagging fear creeping over her body. The shirt was short, only reaching to mid-thigh, leaving little protection against Mathew's wandering hands, and as she felt his large hand softly caressing the inside of her thigh she began to push, but this time she became desperate to get away. She was not some wanton doxie. She was Sorrel Morgan, and no man had ever dared to be so bold as this one. She could not let this proceed any further. She must put an end to it and now. "Please," the word was pulled from the depths of her chest. "You cannot. Let me loose."

Her words reached Mathew's ears as though from miles away, so enraptured was he. The silky touch of her skin drove him ever on.

A gush of fear began to spill out of Sorrel. She was frantic, and like a wild animal she began to lash out at Mathew, fighting for her freedom like a wild cat. "No!" she was now screaming and kicking out with all of her strength.

Some form of reason seemed to come to Mathew for a moment, and in the dim light of the hearth illuminating the room he tried to look deep into her face, and as he did what he saw brought him to a complete halt.

Tears were streaming out of huge, frightened green eyes as she pushed and shoved, and as his arms relaxed somewhat with his looking into her face she quickly jumped to the other side of the bed and crouched low on her knees with a fur clutched tightly over her chest.

Rising up and sitting upon the bed Mathew looked at the woman he had only seconds ago been holding tightly in his embrace, wonder in his face. Never before had he forced his attentions on any woman.

Tears were still falling down Sorrel's cheeks, and with a slow movement Mathew's hand reached out and gently wiped them away. How could he have acted in such a brutish manner? he questioned himself. What had come over him?

Sorrel flinched at his touch, not knowing what to expect next from this man who stirred such strange feelings in her. She was as much angered with herself as she was with him. How could she have let herself become so carried away?

"I—I," Mathew started, feeling her jump from his touch. He knew that words of apology were needed, but for the life of him he felt his tongue tied. He could not form in his mind what best he should say.

A noise outside of the cabin drew his attention, and with one final look into the emerald eyes Mathew rose and went to the cabin door.

As he opened the door the noise of animals fighting came to his ears. He had thought that afternoon that he had heard the howling of a wolf, and now with the noise coming closer to the cabin he was certain that Lancer had found himself some sport for the night. He had no fear about his pet for he had on more than one occasion seen the great beast attack a pack of the wild animals and come out the victor. In fact, Mathew felt envious of the animal—he would give anything at this moment for a good fist fight. Then perhaps he could wipe from his mind the image of the woman who was sharing his cabin. If he did not begin to gain some form of control over himself she would be sharing more than just his home.

Shaking himself as though he was a man possessed by an angry demon he stomped out of the door and out into the coldness of the night.

There was no such easy escape for Sorrel. As she heard the door slam she threw her head down upon the deep furs and wept loudly into their softness. She had dared, even in her sleep a dangerous game, and now her folly had been found out. She felt those bold lips upon her own now as she had only moments before, the thoughts bringing her tears racing down without let-up. She had been brazen, almost without fear in his arms, as she had been the past two nights in the deepness of her dreams. And with a sense of relief but a deeper sense of sorrow she had caught herself just before surrendering all to this man that she hardly knew.

"How could I have done such a thing?" she cried to the empty room. How could she face this man again after what she had given and taken in those few minutes in his arms? He would know with her every look her deepest thoughts. Perhaps know them even better than she did herself, for her mind was a scramble of emotions. She had wanted his arms about her and his lips upon her own, but then, at the same time, she had despised herself for wishing such boldness from a man she knew nothing about. The only thing she knew of this man was his name. She knew nothing of his past nor what kind of man he really was. Never before in Sorrel Morgan's life had she let herself become so frivolous. She had always known what it was that she wanted, and in short order she had had within easy grasp the object of her desire.

It was true, though, that she had never played deeply at the art of love. Her path had been made straight for her by her father and her aunt at an early age, and she had always had them near at hand to steer her straight. She had, of course, enjoyed light flirtatious affairs with handsome gentlemen, but never had they gotten out of hand. So now she knew that she was at a loss. This large, handsome mountain man was not one of those stylish, courtly young men that she had been brought up around. He was just the opposite. He was not the type to be flirted with and then pushed aside; there was something underlying his passion that was ruthless, almost dangerous.

Beating the pillow under her head Sorrel wept again. It was not just the man that worried Sorrel, but herself. She was different from the light, uncaring girl she had been at her Aunt Corry's house. It now seemed like years ago that she had led that pampered and sheltered life of rich man's daughter. Life here in this cabin was real, and she had no one but herself to rely upon. And now the full realization hit her that she could not really count upon her own good senses to see her through. What if once again this Mathew Danner were to enfold her in his arms? Would she be able to pull herself away or would she be swept up in the feelings that he evoked in her body and be lost to true reasoning?

Her tears coursed over and over her cheeks as the time slowly crept by, leaving her body weary and her eyes heavy.

The next morning before the sun touched down upon the earth Sorrel's eyes opened, and though the cabin lay in complete darkness she could make out the form of the man sleeping upon the pallet near the now cold hearth.

As soon as she saw Mathew her mind filled with the events of the night before. How could she stay here in his cabin and act as though nothing had occurred between them? It would be impossible, if not for her then for him. At every turn they would be reminded of their lips enjoying the sweet taste that had been hidden from them until they had touched. They would with each look be reminded of the feel of each other's skin under their hands as they had held tightly to each other. She felt as though her mind would burst from these tormenting thoughts, and without thinking where she would go or exactly what course she would take Sorrel quietly got up from the bed and slipped into the dress that Red Hawk had brought her. She would only take two of the leftover biscuits from the night before, she thought. She did not want this man to think her a thief, even though the thought had crossed her mind that it would be much easier if she were to take his horse than to try to walk in the deep snow.

It was only a short time later that Sorrel was indeed standing outside of the lean-to that housed Mathew's large black stallion. Quickly she set aside the small packet that held her shirt and the pants that were hers and the biscuits that would be her only nourishment until she could find help. She had saddled and taken care of horses many times in the past, so this job was not one new to her and was quickly finished.

Within only a short few minutes Sorrel Morgan and Mathew Danner's great beast were slowly making their way through the thick white snow covering the valley, Sorrel casting from her mind that the taking of Mathew's horse had indeed made her a thief.

Trying to remember the route that Red Hawk had taken that first day, Sorrel turned the horse's head in what she hoped was the right direction. If she could somehow find her way back to where her father's camp had been perhaps she would be able to find some kind of help. She did not think of how long it had taken Red Hawk to bring her to this cabin nor did she remind herself of the long ride through the forest. Her only thoughts were to put as much distance as she could between herself and the man who had inspired such deep, and almost hated, feelings within her.

The darkness slowly vanished and made room for the light of the day. Sorrel shivered uncontrollably as she huddled upon the back of the large stallion. She had thought once to stop and to put on the clothes she had tied together to form her pack, but the idea of stopping and getting down in the cold whiteness sent cold, piercing horror over her body. Even her mind seemed to be growing numb with the cold, and as she weaved in and out of the trees her imagination began to play wild tricks upon her. In back of each huge tree she began to see fierce Indians. She knew that the woods were home to these warriors, and they were not all as friendly as Red Hawk. She even began to wish as the day drew on that Red Hawk would appear from behind one of the trees and find her and return her to Mathew's cabin. Anything would be better than to stay here in the freezing cold and be scared out of her wits.

Indians were not, however, to be the cause of Sorrel's turnaround that day. Instead, a small rabbit running out from the thick foliage and scurrying between the stallion's hooves was to change her course. As the small animal darted close to the horse's legs, the stallion, who all morning had been sensing the fear of the woman riding him, rose nervously on his back legs, and, accompanied by the piercing scream that came from the woman, he began to run through the trees, barely noticing that he no longer had a rider on his back.

Sorrel lay in a heap, her dress pulled up to her thighs and her freezing legs now exposed to the coldness of the snow. She lay stunned for a full minute before she rose on her elbows and tried to grasp what had just happened to her.

She had always been an excellent horsewoman, and she now felt shame for her behavior. She could not blame the stallion for his fear of the rabbit, she knew that she was mostly responsible for his nervousness and that his throwing her was not a deliberate act but one of desperation and fear. She could only hope that he would run himself for a time and then return to where he had lost his rider. She swore that she would not again be so foolhardy. She knew that horses were intelligent animals and could sense what their riders were feeling. She should have known better than to let her fear of this forest make her act as she had.

Now, though, she looked about herself with a taste of true desperation. She would be completely on her own if the animal did not return soon. She started to stand, but as she pulled her legs from under herself she felt a small, wrenching pain in one of her ankles. She prayed silently as she put a small amount of weight on the aching foot that it would hold her weight and was not broken.

To her relief she found that it was only sprained, and not too badly at that, but still, with each step she took, a piercing pain shot sharply up her leg.

With the break of daylight Mathew rolled over on his pallet, pulling his covers up about his chin. It was freezing in here, he thought as he felt the cold circle about him. He dreaded getting up and lighting the hearth, but pulling himself from his warm pallet he threw logs upon the now cold ashes and began to build up a roaring blaze. After warming himself he turned about toward the bed, daring a look in that direction as he remembered the night before.

When he had finally come back into the cabin last night Sorrel had been asleep, and as he had walked to his own pallet he had caught a glimpse of glistening tears still damp upon her face.

He had railed at himself for over half of the night, not finding sleep until the early hours, for what he had done to Sorrel. She had trusted him not to harm her and had been sleeping trustingly in his bed when he had dared his foul act. He expected that today, and for the rest of the days that she stayed here in his cabin, she would treat him with a cool disdain for his rude behavior.

As his deep blue eyes lingered on the bed, hoping to be able to watch her for only a moment as she slept, he rose up from the hearth with some surprise. The bed was empty, and now he noticed for the first time that Lancer was in the cabin. He had left the animal out last night, hoping that if there were any more wolves he would scare tham away from the cabin. Now, though, the large dog was scratching and whining at the door.

"What is it, boy? Did she shut you up in here while she went for her morning toilet?" This was the only reason that Mathew could fathom for the girl to leave the safety of the warm cabin, though he thought it a bit odd that she had not built up the fire before going outside. Perhaps she was afraid that she would have awakened him, the thought hit him. And he could not blame her for not wanting to face him after his brutish manner of the night before.

He would put some coffee on and start breakfast, he thought, and quickly set about his task. Raising his head toward the dog he scolded him and ordered him to lie still. His infernal noise seemed to become louder with each passing second. He wished to have at least started the meal before Sorrel returned; perhaps he could make up to her a small bit, he thought, by having a warm cabin and a cup of coffee awaiting her.

Time passed slowly and as Mathew finished frying the venison he once again wondered as he had now for the tenth time what was keeping the girl. He hated to go in search of her and offend her even further by finding her attending to personal needs. But as the minutes ticked by he, like Lancer, began to become anxious.

Finally he gave up and began to pull his coat on. The girl had to be out of her mind to stay this long out in the cold when she did not even have a jacket of her own. All she owned was the dress Red Hawk had brought her and that was by no means warm enough for her to be staying this long out in the freezing weather.

Lancer jumped to his feet as he saw his master putting on his jacket. His dog senses were in tune, and he knew that the woman he had begun to love was in some kind of trouble. He had wanted to follow her this morning and had resented being locked up in the cabin, so now, if his master was going outside, he would not be left in again.

Mathew saw the anxious worry of his animal and as he opened the cabin door the dog shot through it and ran about to the back of the building. "Here boy," Mathew shouted and followed the animal, hoping that neither he nor his dog was disturbing the woman.

He had just rounded the cabin when Lancer charged into the lean-to that he had built for his horse. His curiosity piqued, Mathew followed, and as his blue eyes adjusted to the dim light his face became dark and distorted with anger.

His horse was gone. Sorrel must have taken the animal and fled. How stupid he had been—he could kick himself. There he was in the cabin not wanting to disturb the girl and fixing breakfast for the both of them and she was more than likely miles away by now, and with his horse.

She must have left early this morning, he thought, as his eyes followed the horse's hoofprints in the snow. It had not yet snowed that morning, so nothing had covered the tracks. Perhaps if he hurried he could try and find the girl. There was no telling what she could get herself into in this country, and there certainly would be no help coming to her except that of an Indian, and none of them would be willing to give her the kind of help she wanted. Hurrying, with this thought in mind, Mathew went inside the cabin bringing out with him a packet of the food he had just cooked and his long gun. "Come Lancer. Let us find the woman before she comes to some harm."

The tracks made by his horse were easy to follow, and by mid-morning Mathew and Lancer were out of the valley and headed into the forest that bordered it. Mathew tried to hurry his pace as he felt the soft tiny flakes of snow gently coming down on him. If the snow covered the tracks it would be only with luck that he would find the girl and his horse.

Something from the corner of Mathew's eye pulled his attention around and with Lancer's barking Mathew stared hard at the large black moving object that stuck out starkly against the white of the snow.

Why, it was his horse, he thought, as he watched the animal slowly making his way through the forest. At the loud, piercing whistle the large animal stilled and cocked his ears in the direction the noise had come from. Again the whistle, but this time the animal did not hesitate, he came at a full gallop toward the man who had cared for him since he had been a colt.

"There, there, boy," Mathew soothed the beast as it stopped in front of him. The horse's eyes rolled in his head and his sides quaked and shivered from what he had been put through that day. He had been on his way to the valley and to home when he had heard Mathew's whistle, and now he nuzzled softly at his master's hand.

"Where is the lass?" Mathew asked, knowing now that since she was no longer on his horse's back she was either in some kind of trouble or had perhaps been found by an Indian. If she was afoot that could be even worse for her in this snow.

Taking only a few more moments to calm his large stallion Mathew jumped upon the great steed's back and made his way through the forest.

The snow had begun to fall ever harder, and it was late into the afternoon when Lancer broke the quiet of the woods with his loud yelps and barking as he hurried through the trees. Mathew pushed his mount, knowing that Lancer must have picked up Sorrel's scent.

He soon came upon Lancer licking and prancing about a still form lying curled into a tight ball at the base of a large tree. Quickly he was on his feet and running to the thing that had Lancer's attention and as his eyes fell on the woman before him his heart seemed to break within his chest.

She only moved feebly as Lancer kept up his licking with his great tongue on her face, trying to get a response that would tell him that this woman he loved was all right.

"Lancer, down boy," Mathew called as he leaned down and gathered the cold form up into his large arms.

For a second Sorrel's green eyes fluttered open but the movement seemed too much for her to bear and instantly they closed once again.

She must have grown weary and lain down to rest, Mathew thought as he started to his horse. And that was the worst thing she could have done. There was no telling how long she had been lying there in the freezing snow. Her hands were blue and her face was pale, her lips shivering and purple.

Climbing onto the back of his horse Mathew began to try to bring some warmth to the woman in his arms. Opening his jacket he brought her body up tightly to his chest, enfolding her within the softness of the inside furs of his coat. He then rubbed and blew on her hands, trying to bring the circulation back to them. Slowly and painstakingly he worked over the still form in his arms. He felt desperation as he laid her cold cheek against his neck. He could not let her slip away from him. This was all his fault. She would not have tried to run away if he had not forced himself upon her.

Slowly Sorrel began to feel the life beginning to flow back into her body. She felt prickling pains shooting through her numb hands and feet and soft moans began to escape her lips.

Mathew felt her response and began to soothe her with soft, gentle words as his hands constantly stroked and worked the blood back into her body.

Sorrel realized who was holding her the moment her senses returned, but instead of fear or anger she felt relief and relaxed back in his arms. His warmth and strength were far better than what she had suffered today.

"Ah, my little love, you were foolish to try to venture forth in this weather. I told you there was no way out until the snows thaw." Mathew's words were a gentle caress spoken against her cheek as he felt her first movement, and with this movement he felt some of the pieces of his heart being put back into place. He snuggled her more tightly in his arms, wrapping the jacket about her, and then softly called to his horse to begin the journey back to the cabin.

It was way into the night before Mathew pulled up in front of the cabin and carried Sorrel into the safety of his home. He placed her upon the bed and then at once set about to build a fire to warm the cabin and her. After this, without a word spoken between them, he went outside to rub his horse down and put him in his lean-to.

The ride back to the cabin had been a torturous one for Mathew Danner. Holding Sorrel's soft form tightly against his chest for the whole afternoon and evening had been a sweet, searing agony. Even his thoughts of Elizabeth had not been enough to take Sorrel Morgan from his mind. He could barely even remember what Elizabeth Strickland had looked like. Instead of the pale, cool features that he had thought he loved, he now saw only honey curls and emerald, flashing eyes.

While rubbing his horse down he came to a decision. There was no possible way that he could stay in this cabin with this woman for the remainder of the winter and play the gentleman. If he did not leave, and soon, he knew that he would make the final mistake that would more than likely have the girl once again fleeing him and risking her life to gain freedom.

Chapter Nine

Whiteness covered the valley, and an icy chill surrounded the small cabin. Sorrel huddled before the fire trying to keep herself warm. It had been two days since she had tried to gain her freedom from this cabin, but all that she had truly gained was this feeling of being constantly cold and in complete solitude. Except for Lancer she was as alone as she had been when Red Hawk had brought her here. But even then she had had something to look forward to. At least the Indian had made his daily visits, making sure that she was all right and that she had plenty of wood and water.

True, there was enough wood cut to last her several more days, but Sorrel felt a deep resentment that she had been left to herself, even though this had been her own intention when she had run away from Mathew Danner. She understood that her anger was based on the fact that the large mountain man had dared to leave her. She had been the one who should have left him, not the other way around.

Rising from the chair she once more walked about the small cabin. At least on the morning that she had awakened and found him gone she had found Lancer here. She had also found a small handwritten note, telling her that Mathew had decided during the night that he would leave for a time to hunt. That was all that the note contained, with only Mathew's neat, flourishing scrawl at the bottom. Sorrel did not know what she had expected, but now, after two days of solitude, she knew that she had wished more from him than those few words.

What was getting into her? she had scoffed at herself over a dozen times. She had been the one trying to flee him, but now with him gone she thought of nothing else, night and day, but his tender lips. Her nights alone had been the worst. She had lain awake all night long, and imagined tender love words coming from the mountain man's mouth as his lips descended on hers with a consuming vengeance. As soon as she felt those lips, though, her eyes would open with an expectancy of desire, but she would be left empty and without any hope. But she had never loved before, so she shunned the very thought that she might be feeling more for this man than for any other in her past.

Lancer scratched at the door, wanting to go outside, bringing Sorrel from her deep thoughts. "Ah, boy, do you wish to go out into the cold?" She hurriedly went to the door and held it open for the large, furry animal.

Another night faced Sorrel and now she reluctantly set about preparing herself a small meal. Her thoughts were only of getting quickly through the motions and hurrying the arrival of the next day. The sooner the days passed the more quickly she would be able to be free of this valley prison and the distressing thoughts of the large mountain man.

Sorrel's wishes were not to be fulfilled. As she lay down upon the soft, deep furs and tried to shut her eyes the vision of Mathew Danner somewhere out there in the cold and shivering under a thin blanket came to her mind. It was not her fault, she told herself over and over. Was she to blame that he had chosen the freezing snow over her and a warm cabin?

She was beginning to think of Mathew's leave-taking as more of an escape of her than a hunting trip. He would rather face the freezing cold than be alone with her—and hadn't she been cause enough for him to flee?

All the long night these thoughts plagued Sorrel, and with the coming of morning she felt her body's weariness as she rose and let Lancer out the door. If she did not pull herself together and put all these thoughts from her mind, she scolded herself harshly, she would be a worn-out old hag in the next few months.

Though the snow outside was like a white blanket thrown about the valley, Sorrel found with the opening of the cabin door that the sun was shining as it had not in days. Feeling the sharp confines of the small cabin that she had stayed in for so many hours she quickly gathered up a large fur and went out. She was not one to let an invitation such as this pass without a quick sampling. Calling Lancer to her side she went to the back of the cabin. Near the stream she found a large dead tree lying on the earth next to the path. The chill of the air was lessened by the rays of sun shining down upon the valley, and

Sorrel spread the fur over the tree and sat back against a huge branch rising up disjointedly from the body of the massive trunk. Sitting thus she began to brush out her long golden curls as Lancer, enjoying the feel of the unusual sun, decided to stretch out his muscles by giving chase to a fleeing rabbit who had dared show himself as Lancer sniffed in the brush.

Seeming lost to the beauty around her and deep within her thoughts, Sorrel was startled as she heard a horse pull about to the back of the cabin. Turning around she looked up with some surprise as she saw Red Hawk jumping from the back of his horse.

Her smile was large and genuine as he approached. Even his company was welcome to the girl after her days of solitude.

The red man's small frown turned to a huge grin as he saw her welcoming smile. Everything about her interested him—her glowing golden curls cascading all about her and her soft gentle beauty radiating with her tender smile absorbed him as he approached her.

"It is so good to see you, Red Hawk," Sorrel started, moving over on the fur to make room for her visitor. "I am afraid that if you have come to visit Mathew he is not here. He left a few days past to do some hunting." She hurried through this, feeling her face beginning to turn red.

The Indian did not answer but watched her features as she spoke each word.

Sorrel was not to let this chance of company easily slip by, and barely realizing that the Indian remained silent she went on, "It has been some time since you have been here, Red Hawk. Have you also been hunting?" She smiled brightly at him and watched his dark eyes silently appraising her as he sat across from her.

Lancer at this moment ran back to where he had left Sorrel, and seeing the Indian sitting across from the girl he now loved he growled deeply within his chest. Though he at once recognized the Indian as being a friend of his master's, he still did not trust the other man and especially not around this woman.

Sorrel with a gentle but stern voice silenced the dog and ordered him to leave the two of them.

Going only a short distance away Lancer lay down near the stream and watched over the girl, keeping the red man ever in his sight.

"Mathew's great animal still does not care for me." The Indian's first words came softly but seemed directed to no one, so Sorrel did not answer but sat watching the water in the stream slowly make its path down through the valley.

"You have asked me where I have been these many days, Sorrel Morgan, and I shall tell you."

Sorrel's attention now was pulled back to the man at her side. Something in his voice caught at her. The softly spoken words seemed pulled painfully from deep within his chest. She looked this time with more deliberateness into his handsome face. She did not speak. For some reason she knew that she was not expected to say a word.

"I did not go hunting, though I did go deep into the forest. The last day I was here and brought you the dress that my wife had made," his dark eyes kindled brightly as they again went over the body that that article now was adorning, "Mathew said words that touched deeply within my chest." Here he paused as though trying to find how best to proceed.

Sorrel looked at him expectantly. Was he bringing her some word from Mathew? Was this what his visit was all about?

"I left this valley and went to the forest to search out my soul and what I found was not to my liking. I made a mistake by taking you from your father's arms and bringing you here."

Sorrel now understood what was going on in his mind. He was sorry and now wished to apologize. But she no longer felt there was anything for him to be sorry about. She held no grudge against this red man. She felt she had grown since she had come to live here in this valley. And for some reason she felt no anger at this man. She truly felt pity for him for his own concern with what he had done. She slowly raised her hand and touched her finger to his lips. "There is no reason to go any further, Red Hawk. It is all in the past, and I do not feel any anger at you."

She felt a small smile grow beneath her hand as the Indian watched her.

"There is more to my story, Sorrel." He brought her fingers down from his face. "When in the forest I was plagued by Mathew's words of anger and I realized that I should not have brought you here for him. His anger can be great when he is provoked, I have seen this for myself on occasion. I wished to find my reasons for concern for Mathew and you, and as the days passed I did." Here again he paused and his dark eyes probed deep into those opposite him. "You were this reason, Sorrel Morgan."

Sorrel's breath caught at the seriousness of his words.

"My days and nights became tortured with your vision. On every hand I saw within my soul your beauty and gentleness. At the pond where I would swim in the icy waters I could hear the soft, tinkling whisper of your voice gently hitting the water's edge from the waterfalls. All the forest seemed to bear my pain and in each tree and in the very ground that I lay upon for my bed I saw the sparkling green of your eyes. The great sun who has always brought my people its warmth and even the moon in the darkness of the night spoke of your golden mane that even now is draped about your body as your cover. Even the gentle falling snow covering the earth told me of your soft loveliness."

As he was silent for a moment as though reflecting on his own words great diamondlike tears began slowly to come from Sorrel's green eyes and make a path down her cheeks.

Red Hawk looked in wonder and slowly his large hand reached out and gently wiped away the tears that seemed to cut into his heart. "As a child I grew up with the story of my birth from my father's lips. On the day that my mother left their lodge to make her way to the birthing hut my father left the women and went to the forest to hunt away the time it would take for my birth. As he grew weary he lay down under a huge oak tree, and deep in his sleep a large red hawk came to the lowest branch and the words softly came to my father that a son had been born to him. As he hurried back to the village he was greeted with the news that indeed he did have a son and that son he named Red Hawk after his strange dream."

Sorrel looked at him not understanding why he was telling her this strange story.

"My father is also the shaman of our village and I have told him of you and your beauty. When he was a younger man he lived with a white family and went to the white man's school. The name Sorrel, my father has told me, is also the name of a color, and that color is also the same as the red hawk."

Sorrel was truly amazed at his words.

"You and I have been linked by destiny. From the first when I saw you bathing in the pond I knew that I could not be away from you. I saw Mathew yesterday in the forest, and I have told him that I wish to take you for my wife."

"For your wife? You saw Mathew?" All his words now seemed to be a jumble in Sorrel's mind. How could she be his wife when he already had a wife, and what had Mathew said when he had told him that he wanted her for his wife? Had he not cared what would become of her? Had he told this Indian to take her and do as he wished? Tears once again came quickly to her eyes, only this time she felt a weight as large as a great stone filling her heart.

Red Hawk watched the girl and over and over he repeated her words to himself. When she had said Mathew's name there had been something in her voice that he had never heard before. "Do you not wish to leave Mathew Danner's cabin?"

No longer able to control herself Sorrel burst out weeping and shook her head from side to side.

"If it is because I already have one wife—" he

thought that this perhaps was the reason for her distress. The white people had different ideas and he already had heard Mathew's views on this subject. "My wife, Tame Elk, is a good woman and she would love you as I do. She would be like your sister and show you many things. I would love you as my first wife in my heart, Sorrel." His words were almost a whisper now as he saw that her tears were reinforced.

"No, no," Sorrel got out from between sobs.

Red Hawk knew of only one other reason why she would refuse him and that was that she cared for another, and the only other man who could have touched her heart would have been Mathew Danner. Though the Indian thought that Mathew did not care for the girl—for when he had seen him and had told him of his wish to make the girl his wife he had seemed angry at the mere mention of the girl's name and had told Red Hawk he did not care if the girl wanted to wed him, it would be fine with him. But now he thought that perhaps the girl had a heart of her own, in which she did hold Mathew dearly, while Mathew, with his built-up shell of hardness, was blind to her feelings. "Is it Mathew Danner who is the wedge between you and me?"

For a second Sorrel felt genuine fear for herself and for Mathew as the Indian spoke these words, but knowing that she could not hold back the truth she nodded her head, and then, as her tears kept flowing, she bent her head down and stared at her folded hands in her lap. "I cannot help it. I did not truly know myself until this very moment how I felt for Mathew." Her words were so softly spoken that Red Hawk had to bend to hear them. "I thought that what I was feeling was anger and hatred, but I know now that I love him."

Red Hawk felt his heart constrict as though a sharp lance had pierced it. His first reaction was a deep, burning hatred toward Mathew, and he could envision his knife cutting the man he had called brother and pulling his heart from his body for the injustice that he was now receiving. He had not thought for a second that the girl could have fallen in love with the large mountain man. But as he sat for a few moments and watched the pitiful sight of the woman in front of him he knew that he could never harm Mathew Danner. He had spoken the word *brother* in truth, and he knew that nothing could ever come between him and the love he held for the other man. Mathew had come to this valley some time ago, and on the day he had arrived Red Hawk, for the first time in his life, had needed the help of a white man.

He had been hunting the forest for a large buck he had spotted, and as he rode out of a large group of trees he had heard a shot and at the same time he had felt something hitting him in the side. He had fallen from his horse, frightening the animal and sending the beast into a frantic run in the opposite direction. He had lain on the ground and felt the blood beginning to flow from his body.

He knew who had shot him; he had spotted two white men that morning. They were trappers, and he had silently passed their camp. He did not wish to cause trouble, there were enough young bucks from his village who did, and if they found white men so close to their village trapping animals he knew that they would not easily let them pass. But Red Hawk that day had cared for nothing but the animal he had been in pursuit of, and now, to his regret, he found that he had been careless.

It was the next morning before help had come to the injured Indian. Mathew Danner had been riding through the forest and had almost missed the sight of the injured man, but his horse had scented something unusual and had pranced about, drawing Mathew's attention. Mathew had quickly tended the red man's injuries and had fought to keep him alive. He had found the abandoned cabin in the lower part of the secluded valley and had taken Red Hawk there and nursed him back to health, and from that day Red Hawk had loved the white man as though he were indeed his own brother. He had taken him to his village and had even had a fight with another brave over the fact that he had brought a white man to their homeland. So now as the Indian looked at the young woman he knew that he would never harm the man who had given him back his life. He owed him all that he could give him, and that was why Sorrel Morgan was here at this very moment. He had brought her as a gift to his friend.

"Mathew Danner is a lucky man to have your love, Sorrel Morgan." Red Hawk took her hand, and, lightly caressing it, he brought it to his lips. He felt some of her pain as he watched her and he knew that he would do anything for this woman whom he loved so dearly.

The sun was shadowed by huge, dark clouds when Red Hawk led Sorrel back to the cabin, promising that he would be watching over her from a distance and that he would return on the following day to see to her needs.

Sorrel felt some relief at knowing that she had someone who cared, but still she felt the wretched bite of a love lost. She went into the cabin and fell asleep almost as soon as her head hit her pillow.

It was not Red Hawk who returned the following day, but instead Mathew who came through the cabin door late that afternoon.

Sorrel jumped to her feet at the opening of the door and then stood as though stunned with mouth gaping at the large mountain man as he entered the room.

Mathew did not act as though he even noticed the girl standing across the room. He strode to the table and threw down his saddle bag and another larger sack.

Lancer was the only one to show any emotion as he lunged at his master, excited to have him home again.

Absently Mathew rubbed the dog's huge head, his thoughts seeming a thousand miles away as he stood near the table, his back to Sorrel.

Finally, though, he broke the quiet. "I trust that you made out all right in my absence?" His words sounded cold and hollow.

"Yes—I—I mean everything was fine." Sorrel was brought back to her senses by the icy tone of his voice. Once again she sat back in her chair, but now, having admitted to herself and to Red Hawk yesterday her true feelings for this man, instead of finding herself angry at his cold manner and his callous treatment of her she found herself quietly studying the large man's back and the way his dark hair curled softly at the nape of his neck. Her emerald eyes caressed him with a longing as her heart cried for him to send a tender word her way. If only she could dare her heart's desire and reach out and touch that soft black hair at his back. A soft sigh escaped her with this thought. More than likely he would give her a thrashing if she were to try to do this simple thing, and as she thought of her own treatment of him a few days ago and how she had acted the child and run off with his horse, almost injuring his animal and killing herself, she could not blame him if he were to strike out at her in anger.

That soft, wistful sigh reached Mathew's ears and seemed to magnify itself until Mathew felt his own heart jump a beat. Slowly, without a word spoken, he turned about and looked toward Sorrel. Her beauty caught his blue eyes instantly, but something deep in her eyes also caught at him almost bringing him to his knees in front of her. He had to clamp an iron band about his emotions, he warned himself. He said, "Red Hawk came to my camp late last night."

His words, though spoken softly, reverberated in the small cabin and fell upon Sorrel with embarrassing effect. As his bold blue eyes watched her face intently she felt her own features beginning to turn scarlet. She felt completely mortified. Red Hawk must have left her yesterday and gone right to Mathew. She could imagine what the Indian had told this man to bring him quickly back to his cabin. "I—I . . ." Words seemed to be lost to her. She slowly lowered her eyes to her folded hands and sat quietly, waiting for this man to laugh at her and to scorn her for the feelings that Red Hawk had told him she harbored for him.

Laughter was not in Mathew Danner's mind at that moment as he stood and watched the beautiful woman before him. He had argued with himself all the day on the ride home just what he would say to her but as of this moment he still did not know what to do or what words should be spoken. He was not truly sure of his own feelings for this woman. He knew that he desired her, he had desired her from the first moment he had set eyes upon her, but was that all that he felt? When Red Hawk had found him the evening before and had told him of his talk with Sorrel, Mathew had at first laughed at the Indian's words. "The white woman would not leave your cabin to become my wife, she is in love with you, Mathew Danner." As quickly as these words had left Red Hawk's mouth Mathew had burst out laughing. The one thing that the large mountain man had been sure of was that Sorrel Morgan had wished no part of him. That was why he was out here in the freezing cold—because he had not wished to frighten the girl into trying to run away again. But as his laughter had died down his friend had stood solid and stern.

"I do not think that my words deserve your amusement, my brother."

Watching the anger beginning to form on his friend's face Mathew realized that the man was telling the truth. "I am sorry, but I have felt nothing but the bitter sting of Sorrel Morgan's beauty since first meeting her. Does she change from hatred to love so easily?"

"I do now know of her hatred, my brother, but I have seen and heard of her love." Red Hawk's words had no doubt.

Mathew had turned from the Indian and gone to the fire, throwing more logs on the flames. For a moment quiet descended on the two men, but then Mathew's voice reached Red Hawk's ears. "What would she have me do?"

The Indian knew that the words were not easily spoken by this large man but were being torn from his insides. For he could read the confusion and indecision written on Mathew's face as he looked up to him.

"I do not know your heart, Mathew Danner, but I do know that the woman is worth much and that if I could redo what I have done in the past I would have left her with her father. She does not deserve this pain that she has had forced upon her."

It was the first time that Mathew had ever heard Red Hawk speak in such a manner, and as he rose from the fire their eyes met in a deep communion. He read deep within the Indian's piercing black eyes that the latter wished for the girl not to get hurt. But Mathew himself had no idea what his true feelings were. And now, as he stood before Sorrel, he was at a loss. Still, after all the night before and the long ride back to the cabin he had no idea what he would say or do.

His blue eyes softly went over Sorrel as she sat with her eyes looking at her lap, and the night came to his mind when he had held her close and had placed light, tender kisses on the lids of those emerald eyes. A light, hazy feeling came over him with these thoughts. Could it be true what Red Hawk had said? Could this woman truly feel love for him? Without realizing how, he found himself standing directly in front of Sorrel.

Sorrel heard each of his steps, and with each footfall her heart beat erratically. She felt his blue eyes upon her and her breathing came in short, tiny gasps.

Taking up her small, delicate hand into his larger one Mathew forced Sorrel's gaze upward. For a moment the wish to grab her up from the chair and to grasp her in his arms until he could force a confession from those tempting, teasing lips came over him, but Mathew Danner was not that type of man, and slowly he tried to say the words that would lead him to the truth. "Red Hawk told me that he came here and asked you to leave my cabin and become his wife."

Once again Sorrel felt her face flush. If Red Hawk had told that to Mathew he must have told him everything. Her eyes lowered again as she worried her lip with her small perfect teeth.

Mathew reached out and slowly brought her chin up. "He told me of your reasons for saying no to him." He stood back quiet now, wishing for Sorrel to make some sort of answer.

Not knowing what to say next Sorrel took the easiest way out for herself. "Why—why, of course I did not accept his proposal."

Mathew stood there expectantly, waiting for the words that—though he had told himself did not matter one way or another to him—he had, in fact, hurried with all the speed that he could muster to get back to this cabin to hear come from her lips. Sweet, soft words of love formed in his mind and lay at rest waiting to be spoken.

Instead of saying what was in her heart as she had done with the Indian, Sorrel tried to form a hard anger as her shield. "Is that why you rushed back after leaving me here and not worrying about what would happen to me? Is that why you hurried back, with the hopes that I would be leaving to marry that red man?" She rose from her chair and put it between the two of them, the closeness of this man putting her off her ease.

What was happening here? Mathew had thought that this meeting between them would be different than those in the past. Had Red Hawk lied when he had told him that Sorrel had loved him? Anger began to grow in the depths of Mathew's chest. He was not the type of man who took lightly to jesting. If she had only told Red Hawk what she had in order to dissuade him from pursuing her she had made a mistake. "You know my reasons for leaving you here alone, Sorrel. I could not bear the thought that you might run away again. The next time you might not have been lucky enough to be rescued from your own foolishness."

"Foolishness! How dare you!" Sorrel's voice was filled with deep outrage as she pranced about the room. "You try and attack me during my sleep and then when I try to gain my freedom from you, you call it foolishness?" Going to the cabin door Sorrel threw it wide for Lancer to go out. The dog had started to become uneasy with the rising of their voices.

But before she could pull it closed she felt a hand of steel grab hold of her wrist. "Deny to me that my attack on you was so unwelcome."

The words spoken so close to her face left her breathless. How could she deny what he was saying when he was speaking the truth? She tried to pull her arm free, but to no avail. He was relentless, not saying another word but pulling her emerald eyes to his blue ones with a force of will that was shattering.

"Tell me you do not want me and I shall leave." His words touched her like a soft caress.

She shook her head, and crystal-diamond-shaped tears began to form in the depths of Sorrel's eyes and to escape one by one.

The hand that had been so hard and unyielding holding her prisoner slowly relented and gently reached out to touch one of the salted drops. He still did not know how he felt about this girl, but he knew that no other had affected him as she was now doing. Even Elizabeth had not brought him such a sweet aching pain when he looked at her. "You are beautiful."

Sorrel's eyes rose to his and within seconds she was clinging to his strong, sturdy frame.

"I cannot be away from you and I cannot stay here alone with you." Mathew's words were torn from him as he held the small, lovely beauty tightly in his arms. "I think that my brother Red Hawk had the right idea when he brought you to me."

Sorrel heard his words, as though coming from a faraway space and time. She could not fathom their meaning. She only knew that she was finally where she had wished to be for so long. The man she loved was holding her in his arms and nothing else in the world mattered at this moment.

"We shall ride to Red Hawk's village and have his shaman marry us before this very evening." Mathew's lips descended upon hers and Sorrel felt herself melt against him. Everything held within her was drawn out and made visible with that one tender kiss. She cared not where he took her or what words were said to join them—she only knew that she wanted to belong to this man. She loved him beyond anything she had known before and only wished to share everything with him.

Mathew set her from him at arm's length for a moment and looked down into her heart-shaped face. "Do you wish to be my wife Sorrel? I cannot offer you much." He looked around the cabin and for a second a vision of Crescent Mist came to his mind, but he quickly cast it aside. That had been another time, and he would not look back on it now.

With tears still wetting her cheeks Sorrel nodded her head, and then with a cry of joy she flew into his strong arms. "I am yours, Mathew Danner!"

Chapter Ten

Sorrel awoke with a slight shiver and automatically reached out and snuggled herself against the warmth of the man who was now sharing her bed. For a moment her sleepy mind went back over the day and the night before.

She had gone with Mathew, sitting in front of him on his large black horse, to Red Hawk's village. The whole afternoon now seemed like a hazy dream. As they had ridden through the valley Mathew had held her in his arms and kissed her, keeping her senses shattered and her limbs trembling.

She had watched as though from a distance as the Indian village had come before them and then as they stood before Red Hawk's lodge. Even then, with Mathew's arm around her and his nearness filling her senses, she had not been able to breathe right and let her mind settle.

She could remember meeting Red Hawk's wife, Tame Elk, and she remembered how beautiful the young woman had been. She had wondered how Red Hawk could ever have wished to have another wife, with the one he already had.

She could also remember Red Hawk himself greeting her and Mathew and the way his eyes had held her as Mathew had told him of their wish to marry here in his village. Deep in his eyes Sorrel could read pain, but she could also read on his face that he would bury this pain deep within his soul in order not to hurt his friend.

The marriage itself was a hurried affair performed by a grizzled old gray-haired Indian man who someone had said was Red Hawk's father. She had not understood a word of the ceremony but Mathew had and had spoken for her as well as himself.

Sorrel had thought for the briefest of moments as she stood before this Indian chief that her father and Aunt Corry should have been here to see her wed. But that thought, like all her others that day, had not lasted long.

It had seemed only moments before the pair were once again upon Mathew's great horse and heading back for his cabin. Barely any words were spoken between them on this ride back, and once in the cabin they were both ill at ease.

Sorrel did not know which way to turn, what was expected of her now that she was a wife.

And Mathew, feeling her unease and his own, as well, excused himself and grabbing up clean shirt and pants and a bar of strong-smelling soap headed for the icy stream at the back of the cabin.

Sorrel began to place cauldrons of water upon the hearth for her own bath as she set about preparing supper for herself and her new husband.

In short order bowls of venison stew and biscuits were on the table, and as soon as Mathew returned from outside they ate their meal, in silence. Sorrel began to clear the table and pull out the large tub that she used for her bathing. She placed this upon the fur rug before the hearth and as the water heated she poured it into the tub.

Mathew, at a loss as to what to do next, struck upon an idea as he watched his young wife preparing her bath. Rising and pushing his large frame from the chair he picked up the two water buckets and at Sorrel's questioning look he said quietly, "I shall fetch you more water."

Upon his return from the outside cold Mathew found himself struck still as he closed the door. Sorrel sat in the large tub, her golden hair piled on top of her head and the curls hanging about her face glistening from the firelight. She also stilled as she heard the front door opening, her leg raised in midair with soap on it.

Clearing his throat Mathew regained his composure, and forcing his eyes from the beauty before him he poured the buckets of water into the cauldrons upon the hearth. Once more he hurried from the room with the buckets in hand.

A small smile played upon Sorrel's pink lips as her husband left the room. He had seemed so sure of himself this afternoon before their marriage, but now he was as nervous as a young schoolboy. She herself was nervous, but seeing Mathew's discomfort she felt a little better. She loved this man, so whatever happened tonight she was more than willing to share with him.

As Mathew entered the cabin once more Sorrel hit upon an idea, and delighting in the slight flush that slowly rose upon his bearded face as she turned in the tub and looked him full in the face, she held back a small giggle and softly questioned, "Would you please pour some of the heated water into the tub, Mathew?" One finely curved brow rose with her words. "I could do it myself if you would prefer not to." She placed each slim hand upon the rim of the tub as though she was about to raise herself and have done with the job at hand.

Not realizing that she was teasing him, Mathew rushed to the hearth with the pails of water in his hand, set them aside, and hefted up the heated water and started toward the tub. Taking a large breath of air into his lungs before he looked down upon his young, beautiful wife Mathew slowly began to pour the steaming water into the tub.

Sorrel luxuriated in this new warmth, and with an inviting purr of contentment she squirmed seductively beneath the surface, the new heat adding a rosy hue to her cheeks, and from the top of her breasts and along her slim neck her color heightened.

Mathew groaned inwardly and hurrying with his task he once again left the cabin, buckets in hand.

Sorrel's soft, tinkling laughter filled the small cabin. What did this man she had married think, she smiled, that she would spend the evening in her bath? Hurriedly she stepped from the tub and dried herself. She then put on the only night clothes that she owned, one of Mathew's large white shirts. Fleetingly and with some regret she wished that she had a soft, appealing gown with which to adorn her body for this first night she would share with her husband, but with a large sigh she pulled back the covers and climbed into the soft bed.

Though she could not tell herself that she was pleased with her surroundings and the things at hand, Sorrel knew that she had wished for this man above any other. She was no longer Sorrel Morgan. As Sorrel Danner she knew that her comforts would be provided by the man that she loved.

To look back at her past life would be to look only as far as the day in Richmond at Langston's emporium and that night at the inn, for she was sure now that this man she had wed in an Indian village was the same man she had viewed from afar and had shared a few stolen moments of sweet kisses with in the inn. As she lay there awaiting her husband's return she thought back and realized that most of her life she had been searching for something, and she knew now that this something was the man she had found here in the Cumberlands. Their destinies had been linked from that first day in Richmond, and now that she had found this mountain man called Mathew Danner she would not be easily tempted away from him.

She had been taught by the good nuns that a woman, once married, was to love, honor, and cherish her husband. She could remember how, at the time of hearing this, she had laughed with glee at these foolish words. At that time she had only the prospect of marrying Clifford Sumter, and she had known that she could never love and honor a man like him. For a fleeting second the features of this tall, slim, almost angular man came to her mind. She had forgotten completely about her betrothal to Clifford Sumter, and now she saw him again as she had the night of the Shatners' ball. The arrogant twist to his lips and the dead-cold chill of his gray eyes filled her mind's eye for a full minute. A slight shiver went down her spine, but with a small sigh she put the thoughts of Clifford Sumter from her. She would not be plagued with these memories tonight. Her father would take care of whatever was necessary as a result of her having broken her marriage contract. She had no doubt that her father would be angry for a time about her inopportune marriage, but after he met her husband and saw what a good man he was she was sure he would swiftly come around. He had always said that he wished only the best for her.

Mathew brought her from her thoughts of her father and her now ex-betrothed as the door opened. Glancing about the small cabin he saw that she had at last finished her bath and awaited him in the bed.

The fire on the hearth had burnt down somewhat, leaving most of the cabin in dark shadow. Going to the cupboard Mathew pulled out his saddle bag, and though Sorrel tried to see what he was doing she could not make out his movements.

She waited in anticipation as any young bride waits for the moment of total surrender. In a few moments she felt the motion of the bed as Mathew placed his large frame on the opposite side from her.

His nervousness and shyness were no longer apparent as Mathew slid beneath the covers and his strong, large hands made their way to Sorrel and pulled her ever so gently into his embrace.

Sorrel felt the quivering of her body as she neared the man she loved, and without any restraint she let herself be pulled toward him.

Soft, lilting words of praise for her beauty gently touched upon her ears as she was pulled against Mathew's naked form. His lips lightly kissed that ear and then made a small trail of tiny kisses along her throat as his fingers lingered on the soft, velvety texture of her hair.

Sorrel felt herself once more, as she had that afternoon, slipping into a world of hazy unreality. Never before had she experienced such a feeling of desire and tenderness overwhelming her senses. She gave all to this man who was now her husband, she did not hold back. Touch for touch, caress for caress, and kiss for kiss. They were as one, as far back as from the beginning of time, and as man met woman they both discovered the true meaning of their beings.

Sorrel felt herself completely devoured. There was no pain, only tenderness given to her by this large man who brought her to the pinnacle of her womanhood.

Mathew stormed his new wife as though she was a castle, boldly breaking down every fortress and gently pushing aside each obstacle until he found the prize he sought. And with the finding of it he gloried, holding on to her as though time had become eternity and all else besides this moment was unreality.

Afterwards, as Mathew held Sorrel tightly in his embrace, her soft words of love touched at his heart. "I love you, Mathew Danner." Her soft sigh brushed upon the dark mat of hair on his chest.

Still not understanding his feelings for this woman Mathew lightly caressed her soft cheek. "Go to sleep now, my sweet," he said softly still holding her tightly against him. He lay awake far into the night and long after he felt the deep breathing against his chest that told him that his young wife had fallen into a deep sleep. What had he done? he asked himself. Had he taken this young girl for his wife only because of his desire? Had he married her only because of his baser needs? But if not, what kind of man was he? The reason for his being here in this wilderness was the fact that he had loved Elizabeth Strickland. But now, as he had in the past few weeks, he had tried to bring her vision to his mind and was at a loss. How could he have loved her so much and now be able to put her so totally from his thoughts? Was he the type to profess to love one woman with all of his heart and then just as easily to forget her in a short amount of time and turn to another? These tormenting thoughts plagued him most of the night through, but when he finally did shut his blue eyes he still did not know what his feelings were for the woman at his side.

Sorrel once more felt herself shiver from the cold and as her husband rolled over from his side and faced her she kept herself this time from cuddling up to his warmth. She lay silently, her emerald eyes studying her new husband. She saw now what she had not noticed the night before, that he had shaved his beard. That must have been what he had been doing while she awaited his coming to bed. She looked with deliberate care over every inch of his face. He was much more handsome with a clean-shaven face, she decided. His face was strong and lean, each feature finely chiseled. His dark brows were arched over eyes that she knew were as blue as the dark sea. Sorrel went over them again as she had so many times in her mind in the past. His nose fit his face to perfection, with but the slightest curve to it, adding a touch of strength and dashing appeal to his otherwise pleasant features.

As his dark blue eyes opened and stared out at Sorrel she looked back with some surprise. It was not surprise at being caught observing him in his sleep, but surprise at the recognition that dawned within her mind. He was indeed the man of her dreams, and she had thought to keep this her secret, not even to share it with him. But now, his features no longer hidden by the removal of his beard, she knew that she had also seen him thus, in a portrait hanging over a large stone mantel. Before she could think any further about this, he spoke.

Mathew stretched his body out full length and then pulled her tightly up against him. "Good morning, my pet. I hope you have slept well?"

Sorrel's smile filled his eyes. "Aye, my husband, I slept wonderfully well."

Mathew felt the bite of her words as she said *husband*. He felt uneasy at this word she so easily let flow from her lips, somehow like a betrayer or a user.

"Are you hungry, Mathew?" Sorrel questioned, starting to rise on her elbows. She wished to please Mathew in all things and not to let him find any displeasure in her actions.

"Not hungry, my pet," he rolled atop of her, "but completely famished." A leering grin came over his mouth before he lowered it to her soft, pliable lips.

"My strength seems to be sorely strained, but for the life of me I cannot understand why." His laughter now filled the cabin as he leaned over Sorrel and watched her face turn a bright red at his words.

Sorrel tried to pull herself from his arms, intending to rise from the bed and to prepare her husband his meal, but with a little pressure Mathew stayed her.

"Do not try and flee me so soon, my love." His lips again sought out those below him, and, gently, with a searing tongue of desire, he probed and delved into the sweetness of her mouth.

Their love was like the night before, a blinding, consuming, overwhelming passion that spiraled to heights that neither had ever before experienced. Their senses were so fully attuned, so deeply enmeshed within the intensity of the moment, that there was no room for thought or deed of the outside world. All that mattered was here on this soft bed of furs.

Their kisses were full and inviting, giving without reserve, sending both to dizzying heights of abandon as their bodies melted and fused, becoming one with their total consummation.

Their bodies strained together, eagerly devouring this strong draught of love, Sorrel delighting and responding to her husband's every touch, lost to all but the sheer, burning ecstasy that had built up so brilliantly within her. With a towering clash of bursting embers, she was brought to a consuming passion.

Mathew also was brought to new heights in their burning ardor. And as their passions ebbed and he was brought back to the reality about him he held tightly on to this radiant flower that had swept so unexpectedly into his life. He reflected over the short time he had known this woman and the sweetness of her giving to him. There was more here, he knew, than the delicate intimacies of the everyday man and wife. There was a binding of the senses, a complete giving and sharing that he had never known before. But still he felt a pull to stay apart, to keep at a distance before he became totally lost to the feelings stirring within his soul.

After a few moments of this quiet reflection over what they had just shared, Sorrel pulled from her husband's side and started to climb from the confines of the bed. "I will put on your coffee and start the biscuits," she said, hurriedly pulling the shirt from her young body and putting on in its stead the dress that she had received from Red Hawk.

Mathew fluffed the pillows behind his head and watched his young bride scamper about the cabin, first building up the fire in the hearth and then starting their meal. She was beautiful, he thought, letting his eyes roam over her curves, his mind going over the night past and the moments just before. As his thoughts took flight he brought his hand up and rubbed his chin. Finding his beard missing he was once more reminded of the eyes watching him so intently as he had awakened. What had she thought on seeing him without his dark beard? Had she liked what she had seen, or had she somehow been disappointed? Knowing that the only way to get an answer was to ask her, he started. "Tell me sweet, what do you think of the real me?" Still his hand rubbed his chin as she looked up from putting the coffee on to boil.

A slight flush caressed Sorrel's features as she thought over how she had lain and gone over her husband's face, and now for the first time she realized that he had caught her in her admiration of him.

Mathew sensed her embarrassment and his deep-throated laughter bounced off the walls of the small cabin. "Come now, sweet, I assure you it was a pleasure to awake and find such beautiful eyes looking up into my face. After sleeping on that hard floor for the past weeks I more than promise you that everything about sleeping with you here in this bed was a pleasure."

A small smile came to Sorrel's face at his words, and as she turned back to her meal the soft words came to Mathew, "I think you are indeed quite handsome, Mathew."

Mathew's pleasure was more than obvious as he smiled at her words. He would not have known what else to do but grow back his beard if she had found some fault with his looks, but from her soft words he knew that she was speaking the truth and was pleased with him.

His mood seemed to grow serious as he watched her preparing their meal. Still in this mood he rose and dressed and sat at the table.

Sorrel smiled at him as she placed a steaming cup of coffee in front of him.

"Perhaps we could go for a ride later in the day when the sun comes out."

Sorrel looked up expectantly. "I would love to."

"We won't go too far to tax my steed's strength, but perhaps a small way." Mathew started to eat the food before him, feeling some pride in seeing the way Sorrel's face lit up at his words.

Sorrel remembered their ride yesterday to the Indian village and a flush covered her face. She could not wait to be gone from this cabin and once again to be held in her husband's strong arms.

As soon as the meal was cleared away the couple made their way to Mathew's horse. They went in the opposite direction from the Indian village and Sorrel thought they seemed to go deeper into the forest. Lancer happily followed, either running on ahead or trailing behind, his nose always at the ready for the scent of a wild animal, be it large or small.

Mathew told Sorrel much about their surroundings that she had not known before. He pointed out whatever naked vegetation could be seen sticking out of the snow, explained the name of each and the uses they had in either healing or harming.

Sorrel was amazed at the knowledgea that this huge mountain man possessed and once again she wondered what kind of man she was married to. He seemed so strong, but then he could be so gentle. He had knowledge of everything about him and seemed at ease with every subject.

She did not have time to dwell on these thoughts for long. As they rode on they came into a clearing. She spotted a pond at the far end, a sparkling waterfall showered down crystal water.

Mathew jumped down from the back of his horse and brought Sorrel down beside him. Before releasing his hold upon her waist his lips descended to her own, and for a time she was held captive by his mouth.

"I want to show you something." Mathew gently released her with a smile that left her standing breathless. Laughing loudly he took hold of her hand and pulled her along after him. "If it is to be a trapper's wife you are going to be, madam, you had better learn to be a bit quicker on your feet."

Sorrel took his words, though he had said them jokingly, as a rebuke, and tried to hurry her pace behind him. "I am sorry for lagging, Mathew." She was truly sorry and wished to please him, but for the life of her she didn't know how she could change. Each time he touched her she seemed to melt. And if he wished for her to be quicker about his business, she reasoned with herself, then he should not kiss her in the manner that he did, though she would not dare to tell him this.

The scenery about them was beautiful. Sorrel looked to the water's edge and could see in her mind the lush green of the summer grass surrounding the pond and teeming with flowers.

Though Mathew had tried to cast everything of his past from his mind, something about this special spot pulled at him each time he came near it. Something of the Lord seemed to call out to him, to make him turn about and look back down his path. So many times since first finding this pond he had told himself that he would not return, but always he found himself standing in this same spot.

Sorrel, after taking it all in, looked up to her

husband, and as she watched his face she was struck again, as she had been that morning, with the conviction that she had somehow met or seen him somewhere before in her past. This was impossible, she told herself, as she looked deeper into his face, finding this task now an easy one, since he was totally engrossed in his surroundings. If she had somehow ever met this man in the past, she would never have forgotten him, she was sure of that.

"Are you going to make it a habit of watching me, my pet?" Mathew's deep blue eyes twinkled as he brought them down to her emerald ones.

"Oh, I am sorry. I did not mean to stare." Sorrel tried to apologize and was truly distressed at being caught in her perusal of him again.

"Come along, Sorrel." He seemed not to have heard her words and once again took hold of her hand and started around the edge of the pond. "One day I was here fishing, and I found this." They were nearing the waterfall, and Sorrel covered her ears at the loud noise the gushing water made.

She pulled back as Mathew started toward the falls, making his way up a small incline at the base of the water.

"Come pet, I would not let any harm befall you." His blue eyes looked deep into her own and all her resistance seemed to vanish. Sorrel knew at that moment that anywhere this man led she would follow.

Keeping hold of her hand, Mathew, as though by some twist of magic, pulled Sorrel behind the falls. Barely a drop of water touched either of them as he pulled her into his grasp and turned her about facing the water.

Gasping aloud Sorrel now looked out at the pond from a different angle. She turned about to question Mathew. "But how?"

"It seems that beyond these falls there is a cave. I had no idea about it until one day, when I was fishing, I decided to go for a swim. I wanted to dive into the falls and I came up on that ledge. I ventured a bit further and found what was behind the water."

Sorrel now looked over her husband's shoulder and saw the cave he spoke of. It was actually only a large indentation in the cliff, but it was large enough for the two of them to stand comfortably and watch the outside world. Sorrel shivered a bit, feeling even in her husband's fur jacket the coolness of the falls and the crisp weather.

"We had best start back," Mathew said, taking her lips once more before letting her go. "It is getting late and besides I see Lancer sniffing about at the pond's edge and not able to see us. If he finds our scent leading behind these falls he will surely set up such a howling that our ears will ring for days."

Sorrel's laughter joined her husband's as he took her hand and started back out of the cave and down the cliff. Upon second reflection, though, Mathew gathered up his small wife into his arms and began to carry her snuggled tightly against his chest.

Sorrel did not argue, she rather liked being in his arms and delighted in the feel of his large muscles through his jacket.

The ride home was slow and leisurely, with stolen

kisses and tender caresses on the way.

As the great black beast stopped outside the cabin door Mathew slid to his feet, and taking Sorrel in his arms he pushed the door open and carried her over the threshold, depositing her without much preamble in the middle of the bed.

As she started to her feet Mathew held her with his hands reaching out and pushed her softly backwards.

"But, Mathew, you must be starving. It will only take a moment to prepare something for you." Sorrel was trying to be an adequate wife to this man, and as they had been riding home she had thought over what she would prepare him for his dinner.

"I can see that I shall have my work cut out for me, Mrs. Danner," Mathew smiled down at her as he pulled his jacket from his shoulders.

"What do you mean Mathew? Is there something wrong?"

He did not let her finish, but fell down on the bed beside her. Taking great care he pulled her fragile chin up toward him and murmured before his mouth overtook hers, "Your thoughts are always upon my belly and not where they should be, my love."

Sorrel released a small giggle before his mouth worked the usual effect upon her senses and brought her into the world where only he could lead her.

Mathew's smoldering sapphire eyes stormed with their desire, and as Sorrel looked into their depths she became breathless as they boldly raked over her delicate features.

Within seconds Sorrel found herself helping him

discard their clothing, and when they were naked Mathew once again let his gaze wander over her, taking in all her finely hewed curves.

Sorrel felt the eyes upon her as though a physical invitation to desire, and trembling with the intensity of her need she wrapped her sleek arms about his neck and pulled his head toward her, pressing her soft lips to his, her small, tempting tongue going in and out between his teeth and then meeting his own with a fiery explosion.

Like Sorrel, Mathew felt his need greater than any he had had before, and with purposeful intent they came together as one. Their love, union, and hearts joined as binding as a reed. As far back as time immemorial this was meant to be. This woman was his, and this man was hers, and if the very earth were to open up its bowels and swallow them, they would still be one. For this great love was meant to be and nothing could set them apart.

They were caught upon the bed, the light growing dim and the air growing chilled, but they took notice of nothing but the rapturous bliss they were giving and sharing with each other.

As the days passed the young couple's life was like that of any young married pair's. Their isolation was their honeymoon, their chance to learn each other's ways, likes and dislikes. The snowflakes that covered the outside world wrapped the two inside the cabin into a cocoon of sharing, and they grew close.

Sorrel was more than pleased with the man she had

married. Each day was more wonderful than the last. The Mathew Danner she had met so long ago now seemed to have completely vanished. Where there had been his cold anger there were now only tender and consoling words of concern. Their days were shared in walking the forest and talking, and their nights were shared in each other's arms, learning each other's wants and desires. These nights were the most special to Sorrel, for afterwards, with only the hissing and crackling of the fire in the hearth filling the quiet cabin, the pair upon the bed would quietly talk.

During these nightly talks Sorrel had told her husband all about her past. She told him about her father and her Aunt Corry and what her life had been like before. She left nothing out. Mathew's laughter had filled the small room as she had told him of her exploits at school and how wild she had been as a young girl.

"You still have not much changed on that account," he had laughed aloud, pulling her tightly into his embrace and putting an end to their conversations for that night.

Mathew though, was not as free with his words as his wife. Still Sorrel barely knew anything about the past of this man she called husband. He had volunteered one evening that he had gone to Europe and been in school there, and he had told Sorrel about some of the adventures he and friends had had. But he never told too much, and Sorrel found that no matter how much she tried to pry he would easily turn the subject about if he did not wish to talk about what she wanted to hear.

The fact that he had had his schooling in Europe disturbed Sorrel. Why was a man of Mathew's intelligence and obvious breeding hiding himself away here in the Cumberlands and hunting and trapping for his survival? All manner of thoughts came to her mind, but she cast each one from her. She had wondered one day if perhaps her husband was a criminal and was fleeing from the authorities, but quickly she tried to dash this from her mind. He was too good a man to get himself into serious trouble. But still this doubt plagued her at the strangest times. He seemed to be hiding from something or someone, and though she was his wife she felt—or rather, knew—that he was holding things back from her. She could only hope that with the passing of time he would trust her more.

The days seemed to slowly, as they are wont to do, glide into weeks, and those weeks turned to months, and still the snow lingered on.

For the past several mornings Sorrel had not felt too well on first rising, so Mathew had taken it upon himself to get up and start the fire in the hearth and put the coffee on to boil.

But this morning shortly after his rising Lancer began to bark, letting the couple know that someone was approaching.

Mathew went to the window and peered out, remarking quietly as he went back to the hearth and warmed his hands that Red Hawk was making his way down the valley.

Sorrel hurriedly scampered from the confines of

the furs upon the bed and rushed about dressing herself and brushing her hair.

For the first time Mathew looked askew at his young wife. "If you feel unwell this morning, Sorrel, you do not have to rise. I can talk to Red Hawk outside." What was this small stabbing pain he felt as he thought back to the way he had seen the Indian watch the young girl who was now his wife? He tried to push this thought to the back of his mind, reasoning with himself that he only wished to watch over what was his.

"I feel fine, Mathew." Sorrel patted the curls about her face into place. "I would not wish for your friend to think that your wife stays abed all the day." She smiled up toward the man she was so in love with, but shortly her smile froze upon her face as she saw the scowl that was cast toward her by the man she most cherished. She was reminded again of the long ago days when each word she uttered seemed to bring about Mathew's anger. "What is it Mathew? Have I done something to displease you?" Her apparent fright at being the object of his wrath so unnerved him that he went to her and took her into his arms.

"You could never do anything to so upset me, sweet. I am sorry for letting you think that I was angry. Come, let us greet our company together." He pulled her to the door and opened it wide, his arm about his bride as his Indian brother halted his horse outside the front of the cabin.

"I see that you and your wife are well, Mathew, my brother," Red Hawk greeted them as he jumped from his horse and made his way to the cabin.

"Aye, my friend. We are fit indeed." Mathew turned about and stepped into the cabin, letting the Indian into his home. "Come in and sit and have a cup of coffee."

"I would like that, Mathew." Red Hawk followed them into the cabin and took the opposite chair from Mathew.

Sorrel quickly poured the coffee into the cups without looking directly at either man, for she was still confused by Mathew's earlier actions. She set about making up their bed and putting their home into order.

The two men talked quietly about matters that only concerned themselves. Leisurely as they sipped their coffee Red Hawk told Mathew that he was planning a hunting trip. That was the reason for his visit. He would be gone only two weeks and would like for his white brother to come with him. It was a long time since the two of them had been together on a hunting trip and he was anxious for them to make one now.

Mathew had not answered right away but had let his blue eyes go to Sorrel as she leaned over straightening out the bedclothes. He had no wish to leave his bride so soon. He had spent too many long, lonely nights. Perhaps Red Hawk relished the idea of a hunting trip with just the two of them but Mathew was of a different mind now that he had tasted the joys of sharing each day and night with his beautiful wife.

Red Hawk also followed Mathew's eyes and watched the young woman at her task. He studied her for a moment and as she turned about and looked toward them and then hurriedly went about straightening out the rest of the furs a small laugh came from the Indian. "I see, my brother, that you have not wasted these cold nights that the great Father has sent to us. Your woman shall bear you a fine son."

Mathew watched the Indian's face as he said each word, the meaning slowly making contact with his brain. "What are you saying, Red Hawk? My wife is not with child."

"You may know the forest almost as well as an Indian, my brother, but you do not know your own woman?" Red Hawk asked in some surprise. How could a man not know when his own woman was to bear him an offspring? "Have you not noticed the new beauty of your woman, my brother? Perhaps I do more easily than you because I have not been to your cabin in some time." He tried to find an excuse for Mathew's no knowing this simple fact about his wife.

Things seemed to crowd in at Mathew's brain. The sickness in the mornings, the new softness that radiated from her gentle features with each look she sent his way, and then the most important fact of all hit his mind: They had been man and wife now for well over ten weeks, and she had not in that time had her womanly time of the month.

Red Hawk watched his friend intently and knew the moment that Mathew realized that his words were true.

"I did not even think." Mathew wiped at his brow,

his eyes once more going to the woman across the room. She was carrying his child within her? What had Red Hawk said—she would give him a fine son? Was this red man so knowledgeable that he could even tell the baby's gender? The blue eyes turned again toward the man sitting opposite him.

"Mathew Danner, do not worry over this. Your woman probably does not even know herself yet. My people live by nature and learn at a young age the things of this earth."

Mathew could only nod his head in agreement. Of course Sorrel did not know as yet that she was with child. It was a rare occurrence that a man knew even before his wife that he was to be a father.

Mathew's mood turned solemn and quiet, and after he had barely murmured a reply to Red Hawk's conversation, the Indian rose from his chair and started to bid his good-byes.

"You will not wish to leave your woman now, my brother, so I shall go alone up to the great forest. I shall bring you back some meat," he added, laughing over his shoulder as he went through the door.

Not even rising from the table to see his friend out Mathew only nodded his head at the red man's words.

As the Indian made his departure Sorrel came to the table and looked down toward her husband. He looked so enraptured that she dreaded disturbing him. But as she refilled his coffee cup his head rose and his blue eyes stared up into hers.

"Would you care for some breakfast, Mathew?" she ventured, feeling a strangeness in the intensity of his gaze.

"No-no, do not bother yourself."

"It would be no bother, Mathew. I enjoy cooking for you." Sorrel thought she heard displeasure in his tone and wished for nothing more than to please him in any way that she could.

Mathew's gaze softened somewhat as he saw the expression of bewilderment that crossed over her lovely features. Should he tell her what Red Hawk had imparted to him? he wondered as he watched her. Should he tell her that she was at this moment carrying his child? But, thinking these thoughts, he could not come to frame them in the right words to come out of his mouth. In fact he did not even know what his thoughts were. Everything seemed to be happening so quickly. First he had found this lovely creature here in his cabin, and then, when he discovered that he could not resist her, he married her, and now, in only a short amount of time, he found that she was to bear him a child. His hand rose to his brow and he rubbed at his temples, trying to clear his mind.

Sorrel caught this movement at once, and with a worried look she questioned, "Do you feel unwell, Mathew? Are you taken ill?"

Her look was genuinely filled with concern. She had no idea what she would do if this man were to become ill. She had never learned the art of medicine or healing, in fact, she had never even been around any sick people before in her life. Oh, her Aunt Corry had always seemed to have attacks of her head, but Sorrel had the idea that these attacks were always brought on when her aunt wished to have her own way. For a fleeting moment the thought filled her mind's eye of her large, healthy, virile husband lying abed ill, with only her to help in his care.

Her worry registered quite clearly on her face, and with a small laugh Mathew rose to his feet and took his wife into his strong arms. "Do not be concerned with any fears on my account, my pet. I am as healthy as an ox." He brushed her lips lightly with his own and felt the sweet magic that was always there for him. It was a blinding conjuring of spells, which could sweep him up into a world of unreality and passion when he was with this woman.

Sorrel felt the truth of his words. He was as strong and sturdy as ever before, she thought for a brief second before his lips and tongue drove all thought from her mind.

"Must I prove to you every hour, my precious, that I am hale and hearty?" His deep-throated words softly caressed Sorrel's ears as he scooped her up into his arms and slowly made his way back to the bed they had only left a short time ago.

"Aye, Mathew, every hour." The softly spoken words mingled with his own as Sorrel lightly brought her hands up and rubbed the black hair matting his expansive chest. She never seemed to grow tired of this man. She felt empty without him near, and without his arms about her she seemed always on the edge of wanting. He was her substance, her sturdy support to lean upon, and she would not wish to exist without him now.

Mathew was as eager for this woman as she for him, and chasing away Red Hawk's visit and his words of nature and babies, he, with only one thought now in his brain, began to place small, tantalizing kisses upon her face and neck, and before more time passed the delicious, giddy feeling of rapture totally consumed the both of them, leaving room only for them to touch, feel, and smell—to delight in the realms of their own making.

Chapter Eleven

Often lovers lose themselves in the giving and taking of the simplest of acts, and for the next few weeks Sorrel and Mathew became even more involved with each other and their mutual life than they had been before.

Sorrel felt that Mathew grew more loving and caring with each passing day. Upon occasion she would catch Mathew watching her at unexpected moments with that same quiet, wondering look that she had seen for the first time the day that Red Hawk had paid his visit. This unexpected watching of her never lasted long, though, as she always questioned him about what was the matter and was reassured by his words that her concern was for nothing.

She never stopped wondering what the following day would bring. She seemed to be living in a fool's paradise, playing games with the truth. She still knew little of this man who was her husband, and with each passing day her curiosity grew bolder with her need to know more. What was it that he thought about at those odd moments? she wondered almost daily now. How could he not give her some clue as to what was eating at him? She was so wrapped up in thinking about Mathew that she didn't notice the changes that were beginning to come over her own body.

Mathew, however, noticed them all. She seemed to grow more beautiful each time he looked at her. Still he did not confess to her that he knew that she was carrying his child. Some small, nagging fear would come over him every time he would begin to bring up the subject of children. He was still not even sure that he wished for children, and once he voiced the fact aloud to her that they were to have a child he felt that everything would be put into motion and there would be no way out. He knew that this was irrational thinking, for it was already too late to change what was to be, but still he dreaded the moment that she would know the truth for herself.

And for Sorrel the truth was not long in coming.

Sorrel's morning sickness had left her days ago, but one morning as she wriggled into her dress she looked with a new eye at her figure. The dress seemed to be tighter as she smoothed it down over her hips. Had it shrunk in the washing that she had given it yesterday, she wondered as she tried to peer over her shoulder and look down her trim back. She had never had to worry about her weight before, but now she began to think back on the other day when she had been bathing and had noticed for the first time that her breasts were a bit fuller.

When Mathew rose from the bed and sat down to his breakfast he found that his wife was not going to join him. "What is it, Sorrel?" he questioned as he peered at her with one brow arched.

"Nothing is the matter, Mathew," she responded, pouring his coffee.

Starting to take a bite of his food his eyes went once more to his young wife, who was sitting across from him and watching his every movement. "Is it something that I have done that is disturbing you, madam?" He placed his fork back upon his plate and looked her full in the face.

"Why no, Mathew." She flushed at being so rebuked for her impolite staring. She always wanted to watch him and now she had caused him to become angry.

"Then why, pray tell, have you not fixed yourself a plate? Do you intend to sit the meal through watching my every move?" There was a tender chiding to his tone that was lost upon his wife.

Quick tears came to Sorrel's emerald eyes. "I do not wish to eat this morning, Mathew." She hung her head now, not wishing to tell him that she had planned earlier this morning not to eat breakfast and to eat sparingly from now on. Married life seemed to have agreed a bit too well with her, she thought, and if she did not put some restraint upon herself she would soon be as large as a house. She was sure that such a woman would not be able to keep her husband's eye for long.

Mathew once more picked up his fork and began to eat. Chewing a tender morsel of meat he watched his wife and reflected on her words. Was she not feeling well this morning? Was it normal for a woman in her condition to not wish to eat the first thing in the morning, or was there something else the matter? He would have to watch her and make sure that she was not becoming ill. This marriage of his seemed to be becoming more and more of a problem.

Finding herself alone in the cabin after breakfast Sorrel decided that she would give the small building a thorough cleaning. She and Mathew had been in each other's company so much these past weeks that she had barely spent any time cleaning the cabin. Now, with Mathew out chopping wood and tending to his horse she would have some time to do it. She had always loved to help in her Aunt Corry's home, and now here in the wilderness with only herself to tend to all that needed doing she relished the work. She did the dishes, and then, reasoning that perhaps she was gaining weight because she had not been as active as she was used to being, pulled out a bucket of water and started to scrub the wood floor of the cabin.

Time went by slowly and Sorrel had to stop often during her work and straighten and rub the small of her back. Down here on her hands and knees the small cabin seemed to take on monstrous proportions. She could barely wait to finish the job. When she was almost done the door swung open and her husband stepped into the room.

"Wait, Mathew," she called from her position on the floor, looking up at the looming figure over her. She hoped to dissuade him from stomping across the floor and dirtying it after the time she had spent getting it clean.

"What are you doing?" His voice was not loving and kind as she was used to but was hard and cold. "Are you out of your mind, woman?" He stepped into the cabin and reached down and pulled her up by the arms.

Sorrel could not understand him. "I was but scrubbing the floor, Mathew. It was in dire need of this scrubbing, and I should be ashamed that I have left it for so long." One of her hands brushed at the curls that were now hanging loose about her face and enabling her to view her husband as she wished.

Mathew took a deep breath before he continued. He cautioned himself that this was really his fault. He was the one who was not confiding in this woman and if any harm were to befall her because of this affair he had only himself to blame. "I do not wish you to do such labor again, Sorrel." His tone was still firm as he also brushed at her unruly curls.

"But Mathew, I am only doing the job of any housewife." Her confusion was plainly apparent upon her features.

"Do not argue with me on this subject. You are my wife and I alone shall decide what is your job. You do enough by preparing my meals and keeping my bed warm at night." He looked about at the sparkling clean room and once more red-hot anger filled his face.

"You will tell me what I can do?" Sorrel's voice rose as she looked up into the angry face. "How dare you! I have never been told what I can do and what I cannot, and if I wish to scrub a floor I shall." This was the first time since their marriage that she had raised her voice to her husband but Sorrel felt great anger at his words. Fix his meals and warm his bed, indeed. She was not a servant to be told what to do and the sooner he was made aware of this fact the better off they would both be. Swinging about she once more stooped to her knees and picked up her cloth from the bucket of now filthy water. Sloshing the wet cloth upon the floor at his feet she began to scrub.

"Sorrel, I am warning you," Mathew seethed between gritted teeth. He was not used to being disobeyed and he would not have this slip of a girl bringing harm upon herself because of her stubbornness. "Get up from that floor this minute."

Sorrel's only answer was to glare back at him from her position on the floor.

Reaching down Mathew took hold of his wife once more. "I shall tell you what you can do." He took the rag from her clenched hand and carrying her over to the chair before the hearth he put her down. Turning about he went to the bucket of water and looking down he saw the small spot where she had not yet scrubbed. For a moment his thoughts ran wild but finally he bent down and mopped up the rest of the wood floor. Finishing, he took bucket and rag and without a backward glance at his wife he went through the door and outside.

Sorrel watched her husband's retreating back in amazement. What kind of man was she married to? He would take it upon himself to scrub a floor in order not to have his wife do it? She shook her head trying to make some sense of the last few minutes. She squirmed a bit in the chair, feeling the tension pull in her back, and though she would never have admitted it she was glad to see the last of the bucket of water.

The rest of the afternoon passed in relative silence. Mathew came in for a few minutes at lunchtime but as soon as he finished he went out again, leaving

Sorrel to the quiet of the cabin.

Late in the afternoon Sorrel took water bucket in hand and started toward the stream. She glanced about trying to see what had kept Mathew the whole day out in the cold, and there on top of his horse's lean-to was her husband putting the finishing touches to the repairs on the roof.

On seeing Sorrel and noticing what her intentions were Mathew jumped down from the roof and quickly caught up with her. Taking the bucket from her hand he said, "I'll help you, love." His words were softly spoken and Sorrel knew that he wished to make amends, but her ire had been roused and it was hard for her to relinquish her anger.

"I am quite capable of doing this small chore," she replied.

Mathew knew that she was still angry and he felt she had good reason. He had been a bit cruel to her that morning, and all day as he had worked he had thought of ways to take back what he had said. It was indeed past time for him to talk to her about what had been plaguing him and put some kind of order into their lives, but for the life of him he did not know how to approach the subject. Each time an idea came to his mind he discarded it. Was he to come out and say, you cannot do such work, for you are to bear me a child? And then what of her joy—would he dash that with his not knowing how he truly felt? Would he perhaps turn her from him and from the child in her womb? He did not speak to her again but went to the stream and dipped the bucket and pulled it up filled with icy water.

"Thank you," she said, her tone as cold as the

winter wind blowing through the valley.

Not answering, Mathew started back to the cabin with Sorrel following. He did not tarry long inside but hefted up the buckets once again and started back to the stream. He knew that bath water would be needed and he did not want to find Sorrel again carrying the heavy buckets of water from the stream to the house.

Sorrel was truly relieved, for her day's activities had drained her strength somewhat, and with the tension she was feeling from her displeasure with her husband she wished nothing more than to fall across the bed and cry out all of her frustrations. This, though, she knew she could not do. She had never in her past been so easily upset, and bracing her backbone she promised herself that she would not now let her true feelings show.

It was much later that evening before Sorrel was able to set her tired body down in the warm water of her bath. Mathew sat near the hearth reading, his eyes seeming to stare through the pages and not notice his young wife as she disrobed and set about her nightly toilet.

Sorrel sighed with relief and pleasure as she felt the warm, soothing water healing the tension and tightness of her limbs. She was thoroughly amazed that such little work could weary her so. But then, she reasoned, this was the first time in her life that she had bent down and completely scrubbed a floor.

After lathering her body with the creamy soap and rinsing each portion of her well-cleansed skin with her sponge she leaned back against the rim and shut her eyes, now wishing only to enjoy the radiating warmth that was all around her.

Mathew, who had tried to concentrate on reading but had been sorely tested with each movement of his wife, finally put the book aside and let his dark blue eyes feast at their leisure. She seemed almost asleep there in her bath, and he found that he could watch her without her knowledge and this fact pleased him. She was so beautiful, he thought to himself. She could almost bring tears to his eyes with her beauty and her soft, gentle ways. His heart pained him for a moment as he thought over his cruelty toward her that day. Rising from his chair he went to the side of the tub on silent feet, bringing the chair he had been sitting on in his wake. Setting it down, he sat and watched her from a closer distance.

He had been right in his assumption that she was asleep, her small, shallow breaths told him that she was indeed sleeping. With what seemed a will of its own, his large, sunbrowned hand reached down into the water and gently touched the soft skin that covered his child. A tenderness filled him at this moment that he had never known before. His child was in this woman's body. A babe made out of their bodies and their love.

Sorrel slowly woke as she felt herself being touched. Her large emerald eyes looked up into Mathew's. The first thought that came to her mind was that he also had noticed the extra weight she had gained and for some reason he was feeling her new roundness. "I seem to be gaining a bit of weight." She blushed at her own words, but when none were forthcoming from her husband she continued. "It must be that I am used to a more active life, but it will be only a short time before I am back to my usual self."

At her words Mathew now understood why she had skipped her meal that morning and why she had only picked at the food before her during the rest of the day, and he even realized now why she had scrubbed the floor as she had. She thought she had a weight problem and that she had been lax and eating too much! Laughter started to ripple from Mathew's lips as he saw the seriousness in her gaze.

Sorrel saw no reason for his mirth and started to push at his hand. She would not have him rubbing her belly and laughing at her as though this were some great joke.

"Oh, pet, how sweet and innocent you are," he murmured, not letting her disengage his hand from where it wished to go. "You truly have no idea, do you?" Mathew's words were softly spoken, as though to a young child.

Something in his words, perhaps the tone in which they were spoken, drew her attention and she stopped pushing him away and watched his blue eyes intently. Shaking her head back and forth she worried her lower lip. "What do you mean? I have no idea about what?" Deep within her there was a dawning of his meaning and something vibrant stirred within her being.

"You are carrying our child in you, Sorrel."

Sorrel's emerald eyes became twin saucers of wonder as she looked deep into her husband's face to find the truth of his words. "But how . . ." She could not finish she was so confused.

"How do I know? I must admit that it was by no

means my own genius, sweet, that I came up with the knowledge of your delicate condition." Mathew paused here, taking a deep breath of air into his lungs before he went on. "You remember that day weeks ago when Red Hawk paid his call?" He waited for the nodding of her head that indicated that she did indeed remember. "I am afraid, love, that our friend Red Hawk is quite a bit more observant than your husband."

"You mean he knew that day that I was pregnant?" Sorrel could not believe her ears. How could he have known so soon? She and Mathew had not been married very long, in fact she thought back and knew that it had not been much longer than a few months.

"He explained that morning how he knew, and I guess I did not fully take him at his word, but I have watched over you and after today's episode of your scrubbing the floor I decided that it was time for me to announce the good news." Mathew left out that the truth of the matter was that he was not sure of his own feelings, and that that was why he had lingered with his news, but he knew in his heart that speaking his confusion aloud could only bring heartache to Sorrel, so he bore his feelings in silence and smiled down upon her.

Sorrel still could not fully grasp the meaning of the words that were falling upon her ears. "But it is not possible, Mathew." She tried out of desperation to reason with herself and her husband. "Every woman knows when she is carrying a child in her body. How could I be so different?" Was it true that she was to bear a babe, and that she was not just growing lazy and a bit plump?

Now that Mathew had set the thing into motion his patience was enduring and he began calmly to explain. Rubbing his knuckles gently across her cheek he started. "Have you not noticed that we have been married now for a few months and during that time you have not had even once your monthly time?"

"But . . ." Sorrel started to interrupt, her face flaming at his personal words.

"Do you not remember the sickness that struck you for a few weeks each morning? I have been told that some women keep this sickness during the whole course of their pregnancy."

Sorrel did remember this and now she began to remember other things about her body—the soreness of her breasts, and the way that she would suddenly, at the oddest times, get the wildest cravings for the strangest foods, things that they did not even have here at the cabin. Were these the signs that most other women knew and expected in order to tell that they were to have a child? All of a sudden she felt really bewildered—she had thought she was getting fat and now here was Mathew telling her that she was to have a baby.

As though reading her mind, Mathew knew exactly what his lovely wife was thinking, and seeing the lost look on her face he silently reached down into the now warm water and gathered her up tight against his chest. "Everything will be fine, pet. Do not fret so."

"But Mathew, a baby!" she moaned as though all her world were coming to a calamity. With the reality fast sinking in, Sorrel's mind was quickly touching on the disadvantages of having a child at this time.

"That's right, sweet, a baby. Our bond is truly sealed now, for all time." He set her down and dried her body with tender ministrations and then once more picked her up and brought her to the bed. "You will make a fine mother to my son, my pet."

Snuggling beneath the fur covers Sorrel looked at her husband. "It is true, then, Mathew? We shall have a child?"

He noticed for the first time as he began to undress himself the light of growing happiness streaming from deep within the emerald eyes gazing up into his own. "Aye, love, 'tis true." And with this first stirring of gladness in her, Mathew himself began to feel a growing pride. Perhaps all of his worry over the babe had been for naught, what harm was there in a tiny infant? He grinned boldly as he sat on the bed and jerked off his boots and then his pants. In the past he had always been fond of children and had even dreamed in days gone by of children of his own. He tried to strike from his mind the small, perfect-featured blond-haired children that he had wished to have with Elizabeth. What if this child of his dreams did not have Elizabeth Strickland as its mother? Would he not feel still the instinct to love his own son or daughter, given to him by Sorrel? He had not let himself think along these lines before, and now for the first time in weeks he felt a great relief fill him.

Resting her hand lightly upon her abdomen Sorrel smiled in wonder to herself. She was to be a mother. All that she had been dealt in the past was as nothing, all the twists that fate had made in her life, she now knew, were only to lead her to this isolated cabin and to let her receive this most treasured prize. A babe born out of her love for this man. What had Mathew said? "Their bond was truly sealed now, with a child on the way." Her bond had been sealed that day in the Indian village, but if this child was what Mathew needed to link them more closely, let it be so. She loved this man beyond all reason and to have his child was a part of this love. She would give this babe the most tender mother's care and with a mother's loving eye she would watch it grow as strong and as good as its father.

"What is it that has you smiling, Sorrel?" Mathew climbed between the covers and pulled his wife up tightly in his embrace. "Does the thought of the child please you so much?"

"Oh yes, Mathew," she breathed as she placed a light kiss upon his firm chin. "I am more than pleased, it is as though I have only started to live." She could not seem to tell him in words how she was feeling within her heart.

"I should have told you sooner pet, so we could have been sharing this joy." His lips swooped down upon hers as though they were birds of prey, and within minutes all thoughts other than those of themselves had flown.

Their loving that evening was as no other time in their past. Mathew held himself back with tenderness and regard for her wishes. Each touch between them was lingering and desiring of special response.

Their bodies molded together to form one, one desire, one will, one object, striving to gather together all their hidden feeling and to consummate that feeling in a building, crashing maelstrom of total surrender and love.

As though passing by on the swift golden wings of love, time quickly flew. Each day followed a fleeting pattern of swiftness, devouring all lingering moments. As the snows upon the passes began to melt and all the land throughout the Cumberlands became a majestic picture of green and beauty, Sorrel Danner flourished, becoming lovelier with the changing of the season.

Her belly grew as swiftly as her beauty, and by the time that it was finally possible to leave the valley, it was apparent that Sorrel was in no condition to make such a journey.

"Try to put such thoughts from your mind, love." Mathew lightly let his large hand pat the protruding mound that was now his wife's shape. "You are in no condition to make a long journey and I would not chance such a trip."

"But, Mathew, you must realize that we can no longer stay here in this valley. My father will be sick with worry as it is. Any further delay would be much more than cruel." Sorrel tried to reason with Mathew once again. For the past month, ever since the weather had shown signs of warming, she had on every possible occasion tried to sway his mind about staying here in the Cumberlands until the birth of the baby. "I would surely be able to ride, Mathew." Even her own look as she glanced down at her figure betrayed some doubt as to the truth of these words.

Mathew pulled her into his arms and tightly molded her form to his own, his laughter filling the confines of the room. "You, my pet, would not be able to endure even a small trip, let alone days of riding." As he looked down into her face and saw her lip slightly quivering his tone softened. This was the only time that he felt close to losing his temper at his beautiful young wife—whenever she broached the subject of their leaving this valley and going back into the outside world. He knew within himself that he was not yet ready to make such a step. He still felt the need to stay here in this isolated area as though hiding away from all reality. He argued with himself time and again that all he needed was this cabin, and that now that he had Sorrel his life would be complete when their child was born.

Sorrel let out a soft sigh knowing the uselessness of her pleas. He was set on this one subject, and she knew that she would not be able to turn his mind about. For a moment she relaxed within the warmth of his arms. Each time he touched her she seemed to come alive. Even after the months of being married to him he still had the power to turn her very limbs soft and yielding, wishing only for his touch and nothing more.

Mathew could feel the effect that he had on Sorrel, and a strong feeling of guilt came over his heart. Why could he not be fair to her and give her the one thing that she wished the most? He tried in every way to be a good husband to her, and in her condition he now was most tender, watching over her every movement and trying to please her and be as much help as he could. But he knew without the words having been spoken that she would give all that her soul could afford to hear him say that he loved her. He saw it each night as he held her in his arms, the look within her emerald eyes was all but begging, pleading with him to tell her more, to give the part of himself that he was holding back. But instead of the words that she wished to hear he would take her lips and kiss them into the silence that he desired for his troubled mind.

Sorrel pulled herself from his arms with a strong will. Silently she went to the chair near the hearth and sat down, taking up into her lap the piece of material and thread that Red Hawk's wife Tame Elk had given to her for her babe. She admired the cloth once again, letting her fingers lightly caress the soft texture of the shimmering material.

Tame Elk had come one day with her husband on a visit and one of the many gifts she had brought with her had been this fine material. Red Hawk had told his wife that Sorrel was pregnant, and with the news the other woman would not let her husband have any peace (these were Red Hawk's words on the matter) until he brought her to Mathew's wife. Sorrel had liked the beautiful dark-skinned woman when she had first met her on the day of her marriage, but she had never expected the other woman to come with her husband to pay a visit.

Sorrel had truly been entranced with the other woman. She had a soft manner and gentle ways, and the love that she bore her husband was apparent. The two women had spent a wonderful afternoon visiting with each other, and Tame Elk had shown Sorrel the cloth she had brought and had shown her how to arrange it into a gown for the babe when it arrived. This material, she had told Sorrel, her father had gotten from a white man as he had passed through their village one spring, and the color, such a light yellow, had so pleased her father that he had quickly brought it to his only daughter and told her that it was for his first granddaughter.

Sorrel had been stunned by the woman's generosity and had at once told her that she could not accept such a treasure, but Tame Elk had laughed the matter aside and assured Sorrel that her father would be more than pleased with any color of cloth that she put on a child for him.

She had brought more material, too, in fact, she had brought with her a fur sack filled with cloth and also two more dresses for Sorrel, larger than the one that Red Hawk had brought to her.

Sorrel had been more than pleased with the fine gifts from the other woman, but even more, she was pleased with the woman herself. It seemed to Sorrel that an eternity had passed since she had visited with another woman and this woman who talked so easily and laughed about her life, her village and family, somehow brought a brightness to Sorrel's days that she had hardly known she was doing without.

From that day forth, whenever possible, Sorrel would have Mathew take her to the Indian village to visit Tame Elk, or the Indian woman would come with her husband to the secluded valley and visit with her. Now, though, Sorrel thought as she took a tiny stitch in the material, she would not be seeing her friend for some time. She and her aging mother were making a trip across the Cumberlands to visit for a time with her mother's people.

Mathew watched his wife fingering the soft cloth

before she finally began her sewing and something in her look told him of her despondency. "Why do you not set that aside for now, Sorrel, and we will go for a short ride?" He did not wait for her answer but went to her chair and took the material from her hands.

Her mood seemed brighter at the prospect of leaving the tiny cabin and getting out into the fresh air. She rose to her feet and started to the door.

"Just one second, my little impatient mouse." Mathew followed her, but passing the bed he grabbed up her fur jacket. "The weather may be warming, but still you need this." He draped the soft fur about her shoulders. "We would not wish for you to become ill." With these last words he dropped a light kiss upon her forehead and went ahead of her out the door to saddle his horse.

Their ride was slow, Sorrel sitting contentedly before her husband as the huge, black beast picked his way delicately through the familiar paths in the valley.

Mathew kept his horse on a tight rein, not daring to let him have his way, which this fine day would have been to go charging over the valley. He could feel in his large hands as they held on to the leather reins the fine spirit of his mount. Mathew had to admit that the sweet spring air did much to revive his own flagging spirits, so he could not find fault with his horse. But he held a more valued treasure upon the back of the horse than himself alone, and he was taking no chances with Sorrel and the child.

Relishing the fresh, warm air and the tender arms circling her waist Sorrel looked silently at the beauty all about her. All the forest seemed to be alive with a new, invigorated pulse. Small animals scurried about, lively objects for Lancer's practiced eye. Soft, lilting peals of laughter filled her husband's ears as she watched Lancer scurry up a small brown rodent. The tiny creature was not about to run any further and turned with ferocity. Lancer, thinking this whole affair great sport, tried swatting at the little animal, which to him was nothing more than a way in which to relieve some of his built-up tension of the past few months. Lancer was in for a surprise, though, for instead of a little bit of fun he received a stinging bite to his front paw and jumped back with a yelp.

"That will teach you, Lancer," Sorrel laughed, bringing a smile to Mathew's face. "Leave the little fellow alone."

Lancer was more than happy to oblige, and with a last wounded look at the fierce-looking little creature he ran after the horse carrying his master and mistress.

The forest was beginning to abound with a rich lushness that Sorrel had not seen before. It seemed that every color imaginable was before her eyes—the green, red, and gold of the huge trees standing sentinel above them, the deep green of the grass, which now, with the snow not covering it, was free to grow lush and thick, and the different-colored profusion of the flowers.

It was only a short ride to the pond with the waterfall, and as the horse approached the area Mathew jumped down and lifted Sorrel down. "Here we are, pet." He looked about at the beauty for himself before he spoke again. "Not much has changed, it is still magnificent."

Sorrel could feel the tenderness of his words and she felt her heart constrict with the love she felt for this man. How easily it seemed for him to express himself over something as beautiful as the scene before them. For a second a small doubt wedged itself into her heart. He seemed not so easily to find words to express himself as far as she was concerned, or even in regard to their future. Each time she tried to press for more of a commitment he seemed to pull away from her. Oh, she could not fault him for the tender care that he showered upon her—never had she been treated so thoughtfully. But there was something missing, though she could not put into words what it was.

"Come, sweet." Mathew took her out of her thoughts by grabbing her hand and pulling her after him. He had brought a blanket from the back of his saddle and now he laid it next to the water's edge. "Sit here and relax for a time." He gently helped her to lower herself and then sat down next to her, pulling her tightly against his chest.

Neither spoke for a time, both lost in their thoughts and the beauty about them. Sorrel was the first to break the quiet. It was as though this place was affecting her in some odd way, she felt suddenly desperate to hear the words from her husband that would give her more of him than he had shared with her thus far. "Mathew?" she ventured, barely daring with her thoughts to look him in the face.

"What is it, love?" he leaned back upon his elbow and watched her intently, awaiting her next words.

"What will happen to us?" She did not know how

to phrase the words that she wanted to say and this was the only thing she could get out.

His fine, dark brow rose as he saw the confusion on her face. "What is it, pet? What do you mean, what will happen?" He seemed not to understand her question. "We shall, of course, be like any other married couple. There will be children, and good times and bad."

Sorrel's frustration overwhelmed her with his answer. Could he not understand what she wished to know? Did she have to come right out and ask him his true feelings? "Is that all, Mathew?" Great, large tears formed in the depths of the emerald eyes.

Mathew sat back up, now knowing what it was that she wished to hear, but feeling uneasy. "Why, of course, sweet. What else is there?"

"And what of staying here in the Cumberlands? Will we also raise these children of ours here in this wilderness?" Her voice cracked with a soft sob at the finish of her question.

Her sorrow and tears were as visible and apparent as the huge waterfall cascading down into the pond but still Mathew could not force himself to offer the comfort that she wished. Rising to his feet he started to walk away from the blanket, but knowing that he must answer her in some way he began softly, "After the babe we will decide about this, Sorrel. What good is there in becoming upset when we cannot leave this place now even if we wished to?"

Sorrel did not look up toward his face. Instead, she watched as the droplets of her tears wetted her tightly clasped hands upon her lap. How could this man that she loved so with all of her heart be so cold and hard? Had she ever given him reason to treat her in this manner? Why was it impossible for him to tell her how he felt about her? For the first time in the months that they had been man and wife she struck out at him with hate-filled words. From the very depths of her inner being welled up doubts and fears that she now put into words. "Is it me, Mathew?" She finally lifted her tear-streaked face, and with eyes pleading for him to somehow put a stop to her words she went even further. "Or is it that it is not me but another woman?"

Mathew's face turned a shade paler as he looked at his wife and was confronted by the truth of her words.

Sorrel saw his look and took it for an admission of guilt. "Is there another woman, Mathew, who even now bears your name? Is that the reason that you will not take me from this place of nothing but trees and animals?" She could go no further, but instead burst into great gulping, wrenching sobs, taking his look and the fact that he had not said a word but stood looking down at her as the confirmation of his guilt.

Mathew stood as though she had slapped him in the face. He had thought at first that she had struck upon the reason for his cool reserve at odd times, the reason why he could not so easily say what he thought was within his heart. It was not she, she was without fault, playing the loving wife as though she had been made for the very part. It was he—he was the one who was not worthy of her trust or her love. It was he—who had so easily loved in the past and had carelessly forgotten that love. Why did he not reach down and take this woman who meant so much to him into his arms and confess it all to her? Tell her what he felt for her, and that she was all that mattered. But, shaking his head, he turned in the opposite direction. If he dared to allow such words to leave his mouth he would be admitting that Elizabeth had not been what he had thought, and that all he had left in the past—his home, his church, and even his father—had been in vain, the leaving the act of a selfish man.

Sorrel could not see through her tears, but she could hear him leaving her side by the soft crunching sound of his boots upon the thick grass, and with each step she felt the tightening of her heart. It was true. She had wondered at times if this could be the case, but she had each time put such thoughts from her. But now she knew—there indeed was another woman. And from his not answering her last question she must also assume that that woman was Mathew's wife. Tears once again streamed down her flawless cheeks. Had he only married her for his convenience? Had he taken his friend Red Hawk's idea of marriage as a means to gain her through the winter, and had he planned when the snow thawed to let her return to her father and not give her a second thought, except perhaps on a lonely night when he would pull her from the depths of his mind and remember the small pleasure he had taken in a woman-girl who had been so in love with him that she had foolishly let herself be talked into a wedding in an Indian village? Well, his plans had been turned against him, she thought, rubbing furiously at her eyes now, trying to stop her tears. For there was a child coming, a child that she had thought had been made from their love. Now she knew that it would only know its mother's love, for as soon as she was able she would take her child and leave Mathew Danner and let him be free to go to the woman who he apparently cherished so much.

She would no longer think of herself as the woman who had stood before that old Indian with Mathew at her side, listening to the foreign words and saying in her own mind in English the words to love, honor, and obey. She was no longer bound by those simple words, she told herself as she dashed the last of her tears and tried to straighten herself somewhat. She was Sorrel Morgan once again. She thought back to the days at her aunt's house, daring any to tell her nay. She had stood up to the boldest of men, standing up for herself and not letting any become her master until she had met this mighty mountain man here in the Cumberlands. And now, to her horror, she found that these months of bliss and love had turned into a terrible nightmare.

Well, she would survive. Not necessarily because she wished it, for if the truth were known she would rather have perished here, this moment, than to have to face her future now, but she knew she had no choice. Her destiny had brought her this route, and if only for the child in her body, she would survive. She would let no harm come to herself or her infant.

Mathew had gone to his horse and stood gently rubbing him down with handfuls of grass, every now and then his blue eyes going to the woman at the pond's edge. What was she thinking? he wondered as he patted the animal that was as close to him as a well-known friend. He could well imagine her anger. He should have said something to her when she had asked about another woman. Even denying it would have been better than walking away, he realized now. In Mathew's mind the only words that had registered were those asking him if there was another woman, and, with his guilt about Elizabeth, he had been stunned. If he had been listening to her words and not looking so intently at her tear-stricken face he would have been able to assure her that no other bore his name besides her, but instead he had walked away leaving her to her own imaginings. He would say no more on the subject, and he would hope that she would not broach it again, either, not until he was ready to talk about it. He knew that one day he would have to tell her everything about his past, for what man could keep his life forever hidden? But that day, he hoped, would not come too soon.

With a resolute picture of her future holding only the joys that would be brought to it by her child, Sorrel pulled herself to her feet, and gathering the blanket in the crook of her arm she went toward Mathew and his horse.

Mathew smiled at her approach and gently lifted her to the horse's back. "There, sweet, let me just tie this to the saddle." He took the blanket from her hands and folding it tied it to the back of the saddle.

He was acting as though nothing was amiss, Sorrel thought in amazement. How could he be so callous? she wondered sending him a scathing look.

Mathew looked up just in time to see the heated look shooting from the depths of her emerald eyes and he knew that her anger had not abated. He would just give her more time, he decided, pulling himself up behind her.

For the short duration of the ride back to the cabin Mathew was presented with the stiffness of his lovely wife's back. Each time he called her attention to some small wonder of the forest he was quickly quieted by the stiff lifting of her fragile jaw. She was in no mood to be easily placated, he realized, and he too fell into silence.

That evening the quiet that filled the small cabin was like an invisible, tautly stretched barrier between Sorrel and Mathew. Sorrel went through all the motions of being the wife she had been in the past, but there was a difference. There were no small smiles or light touches for her husband as she set about preparing the meal and setting the table. Each time her emerald eyes happened upon Mathew as he sat near the hearth and cleaned and polished his rifle, she felt the sting of bitter tears blinding her vision and making her quickly draw her head from his direction and toward the food in front of her.

Mathew, upon occasion, glanced his wife's way with some concern. He knew that she was still angry and he wished to give her a cooling-down time to regain herself and calm her thoughts. But soon he realized that her mood had not changed and began to feel quite unsettled.

If Mathew had expected Sorrel to relent easily and let things go back to their usual routine, he was in for quite a surprise. For Sorrel was dwelling continually now on Mathew's face as he had looked at her at the pond. His guilt had been written all over his face, and each time she thought of his expression she was reminded of how big a fool she had been.

Their meal completed in silence, Mathew rose

from the table and calling Lancer to his side went out, thinking to give his wife some time to herself. Perhaps this was what she was in need of, he thought; since their marriage neither of them had had much time alone. Maybe this constant closeness was the cause of their friction.

As soon as he was through the door Sorrel hurried with the few dishes and straightened up the kitchen area. Then, not wishing to face Mathew anymore she put on her nightshirt and lay down, scooting far to the side of the bed and presenting her back to the room.

She felt such despair within her heart that it was as though some great stone was lying on it. How could she go on acting the part of wife while all the time she would be knowing that she was not loved, that there was someone else. She and her child meant nothing to Mathew.

Large tears flowed from her eyes as she thought of how much she loved the man who could, without a care, use her in such a way. Trying to harden herself she concentrated on what she would do when her baby was born. She would not stay at the cabin any longer than she had to. If she had to take her child up in her arms and walk her way out of this valley, she would. This affair of being deceived by one's heart was the most painful experience that she had ever encountered, but she would force herself to put her love from her; she would make her heart become as hard and unyielding as his.

By the time that Mathew returned to the cabin, Sorrel had already wept herself to sleep, and standing over her still form on the bed Mathew felt his heart contract.

She seemed so beautiful and frail in her sleep, and as the small gulps of her sobs came softly to his ears he felt the full measure of the hurt he was inflicting upon her. He truly wished that he could change things, but he had no idea on how he could approach the subject of Elizabeth Strickland. For a moment the impulse was strong for him to reach down, shake her awake, and confess everything, but then some inner voice cautioned him that to do so would be to destroy himself, to lay bare the fact that he was not as strong as he had always thought and that his feelings could be so easily swayed.

Shaking himself he took himself away from the bed and sat in the chair near the hearth. Given time, he thought, she would return to the way she had been in the past. He knew that one of the reasons for her distress was the fact that she was with child, he had always heard that women were especially moody when they were pregnant. So why would Sorrel be any different? he asked himself, trying to find other reasons for her anger with him. All things worked out with the passage of time, he assured himself.

Chapter Twelve

With each passing day Sorrel's movements became more limited by the extra burden in her body.

Her mood more often than not was irritable, and she seemed on the fine edge of a breaking point more times than she even wanted to think about.

After that afternoon at the pond's edge when, to Sorrel's mind, her husband had confessed his darkest secrets, she seemed to become a different person. She no longer smiled and sang softly as she stitched the soft material that would be the gown for her child. Oh, she performed that duty that she knew was hers, but she now did it quietly, her thoughts never far from that afternoon at the pond's edge.

She could not seem to shake the shock of her betrayal at the hands of the man she loved and had thought of as her husband. She prepared his meals and kept the cabin clean, but more than that she did not offer, and Mathew, sensing her anger and knowing that he was not at that time prepared to tell her all that was walled up within him, also maintained his quiet and lived in solitude.

Though the two shared the small living space, they

became like strangers. The only time that their bodies betrayed their thoughts was deep in the darkness of the night when they would fall asleep, each far to his own side of the bed. But deep within their souls was the desire to draw near to each other, and though Sorrel scolded herself each morning, she would without fail find her body, upon awakening, snuggled up to Mathew, her limbs entangled with his.

Neither mentioned this, but during each day the feel of the other's body lingered on in each of their minds. How could they put such thoughts from them after the intimate life that they had shared?

Mathew delighted in finding his wife in his arms during the night, hoping that she had at last come to her senses and had forgotten their quarrel. He could not bring himself to confront her openly, but each time her soft body pressed close to his he would smile contentedly and fall back to sleep, hoping that with the morning she would be changed from the Sorrel she had been in the past few weeks to the one she had been in the past. He remembered well how she had been in the past, loving, giving and receiving—all that a man could ask for in a woman.

Thinking over the past weeks Mathew had reasoned with himself and had come up with the idea that her pregnancy must be causing this hardness within her. He was sure that as soon as the child was born she would forget the words that he had spoken (or not spoken) and then they would go on as before.

Not once did it enter Mathew's mind that his wife would wish to leave him and return to her father. He knew that couples went through valleys and over mountains and he decided that, for them, this was just one of the valleys and that soon they would once more be starting up the mountain.

Sorrel's mind, though, was not so easily eased. With each passing day she tried to harden her heart to prepare herself for the day when she would take up her child and flee this cabin and the man who had such power over her.

When Mathew looked at her with a smile and kindness in his eyes she would turn her head and make herself think of the woman that somewhere must be waiting for this same man who could look so tenderly at her. When he thanked her for a meal or a service she performed for him she would answer politely, but quickly she would get herself busy doing sewing or cleaning, wishing not to let her defenses down. She was convinced that she had been treated harshly and was determined that she would not submit to this man who now was, to her, vile and worse than any rogue she had met in her entire life.

She only waited for her baby to be born, and now, with each passing day, she wondered if it would not be soon. She did not think that she could grow any larger as she looked down to her belly and rubbed gently at the spot where the tiny being within softly kicked. For the last few days she had been having small, stirring pains at different times in the small of her back, and she knew that these pains were a sure sign that her time would indeed be soon.

Sighing loudly Sorrel straightened and rubbed her back. Cooking seemed to be more of a chore today than she wished for, but there was no one else to do the work with Mathew gone, and he would be back expecting something to eat. He had left early that morning to check on some of his traps, and now, with the sun starting to lower, she knew that he would be coming in at any moment, and she could well imagine his hunger. Though she tried at each turn to harden herself against him, she could not bear the thought of him hungry or lacking for any kind of comfort. This, she tried to tell herself, was normal for a woman. She tried to cast from her mind the thought that she truly cared for his comfort, trying to make the things which she did in his house into a mere job.

The aroma of the bubbling stew filled the tiny building and Sorrel sat down for just a moment after setting the table. She was so weary she could barely stand. Her only thoughts now were of lying down upon the soft bed. For a moment her emerald eyes lingered on that appealing piece of furniture, but with the slamming of the door her eyes swung about to the tall frame of her husband.

There was no pleasure in her gaze as she looked at the man entering the room. No greeting or welcome came from her soft pink lips, and in return the look of genuine concern and pleasure at being home fled Mathew's own visage.

Without preamble Sorrel went to the hearth and taking up a large dipper she filled the two plates with the stew. There was no talking as Mathew sat down to the table and started his meal. He did not know the words to break into her cold reserve, and after the long day of hunting he was not in the mood to try and woo her.

Not being able to eat more than a small portion of

her food, Sorrel was soon starting to clean up the mess left from the meal, and this done, she began in short order to make herself ready for bed.

Mathew watched her movements thoughtfully as he sat back in his chair. It would not be long, he thought, before she would have the child. He had not really given this much thought, he realized suddenly as his blue eyes filled with her protruding stomach and swelling breasts. Perhaps in a few days he would go to Red Hawk's village and ask his friend if there was a woman from the village who would come and stay for a time here at the cabin, to be with Sorrel when her time came.

For a few minutes he let his mind wander to thoughts of having a baby. He could view in his mind the tiny form of an infant held in his large hands. What would it feel like to have a child and know that it was a part of his own body and that the tiny being would be completely dependent upon him? This thought staggered Mathew, and again he looked toward Sorrel. Perhaps he had been wrong. Perhaps he should have taken her while she was not too far along in her pregnancy and gone back to Crescent Mist or somewhere else—*anywhere* else, he suddenly realized, would have been better than here in this wilderness. What could he have been thinking of, he questioned himself, rising from the chair. He indeed had not been thinking! How could he have risked such a thing as to endanger this woman and the child that she was carrying? And suddenly he knew that staying here was just that—a risk.

Seeing her climb under the covers on the bed Mathew went to the door and stepped out into the cool night air. He felt like a man trapped and without any means of finding his way out.

Mathew stayed outside for some time, trying to sort out in his mind the reasons for all the actions that he had taken since first he had set eyes on Sorrel Morgan.

When he went back into the cabin the fire in the hearth had burned down low and the sleeping form of his wife was softly illuminated in the dim light of the room.

Quietly Mathew undressed and climbed in beside her. Her easy breathing proclaimed her to be asleep, and he silently laid his large body as close as possible to her without waking her. The feel of her soft, satiny skin brought him to peaceful dreams in short time.

Mathew was reluctantly hauled from the depths of his sleep by someone calling his name softly, and with the realization that it was Sorrel who was calling he rolled over and enveloped her in his strong arms. Shortly, though, he sat up, rubbing his eyes and trying to see through the dark and into his wife's face.

Her silent sobbing and the feel of something wet on his chest had brought him fully awake. "What is it, Sorrel?" And with no answer forthcoming he tried again. "Did you have a bad dream?" Never once did it enter his mind that she could be crying from pain, but he tried to no avail to see the cause of her distress.

Sorrel had awakened some time ago to a series of small, sharp, piercing pains in her abdomen. She had at first tried to ignore them but soon she found herself bent double in the bed and clutching her middle and biting her lip to keep herself from yelling out. It was with some reluctance that she had called Mathew's name and taken hold of his arm. She not only did not wish to wake him from his sleep, but she had told herself over and over these past weeks that she would be able to handle this affair of birthing her child all by herself.

Another pain hit her at this moment and she gasped aloud, grabbing hold of her distended belly.

With her loud gasp Mathew took hold of Sorrel and pulled her up against him. "It is the babe?" He wished for her to answer and to tell him nay, but he knew with no words spoken that this was not going to be the case. Once again he felt her hot tears against his chest, but this time he gently pushed the hair from her forehead, and after placing a kiss on that most tender spot he laid her back down against the furs.

Rising, he rushed to the hearth and started up a fire from the banked coals. He was frantic the whole time, not knowing which way to turn now that the time had come for her to deliver.

Grabbing up his pants and pulling them over his lean frame he looked down to the bed. Now, with the light given off from the built-up fire, he could see the pain etched upon Sorrel's lovely features. She seemed to relax and she closed her eyes for a moment, and Mathew used this time to run outside with a bucket to fetch water.

He was only gone for a few moments, and with his return his blue eyes went automatically to the bed. Sorrel had pushed the covers from her body and beads of sweat now drenched her and the sheet beneath her.

Taking the bucket of cool water he poured some into a bowl and set this with a rag next to the bed. The other he poured in a pot and set this over the fire.

"There, sweet," he softly cooed as he sat down upon the bed next to her and wiped her forehead with the cool water.

Sorrel had not said a word to her husband since she had awakened him, but now, seeing the concern plainly written upon his features, she wished to give him some comfort. "Thank you, Mathew. I feel somewhat better now."

As she finished these few words another spasm of pain coursed through her body leaving her gasping and trembling with tears brimming brightly in the depths of her eyes.

Mathew did not know which way to turn. The only comfort he knew to give was to speak soothing words and to wipe her brow. "I'm sorry, love," he murmured gently as he bent down and left a kiss on her trembling lips.

Something in his tone drew Sorrel's emerald eyes to his. She had tried for the past several weeks to harden herself to this man, but now, like a shattering blow, came the knowledge that she would never be able to keep herself away from him. He was like breath to her. How could she break herself away from her own reason for living and breathing? She smiled up into his face with this realization. The gulf that had been built up between them was now broken and torn into a million pieces.

Mathew saw the smile, but with his harrowing thoughts he did not quickly discern its meaning.

"Try to rest between each contraction, love," he cautioned as he saw her body's release from its last pain.

"Do not worry, Mathew, I shall be fine," Sorrel murmured, shutting her eyes with the few moments left to her free from this tearing pain.

Mathew knew that his wife's pain had only just begun and that with the first child sometimes the labor could be long and drawn out. He had helped to deliver a child one night long ago when a farmer had come to his house and had begged him to help his wife. He was unable to get the doctor for her or any midwife. So the only other person that the worn and weary farmer could think to ask for help was Mathew, he being the only preacher in the area.

Mathew thought back to that long night with some reflection now that Sorrel lay quiet, trying to rest. It had indeed been a long night, and Mathew admitted to himself even now that he had been more than a little frightened as he had entered into the two-room farmhouse.

The good man and his wife had had several other children. These, all being young, had sat before the hearth in a small group and listened to each sound coming from the other room. Mathew on first entering the house had wished that he could sit with the children and stay near the fire, but the man had taken his arm and led him into the single bedroom. With each step up the stairs and toward the room, from which soft, muffled groans of pain were clearly heard, Mathew had prayed, calling on a power much greater than his own to help the woman.

The person on the makeshift bed across the room

had seemed hardly lifelike as the two men had entered the room. Only a graying head showed out of the large comforter thrown across the bed. The woman was so frail and worn from years of childbearing and heavy labor that Mathew felt his heart contract with his pity.

He had not known the family too well; only on rare occasions were the couple and their children in church. But Mathew knew that they were hardworking people who deserved a chance to survive.

When they entered the room the farmer had gone straight to his wife, and without any further delay he had rolled up his sleeves and begun to tend the painwracked woman.

Mathew had stood for a time not knowing what he should do, but soon he also was over the bed and trying to encourage the woman to bring the new life from her body.

During this time and between contractions the woman had bravely told Mathew as he sat and held her hand about her other deliveries, telling him that the only other birth to cause her much stress had been her first, but this, she had said, was more usual than not. She had even mentioned other women who had been in labor more than two days with their firstborn but had come out of the ordeal fine.

Mathew had comforted the woman as best he could, praying that this would be the case with her for this pregnancy, but with each look in her direction he could not help doubting that she was strong enough to bear much more.

He had been wrong, though, for several hours later the woman was sitting straight up in bed and smiling down with love at a beautiful baby girl.

Mathew had marveled at the birth as he had watched the farmer deliver his child, thanking God that he was privileged to view such a wonderful creation.

And, indeed, he had been privileged, he thought, as he watched the still form of his wife, trying to find some rest for the ordeal ahead. For if not for that night at that farmer's house he would be at a complete loss as to what to do or what to expect.

Sometime in the early hours of the morning Mathew found sleep as he sat beside the bed and watched over his wife. She also had fallen into a light, pain-free sleep, but with the dawning of morning and with the opening of her eyes she again felt the gripping of her insides, and with the day the pain seemed more fierce.

Mathew's eyes flew open as he felt movement upon the bed, and there before him was Sorrel's beautiful face trying hard to hide her pain.

Scolding himself for falling asleep, Mathew stood to his feet and stretched his aching muscles. Bending back down to the bed he placed a light kiss upon Sorrel's soft lips. "Is the pain still bad, sweet?"

Her answer was the nodding of her head, but she tried to smile and not to be a burden. This was not to last long, though, for a searing pain brought a gasp from her lips and her body rolled on the bed from side to side.

Mathew wished that somehow he could take this pain from her and bear it himself, but things were not this easy, he realized as he sat down and gently stroked her face, trying in some way to ease her torment. "Ah, love, love, if only I could do something to ease you," he murmured, his mind a blank as to what to do.

The sheer torment in his tone struck Sorrel and pulled her from the depths of her pain. He seemed more in agony than she was, and this helped her to get a hold on herself. She reached up and took the hand that so gently was stroking her face and placed a small kiss in the palm. Such a large hand he had, she thought for a second, so large and strong but so gentle and loving. "Do not frown so, Mathew. Every woman goes through this same thing. It is what we are born to the minute we are ourselves brought forth from our mothers." With the mention of mothers Sorrel thought back to the few times she had heard her Aunt Corry or her father make any mention of her own mother. Aunt Corry had told her when she had been a very small girl that her father had loved her mother very much and Sorrel had never doubted this statement. But over the years little else had been said about Leona Morgan. Most of what Sorrel had learned about her mother had been from overhearing her aunt talking to one of her lady friends or when, during her father's and aunt's conversations, something would slip about the mysterious Leona.

As Sorrel had grown older she had realized that the reason that Leona Morgan's name was rarely mentioned was the fact that her father still had not fully gotten over her death. She had watched his face on more than one occasion while he was talking to his sister about his long-dead wife, and then, on their trip on the boat, she had finally fully realized the depths of the love he had shared with her mother.

Sorrel had questioned her aunt the morning after one of the conversations she had had with Graylin, about the death of her mother. Her aunt had warned her not to bother her father and had told her in a very few words that her mother had been a lovely woman who had died early in life after her delivery of her daughter.

Sorrel, after this conversation, had felt a closer bond to her father, realizing what he must have gone through losing his treasured wife and only being left with a daughter. That, though, she realized, was why Graylin had loved his daughter so much and had always wished for her happiness—in Sorrel he saw a part of Leona that could never be found anywhere else.

Ah, if only Mathew loved her with this same burning, fierce love that her father had had for her mother! Even after her death he had not let it go.

"I'll fix you something warm to drink, love." Mathew squeezed her hand and let it drop, not knowing her thoughts.

"Yes, Mathew, that would be wonderful." Her tone was soft but her thoughts were far elsewhere. Why could this man whom she loved so much not love her in return? Was he only waiting for the babe's birth before he would leave her and return to his other woman? Mathew had left her side and now tears of anger and remorse clouded her vision. She had viewed love in the depths of her father's face that evening aboard the *Seafare Lady* when he had talked about his wife, and now she knew that she would even give her own life if that could somehow bring that same look to Mathew's face as he talked about her.

For the rest of the morning and afternoon Sorrel lay in agony between the pain of her body and the misery in her mind. With each contraction her small hands gripped on to the sheet and she gritted her teeth from the searing pain that seemed to consume her. But with the let-up of the pain she was doubly tormented. Each time she looked into Mathew's dark blue eyes she wished to beg him to love her, to beg him to forget that other woman and to stay with her and their baby. Though the words would not come so Mathew could stand in his own defense, the thoughts were always there.

The sun had begun to lower in the sky, leaving the outside in a quiet, soft, darkening haze when Mathew once more left the cabin to seek water.

His thoughts went back to the evening before when he had thought that he would have enough time to go to Red Hawk's village to seek out someone to help with the birthing of the babe. Whatever had possessed him to wait so long was a mystery to him, and he had to admit that he had not fully thought about what was to happen. Perhaps he had thought that he would be able to handle the situation, and under different circumstances perhaps he could have, but now he knew, with a sinking feeling in the pit of his stomach, that what was happening in that cabin was out of his control. Sorrel seemed to be growing weaker with each passing minute, he doubted now that she would have much strength to bear up to much more of this pain. With each new searing torment to her body Mathew himself began to feel his own insides being pulled apart.

Large droplets of sweat rolled down his forehead and into his eyes as he bent to dip the buckets into the stream.

What would he do if something happened to Sorrel or the babe? How could he have been so stubborn and foolhardy? All the day she had lain in agony, and from the first he should have ridden for help. If nothing else, the women at Red Hawk's village could have given Sorrel something to help ease her pain. Some herb or drink, perhaps. He could have kicked himself for not going for help, but now he knew that his time had run out and it was too late for such action. It was he and he only who stood between Sorrel and death. Death had been a traitor to him in the past, and he was determined now not to let Sorrel be given up to that fate. She could not be lost to him now.

Hefting the buckets up he started back down the well-worn path to the cabin. He dreaded entering that door and facing that beautiful face so pinched and strained with suffering. How could he have let this woman down so? he questioned himself. She had depended upon him from the first and he had brought her nothing but this pain. Tears came easily to his eyes for the first time since he had been a boy. Had this not been his life's story—letting down those who most counted on him? He had left all his past and had come here to the Cumberlands trying to hide from all that he had known, wishing to shun all those who needed him.

For a second he stopped, and as he stood and held

the two buckets of water his life flashed through his mind. His past, and the present. He found himself near a fallen tree, and, sitting down, he took a long, well-needed breath of air. How could he have been so foolish? Had Elizabeth Strickland had such a hold upon him that he had cared for nothing else? For the first time he let his thoughts be truthful.

It was as though for the first time Mathew realized what he had done. "My God, my God," he cried aloud. "I have even given you up, and for what? I can no longer even see Elizabeth in my mind. She is gone from me, while the woman who I love lies in agony there in that cabin, while I am helpless to do anything to help her." As he said this, a time long ago came to his mind, when he had stood in defiance to his father for the love that he had had for his Lord.

Silent, agonizing tears slid down his strongly chiseled face. Tears that were for more than the woman in the cabin—tears for himself, and for a way of life that had meant all to him, and from which he had turned for little reason.

As he sat thus a soft cooing sound came into his consciousness, the gentleness softly touching upon his ears. Looking up and through his tears, he saw a small, perfect dove. As he watched the small bird hopping from one tree limb to another he thought of a time in the far past when a fisherman called Simon Peter had stood before his Lord. "Simon son of Jonas, lovest thou me?" were the words spoken to the large, quiet man. And as though hearing these same words directed to himself over and over throughout every portion of his soul, Mathew began to speak to his Lord. And as the prayers came to his lips that he had never thought to speak again, he asked his Lord's forgiveness, knowing that with the asking he was no longer bound down by his past. Elizabeth was no longer his jailer. He was free at last.

And with thoughts of Elizabeth his wife's image filled his mind. How he had wronged this woman who meant so much to him. He would beg for her forgiveness also, he told himself. He would make her understand all that he had been withholding and then tell her of the deep-burning love that he had for her, which he had, through his own stupid foolishness, been hiding from her and from himself.

He saw her again as he had last viewed her only moments earlier. Would she forgive him all that he had put her through these many months? His Lord would forgive him, but would his wife?

His time of settling his past mistakes and planning his future was cut short by a piercing scream, filling his ears and leaving his body cold and shaking.

Quickly picking the water buckets back up he hurried to the cabin. Mumbling a prayer to the Lord, he asked his help with what lay ahead. But with this prayer he knew a difference from those he had desperately prayed those long days and nights in Elizabeth Strickland's room. This evening outside the cabin he asked the Lord's help, but he knew that he would abide by his will and would never again turn his back upon him. What ever happened to his wife and child he knew that the Lord would be there by his side.

Catching a last deep breath of air he entered the door and hurriedly went to his wife's side.

Desperately she clutched his hand with her own,

her features showing the sheer pain that was being raked over her body.

"There, sweet." Mathew took in the scene before him, knowing that it was either time for the babe or that his wife would lie here and be completely pulled apart. "Push down, Sorrel. With each pain push," he coaxed her.

And from deep within Sorrel's tortured mind she heard her husband's voice and she pushed, straining with her pain.

"He is coming, love!" Mathew shouted with wonder as he saw his baby's head beginning to push out.

Her pain now almost unbearable, Sorrel bore down with all of her might, and though she felt some relief it was only short-lived, for almost immediately the pain started back up, even more excruciating than before.

Mathew gathered the baby into his hands and placed him off to the side of the bed, wishing for a free hand to tend his wife. The pain should have left her, he thought to himself as he watched her writhing upon the bed, her nails digging deep into the covers. As soon as the baby had been delivered of the farmer's wife she had immediately been relieved, and within moments she had been smiling down at her new daughter and laughing with her husband.

Sorrel, through the haze of her pain, was having the same thoughts and wondering if she were going to die. Would she be torn apart with these knife-sharp pains until she could breathe no more? She looked through the dim fog of her brain at her husband's concern-written features. Did he know that she was dying? Would he be glad to be rid of her? But what of the baby? She could hear him crying with lusty little calls to be cared for and she wished for nothing more than to reach out and take him in her arms, but she was unable to. All of her strength was concentrated in the depths of her body, trying not to give up, to hold on and fight.

Mathew looked at Sorrel's face and saw deep within her eyes a new glint of determination, and this alone bolstered his courage, for only seconds ago he had felt sure that he was going to lose his wife, the woman he had only a short time ago truly realized that he loved beyond all reason.

Sorrel was the first to realize what was happening to her body, and with a gasp she pushed down with all of her might. "Mathew!" she cried, drawing his attention to the lower portion of her body.

Not believing his eyes, Mathew went once again to the foot of the bed and coaxed his wife to push down, and within moments he was reaching down and holding another tiny body.

With the ending of her pain Sorrel seemed to sink into the softness of her bed, her emerald eyes closing with the need for rest.

Mathew stood holding one child and looking down at the other one lying on the bed. For a moment he could neither speak nor move, but then, shaking himself, he forced himself to function. "Twins," he breathed at last, but looking at Sorrel he saw that she was already asleep.

Lying the baby in his arms down next to the other one, Mathew went to Sorrel's side and bending down he lightly placed a kiss upon her lips. A soft, satisfied smile came to her sleeping face, but, disturbing her once more, Mathew brought water and cloths and proceeded to bathe his wife's body.

With tender, loving movements Mathew rinsed Sorrel's body and changed her into the only other white shirt that he owned, his thoughts filling with a small pain that his wife had to be treated this way when, for no reason but his own stubborn pride, he had kept her here in this valley and made her do without.

All of his faults seemed to be coming back to roost tonight, and he knew that he had a lot of making up to do.

As he wiped his wife's brow with the cool water, her emerald eyes fluttered open for a moment and their eyes met and locked. "I am sorry, love," was all that Mathew could get out, as his throat constricted.

But no more was needed, for after those few words the green eyes shut once more.

Mathew's chest swelled with immeasurable pride as he looked at his wife's sleeping face. What a woman she is, he thought. She had given him not one but two children. Two fine, healthy babies, their cries filling his ears and bringing a deeper smile to his face.

After cleaning up the tiny infants, dressing them in the soft gowns that Sorrel had fashioned, and laying them in the small cradle that he himself had built, he sat back in the chair and studied the creations before him.

The twins were even more than he had expected. Their tiny forms were perfect. Each head was tufted with his own dark curls, and from the sounds that they had made while he had given them their baths he knew that each would be hale and hearty.

For a second Justin Danner's face came to his mind. His gray-haired father would be bursting with happiness if he could see his grandchildren. He could see the elderly man's face breaking into a huge grin and could almost hear his congratulations.

Mathew shut his blue eyes, a satisfied smile upon his own lips. As soon as Sorrel and the babies would be able they would go back to Crescent Mist. Mathew felt a deep eagerness for his home. Sorrel would love Crescent Mist and his children would thrive. Crescent Mist's old black cook, Mally, would think herself in heaven with the two babies to tend.

A peaceful sleep came over Mathew as he sat in the chair next to the bed, the past day and evening's ordeals passing from him as though a heavy weight had been lifted.

Sorrel's eyes fluttered open as the crying sounds of her babies reached her ears. At first she did not move but lay still, her emerald eyes touching on her husband's sleeping form next to her. He seemed so handsome, almost boylike with his eyes shut and his features softened with his vulnerability.

Once again the crying noises came to her ears, and she at once remembered that she had had not one child as she had thought she would but two. "Twins." She sighed aloud. The crying stopped and she relaxed.

With the slight sound from the bed and the small movement as Sorrel turned her body to a more comfortable position Mathew's blue eyes flew open.

For a moment his look was all concern but shortly stirring, happy lights were touched off within the depths of those sapphire orbs. "Do you feel well?" His question directed to his wife was a soft caress, as though he was holding his breath awaiting an answer.

"Quite well, Mathew." Sorrel's smile filled his vision, and he grinned.

"Well, love, can I get you something?"

Sorrel ignored his words and spoke her own. "We had two babies?"

Mathew thought that perhaps she could not remember, her pain having been so harrowing and she having been so weary. "Aye, sweet. Twins, two perfect boys." His grin was so large as he said this that in the darkness of the room his white teeth gleamed.

With their smiles aimed at each other their eyes locked in a warming gaze. And Mathew, making the first move, bent over the bed and took the soft, petal-pink lips below his own. Lingering delicately, Mathew drank of the sweet nectar that was his wife's, alone, not seeming able to content himself with a small amount.

Sorrel was the first to try and disengage herself from her husband's grasp. From the deep recesses of her mind she cautioned herself that this was the same man who had another woman besides her. She had thought while she had been in labor that she would forget this and try to bring things back to where they had been before that day at the pond, but she knew, though the fact was that she could not live without this man, that she could never forget that at any time he might tire of her and leave her for another.

Mathew laughed aloud at his own overexuberance as he felt her hands pushing at his chest.

Sorrel felt her cheeks flaming from his laughter.

"Ah, love, you wound me, I wish but to hold you for a moment."

"Mathew, bring me my children." Sorrel tried to quiet him.

"Nay, love, let them sleep for a while longer. You and I have much to talk about."

"You are wrong, Mathew, there is nothing that needs saying." Sorrel felt a fear growing deep inside her. Was he now going to tell her about his other woman? Was her time with him already cut short?

Mathew saw the fear registering deep within her eyes, and for a moment he wondered what could have brought this on. He wished only to straighten out their relationship. "There has been much that I have left unsaid since I have known you, Sorrel."

"There is no need Mathew. Leave things as they are, please." She tried to pull her hand away and turn her back on his words. Now that it was finally time for it all to be out in the open she had no wish to hear it. Once the words were said she would have to make a decision for herself and her children and to her mind there was only one course open to her. She would have to leave this life and the man she was so helplessly in love with.

"Leave things as they are? But Sorrel, do you not see that this life that we have shared has been a sham on my part?"

Sorrel could bear no more and the tears began to flow down her cheeks.

Mathew was amazed at her reaction. He had thought that she would have been more than glad to finally know who he was and what kind of man she was married to. "Listen sweet," he rose from the bed and sat down on the chair to see her better, automatically reaching up and tracing a tear making its way to her chin. "I do not understand what happened to the curious little minx that I married who wished to know all about her husband?" His words were tender, not wishing to hurt. He was beginning to think that perhaps this birthing had been too much for her.

"You needn't tell me anything, Mathew," she sobbed. She did not think she could bear this horrible betrayal so soon after the ordeal of her children's birth. She only wished to be left alone, to fall into a deep sleep where only her dreams of love and faithfulness were real.

But Mathew had ventured this far and he was determined for her to know about all of his past and his desire for his family's future. "I have done you a great disservice, Sorrel, by not telling you of my past, and with this realization I am bound not to be swayed." With one last look down at his wife's stricken face, he began. "My family is from Kentucky and owns a large plantation called Crescent Mist."

Sorrel rocked her head back and forth trying to block out his words. She could not listen, she told herself over and over. For if she did she would be lost.

"Sorrel, you must listen to me." Mathew's voice was a commanding plea.

"No! Do not do this to me!" she cried desperately, trying to think of some way to stem his confession. "I do not care anymore about your past, I only care about now. How can you be so cruel, Mathew?"

Mathew looked at her tear-stained face and felt the breath leave his body. Had she completely lost her senses?

"Please Mathew, I cannot live without you. Your babies and I need you. Can we not stay here in this valley? I shall never again treat you unkindly, I love you Mathew." This final plea was the one that Sorrel thought the only option left her if she had any chance of keeping this man whom she knew she loved more than life itself.

Pulling her tenderly into his arms Mathew soothed Sorrel's brow with small, tender kisses, trying to put her at her ease and to curb the agitation that she had worked herself into. What on earth did she think he was going to do? he wondered as he went over her words once again in his mind. She had said that she could not live without him, that their children needed him. Did she think him capable of leaving her and his sons? Mathew shook his head trying to clear his thoughts. He had to admit that she had not been at all at fault if this was what she imagined. He had not been exactly the most kind and thoughtful of husbands—in fact, he had to admit he had been quite the opposite.

Kissing her lips as they quivered delicately from her upset, he looked deep into her eyes. "Let me talk, love. Let me explain." With the shaking of her head he pulled her tighter into his embrace. "I love you, Sorrel," were the only words he said.

The quiet that filled the room seemed to grow for the space of an eternity. Sorrel's breathing grew in tiny, frantic gasps as these few simple words reverberated over and over in her mind. "I love you, Sorrel, I love you, Sorrel." She dared not even breathe very loudly with the fear that she was only imagining that he had said these words that she had for so long wished to hear.

Finally Mathew broke the quiet, as he feared that she had fallen asleep in his arms. "Did you not hear, sweet? I said I love you." A huge grin appeared upon his face at the pleasure that he felt with the saying of those words.

Sorrel pulled back from his grip and looked up to his face, seeing for herself the truth of his words and the happiness that had been evoked in him by saying them.

She did not realize how critically she was looking at her husband until he spoke again. "Are you not pleased with my words?" His smile began to fade as he thought that perhaps he had not told her what she wished to hear.

Rising up she placed a kiss upon his lips. "I have waited it seems forever to hear those few words from you, Mathew." Her own soft smile touched him lightly.

Mathew wanted to shout with his happiness as he looked at his wife, but instead he grinned even more broadly. "Now perhaps, madam, you will let me continue with the telling of my past?"

Sorrel was still not too sure if she wished to hear what he had to say, but as long as she knew that he loved her she knew that she could face anything. Slowly she nodded her head.

Mathew's tone was serious as he proceeded to tell

her all about his past, leaving out nothing. He could not see her face, for he still held her in his arms with his chin resting gently atop her golden curls, so he did not see her reactions as he told her of Elizabeth and her illness and how he had turned from his family and his Lord.

Sorrel had no jealousy for this other woman who was now dead and gone from this life. Perhaps at one time she had had a place in her husband's heart, but now that heart that beat so warmly beneath her soft cheek did not have any room for any other besides herself. She had learned that much of this man who was her husband—he was not one to do anything in small measures; it had taken him all these months to discover his love for her, and she had no doubt now of its strength.

She would not in her wildest imaginings have thought of the man that she had married and shared a life with as having stood before a congregation of people and talked to them of the Lord. But this man who now held her in his arms was a different man from the one she had known in the past, and this one she could now well see standing up and proclaiming to all his belief in the Lord.

Quietness was all that greeted Mathew's final words of how on this very day he had discovered the great love for his wife that he had tried to hide from himself, and how he had once again found his Lord and master.

Only moments ago Sorrel had thought that her life here in this valley was to end tragically, but now, incredibly, it all had turned in her favor. What more could she ask for than for this man to love her and to stay by her side for the rest of their lives? It all seemed unbelievable to her.

Now, instead of tears, tiny, brilliant lights of pleasure swam in the depths of Sorrel's emerald eyes.

Mathew reached down and pulled her fragile chin in his direction, his gaze filling with the lovely slanted eyes before him. He read the pleasure that was there and relished her delight. "You are pleased?" he softly questioned.

"Aye, my love. I am very pleased," she breathed, hardly above a whisper.

"Do you think that you will love me now that you have heard of my past? Perhaps the reason for your love was the fact that you were intrigued with the unknown?" His voice was jovial as he caressed her cheek.

Sorrel grasped the hand that was so near her face and in a serious tone she began to answer. "Nay, Mathew, that is not the way it is. I admit that the unknown is not to my liking, but I am afraid that my love for you has nothing to do with what was before I knew you. You are all that I could ever wish in a husband and the mere thought of losing you has the power to completely shatter me."

"Never will you lose me, love. Now that my stubborn heart has finally figured things out it will never change. I love you, and no small amount. All that I have, all that I shall ever be, I give willingly to you, to keep and to nurture until nothing else can stand between its love's bloom."

Tears came easily to Sorrel's emerald eyes from the tenderness of Mathew's words, but before another one could be spoken a small, impatient cry filled the cabin.

"I am afraid that our sons, madam, have a mind that it is time for us to give attention to them." Mathew started from the bed but turned back before he had taken many steps and once more took Sorrel's lips with his own. This kiss was like liquid fire, full of rich intensity, until all was out in the open between them. "I am the richest man alive, Sorrel Danner. A wife like you, and two fine sons to share my name. What more could any man ask of this life?" His words were shared with her, but he said them as though to himself.

Sorrel did not speak but smiled at her husband as he left her side and went to bring her sons to her. How fortunate she was, she thought, as she watched Mathew's strong back bend to retrieve her children. Fortunate, indeed, to have such a man for a husband—and to think that she had almost destroyed what they had by her own foolishness! She shuddered to think of this. Never again would she mistrust this man—their future would hold only love, from this day forth.

Chapter Thirteen

In the lonely valley, far from any other human habitation, Mathew and Sorrel and with their infant sons discovered their own Garden of Eden. The beauty that was all about them seemed to come alive, to vibrate with new meaning as they took the time for healing and growing, and for learning again one another's wants.

The twins, Joshua and Joseph, waxed strong and healthy, their father delighting in the special times of the day when he would help Sorrel to give them their baths or sit and watch as one of the tiny beings was snuggled to Sorrel's breasts greedily devouring his meal.

Each day, Mathew thought, his children grew bigger, and with the summer months bringing warmth and beauty to everything around them, Mathew watched Sorrel carefully, biding his time until he would no longer see his wife's grimacing from discomfort with each step of her walk. He was like a horse prancing and biting at the bit, wanting only for the days to rush by so that he could take his family from this wilderness and back to his home in Kentucky.

More and more often he spoke to Sorrel of Crescent Mist, seeing in his own mind his new family taking their rightful place in his old family home.

Sorrel thought that she could not have asked for a more idyllic life. Mathew showered his love upon her, at every turn showing her what was within his heart. He seemed to be trying to make up for the time lost, to set aside any doubt that still might linger in Sorrel's mind about his feelings for her. And the time not spent lavished upon his wife was spent with his sons. Sorrel thought there could not be a man prouder of his children. He helped her at every turn to tend them, no job seeming too disagreeable to him.

As Sorrel sat rocking Josh back and forth, readying him to be laid beside his brother for his afternoon nap, she thought back to the day before with a light smile on her lips.

As she and Mathew had been giving the boys their morning baths they heard a horse racing down toward the cabin. Mathew dried his hands, a broad grin upon his strongly chiseled features. He knew without a doubt who the rider would be, and his excitement mounted as he gained the door.

Red Hawk stood outside the cabin. "It is a grand host who meets his guest at the door, my brother," Red Hawk greeted Mathew with a smile.

"Come in, my friend." Mathew swung the door wide allowing the Indian to enter.

Red Hawk's dark eyes automatically sought out his friend's woman as he entered the room; one of the delights of his visits to Mathew's cabin was always to see her. Today, though, instead of finding her still huge with child, he saw a tiny babe in her arms, and to Red Hawk she was lovelier than he had ever seen her as she made soft, gentle noises to her child and held him so tenderly. "My congratulations, my friend." He looked at Mathew, and then his piercing black eyes were drawn back to Sorrel and her babe.

"Come, Red Hawk, I would have you meet my son." Mathew placed an arm about the Indian's back and steered him toward the table.

"A son? You are indeed blessed, my brother," Red Hawk said as they approached the woman and her child.

"Aye, that I am, my brother, more so than you even realize." Mathew gave the Indian little time to think over his words but reached out and took the cloth that was used as a blanket for the babies and easily gathered the small infant from his mother's arms. Wrapping him in the soft material he held him out to his red brother. "This is Joseph."

Red Hawk took the bundle handed him and for a moment did not speak as he looked down at the tiny pink face and now wet black curls. As the Indian's eyes rose they went to Sorrel, and touching the babe's cheek lightly with one of his long, tanned fingers, he spoke to her softly. "He is a fine man child, Sorrel Danner. You could not have done better for my brother." In the Indian's voice there was a sadness that only Sorrel was aware of, and she knew that Red Hawk was thinking that if things had worked out differently this child, perhaps, would have been his.

Mathew broke the tenseness of the room with a hearty laugh. "You think she could not have done a finer job?"

Red Hawk pulled his eyes from the woman he thought more beautiful than any he had ever seen and looked at Mathew, his gaze saying that he indeed thought that Sorrel had birthed a perfect child. To Red Hawk there was nothing finer that a woman could do than to give birth to a male child. This woman whom he had desired for his own wife had given his friend a fine son, and he not only was happy for Mathew, but he also felt envy.

"Come over here a moment, my brother." Mathew walked to the other side of the hearth to the small cradle.

Red Hawk followed, thinking that he wished to lay the baby in his bed.

Smiling with excited anticipation Sorrel watched as her husband led the Indian to where their other son slept.

Mathew stood next to the cradle, a large grin upon his face as his eyes looked down into the small bed.

As Red Hawk reached the cradle he held out the babe for its father but as Mathew seemed to pay no attention to him but be absorbed in looking at the child's bed, Red Hawk also looked down. As his eyes fell on the small bundle in the cradle he again looked at the child in his arms. "Two, Mathew?" He looked back and forth once again, not believing what was before him.

"Aye, my friend two." Mathew reached down and picked up the sleeping babe, identical to the one the Indian was holding. "This one is called Joshua." He brought him around and held him up to his brother.

"They are both sons?"

Mathew laughed lightly at his friend's disbelief.

"Both sons."

As Sorrel had seen the shock upon the Indian's face she had gone to her husband's side to enjoy the surprise of his friend. As she approached, Mathew wrapped his large arm about her shoulders and drew her up tightly to him. "Indeed, my wife has done me more than proud. I cannot express to you, my friend, what this woman means to me."

Red Hawk watched the pair and something within him seemed to be pierced. Perhaps in his heart, he thought, he had wished that still there was some way he would win this woman for himself, but now, as he held his white brother's child and viewed the joy upon his wife's features as she looked up with loving adoration to her husband, he felt an emptiness inside. He made an effort and said, "The Great Father must be watching over you, my brother. It is truly a great blessing to have two fine sons at one time." His tone was soft and full of longing.

"I agree fully with this observation. The Lord surely has blessed me." Mathew's grin broadened. Handing the babe in his arms to its mother Mathew started to take the other one from Red Hawk. "Come, my brother, and let us share a cup of coffee."

Red Hawk pulled away a bit from his friend. "I enjoy holding your son, Mathew. It is not often that I am so privileged. Do not take him from me just yet, when he is in need of his mother he will let it be known."

Mathew felt renewed pride with the knowledge that this red man, that was as close to him as any brother could have ever been, felt this close bond, as well, with his sons. Going to the hearth he poured them all cups of coffee and placed the cups on the table.

As the pair talked Mathew watched his child in the red man's arms and the way the tiny hand circled about the leather fringe on Red Hawk's shirt.

Finding herself alone with Joshua, Sorrel went to the bed and turning her back upon the men she began to nurse her child. This quiet time of feeding her infants was the most pleasant in Sorrel's day. During these times she seemed to lose herself with the baby in her arms, softly speaking soothing words of love and admiration to it. This was the time that she spent teaching her children about herself and learning about each of them.

Joshua nursed quietly, his dark blue eyes resting on his mother's face as she sang a gentle tune to him.

More than once Red Hawk's black eyes were drawn away from Mathew to the woman on the bed. What a tenderness filled his very soul as he watched this golden woman caring for her child. Finally, not being able to bear any more, he rose from his chair, gave Mathew his son, and left, promising to return soon.

Sorrel smiled contentedly, like a beautiful cat with a large bowl of cream, Mathew thought, as she rose from the chair and placed her son alongside his brother in the cradle. For the first time today she had seen the pride that Mathew felt for his family in front of another person. A small giggle escaped her as she once more saw Red Hawk's face when he had realized that there was not one but two children. But with this picture in her mind she once again was pricked with a small pain of sorrow. She had seen everything that had been written on the Indian's face, and she could hear once again in her mind his words on that long ago day when he had asked her to become his second wife. She was glad that he had Tame Elk and was not completely alone. One day the two of them would have their own children and he would cast from his thoughts the image of her and her sons.

Mathew had been outside all the morning cutting wood and tending to his horse, so now as the door swung wide and he strode into the room she smiled her pleasure. Without preamble he came over to her and gathered her up into his arms.

Sorrel squealed her pleasure as she was picked up off her feet and swung about the room. Finally stilled, but still hanging in midair, she was savagely kissed, and at this touch of her husband's mouth she seemed to melt against him.

The manly smell of him hit her nostrils, sweat, horse, and leather combining to arouse all of her senses.

"Ah, you lusty wench, I can see that not much work will be getting done with you about." His tone softened and he tenderly caressed her cheek. "You are like a beautiful, exotic spider pulling me into your web at your will. Even within my thoughts you spin your silver web, binding about my mind."

Sorrel laughed softly. "Aye, my gallant husband, you indeed see very clearly through my plans."

"Which are?" Mathew interrupted.

"Why, only to keep you so deeply enmeshed within my soft, shimmering threads of love that you will become lost to all but my charms."

"Why, madam, if that is your intention you have

without doubt done yourself a fine job." He playfully set her to her feet and slapping lightly at her backside he went to the bucket of water and splashed the upper portion of his large body. "Now perhaps you would care to feed a starving man?"

"Ah, I thought as much."

Mathew lifted a fine, dark brow in her direction, wondering what she was to say next.

"I think that all of your silken words of devotion and binding love with silver threads were but a ploy to keep yourself from fainting with your hunger. You are a very wicked man, Mathew Danner." She could not keep herself from giggling, but shortly she was rushing about the table, keeping it between herself and her husband.

"So you need more proof of my devotion, do you, madam?" He began to stalk her around the table, droplets of water falling from his black curls and running down the thick shower of black hairs upon his chest.

"Nay, Mathew, I am convinced. I was but teasing," Sorrel laughed, hurrying around the table so as not to get caught and soaked in the process.

"I have some doubt of this, my beauty," Mathew grinned widely. "This time I will convince you thoroughly of my devotion."

Sorrel read the serious intent in his gaze and with a small squeal she scampered from the table and started to the door.

She was pulled up short halfway there by strong arms and passionate lips.

Collapsing against her husband's chest, Sorrel was

more than willing now to be held close. But soon, as she felt her senses being pulled into another region, one of delight and pleasure, she tried to pull herself from Mathew's grip. "Mathew, the children," she gasped aloud, feeling herself all but faint.

A small groan escaped his lips as he took them from those before him. "It will be more than a pleasure to be at Crescent Mist." Mally could tend the boys while he would be able to take his fine time and tend their mother. He held her close for another moment before once more releasing her.

"How much longer will it be, Mathew?" Sorrel questioned, feeling her own impatience to be leaving this valley and discovering Mathew's home that he talked so fondly of. As much as he had told her of this plantation Crescent Mist she felt as though she already knew all about it. Even the name sounded familiar to her, but she knew that this could not be so. "It has been almost five weeks since the twins' birth and if that is what you have been waiting for, I am fine. Never have I felt better."

"I thought that another week here at the cabin would be necessary, love. I want to be sure that you and the boys are well able to make the trip, and also I am going to have to go up to the forest where I trap and hunt and gather my traps." He had not mentioned this to Sorrel before and now he watched for her reaction, but with none forthcoming he continued, "I shall have to leave you here for a couple of days."

Sorrel's answer was a small kiss placed upon his lips, and then without a word she turned and went to the table and started to fix her husband something for his dinner.

"I mentioned my intentions to Red Hawk and asked him to watch over you."

Sorrel's golden head swung about at this. "I do not need watching here in this hidden valley, Mathew. Why would you bother Red Hawk with such a chore?"

"He assured me that it would be no bother. He will camp for a couple of days at the edge of the valley as he did when he first brought you here and awaited my arrival."

"Oh, then that is where he was. I remember at the time I wondered where he was, for he had told me that he would be watching over me. But surely there is no need now for him to watch over the valley."

"I agree with you, pet, but just to be safe he will be close."

"He will not mind?" Sorrel wondered aloud, imagining in her mind all manner of other things that a strong warrior could have to do besides watch over a woman and her children.

"Nay, he does not mind. I would do the same for him if the need were there."

Tame Elk would not return to Red Hawk's village until the first signs of winter, so Sorrel knew that there would be no such job for her husband to do, but she knew also that there was no sense in arguing with him about this matter. His mind was set, and she did have to admit that she would feel a bit safer knowing that she would not be completely alone here at the cabin.

Since the twins had been born Lancer had elected to stay outside. Sorrel had reasoned that the babies' crying must disturb him, and also the weather now was fair and warm. But now, more often than not, the large dog was not about, being always off chasing some sport, so Sorrel could not fully depend upon him for her protection. So with this news of Mathew's, though she hated for him to have to leave her if only for a couple of days, she was somewhat relieved at the thought that Red Hawk would be near.

The next morning as Sorrel and Mathew rose from their bed Mathew declared in a loud voice, as he clasped his wife tightly to him, that this day would be a holiday. They would do nothing but enjoy themselves and their children. He told her that after breakfast they would go to the pond and spend the day. The following day he would be leaving to gather his traps and on his return they would start back to Kentucky.

Sorrel was more than pleased with his idea and hurriedly she fixed their meal and prepared the boys for the short trip to the pond's edge.

They had not been to the crystal clear water since before the babies' birth, and the thought of a day of swimming and enjoying her husband's company was a thrill to Sorrel.

After a hurried meal and Sorrel's impatient prodding, Mathew lifted his wife and then his sons atop his great black horse. He held back a smile, also excited about sharing this day with his family out in the open under the clear skies.

In the days ahead Sorrel was to look back with longing at this day at the pond's edge relaxing and enjoying her husband and children. Her happiness and love for her family would be the one safe lifeline that she could grasp hold of to keep herself from total despair.

The bright sun shone down upon the sparkling, cascading waterfall, keeping the water in the pond warm. Sorrel and her husband gently held their babies in the smooth water, and then, laying them upon a blanket under a tree and letting them sleep peacefully, they took the available time for themselves.

Sorrel was the first to leave the boys' side. Slipping out of her dress, looking again as sleek and beautiful as a golden otter, she dove into the depths of the water as Mathew stood back with a smile and enjoyed the beauty of her perfect form. Not staying but an extra moment to make sure that Josh and Joe were sleeping comfortably he also shed his clothing and following his wife dove into the warm pond. With sure strokes he made for Sorrel.

In the mood for play Sorrel, on hearing Mathew's splash in the water, hurriedly pushed herself, trying to gain the other side of the pond before he could come upon her.

Seeing her gaining speed Mathew laughed quietly to himself. The little water numph would not get away from him. His arms stroked the blue water faster and faster, and with each second he could see himself gaining on her.

Sorrel was so engrossed with her wish to outrace him that she was brought up short as she felt something grab hold of her foot, and with some surprise she went under the water.

This was the first time that Mathew had ever been in the water with Sorrel, and he had never in the past questioned her on her ability as a swimmer, so as she went under the thought went through his mind that perhaps her foot's being pulled had taken her off balance. Without second thought he also dove under the water, now, though, feeling a touch of panic.

On going under Sorrel had broken loose from the hold on her foot and with her eyes open she had watched her husband. Seeing him starting under after her she quickly began to swim off in the opposite direction, seeing the edge of the pond clearly ahead.

Mathew realized his folly in underestimating his wife's skill as a swimmer as he watched her feet kicking at the water in front of him and he followed after her in quick pursuit.

Quickly Sorrel came to land. Pulling herself up she got to her feet and without looking back to see where her husband was she began to run, the air catching in her lungs.

Mathew was only steps behind Sorrel, and as she came to a tree he reached out and grabbed hold of her arm.

Gasping aloud Sorrel was turned about, squealing with glee as she felt her hand captured.

"Ah, you tempting vixin, you cannot flee me."

Mathew pulled her up into his grip.

Sorrel's laughter filled his ears as their naked forms met and melted together.

Mathew felt his blood raging as he held this woman that was all to him, his very life entrusted to her. And Sorrel, without reason, lost herself in the feel of Mathew's arms. His strength was her support, her sturdy pillar of love.

"How could I ever have survived without you?" Mathew's tender voice touched lightly upon her ears and these words seemed to voice her own deepest thoughts. His finger lightly caressed her small jaw and trailed up to her ear.

Sorrel's body quivered at his very touch, her needs attuned to his own, her desire striving toward its highest peak.

Mathew felt her desire as he knew his own, and gathering her up into his strong arms he laid her down in the deep green grass beneath a tall, majestic oak.

The splendor of their love was brought forth as never before. There was some secret drive that bore them onward. Each touch was filled with a golden desire to please, each breath given for the sheer benefit of the other, bringing delight to the ears as words were whispered of love and wonder. Their movements were slow and lingering, wanting to feel, to capture all. The sweet, sensual bliss of their giving left nothing to the wanting and melted all resistance.

As the couple lay sprawled in the tender shoots of summer grass a sensuous silver cloud seemed to overshadow them and drew them ever on to fulfill their passions. As their fiery abandon reached its highest peak and slowly, with colorful brilliance, cascaded about them, both seemed to reach up and take hold of the promised pleasure lying in wait.

Mathew was the first to speak. In a breathless tone he whispered over and over into the golden curls lying in disarray about his face, "Sorrel, Sorrel."

Not being able herself to speak Sorrel instead lay in her husband's arms delighting in the aftermath of the last golden moments.

"You seem to fill my head with naught but love. With each waking moment my mind is filled with your beauty. I shudder at the thought of being away from you, even for only two days." Mathew's words were soft and husky as he told Sorrel his heart.

Reaching up with a soft, small hand, Sorrel tenderly stroked the strong, lean, handsome face above her own. "Oh, Mathew, I am no different. My need is no small thing that I can lightly set it aside, and though the words two days sound so insignificant I know that the time will go as though at a snail's pace and each sound outside the cabin will have me running to greet you. My heart's only reason for beating is that you are there." Tears glistened deep within the emerald eyes.

Mathew saw where their words were leading, and, wishing only joy for this day, he grinned boldly down upon her and with a grunt he rose and pulled her to her feet. "Aye, love, it will be torture to be away from you, but a splendid torture with thoughts of my homecoming ever in my head."

Sorrel smiled in return, her pink lips quivering as

she tried to pick up his mood and to hide her own feelings. She had not really felt too badly about his trip to the forest, but now here with him at her side she felt suddenly a foreboding, a fear that things would not be all right. For some unknown reason a dark terror crept over her heart, but quickly she told herself that this was senseless. But still, deep within her, the prickling fear grew and would not leave her.

"I shall race you to the other side of the pond. The children may have awakened by now." Mathew dove into the water, making her think of something else besides his leavetaking tomorrow morning.

The rest of the afternoon went by swiftly. Most of the time Sorrel and Mathew played with their twins. But neither could bear to take his eyes from the other, and often their hands sought each other out and lightly touched. For both, although they said nothing, felt apprehensive about what lay ahead. But the dye was cast. Tomorrow would find the lovers separated.

With the lowering of the sun and the dark shadows of the night settling about the valley and the small cabin, Sorrel and Mathew tucked their children into their cradles for the night.

"Come to me, love." Mathew's passion-filled voice came to his wife's ears.

Her own desire as strong as his, Sorrel went to stand before the chair that her husbnd was sitting in.

Mathew pulled Sorrel onto his lap without another word and his sapphire eyes devoured her face. Then, with soft, tantalizing kisses, his lips covered her own. Pulling away a short time later, he groaned, as though painfully, "You destroy me with a mere look, with each glance you tear into my heart. I was nothing before you came into my life."

Sorrel's soft, gentle smile filled his vision. "You also are my heart." She reached up and with a soft kiss she molded her lips to her husband's.

Rising to his feet Mathew set his wife to her feet, and then without a word said he pulled the leather ties securing the shoulders of her dress. With the release of the material Mathew reached down and softly nibbled at each of the satiny shoulders, delighting in the feel and delicate fragrance of his mate.

Sorrel felt herself melting against her husband with these gentle ministrations, and turning in a single motion she let herself mold tightly to his body, her breath ragged in her throat as she felt his hands lightly tugging at her dress to make an end of the obstacles between them.

As she was revealed in all of her beauty Mathew stood back and with a deep breath let his blue eyes take in his wife's beauty. And beautiful she was, he thought, devouring her every portion as she stood before him, proud of the love and desire that he saw in the depths of her eyes.

"You have the very power to bring me to my knees." His words were poured out from the depths of his being. "Have mercy upon me, Sorrel, my beloved. Let me again know the sweetness of your love with our union."

Sorrel wrapped her arms about his neck and rising upon her toes she kissed the mouth before her, slanting her lips upon his own with an urgency that could not be denied. This man was all that she wished for. He was all that she needed to keep her sanity in this changing world, and forgetting her fear at being left alone on the morrow she let herself be pulled into the nether regions of wishing only to please this man before her.

With a gentle ease Mathew lifted his wife and brought them to the side of the bed. Placing her in the center he stood back as he began to undress and let himself drink her in.

This moment, this space of time, was all that was left to the couple, for soon Mathew would be leaving and Sorrel would be alone in the valley with only her children for her comfort. And, this thought uppermost in their minds, their joining was unsurpassed in its giving and taking, each touch bringing only the sheerest of pleasure, each kiss plunging deep and seeking out all the substance of the other, as though striving to pull out, to ravish, and to bind their senses in a total experience of oneness.

Pulsating heart beat against heart, mouth joined mouth, and souls reached out and claimed each other as their passions joined and showered brilliantly about them, leaving their minds and bodies touched with the colorful embers bursting within as their bodies reached the highest pinnacle of love.

In the aftermath of their love, their bodies entwined and their hearts beating at a tremendous rate, Mathew looked deep into the face that he adored. "I love you, Sorrel. You are a part of me that I shall never be able to have enough of. You are my breath, my heart, my very desire."

Sorrel took his words as from the depths of his being and though her own feelings were similar she did not know how to voice them. "I have known little of this word called love, Mathew, but from the first I knew that you were what my heart was to be joined to. You and you alone have made me complete. There is that within me that cares for naught but your needs and desires. You are my world. You and your children have brought me to completion." Small tears came to her eyes as she said this.

Mathew saw them, and reaching out a long, dark finger he wiped them from her cheek. "I shall not be gone long, and we will have all of our lives to share together." He stopped here and brought his mouth to cover hers, and once more they shared their love.

The morning sun broke fair and bright from the east, sending the message that the day had arrived. Mathew awoke with a yawn, and rolling over he gathered the woman in his bed up close to his chest. "It is time, sweet." He kissed her pert nose as she pulled her hand up to stifle a yawn.

"No, Mathew," she murmured softly and burrowed deeper into the covers.

Mathew laughed lightly, taking hold of the covers and pulling them down to bear his wife's face. "I must go, pet, and with me I wish but to take one thing." Bending down he took her lips with his own, losing himself in their sweet ambrosia.

Sorrel came awake with the feel of his mouth upon

her own and reaching up she wrapped her arms about his neck, clinging to him as though he were her very life support.

With a moan Mathew pulled himself from her and sat up upon the bed. "If I do not leave now, I shall not be leaving at all."

Sorrel looked toward her husband with a hopeful light in her emerald eyes.

"Nay, pet, if I do not go we shall never be able to leave this cabin and go to Crescent Mist."

The light dimmed in Sorrel's eyes and once again laughing lightly so as not to wake Josh and Joe, Mathew reached over and kissed her into surrender. "Go back to sleep now, love." He broke away and stood to his feet.

Sorrel sat up and watched as her husband dressed. "I can fix you some coffee and breakfast."

"Nay pet, you need your sleep. The sun is barely up, I can fix my own coffee." He pushed her back down and gently tucked the covers about her chin. "Sleep now and before you realize it the time will pass and I shall be back by your side." One more light kiss upon her lips and he rose and going to the hearth started a pot of coffee.

With a small satisfied smile on her lips Sorrel shut her eyes and fell back to sleep.

A short time later Sorrel was pulled from her sleep by the sounds of her sons calling for breakfast. Her first movement was to reach out to the other side of the bed to find her husband. With a start she sat up and looked about her. Mathew was gone and she and her babies were alone. With a large sigh she rose from the bed and started to dress. She would keep herself busy with the boys so the time would quickly fly.

The room felt cold and empty as she nursed her children. Putting them again in their cradle she sat down. Looking about she felt with a sinking feeling that she was really alone, and she knew that Mathew's presence was what had kept her contented in this lonely cabin.

Chapter Fourteen

Graylin Morgan hobbled his way into the inn, and, glancing up through the side door from her cooking, a young girl rushed to him and placed several pillows in the large wing chair resting in front of the hearth. Before hurrying back to her work she set the footstool close at hand and put a fluffy pillow on it.

Graylin set his large frame in the seat and with a huge whoosh of a sigh he smiled fondly at the girl's retreating back.

Pulling his right leg up he grimaced as he placed it on the waiting footstool. He could almost swear that the tormenting limb was broke in half, but the town's quiet, gray-haired doctor had assured him the day before that he had but badly sprained the ankle. Dad-blast but it felt as though the whole lower portion of his leg was aflame with pain.

His head swung about at the slamming of the inn door, and the dark grimace returned to Graylin's face as he watched the young man entering the large common room and sauntering toward his chair.

The young man was in his early thirties but looked

quite a bit older. Graylin put this down to his skinny frame and large features. There was nothing about the young man that was pleasant to look upon, with his light-colored hair, all but white with its sandlike tint, and his gray eyes. The latter were what made Graylin really uncomfortable. The younger man seemed all but without life when he looked at him with those cold silver piercing eyes. But Graylin knew now, after traveling from Texas to Kentucky with the other man, that his looks could be quite deceiving. His mind seemed quick and always at work, though Graylin guessed that the greater portion of his thoughts involved little of good intent.

The other slowly made his way across the room, and, smiling with his cool, thin lips, he focused all of his attention on the elderly man sitting back in the chair. "You are feeling better, I hope, Mr. Morgan?" The question implied concern but the tone was as cool as a winter breeze.

"Aye, as well as can be expected," Graylin gruffly answered. He was once again reminded that if not for this young man and his choice of horses he would not be sitting here in this chair in such harrowing pain. When he had told the youth to purchase horses for them he had not imagined that his mount would be the type to shy from anything in its path. And with all the luck, he had only been astride a few short minutes when a dog had run out from a house in the town and, barking ferociously, had caused Graylin's horse to nervously skid about and then to rear up, catching Graylin off guard and pitching him to the ground.

As though reading Graylin's thoughts, the

younger man continued, "Once more I wish to extend my apologies, Mr. Morgan. I had no idea that the horse was so skittish. I am only now returning from taking the mount back to Mr. Coil's stable."

"Ho, right there." Graylin brought his hand up. "I wish to hear no more about that bumbling nag."

"I did get you another, sir, that Mr. Coil assured me is much more well mannered."

Graylin took his tone to imply that his horsemanship was somehow lacking, but before he could say another word the young girl from the kitchen approached his chair.

"Would you be wishing for your dinner here in your chair, sir? Or would you be wanting to come to the common table?" Her capped, curly head nodded toward a long table against the opposite wall where several gentlemen of varied description were already busy eating the meal before them.

Graylin thought over her question for a moment before answering. If he ate downstairs here he was sure that he would have the company of this young man whether he wished it or not. "Nay, lass, I'll take my meal up in my room, if you will be good enough to bring me up a tray."

The young girl left with a curt bob of her skirts and a promise of sending a tray up as soon as she saw him going up the stairs.

Graylin glanced up at the younger man just in time to feel another twinge of discomfort as the other's gray eyes rose from the girl's full bosom.

"Well, sir, I believe I shall let you go to your dinner and your rest. As for me, I think I shall seek my meal elsewhere. It is a bit quiet here tonight."

Graylin nodded, expectantly awaiting the other's departure. "Just mind that you get some rest. We leave early in the morning for the Cumberlands and I shall not be kept waiting."

Pointedly the gray eyes rested on Graylin's propped foot. "Perhaps you should wait here at the inn, Mr. Morgan. I and the men I hired this morning could well make the trip and find your daughter."

"Nothing will keep me here, young man, so put that from your thoughts. I know that my daughter is still out there somewhere and I intend to find her and bring her safely home."

"I did not mean to offend you, sir. It is only that you must know that I have as much at stake in her return as you."

Graylin looked questioningly toward the other man.

"She is to be my bride. At least she was to be before she was taken by that Indian."

"Aye lad, I forget at times about that piece of paper that was signed so long ago." Graylin not only forgot at times about the betrothal, he wished there had never been such an agreement between this Clifford Sumter's family and the Morgans. After these past months of having this young man around him he knew one thing for sure, and that was that he did not wish for his only daughter, that is if he could find her, to marry this obnoxious boor. As soon as he found her he would inform this young man that the betrothal was called off.

"Perhaps you can forget, sir, but I have waited for a good many years for your daughter to turn the age agreed upon in the papers. And now, after all of these years of waiting, I am sorely tried having to come to this wilderness and hunt her down. That is to say, if she is still even living after being captured by Indians."

Graylin half came out of his seat at Clifford's words and as his face turned a dark, angry red the other took one step backwards. "My daughter is alive. And if you intend on going with me in the morning you had best not stay out all night. I shall not wait for you." Graylin finished pulling himself from the chair, and turning his back on the younger man he started to mount the stairs.

It had been a long, exhausting day for Graylin and Clifford Sumter in no way eased his plight. Entering his chambers Graylin pulled the door shut, and, taking his jacket off and throwing it carelessly across the foot of the bed, he slumped back against the back of a large, overstuffed chair.

His hand, as though wishing to erase his pain, rubbed across his forehead, his thoughts going as they always did with his loneliness back to his daughter's image. With the passage of the months since she had disappeared he had aged considerably. His hair was now completely white, and his weight was less than it had been the first time he had made this trip to the Cumberlands.

Over and over within his mind the question was there, just the same as how the younger man downstairs had voiced it: Was she still alive? Or had she not survived the cruelty of her captors?

But each time he asked the question he could see her lovely face, and he knew that he had to know for sure. He could leave no doubt to his mind on this score. She might at this very moment be thinking of him, and he, being her only hope, was not going to let her down.

As the serving girl knocked and entered the door he told her to leave the tray upon a small table near at hand, his mind, as soon as she left the chamber, once more going to Sorrel.

He thought back to the morning in camp that he had awakened, and, after having a cup of coffee, had gone to the wagon that had become her sleeping chamber. He knew that on other occasions she had slept not inside but under the vehicle, and with a quick glance he saw the covers piled beneath it. Bending down and calling her name he soon realized that she was not there.

Glancing about, he thought that she had probably already risen from the noise of the stirring camp, and going back to the cook fire he sat down upon a log and spoke with Alex Gentry about the progress they had made the day before.

He had felt good, as so had Alex, about the progress they were making, and Alex assured him that they would be well out of the passes before the first sign of snow.

Alex had been the first to leave the fire, in order to get the men started for the day, and still Graylin sat and awaited his daughter. It had become a habit for them to take their morning coffee together as they talked companionably, and Graylin enjoyed this time and did not wish to start the day without the sight of her relaxed and refreshed from her sleep.

As the cook started to put his supplies back into the cook wagon and started to dose the fire Graylin realized with a start that he had been sitting for some time and waiting for Sorrel. Rising to his feet he went back to her wagon, but still there was no sign of her.

A strong grip of panic overcame the large man as he frantically looked about at the forest all around him. Where was Sorrel? his thoughts rang over and over. Why was she not here as she was each morning? As an overwhelming unreason flooded his mind he began to call her name aloud, but soon, receiving no answer, he stepped into the trees around him and began to shout, calling now with the desperation born of love for a child lost and alone.

It was Alex who came at his calling, and after Graylin told the younger man of Sorrel's disappearance he went hurriedly to the wagon and looked beneath it, trying to find any sign that would give them a clue to her whereabouts.

There was nothing, though, around the wagon. Calling the men from all over the camp Alex set them to scouting about, and soon one of the men found the tracks that Alex expected to find—tracks made by a soft-footed, knowledgeable Indian.

Graylin had been stricken by the news brought to him later that morning by Alex Gentry that, by all the signs, an Indian had come into camp during the dark of the night and had taken his daughter.

As Graylin sat in his chair now in his chambers at the inn, he could feel those words once again falling upon him as though a boulder of heavy doom. He felt his heart contracting with the pain of his loss as he had that morning when the news was brought to him.

"How can you be sure that it was an Indian?" he

had questioned the young man in front of him as he rose to his feet and paced about the camp.

"We have found signs, sir, and now, this very moment, I have some of the men trying to find more clues to his destination." Alex Gentry hated to be the bearer of these bad tidings, but he knew that he had to tell this man about his daughter. The true problem was, though, that this Indian, whoever he was, had not left much in the way of signs. They had been lucky to find the tracks at all. This was one Indian who knew the forest and knew what he was about.

"Let us go now, then, and try to find her," Graylin had stormed at the delaying of the other man.

"Well, sir," Alex hedged, not wishing for the men to discover the full implications of his daughter's disappearance.

"Mr. Gentry, if you have something to say, get it out. My daughter is out there somewhere at the mercy of some heathen, and I aim to find her." Graylin had already started toward his horse.

"We will find her, sir, but I think it best that we wait for my men to report. They may find something that we would miss." Alex's thoughts were also on the weather and the huge, dark clouds that were moving into the Cumberlands. He knew that if they were to find the girl it would have to be soon, for they could not linger at this time of the year; each day that passed brought the snows closer on their heels.

"It would seem, sir, that this Indian knew what he was about when he snuck into our camp last night."

Graylin was halted by his words but his look was perplexed. "What is it that you are trying to tell me, young man?"

"I am afraid, sir, that the Cumberlands forests are quite thick, and it may take some time to find the Indian and your daughter." Alex did not wish to go on and stopped his words there.

"Then I suggest that you mount your horse and come with me. At least we have a chance now—waiting until later might prove fatal to my daughter." Once again Graylin went to his horse, but this time he would not be stopped, and once up in the saddle he sat and waited for the young man that he had hired to see them through the Cumberlands to follow his lead.

"Perhaps you are right," Alex finally conceded, though he doubted that any good would come of their leaving camp before his men returned. Perhaps with a bit of luck they would be able to find the girl before the Indian could get too far. But deep within him he knew that the Indian was smart, and more than likely at this very moment he was half across the Cumberlands.

A week later Alex Gentry finally talked Graylin Morgan into leaving the campsite that they had used since Sorrel's disappearance and to start their trip toward Texas.

The weather had grown worse with the passage of each day, and with the men spread out in all directions looking for the girl the horses were getting nervous, and Alex was afraid that trouble would start if something were not done. They could not chance being snowed into the passes for the winter, for that would surely be death for most of them. They had no shelter or provisions to last them such an amount of time.

Alex himself hated leaving the area that the girl had disappeared from, for he had begun to feel something for Sorrel that he had not felt for any other girl, and each time he looked into the face of her father he saw his naked grief. But as far as he could see they had no choice. Either they left and returned when the passes cleared or they stayed. Chances were that it would take some time to find the girl, and this meant risking all their lives. Even his men had begun to complain as their gazes continually went to the dark clouds overhead.

Graylin did finally leave the Cumberlands without his daughter, and with each footfall of his horse his heart cried out with his raw pain. What was to happen to his lovely daughter during this winter? How could this thing have happened to him? But he knew that nothing could stop him from returning, and vowing this to himself he followed the others and they made it through the passes before the snows fell.

It was a weary, tired, heartsick Graylin Morgan who arrived in Texas with the horses that he had set out for. He gave Alex directions to his ranch, and Alex and his men took the animals there. After Alex paid the men off he took a room at a boardinghouse in Houston while Graylin went to his sister's house to tell her the tormenting news of his daughter's abduction and to try and find some rest for his weary soul.

Corrine Borden had been completely shattered by the news brought to her by her brother and had taken to her bed for a week without seeing a soul other than her brother and her doctor. It had been a great shock to her, for Sorrel had been the daughter that she had never had, the only child that the woman had ever had to love and raise as her own.

But by the end of the week, knowing that she could not completely bury herself and the facts, she pulled her dressing gown about her and went down the stairs to find her brother. At least they had each other, she had reasoned while in her bed, and she could try and be some help to Graylin as she knew he was making plans for his return trip to find his daughter.

Corrine found her brother much changed. He had always been full of life and robust, but now he sat in the library and brooded to himself. She knew that he blamed himself and she hated this, for in her mind she was the one to blame for encouraging the girl to go and for persuading Graylin to take her.

Not much was accomplished by either of their guilt, which did little but pull their spirits down. Alex Gentry was the only bright spot in their lives at this time. He spent much of his time at Corrine's home waiting for the ship to be readied for their return trip to Kentucky.

On every hand he tried to help the brother and sister, encouraging them that it would not be long until they could return and find Sorrel. Never once did he allow his worry of her having been killed or maimed by some Indian into his conversation. He knew how much these two people loved the girl, and his heart went out to them.

He spent his evenings with them, telling them stories of his past exploits, trying to ease their minds, and, though the pain of their loss was always with them, after a while it became like any wound, the hurt only the deepest when it was focused on.

It was one of these evenings when the threesome had just finished their evening meal and had started to the parlor when one of the servants announced that there was a visitor.

Graylin called for the maid to show the guest into the parlor, already suspecting who it was. He had sent a letter to Clifford Sumter, explaining all and telling the man that he would be leaving as soon as possible to return to the Cumberlands. He had expected the young man at any time, and he supposed as he sat back in his chair that this time was as good as any other.

Clifford entered the small parlor immaculately tailored, as usual, but as his chilling gray eyes took in the small group and the young man sitting across the chair from Graylin Morgan his back straightened and without preamble he started his questions. When he had received the short letter from Graylin he had thought the whole affair some grand hoax on the part of the Morgan family to back out of the betrothal. No one was kidnapped by Indians, he had thought. They were trying to pull something over on him, and now, as he looked at the young man sitting so casually in Graylin's sister's home, he knew that there was something amiss here.

Perhaps this man was some new swain that Graylin had found for the girl and they only wished for him to tear up the agreement. Well, he would not so easily be duped. He had a stake here, and he intended to get all that was coming to him. He had waited too many years for the girl to come of age and for the papers to be signed to casually turn away.

"I received your letter and have come as quickly as possible. What is the meaning of your words, Mr. Morgan? I do not understand, how could your daughter have been kidnapped?"

Graylin drew a ragged breath and then spoke to the irate man before him. "If you will be good enough, Clifford, to take a seat, I shall try to explain all that happened on our trip." Graylin had no patience where this young man was concerned. He was too arrogant and self-indulgent to suit him, and he had thought many times in the past that his father should have taken a firmer hand with the young man while he was still alive.

With a huff of irritation Clifford complied, sitting in the only vacant chair, near the sofa, which Corrine was relaxing upon. His gray eyes never left the elderly man's face as he waited for the story that was to be offered.

Graylin started, knowing that there was no other way except to finish with the telling so this young man could be on his way. But what truly surprised him was the fact that, at the end of the story, the younger man looked thoughtfully at him for a moment and then, rising to his feet, cleared his throat and proceeded to tell Graylin that he also would be going along on the ship that would see him and Alex to their destination.

"You are sure that it was an Indian that took her?"

This was the only question that Clifford addressed to Alex Gentry. After hearing the complete story from Graylin and deciding that the elderly man could in no way fabricate such a thing, he had decided that the best thing for him to do would be to go along to help find Sorrel. And after hearing everything from Graylin he had been relieved to find that the young man sitting here in the parlor was only an employee of Graylin's and nothing for him to worry about.

Alex had decided at first glance that he did not care in the least for Sorrel Morgan's future husband, and he wondered what could have been on Graylin's mind to betroth such a jewel as his daughter to such a cold fish as Clifford Sumter. His own voice sounded cool and stilted as he replied to the question asked him. "We are sure that it was an Indian, Mr. Sumter, for we found tracks indicating this fact."

Clifford pulled his gray eyes from the man talking to Graylin. At once he realized how deeply this was affecting Graylin Morgan as he glimpsed the moistening of his blue eyes. But his mind and heart were hardened, and all that kept coming to him was the thought that all of his hopes for his future were slipping away with this abduction of Sorrel Morgan.

Graylin jumped to his feet, feeling the dampness of his eyes and not wishing to display this open emotion. He strode about the room without saying a word for a short time. But as silence settled on the small group he turned and faced the man who had asked the question about Sorrel's kidnapper. "Aye, Clifford we are sure that it was an Indian that took her, and we are bound to go back and find her. If you truly want to go with us, then I would suggest that you go back to your ranch and settle things there, for as soon as a ship can be found that is going to Virginia we will be on our way." Graylin left no room for further questions, and with a grunt of displeasure Clifford rose and clearing his throat he bade farewell first to Corrine and then to the gentlemen. "I shall take your warning for my hurrying sir, to heart. You can expect me back before the week is out. My foreman will take care of all that needs handling on the ranch."

Graylin watched as Clifford turned on his heels and started from the room. As an afterthought Graylin added before the young man could leave, "You may want to think about your decision, Clifford." This, indeed, did stop the younger man in his tracks, and as he turned about Graylin continued, "The Cumberlands are not an easy place, lad. You may find the going a bit uncomfortable." He did not wish to come right out and tell the other man that he thought him not up to such a trip so he toned down his words hoping that the other would take his meaning.

And indeed Clifford did take his meaning well, and with a twisted, cold grin he replied, "Do not worry on my account. I can take fine care of myself, Mr. Morgan. You will find me no trouble."

Graylin thought the other was sneering down his nose at him, but he held himself in check until Clifford once more turned and this time left the room. With a large sigh Graylin went to his chair and once again sat down.

Corrine had kept quiet throughout the whole interchange and now, at the distracted look upon her brother's face, she voiced the thought that had been in her mind for the past few years. "Why on earth do you keep that agreement between that young man and Sorrel? I shudder each time I think of our poor girl as his wife." There—she had said what was on her mind, she thought, as she pulled her eyes down from her brother's and looked to her lap.

"I have had the same thoughts of late myself, Corry." And with a soft sigh he continued, "Though now is not the time to worry over such a matter. Perhaps when we have Sorrel once again we will make some changes. I admit that I find this young man quite unsatisfactory." He shook his head as though trying to clear his troubled thoughts.

Corrine gave Alex Gentry a sweet smile as though putting the subject of Clifford Sumter from her mind. "Would you care for another cup of coffee, Mr. Gentry?"

Alex truly liked this woman and even more so now that he heard her objections to this man who was to marry her niece. Standing, he told her that it was getting late and that he would have to be going, for tomorrow he hoped that he would be able to go to the docks early and find a ship. A ship's captain had told him earlier that week that there might be a ship docking tomorrow that would be heading back to its home port in Richmond.

Clifford and Graylin both stood up after Alex did, and after a good night he left them to seek out his room at the boardinghouse. They both went up the stairs and to their own chambers, all their thoughts on the same subject as they laid their heads down for the night. Was Sorrel still surviving?

It was a few weeks before Graylin was able to book passage for himself, Alex, and Clifford. This trip to Virginia was as harrowing as the last for Graylin. He spent most of his time in his cabin in his bunk, his stomach rolling and turning with each shifting of the ship. But this time Graylin did not have his daughter to tend him, and he sorely missed her golden features and smiling face as she brought his trays to him, and with nothing but time on his hands his thoughts were constantly on his missing child.

As the trip neared its finish Graylin's stomach eased up and he was able to stroll on deck and take his meals with the rest of the passengers, but he was more than glad when the call was sounded that land had been sighted.

The days in Richmond passed slowly, and the realization hit Graylin that it really had been many months since last he had seen his daughter. To occupy his time while Alex took several days to hire men and make all the preparations for the trip ahead of them, Graylin visited with his old acquaintance Leory Langston. But now, as he sat in his room and looked down at the cold food upon the tray, he thought to himself that in the morning he would be off, sore foot and all, to find his daughter. He knew within his heart that she was out there somewhere waiting for him to come to her. And he would not give up until he could hold her once more within his arms, knowing that she was safe and secure.

Ignoring the food he hobbled to the brass bed and pulling off shirt and pants he climbed between the covers and tried to find some rest for the night. He would need all the sleep he could get, he scolded himself as he shut his eyes.

Clifford Sumter had stood silent for a moment and watched as Graylin Morgan had hobbled up the stairs to his room. The old fool, he thought. How could he be so sure that the girl was still alive? It had been over a year now and not a single word had he heard from her or about her whereabouts. For the thousandth time he wished he had stayed in Texas. He could at this very moment be lying comfortably in his own large bed, being entertained by a servant of his choice.

But despite these thoughts, he knew well why he was in this backwoods country. He had to be sure of the girl's outcome.

He had been furious when he had received word from Graylin Morgan on his return from this foul country that the woman whom he had been promised since he had been a youth had been kidnapped in the Cumberlands.

At first he had thought the letter a farce of some kind to call off the contract, but on meeting with Graylin that same day he had been assured, if by nothing else than the old man's tortured features, that the girl had indeed been abducted.

Graylin had been sure that her abduction had been caused by an Indian, and the man who worked for Graylin, Alex Gentry, had found tracks and these, he had assured Clifford, had been made by an Indian and one who had been alone. They had spent several days looking for the girl, but the snows had started to fall, so they had to look to themselves and leave the passes before they had been snowed in.

Graylin had started to prepare his trip back to the Cumberlands, and Clifford, seeing no way out but to go along, had volunteered his help. He had planned to have the Morgan's ranch, and if somehow the girl could be found he intended to wed her without further delay.

A cold shudder went through his body as he stood near the chair that Graylin had just vacated. He would marry the girl, but he would never treat her as he had thought to in the past. To his way of thinking a woman was strictly a man's, and for nothing else but his delight. And this would have been her role in his house as his wife. She would have stood quietly behind him and agreed with all he said, waiting only to please him as his own mother had done his father. But now, the mere thought of what Sorrel Morgan must have been put through at the hands of an Indian appalled him. And who was to say that there had not been more than one of the savages? She had been defiled in his mind and would never be worthy of him. The only thing that she now would be good for would be as the instrument by which he gained the Morgan ranch.

Turning about he went through the inn door, and not far from that building he entered another. In this one a foul odor hit his nostrils, the smoke from several cigars stinging his gray eyes and making him squint to find the man that he sought. After only a few seconds his eyes adjusted and he saw the man he was looking for sitting over in a far corner all by himself.

Approaching quietly, Clifford watched the other's features with distasteful disdain. How any man could let himself became as rank and filthy as this one before him was amazing to him. Unconsciously Clifford brushed at his dark blue jacket.

Catching this action from the corner of his eye, a small grin appeared upon the elflike features of the small man sitting at the table. Kicking the chair opposite him out from under the table he gruffly stated, "Sit."

For a moment Clifford debated whether to do as he was bid or not, but as the dark brown eyes rose to his own gray ones, he hurriedly brushed at the seat of the chair and sat.

Never in his experience had Clifford Sumter come across a more dangerous-looking man than this one across from him now. Sitting behind the table the odious little man looked almost childlike, but his harsh-featured face belied this illusion of innocence. The deep white scar running across the bridge of his nose also lent him a feeling of distrust and menace.

"What you be wanting now?" The question was direct.

"I thought to insure that you did not forget that tomorrow morning we will be leaving." Clifford leaned forward, wishing for no other ears to hear what was coming from this table.

"Do you think me dumb?" A dark brow cocked toward Clifford.

"No-no," Clifford hurriedly reassured him. Clifford had chosen wisely in this matter. After asking in each town for the best man to track and hunt down Indians he had on more than one occasion been pointed to this small, disappointing human being. The stories of his exploits had been so gruesome that Clifford had shuddered at the thought of his notorious large hunting knife, which was reported to come down upon a red skin and peal the flesh from the bones. And there were other stories of the tortures that he had inflicted other men who had been born with the misfortune of having red skin. Though the man was small and seemingly inconsequential, Clifford Sumter was no one's fool, and he wished by not even by the smallest word to get on the man's bad side.

"I need no reminding." Again the dark brown eyes went to Clifford's gray ones, their meaning seeming clearer than his words.

"I am sorry to bother you." Clifford started to his feet, feeling his palms beginning to sweat. "All should go as we planned. I shall not see you again until tomorrow afternoon when we meet in the Cumberlands."

"Aye, Cam Brash will be waiting for ye. Don't ye be keeping me waiting long, ye hear?" he added as an afterthought as Clifford turned from the table.

Clifford nodded his head and rushed from the room, his ears filling with the smaller man's strange laughter as he called to the barmaid to hurry and refill his cup.

Clifford left the stuffy inner room and walked out into the cool fresh air of the evening. This chore of seeing that Cam Brash would keep to his word was now behind him, and he was free to find his own dinner and sport for the evening. He would again, as he had the evening before, make his way to Madam Beaufont's. The food there had been delicious and the after-dinner specialties of her girls had been more than he could have hoped for.

The sun had not yet risen and the darkness of the early morning hours filled Graylin's room as he set about getting dressed and started down the stairs, ready to be on his way and get his day started.

A light meal of cold meat and fresh-baked bread was already sitting ready for him in the large common room and there, already sipping a cup of steaming hot coffee and as arrogant as always, was Clifford Sumter.

"I thought I would have to go and wake you, sir," he threw at Graylin as he approached the table.

Graylin felt the hairs on the nape of his neck rise and cautioned himself to remain calm. It would not do after coming all these many miles with the young man to now lose his temper. He would need all the help he could get in order to find his daughter. Without comment he lifted his coffee, took a sip, then he made himself a sandwich with some meat and delicious-smelling bread. Turning about, he threw over his shoulder as he started to hobble out of the inn, "I leave in ten minutes."

Smiling thinly, Clifford swallowed the rest of his coffee and rose following the older man.

The morning went by slowly for the group of men riding horseback into the Cumberlands. Each kept his thoughts to himself as the day progressed.

Graylin had hired several men besides Alex Gentry to make the trip. With each prodding step of his mount he felt the full pain of his throbbing leg, but he refused to stop or slow his pace. Ever on his mind was the vision of his daughter as he had seen her last, so beautiful and sparkling with youth. Just being here in these surrounding woods made him feel a peace he had not felt in over a year, for he somehow felt closer to her. There had never been any doubt in his mind that he would one day find her alive, and he hoped healthy. And now, stronger than ever, this feeling persisted.

Clifford Sumter's own thoughts were somewhat along these same lines. He also hoped that he would find Sorrel Morgan alive. Her health did not at all concern him as long as she was strong enough to survive until the marriage vows were spoken between them. And if she were still alive, he had chosen the right man to help him find her. He no longer trusted the good man Graylin Morgan, and on more than one occasion he had thought that the older man was about to tell him that there was no need for him to continue on with him on this trip, and that he was breaking the contract that had been written up so long ago to bring the two families together. This Clifford would not stand for, and that was why he had begun to put his own plans into motion.

It was late in the afternoon when Clifford finally broke away from the group of men, telling Graylin that he wished to ride ahead and perhaps scout about. He assured him that he would return safe and sound, if not by this evening when the group broke to make camp, then by the morning.

Graylin hardly minded, for he couldn't stand having the younger man about him. All day he had felt the cold gray eyes prying into his back. He readily agreed to his suggestion.

Clifford lashed out at his horse, bringing him into a gallop, leaving the group behind. He had no idea where he would find Cam, for the other man had told him not to worry, that he would find him. So, as the sun lowered in the sky, he slowed his pace to a walk.

Pains of hunger were filling Clifford's belly and he was about to give up and was thinking all manner of foul thoughts about Cam Brash. He started watching for a place to make his own camp. He would stop and eat and rest for a time, it was getting dark and it could be dangerous to go on in the night, he reasoned with himself as he looked about at the thick trees grouped together all about him.

As he rounded a group of these tall trees he saw a rider dimly in the distance, sitting casually waiting. Clifford could tell even in this light who the rider was. There was no mistaking the small shape of Cam Brash.

Riding up to within a few feet of him, Clifford pulled his horse to a stop. "I thought that we could make camp and fix something to eat." He did not mention the fact that he had thought he would not be seeing the smaller man again.

Cam shook his head and pulling his cap from his snarled and matted brown hair he grinned at Clifford. "I been watching ye for the better part of the afternoon. Ye should have eaten some time ago, fer we ain't a-stopping now. No sir, old Cam Brash ain't never stopped just because the darkness sets in."

"But would it not be safer to make camp and eat? We can continue in the morning."

"Ye be wishing to be some miles away from that group of men ye be traveling with, ain't ye?" He spit a long stream of tobacco juice at Clifford's horse's feet.

"Yes, I do, but I would rather not kill myself in the process." Clifford flinched at the other's bad manners.

"Cam Brash always knows what he's about. Ye ain't a-going to get ye self hurt. Who knows, we might even have us some fun and run into some Injuns." Cold, chilling laughter filled the very air about the two men.

"There will be none of that." Clifford tried to sound the part of the one with authority. He should have some say, he reasoned with himself. After all, he was the one that was paying this filthy braggart his wages. "We will go on, as you say, but we will keep to ourselves until we find the woman that I am looking for."

Cam Brash didn't say if he agreed with or opposed Clifford's wishes. With ease he pulled the reins on his horse and slowly started him off. "Some time back I was up here and found a pretty little cabin all hidden and to itself like, in a valley. I think we'll head in that direction. There's a tribe of Injuns that stays on pretty near to that section of the Cumberlands. And if nothing else, we may be able to get some information and some grub."

"Is it far?" Clifford questioned, feeling the extent of his hunger as his stomach growled in protest at their not stopping.

"It be a far piece, but if we keep on through the night we'll make it there by tomorrow noon," Cam threw over his shoulder, and he kicked the sides of his horse, stirring him on to a quicker pace.

With Josh and Joe both tucked into their cradles and sleeping peacefully, Sorrel began to clean the cabin. Going outside, with Lancer following her, she carried in two buckets of fresh water to use for cleaning the wood floors. She hoped that as soon as Mathew returned the following day he would wish to start the trip back to civilization, and if so she did not want to leave the cabin in a bad state. Also, she reasoned, the more jobs she could give herself to occupy her hands and her mind the quicker time would pass.

So she was down on her knees with rag in hand when she heard the sound of pounding hoofs coming toward the cabin. Jumping to her feet and sweeping a stray strand of golden hair back from her brow she hurried to the door. Her thoughts were that for some unknown reason Mathew had returned, perhaps he had decided not to leave her and their children after all.

Opening the door wide she was surprised to see Red Hawk pulling his horse to a halt right before her and jumping down from his back.

Sorrel welcomed her husband's friend with a

smile, but as she saw his stern features all traces of a smile left her lips. "What is the matter?" She barely got the words out, thinking that the Indian had come to tell her some bad news about Mathew.

"There are two riders coming toward the valley." The Indian's words, usually soft and attractive when he talked to Sorrel, now seemed cold and hard to her ears.

"Did you get a look at them?" Sorrel felt a measure of relief that he was not reporting some news about some harm done to her husband. But quickly, at the realization that riders were coming to the valley, she felt her heart beginning to beat with a rapid pumping.

"I followed them for a time, they did not see me. They are white men, but I do not like their looks." As the Indian talked he constantly glanced around them into the trees.

Sorrel was excited at the thought of who the visitors could be. She was sure that she would find one of them to be her father. Of course, he had not given her up and would have made a return trip to find her. She felt almost light-headed at the thought of once again seeing him. She reached out and lightly patted Red Hawk's arm, wishing to reassure him. "It is my father. I just know it is." She began to laugh aloud and without thought she reached up and gave the Indian a light kiss upon the cheek. "He has come to find me, and oh, Red Hawk, wait until he meets Mathew and our children!" She was about to twirl with happiness when the first sound of gunfire hit her ears.

Clifford and his guide had traveled all night without stopping, and most of the morning. Cam did allow one short stop for a drink of water and a quick bite of food. He hurried Clifford with gruff words and angry looks, telling himself over and over that he should never have taken this job. This dandy that he was leading about through the Cumberlands was more apt to fall from his horse and kill himself than he was to find any Injuns keeping a white woman.

He was about to turn in his saddle and once again tell Clifford Sumter to close his big mouth and keep moving when he noticed that right up ahead of him was the valley that he had been seeking.

Grumbling and complaining Clifford pulled abreast of his guide as Cam pulled his horse to a stop. Clifford was expecting the usual gruff words from the dirty little man's mouth, but instead was surprised to see him pointing off in the distance.

His gray eyes followed the dirty finger and came to rest upon a valley. Down in its depths was a small cabin, and from the looks of the smoke rising from the chimney he reasoned that there also must be people. He hoped that the people would be white and not Indians; he had no desire to see this Cam Brash in action.

As the pair slowly led their mounts down the valley and toward the cabin Clifford's interest mounted. From some distance he could see people at the cabin door.

His throat constricted as his gray eyes took in the couple. From a distance away they seemed to be two Indians and a horse. But as they drew closer he noticed that the woman did not have dark hair, but rather her long, thick braids seemed to glow in the sunlight.

Clifford's eyes became more alert, taking in every movement of the woman, seeing her hand reach out and touch the Indian's bare arm and then pulling herself closer and kissing his dark face. From within Clifford came a rage that he had never felt before. His mind became red, inflamed with a passion to destroy, and without second thought he reached down and pulled his long rifle from its case on his saddle, and, with little aim, fired. Without looking back at a startled Cam Brash he kicked his horse's sides and galloped toward the cabin.

Sorrel could not believe what was taking place. It all seemed to be happening in slow motion. From somewhere in the dark recesses of her mind she heard the boom of a shot, and as she stood next to Red Hawk she saw him beginning to fall toward the door of the cabin, his body coming to rest in the doorway with his long, dark legs lying in the dirt.

The scream froze on her lips, leaving her immobile and transfixed as she stared down at the body of Red Hawk as his red blood slowly poured out of the wound on his chest and covered him with its wetness.

Not long though did she have to stand thus, for within seconds Clifford Sumter was standing before her and taking hold of her wrist. Shaking her golden head Sorrel stared at the man before her until finally some sense of reason came to her. "You! Where is my father?" she frantically looked about her and then broke Clifford's grip and rushed to Red Hawk's side.

"How could you have shot him?" Tears were streaming down her face as she tried to stop the flow of blood with the only thing she had, her hand.

Jerking her back to her feet Clifford shoved her away from the cabin door, and, losing her balance she stumbled in the dirt. To her horror another man was with Clifford, and she had landed at his horse's feet.

"I see ye be finding yer woman?" Cam looked to Clifford and jerked his head toward Sorrel.

Pulling herself to her feet Sorrel slowly tried to make her way back to Red Hawk's side. If he was not helped he would surely die, she thought frantically.

"Aye, I found the little Indian-loving baggage." Clifford's anger was beyond control and he kicked out at Red Hawk's thigh.

Sorrel became incensed at Clifford's action, and with all of her strength she threw herself at this man she had for so many years thought to marry.

As though she were no more than a fly Clifford slapped her across the face, sending her back to the ground.

"Take her on your horse with you, Brash," Clifford spat out at his hired man.

Sorrel, realizing that they intended taking her with them, once again pulled herself from the earth and as though on cue she heard the sounds of her sons' crying.

Clifford also heard the noise and his face, which had registered anger earlier, became so hate-filled and enraged that Sorrel thought again before she made another move. She could not endanger her children.

"Where is my father, Clifford? Why is he not here with you?"

"Shut your mouth," came the snarled answer. "Brash, I told you to get her up on that horse."

"You cannot take me with you Clifford. My husband and my sons . . ."

Before she could finish she felt a sharp sting of pain biting deep into her cheek as Clifford brought his hand down and cruelly let his fist fly. "You have no husband, not yet that is." Taking hold of her arm he began to pull her toward Brash's horse.

But Sorrel, never having been one to easily give up, started to fight him, her only thought being that she could not be taken from her babies.

Hearing the loud shouts of his mistress as he rounded the cabin Lancer came at the man holding the arm of the woman he loved and trusted with all the force that his huge muscled body could muster.

"Ye had best look to yeself," called Cam to Clifford as he noticed the large dog coming at a run, large white teeth gleaming.

Clifford glanced about just in time to pull back his rifle and as the dog was about to jump at his throat he brought the butt of his long wooden gun down hard and fast, sending the huge dog into a still pile at the feet of the bleeding Indian.

Sorrel, seeing everything around her being shattered for trying to protect her tried to pull away from Clifford and get to Lancer and Red Hawk, but as before she was stilled by his strong arms. "Let me go, let me go," she wept over and over.

Pulling his handkerchief from his pocket Clifford tied it over Sorrel's mouth, and taking a piece of leather from his saddle he tied her struggling hands behind her back.

Cam had sat on his horse and watched it all with some amazement. He could barely credit that this dandified bumbling greenhorn could handle himself so well. But the proof was there before his eyes—the Indian more than likely dead by now, the huge beast knocked senseless, probably soon to die and here Clifford was lifting this beautiful, struggling woman up into his lap.

Sorrel struggled every second as she was lifted up onto the horse with the foul-smelling little man. She could not be taken from her children and her husband. How could this be happening? Where was her father, or anyone to help her?

"We'll not be going the same way we came," Clifford called to Cam. "I don't wish to run into the girl's father, but need to get to New Orleans as soon as possible."

Sorrel's head swung about toward Clifford at the mention of her father. So he was also here in the Cumberlands—but it was apparent that for some reason Clifford did not wish to meet up with him. And no wonder, she thought, for the moment she were to see her father she would tell him of Clifford's harsh treatment of her, and of how he had shot her husband's friend and struck her dog.

"Aye, laddy, old Cam Brash can take us out of this here forest without a soul seeing us." The small man's tone had a measure of respect in it as he talked to the other man.

"Then let us be on our way." Clifford kicked his horse and Cam followed behind.

Sorrel tried to look back to the cabin but could only manage to find her face against Cam's filthy shirt and the smell nauseated her, so she was left without even one look back at the cabin that contained her sons and all that was left of her heart.

Chapter Fifteen

Mathew approached the cabin with a sense of doom, his dark blue eyes searching the valley, trying to find an answer to his frantic thoughts. Whose horses were those tied outside of his home? There were several, and looking about Mathew could also see a horse tied near the stream at the back of the cabin.

Slapping his mount again upon his sleek flanks he pushed him on, making him go at a breakneck speed down the valley. He could not imagine who the horses could belong to and all that his mind could repeat over and over was that his wife and children were down there.

With urgency born of his love and the wish to protect his family Mathew jumped from his horse's back and grabbing hold of his long rifle he barged through the door of the cabin.

What met his eyes astounded him, and then, looking about at the shocked faces, he let his blue eyes go slowly and deliberately around about the room.

There in the cradle near the hearth were the twins,

their tiny hands and legs waving in the air. All about the room were strange men, and there on the bed—he looked again, not believing what was happening before him—was Red Hawk, and by the stillness of his body Mathew was not sure that he was not dead, but he was sure that he was seriously hurt. He let his eyes go still further, searching out every inch of the small room. Where was Sorrel?

Not a word had been said by the men in the room. Apparently the man who rose to his feet with a slight grimace on his lips was the eldest of the group and all eyes fell upon him and awaited his words. "Who are you?" The words seemed hollow in the quiet room.

Mathew was beginning to feel an unreasoning anger building within the marrow of his bones, and taking a step further into the room he let the full blast of his own voice be heard. "What do you men think to be doing in my home? And where is my wife?" Mathew felt his insides being pulled into a knot. What had these people done with Sorrel? Was she at this very moment outside somewhere fighting for her very life? He felt his large hands grasping a tighter hold upon his gun. He had no fear that he was outnumbered. His strength had seen him through tighter spots before, and where his family was concerned he knew that he could overcome any obstacle. Without a second thought he stalked over to the gray-haired man who had as yet not given him an answer to his questions. This time all the men in the cabin felt the deathlike breath leave his body with the words, *"What have you done with my wife?"*

The harsh anger underlined by the controlled violence of his tone was not lost on Graylin, but now the older man thought that he had made some kind of mistake. He had wished, upon finding this cabin, that he had also found his daughter, but now with this angry young man's words he realized that this must be a futile hope. Sitting back down on the chair as though defeated he sighed, "I do not know the whereabouts of your wife, young man. We found your home in bad condition when we arrived here." He watched the reactions playing over the younger man's features and a part of his heart went out to him. "The Indian over there," he pointed a finger toward the bed and then continued, "was lying in the doorway; he's bleeding from a gunshot wound in the upper part of his chest, almost in his shoulder. I think he'll live, he just lost a lot of blood. We then found the babies." His features seemed to soften as he looked down to the cradle. Graylin had even secretly wished that these children would prove to be his daughter's. But now he knew that he had been nothing more than an old fool. "The babies are all right," he added.

Mathew listened to the older man and without saying a word he went to the cradles. Making sure that everything was all right with them he turned and went to the bed and Red Hawk. If what the elderly man had said was the truth, then only Red Hawk knew what had happened to Sorrel.

"We also found a large dog." Graylin nodded his head to a corner of the room and there Mathew saw a pile that could only be Lancer.

Mathew felt himself wishing to scream with his outrage. How dare anyone come to his home and do such a foul deed? Reaching down, he took the arm of

Red Hawk that was not damaged. "Red Hawk," he called the name, not realizing the force of his voice. "My brother, you must wake and tell me where my wife is."

Graylin felt his heart contract with the pain that he was feeling for this young man. Rising once more to his feet he looked about him at the men he had hired. They had only entered the cabin moments ago, wishing to know his orders. He had thought then that he would not be able to leave until the Indian regained his senses. Of course he could not leave two children to an unconscious Indian and a dog that had a huge gash in his head. But now that this man had come to reclaim what was left of his family he reasoned that he should get on with his own search. Now not only did he have his daughter to find, but also Clifford Sumter was missing.

Graylin felt his own anger when he thought of this young man. Alex had found tracks made by Clifford's horse and also tracks of another horse, and by all appearances the two horses had seemed to be traveling together. That was how Graylin's group had found this secluded cabin, by following the signs made by that bumbling Clifford. "You men go out and water your horses. I shall be coming soon and we shall set back out on our way." As they started to do as ordered Graylin called out to Alex to have his horse readied and he would only be another moment.

Going to the bedside after his men had left the room Graylin reached down and placed one hand gently on the shoulder of the large young man who had come home to find such troubles. "I am sorry son, I only wish there was some way I could help you."

Mathew looked up from the Indian, who he was trying to revive, into the face of the man above him and something deep in those features seemed for a moment familiar to him. Shaking his head he said, "Thank you, sir. I do not know what has brought you here, but I thank you for caring for my family." Once more Mathew turned from Graylin and began gently to prod Red Hawk into wakefulness.

Graylin shook his gray head and turned toward the door, impatient to be off. There was still plenty of time this day to travel and he wished not to waste another moment.

"Red Hawk, you must wake. What happened here while I was gone?" Mathew called again and again to his Indian brother, but nothing seemed to stir him. "Tell me, who has taken Sorrel!" Mathew's voice rose and seemed to fill the cabin, bringing the elderly man to a complete halt as his hand started to reach out for the latch on the door.

Graylin turned about not believing his ears. Had that young man called his daughter's name to the Indian? He could not have been mistaken, the name was too unusual. Without another thought he turned and made his way quickly back to the other man.

"Tell me where she is, Red Hawk." As the older man reached his side Mathew was once again softly shaking the red man.

Graylin looked down at the younger man for a full minute before he drew his attention. "Listen here," he coughed aloud. With Mathew's face turned in his direction, Graylin continued. "The name of your wife? Did I hear you correctly? Is she called Sorrel?"

Graylin felt his breath stop as he awaited an answer.

Mathew rose from the side of the bed to his full towering height as he looked the other man full in the face. "Aye, my wife's name is Sorrel." Mathew could not understand what her name would have to do with this man but he remembered that he did owe this man something for putting Red Hawk on the bed and tending his arm and tending to Lancer and his children.

"Her name was Sorrel Morgan?" Tears came to Graylin's eyes as he watched Mathew's face.

"Aye, that was her name when first I met her."

Graylin could not speak for a full moment. He could not believe he had found his daughter at last. "Then these children, they are hers and yours?" he got out, and at Mathew's nodding of his head the tears that had formed now slowly went down his cheeks. These were his grandchildren and this man standing before him was his daughter's husband. Stretching out his hand toward Mathew he spoke softly. "My name is Graylin Morgan, son, Sorrel is my daughter."

Mathew was thunderstruck and was not able fully to comprehend what the elderly man was saying. Too much was happening around him. The stretched-out hand seemed oddly hanging in mid-air, and without thought he reached out his own and took the one awaiting his. "Her father?" he finally got out.

"Her father, indeed," Graylin said softly. "We came to find her, and now I see that she has a husband and a family started."

"Aye sir, but what of Sorrel herself? What am I to

do?" The words seemed a plea from the very depths of Mathew's soul as he said them aloud to Graylin.

"I think that she will not be much harmed, lad." At Mathew's look of wonder, he continued. "I had hoped that when I found this cabin that somehow I would find my daughter to have lived here and that those beautiful children were hers."

"But sir, she has been taken by someone, what . . ."

"Yes, lad, she has been taken, but I think I know who the foul culprit is and I am sure that he will not harm her. Rather, he would wish to keep her in good health."

"Who is this that you speak of?" Mathew was now ready to give chase and find his wife.

"Has Sorrel mentioned to you that she was betrothed since early childhood to a gentleman by the name of Clifford Sumter?" Graylin questioned and waited for Mathew to answer. His answer would prove much to Graylin. He was not as yet sure of the arrangement that his daughter and this huge man had, and if Sorrel had been trapped somehow into staying through the winter with this man and forced to live here as his wife he would now know the truth.

"Aye, Sorrel told me all, sir. I had in mind upon reaching my home in Kentucky to send the good man a tidy sum for his inconvenience. For, as I said, she is now my wife." Mathew could not understand what Sorrel's old betrothed had to do with what was happening here in the Cumberlands.

Graylin seemed well pleased with the answer that the younger man gave him. If Sorrel had offered all of her past to this man and he was charitable enough to want to compensate a man he did not even know for the loss of his wife, then Graylin knew that there was more here than his daughter's having been forced into anything she did not wish. "This Clifford Sumter is the culprit who has taken Sorrel, I am sure," Graylin let the words fall.

"But how?" was all that Mathew could get out.

"I am afraid that it is as much my fault," Graylin sighed and once more, as though he were aging by the minute, he went to the chair near the hearth and sat his bulk down, his eyes now glued upon the children in the cradle. "I allowed the man to come along with me to find Sorrel, but he must have sensed my displeasure with him and spirited my daughter away. You see, I did not truly know Clifford until now. He has traveled these many miles from Texas with me, and, frankly, I would never have allowed my daughter to marry such a bumbling blackguard."

"Neither shall I, sir. She is mine." Mathew spoke the words as though making a promise.

Graylin did not speak but watched the younger man with respect. Aye, his daughter had done well for herself, he thought. He could never have found a better husband for her. In just this short meeting with Mathew, Graylin knew the type of man that stood before him. "He will not be hard to find, lad. He will be heading back for Texas just as quickly as possible."

Mathew had been used since an early age to taking control and giving orders, and now that he had a set purpose and knew what had happened to Sorrel he began to put everything into order. "I shall be in need of two of your men, sir."

"Anything that I can do lad, and all that I have are

at your disposal." Graylin felt a weight lift from his shoulders and almost felt a smile tug at his lips. This young man was quite capable of handling everything. Glancing down once again he watched his grandchildren as they slept. "We had best get these children a wet nurse soon, son," he absently said to Mathew as he came back into the room after leaving to call two of the men from outside.

"Aye, I know that well, sir. They are both boys; their names are Josh and Joe." Mathew threw this over his shoulder as he helped the two men lift Red Hawk and carry him out to his horse. The two men would take him to his village and there he would recover.

Graylin sat watching over the babies as Mathew next fashioned a litter to be pulled by a horse to carry Lancer. After carefully checking the animal, Mathew found that he had a large, deep gash on the side of his head, and though the dog did not act his usual self and lay still in the corner of the cabin, Mathew was sure that he, too, would recover.

Most important in Mathew's mind was the wish to quickly get his sons to Crescent Mist and secure them proper care. He was not sure how many hours had gone by since they had last been fed by Sorrel, but he did know that it would not be long before they would both be starting to cry out for their milk.

Only a short time had gone by when Mathew entered the cabin and took his boys outside to be carried on horseback to his father's house.

Graylin also was in some need as he hobbled out of the cabin, and Alex Gentry helped him to mount his own horse.

The group of men started off. Mathew was impatient, wishing to hurry each step so he could quickly find his children good care and then be about the job of finding his wife.

Sorrel's life had turned from the paradise that she had shared with Mathew to a tormenting nightmare upon horseback. The ride was never ending, and her body was surrounded by the filth and stench of the little man as his arms encircled her and he held his horse's reins.

Her gag had not as yet been removed, nor the leather thong taken from her wrist. All afternoon and night they rode, neither man seeming ever to need rest, but Sorrel, her body still not as strong as before the birth of her children, felt the weariness of each bone in her body. Her head sagged forward as her eyes shut, but quickly she would feel the pressure of the man behind her and her emerald eyes would fly open.

She was almost in shock. Her life had fallen completely apart before her very eyes. Over and over she told herself not to think of Red Hawk's body lying bleeding in the dust. Nor could she let herself think of Lancer, his head brutally smashed by Clifford's gun barrel. But try as she would she could not force herself to stop thinking of her sons. How would they survive without her? Had Mathew returned early and found his sons alone and her gone? Would he know what had happened and somehow be able to find her?

Tears came to her eyes and she tried to stop them,

afraid that she would make herself sick and suffocate with this vile gag in her mouth. She truly doubted that either man, the one riding behind her or Clifford in front of them, would take the time to undo her gag and let her be relieved.

The scenery before her seemed to blur by her in a hazy cloud as the afternoon sunlight dimmed. All about her was a passage of trees and greenery, and her mind became numb with each plodding step of the horse.

She was suddenly and rudely pulled from the horse's back and then cruelly grasped, and with the touching of hands upon her she came fully awake. She must have slept, she realized. But where were they? she wondered, as Clifford gruffly pulled her along behind him.

She could see some kind of structure before them and the dim light of candles. It must be some kind of inn, she thought. Perhaps she could get some help from inside. For a second her spirits were buoyed, but as quickly they were dashed as she noticed that they were not heading for the front of the building but instead to the back, and squinting her green eyes she could see that someone was holding the door open a crack, as though waiting for them.

Of course, she thought, that was where the dirty little man had gone, to have the back door opened for them.

Without saying a word Clifford hauled Sorrel toward the door. As she tried to pull back, dreading the thought of entering this strange building, he jerked her by the leather straps and coldly warned, "I shall carry you if you insist."

That would have been the final insult to her pride, so, stiffening her back, she went along as he pulled her.

To Sorrel's surprise a young girl awaited them inside a small back room.

"Madam Beaufont told me to be expecting you, sir. I have had a room fixed and it is awaiting you and your, ah, friend here." The girl looked at Sorrel with a kind of wonder, noticing the gag and that the girl's hands were tied behind her back. She also noticed the large bruise upon her cheek, and she was finally only glad that it was not she who was in that position.

"Lead on, then," Clifford gruffly commanded the woman.

Sorrel could not talk so she saw no way in which she would be able to plead with the other woman. But something in the other woman's bearing told her, even though no words had been said, that if she could talk it would only be a waste of her breath. Sorrel knew what this woman was, and she could well imagine who this Madam Beaufont was—*madam*, indeed.

The woman led Sorrel and Clifford up a flight of back stairs and then down a dark hallway. Opening a door she lighted the way into the room with a burning candle.

"I have brought the girl a dress of my own. The little fellow said that she would be in need of some clothing." Her eyes went over Sorrel's Indian dress and her moccasins.

"That will be enough." Clifford threw the woman a few coins, but as she reached the door he called, "Tell Madam Beaufont that I shall be down soon to thank her myself."

"That I will sir, that I will," the girl chuckled as she shut the door.

Sorrel stood in the room and watched Clifford as his eyes took it all in. It was a large room with a four poster bed in the middle and not much other furniture. There was a chair, the only other furnishing besides a small table next to the bed with a pitcher and bowl for washing.

"It is not much but it will do for the night," Clifford mumbled aloud. And then going to Sorrel he looked her full in the face, noticing instantly the twin orbs of emerald fright as she stared up at him. Reaching out he untied the leather thongs from her wrist and then he pulled the gag from her mouth.

The moment the gag was taken from her mouth Sorrel glared at the man who had dared to take her from her husband's home. "How dare you? My father will have you shot when he sees you," was all that she could get out.

"Not so," Clifford said, starting to the door. "Your father would never dare to shoot his daughter's husband. If anything, he will be most grateful for my finding his precious little daughter."

"Husband?" Sorrel was mystified. How could he think that he could be her husband? "If you think to marry me you are mistaken, and all this has been for naught."

Clifford looked at the girl with some distaste. She was certainly as beautiful as he had remembered her, but now her hair was straying out of its confines, and with the bruise on her face and her strange clothing he grimaced just looking upon her. "You have been promised to me since you were a child and with our marriage our ranches will be joined. That has been my dream for the past years and nothing will sway me."

"But I cannot marry you. I already have a husband." Sorrel thought her words simple enough and was surprised at the guffaws of laughter that she evoked from Clifford.

"The only real husband you will ever have will be me, Sorrel Morgan."

"You are quite mistaken in more than one thing, Clifford. I do, in fact, have a husband and my name is no longer Morgan but is now Danner. And my husband is Mathew Danner."

Clifford thought it strange that an Indian would have a name such as this and with his look Sorrel knew his thoughts.

Her own laughter now filled his ears. "You have indeed made a mistake, Clifford, and you had best take care and straighten it all out. My husband was not the Indian that you shot. He was Red Hawk, a friend like a brother to my husband. My husband is a white man and also a man of some means in Kentucky, and he will, I assure you, not take easily to the treatment that you have inflicted upon me."

Clifford felt a raw, piercing anger at her words and her laughter. He had been sure when she had spoken of her husband at the cabin that she had meant the Indian, but now she said that she was married to a white man. How could this be possible? "I do not believe you, Sorrel." His tone was smug, as though he had caught her in her lies. "You were taken by an Indian and you were found with an Indian. There is no way that you could have married a white man and then gone back again to the Cumberlands." He thought he saw her plans now. She wished to make him believe this so that he would release her. But he had waited years for her and he was not one to be easily duped.

The smile died on Sorrel's lips at his tone. "We were married at Red Hawk's village. My husband was hunting in the Cumberlands and found me." She did not wish to tell this vile man what had happened to her, she wished only to tell him enough so that he would let her go back to her children and Mathew.

"Save your lies, woman," Clifford shouted, his face contorting with his anger, and he left the door and strode to within just a few feet of her.

"I do not lie." Sorrel's soft words hit his ears.

"I care not for it. If you speak the truth, what of it? A marriage in an Indian village means nothing. I have been your betrothed for years and you are mine."

"Perhaps my marriage means nothing to you but it does to me and my husband and I assure you that if you ever do get me to Texas that my father will also see my side."

Reaching out and laying hold of her, Clifford shouted, "I care naught what anyone thinks, I only care that you are mine and that your father joins his ranch with mine, and he will, for you are his only child."

Tears began to roll down Sorrel's cheeks from the pressure that he was inflicting upon her arms. "But I have twin sons."

If Clifford had been sickened at the sight of her before, this news only intensified this feeling. Dropping her arms he started back to the door. "Forget that you ever had a child. I never wish to hear those words from your mouth again. When we marry and are living in my home perhaps if you please me I shall let you bear my children."

Sorrel could not believe her ears. He had to be insane. How could he tell her to forget her children and that she would bear his if he allowed it? For the first time she felt the full impact of her predicament. She was being held prisoner by an insane man. Being Red Hawk's prisoner had been nothing like this.

As he opened the door he threw over his shoulder, "Change that dress and clean yourself up." He slammed the door behind him and Sorrel could hear a key turning in the lock.

Her first move was to rush to the window and pull back the curtains. Perhaps she could climb out and regain her freedom. But to her total despair she found that the window had been barred. There was no way out but the door.

Sorrel paced about the room for some time trying to come up with some means by which she could gain her freedom. But it all led nowhere. There was no way out. Feeling total exhaustion she sat down upon the bed, and then for the first time her emerald eyes fell on the dress thrown casually across the end of the satin counterpane.

The dress was a cream color and appealed to Sorrel's eye on first glance. She was surprised as she took up the gown that something so delicately sewn could have belonged to the woman who had led them to this room. But then she reasoned that perhaps this was why the woman had given up this gown. She had been bold and a bit brazen to Sorrel's way of thinking, with her bright red hair and her low-cut gown of a lighter shade of red with shimmering spangles on the bodice.

She let her fingers roam over the soft material. Lifting it she found a chemise and a pair of matching slippers.

The temptation was too much to bear. Sorrel began to unbraid her tangled hair and checking the pitcher to see if water had been brought in she sighed with a small measure of pleasure. At least if she were to be prisoner she would not have to be filthy. An image of the small man who had helped Clifford came to her mind and a shudder coursed through her.

It was only a short time later that she stood before the cracked mirror on the wall and viewed her handiwork. It had been over a year since she had last worn a dress of such beauty and now she smiled her pleasure. The only thing that marred the image looking back at her was the ugly purple bruise on her right cheek. And looking at the dress she still felt tears coming to her eyes. Where was Mathew at this moment? Would he ever be able to see her in a dress such as this? What was her fate to be? Her body began to rock with her sobbing now that she looked again at what had taken place in the last few days. And with little thought she threw herself upon the softness of the bed and wept. She cried for her sons, her arms seeming to ache with the want of holding them tightly to her bosom, and for the man she loved with a love that could never be surpassed. Mathew had grown to be her all, his very presence in her mind filling her with the desire to scream out her anger to the very walls. How could she survive without him by her side? He was her support and future. And now all seemed lost. She would be Clifford's prisoner and would be taken back to Texas, but she promised herself that no matter what, she would escape him and return to Mathew.

Chapter Sixteen

Leading the group of men down the long, tree-lined lane to Crescent Mist, Mathew wished nothing more than to slap his horse's flanks and rush him on. It all seemed so familiar, just as he had left it. But he could not hurry away from his children and father-in-law, so he restrained himself with a will.

As they neared the great house sitting proudly upon the lush green grass and surrounded with a profusion of multicolored flowers, Mathew let his head fill with the scents and sounds that he had grown up around. From the house itself he could hear the loud voice of Mally calling to Justin Danner that company was coming and that he had best hurry his self up.

A large smile came over Mathew's face with the hearing of that beloved voice. How he had missed Crescent Mist! Anxiously he strained his eyes, watching for his father.

And there, as their horses approached closer to the veranda, he caught a glimpse of the gray-haired older Danner. He looked him over with one glance and without a second look he saw that he looked, like

Crescent Mist, not changed in the least. Jumping down from his horse, no longer able to keep himself in control, he ran up the steps of the veranda.

Justin Danner could not believe his eyes as they fell on his son, and he also rushed forward. "Mathew, is it you, boy?" He knew that it was, but he had all but given up hope that his son would ever again return to him.

Mathew smiled happily as he wrapped his arms about his father and hugged him to his chest. He had not so openly displayed such affection toward the other man since he had been a child, but now something within him reached out for the love that only this man could give to him.

Justin sensed some new sadness in his child and pulled back to look him in the face. "You have aged, lad," were the only words that he could get out.

"Aye, Father, I have that." Mathew released his father and turned to the group of men on horseback who sat awaiting his pleasure. "Come down, Mr. Morgan, and meet my father. I shall pay your men their wages and send them on their way. They will not be needed any longer."

Before Graylin could do as bid a piercing scream came from the doorway and a huge black woman ran down the veranda and threw her bulk at Mathew. "Mathew, Mathew! My boy done come home at last!" Mally wept aloud as she kissed him upon the cheek. "I be thinking this here day ain't never going to come about." And pulling herself now out of Mathew's arms she looked toward the group in the front yard. "Here you is and you done brought home company." Mally grinned at Graylin as he slowly made his way off his horse, and as he reached up to Alex and took an infant in each arm the grin became even larger. "Lordy, Lordy Master Mat, what you done and brought home for Mally? Whose younguns they be, Master Mat?" she questioned, looking him in the face as she started to get to the steps of the veranda and help the man carrying the babies.

She saw the pain on the face of the man she had raised and stopped in her tracks. Something was not right here. Why was her boy so upset? She turned about and gave her full attention to Mathew. "Master Mat, whose children these be?" She knew her answer before it left his lips but she told herself that she had to hear it spoken.

"They are mine, Mally," Mathew said softly, and then turned from her to his father. "Their names are Joshua and Joseph, Father. They are twins."

"And their mother?" Justin asked, just as softly, feeling some of the pain that was on his son's face.

"She has been taken."

Justin looked hard at his son, not understanding. How could the mother of his children have been taken? Had she, like Elizabeth, died?

"Perhaps I can clear things up for you, Mr. Danner." Graylin stepped forward and gave the twins up to Mally's care. Graylin stretched out his hand and Justin clasped it tightly to his own. "It is good to meet you once again, though I must admit that I wish it had been under more pleasant circumstances."

"It is a pleasure for me also, Mr. Morgan. Perhaps you would be good enough to tell me what is going on?"

Mathew looked on in surprise as he realized that the two gentlemen knew each other.

"Have a seat," Justin said, pointing to the chairs on the veranda. "If Mally will have one of the girls go and fetch a wet nurse from the cabins out back perhaps she can get the babies settled and then we can make some sense out of what is happening."

"Yes sir, yes sir. It won't be a minute and I have my boys here tended to. Don't you be aworrying yourself none about their care, Master Mat. I done raised you and you turned out just right, and I can take good care of your sons."

"Thank you, Mally." Mathew went over to the black woman and his babies and fondly kissed her on the cheek. "I know that you will see that no harm comes their way."

"Yes sir, I do that for sure." She turned and hurried through the door, her loud voice calling the names of the housegirls and getting things into motion.

Now, after Mally had taken the children into the house and Alex and the men had left for town, Mathew sat down and began to tell his father about Sorrel Morgan.

Graylin also listened avidly to all that had happened to his daughter since last he had seen her. But as Mathew began to tell of his last hunting trip to gather his traps, Graylin joined in, telling what he could of what Mathew had left out.

Justin Danner sat in unbelieving amazement as his son told him all that had happened to him since that fateful day when he had ridden away from Crescent Mist, not believing his ears as Mathew told of his meeting with Sorrel Morgan.

Seeing once again in his mind the picture of the young, beautiful, vibrant girl who had only a year ago sat here on the veranda and filled one of his sad days with a touch of life, he brought his hand up to his aging eyes and covered them for a second, wishing to block out the image he held in his mind of that same beautiful face now being filled with pain at the hands of a cruel abductor. Jumping to his feet, Justin slammed a huge fist against the front of the house. "By all that's right, boy, I shall go with you and find this blighter that dares to lay hold of your wife." Justin Danner had not worked himself up into such a fine temper in some time, and now his face turned a bright red as he stomped about the veranda, chafing at the delay in his urgency to be off and doing something that would regain Sorrel's release.

Mathew also rose to his full height. "Nay Father, you are more needed here, watching that no harm comes to my sons and entertaining Mr. Morgan. He is not able to go on much longer. His ankle is in poor condition and I think he would be much more comfortable here with you than chasing about on the back of a horse after Sorrel. I am well able to find her and bring her back to her family." Mathew's words were said in a tone that left no room for argument. Sorrel Danner was his wife and his concern, and he alone would handle her rescue.

Graylin started to protest but stopped quickly by the look directed at him by a stern-faced Mathew. Then, turning to Justin, he relaxed back against his chair and kept his thoughts to himself. He was sure that this young man was well able to get his daughter back, even if it entailed his going all the way to

Texas, he was sure that it would be done. He also remembered all the pain he had suffered in the past few days on the back of the horse he had been riding, and now a look of pleasure crossed his face. It might not be too bad staying here at this large house and enjoying the company of the elder Danner. He also could take the time to get acquainted with his grandsons. "Fine, lad, I concede. But find my daughter and bring her home safe."

"Aye sir, I shall do that," Mathew answered and then turned toward his father, his look a questioning one, wishing to know if his father also would abide by his wishes.

Justin was not so easily swayed as Graylin and still he chafed at each picture in his mind of the young woman in question. "I cannot easily put the picture of Sorrel from my mind," he said. Mathew's dark brow rose at this statement and he continued, "She spent one afternoon here at Crescent Mist with me while her father looked at our horses. Something about the young woman caught at me that very day, son, and to find that she is now your wife and the mother of my grandchildren and then in the same breath to find out that she is not at your side here at Crescent Mist but is being held somewhere by a man of unsavory character—well, I wish to be doing something."

Mathew was surprised at his words. Sorrel had never said that she had been here at Crescent Mist or that she had met his father. But after a moment's reflection he did remember that she had said that she had traveled to so many different towns and plantations that she had been weary and more than ready to head back to Texas. That must have been her reason for not realizing that she had been to his home. One plantation must have seemed like another to her by then. He set this from his mind for a time and going to his father he put his hand upon his shoulder. "I shall bring my wife back to Crescent Mist. Do not worry or think that you have to ride at my side. You are needed here, Father."

As though doused with the calming effect of Mathew's words, Justin relaxed his agitated stance. Looking deep into Mathew's face he realized that here was indeed a man to reckon with. He was no longer his little boy who he could help out of any situation. He was a man and well able to handle himself in any affair, and this case of his wife's kidnapping would be best left to him. "Aye, son, I shall take fine care of your family."

Mathew grimly smiled and squeezed his father's shoulder a second before turning and starting to the front door of the house. He would get himself a quick bit to eat and see to his sons before he left. Every move he made, though, was an impatient hurrying with his desire to be off. He would have to find some clue to Sorrel's whereabouts and the first place he would start at would be in the last town that Graylin had stayed in before he had set out for the Cumberlands with Clifford Sumter.

Pacing seemed the only option left open to Sorrel as she once again roamed about her prison. She was reminded of a bird in a gilded cage. The trappings were beautiful, and all seemed well, but a fierce fight for survival was really going on.

The only thing that she had to be thankful for was the fact that she was no longer locked up in the room that had been home to a number of women of unsavory reputation. They had stayed at the house that Clifford had taken her to on that first night for only two days. On the second night they had left, as they had come, by the dark of the night, and had ridden for a day until they had come to another town. Clifford, with little fanfare, had gone directly to the waterfront section of this town and to a large ship.

This had been where Clifford and the small, unkempt man had parted company, for Sorrel had not again seen the man called Cam Brash. She had been quickly ushered aboard ship and taken to the cabin that she now walked about.

It had been a couple of days before the ship had pulled anchor and sailed out of port. But this had done little good for Sorrel. She had hoped that somehow she would be able to regain her freedom, but she had been disabused of these thoughts when she saw the small port hole in the cabin. It was the only window, and with each visit of Clifford Sumter, who brought her her meals, she could hear, like a raging sound, the turning of the key in the door.

Clifford only made his visits when he brought her meals and had treated her with cool disdain since that night at the house when she had told him about her husband. He rarely spoke to her now, but in his gray, cold eyes she saw that his determination had not diminished. He still intended to marry her and gain access to her father's property.

Sorrel had not thoroughly given up. The only time

she had broken down had been that first night, at that vile house, when she had cried herself to sleep. On waking the next morning she had determined that she would not again give in to despair. She had little hope that Mathew would find her now. Perhaps if they had remained in the Cumberlands he would have found them, but how could he find her now? He would not in the least know where to look for her. But she was not without hope. Clifford would be taking her to Texas, and her Aunt Corry would be there, and her father. She would seek help the moment that she could break free of the madman who held her captive. And not one time did she doubt that she would find the chance to escape. And that was what kept Sorrel holding on—her thoughts of regaining her freedom and her constant thoughts of her husband and sons.

Over and over in her mind she reviewed the life that she had led in the Cumberlands with Mathew. And most often these thoughts went to the last day they had shared at the pond. How wonderful that day had become in her mind. Her love for Mathew was a never-ending feeling in her heart and soul that could never be swayed no matter who or what the pressure. He was all to her, and even now without him at her side, he was always in her thoughts and the source of her courage, for she had no doubt that she would be with him again.

Her pacing stopped as she heard the latch on the door turning, and Clifford entered the cabin. She wondered mildly what he wanted, since he held no tray.

Gray, chilling eyes went over the woman across the

room, taking in her surprised face at seeing him so early in the day in her cabin, and her body, now dressed in the fine clothing he had purchased for her. He would not have the woman who was to be his wife in anything but the finest, and in Richmond he had found a dressmaker and had purchased the necessary clothing to suit his taste.

"You seem surprised to see me this morning, Sorrel." His tone remained cold while he talked to her.

Sorrel did not speak but watched his every move as though she were a small, defenseless mouse and he a large cat toying with her and awaiting her reaction.

Clifford grew bored easily with this form of recreation, and, losing his patience, quickly spoke. "If you care to take a walk on deck, I suggest that you move quickly."

Sorrel was taken aback by his words and for a moment stood looking at him as though this was some kind of trap.

"I shall not stand here and wait much longer. If you do not care for a breath of fresh air then I shall leave you to yourself." He turned and started back to the door.

"Wait," Sorrel cried, and hurried toward him. He was serious, and that meant she could leave this room.

Clifford turned and waited for her to go ahead of him, then took hold of her upper arm.

As they left the companionway and started to the deck he brought her up closer to him and gruffly whispered, "Do not make any kind of scene here on this ship. I have already told the good captain that you are my wife, but since childhood you have had troubles with your mind." He held back nothing as he gave Sorrel this information.

Shock was apparent on her features as she glared at him. "You have told people that I have lost my senses?" She could not believe anyone could be capable of such an untruth, but she was quickly learning that this man would dare anything. "How dare you say such a thing about me!" She brought her free hand up and tried to slap his arrogant face, but before she could get her hand near him he grabbed hold of her wrist. To her utter humiliation, at that moment the captain of the ship strode by and tipped his hat in their direction. Sorrel saw written on his face, as he took in what was happening between the couple near the rail, that he now needed no more proof: Without a doubt he thought her insane.

The pressure that Clifford exerted upon her wrist was most painful and Sorrel gasped at the pain. He was telling her that she had best watch herself, and realizing that her fate was in this man's hands and that no one now would believe her if she tried to tell them the truth about Clifford Sumter, she turned and looked out to sea. If she did not act in the manner in which he wished she would, in fact, more than likely never see anything besides the inside of her cabin until they docked in Texas.

Clifford smiled grimly at Sorrel's back. Then, turning toward the captain, who was still watching them from a short distance away, he called to him, "Good day."

The captain seemed satisfied that the young man was well able to handle his insane wife, and once more tipping his hat he turned and went about his business.

When the captain was out of hearing range Clifford turned and spoke next to Sorrel's ear. "I shall not be so easy the next time you try something. My wife will obey me, and if you ever again raise your hand to me you will regret it." His voice grated chillingly over Sorrel, but she did not answer, a fear now filling her that this man was more than insane, he was unpredictable, and he would stoop to any lengths to get what he wished.

As Mathew had left Crescent Mist he had been met up with by Alex Gentry, and no matter what he told the other man he could not sway him from riding with him and helping him to find Sorrel.

At first Mathew had tried to turn him from his decision to come along, thinking that he could cover more land and do more to find Sorrel on his own, but now he thanked God for the other man.

It was Alex who had late one night, in a small town, met up with a filthy little man called Cam Brash, and after he had bought the odd little fellow a few too many drinks the man had talked well into the night about his adventures with the greenhorn he had taken to the Cumberlands. He had also told this stranger who was so willing to spend his coins on a new bottle for him of how that same greenhorn had surprised him and turned more than mean as he had killed an Indian and a vicious dog that had looked as large as a wolf and then had taken the Indian's woman.

Alex had played along with the little man and listened to it all, every once in a while prodding him to tell more.

When Alex returned to the inn that he and Mathew had rented rooms in, he had gone straight to Mathew's room, pounded on the door and awakened him from his sleep.

"What is it, man?" Mathew had pulled the door wide, trying to get on his breeches.

"I have found her, Mathew. I have found the man that went with Clifford to the Cumberlands." Alex rushed into the room excitedly.

"What? What are you saying?" Mathew thought that he had heard wrong.

"I said that I know where Sorrel is."

"Where, where man?" Mathew took hold of the front of Alex's shirt, all but lifting him off his feet.

"He took a ship from Richmond only one day ago, heading back to Texas," Alex said quickly, wanting his release from his large hands.

"And Sorrel?" Mathew held his breath awaiting his answer.

"The man said that she was fine but he also said that this Clifford Sumter was insane and liable to get quite angry. I think that we should hurry on our way and get to her before anything happens."

"Aye." Mathew began to throw his clothes into his saddle bag and then quickly pulled on his boots. "I shall meet you downstairs in a few minutes and we will be off." He left room for no argument and Alex hurried off to his own room to get his belongings.

Mathew was possessed with but one thought, and that was his wife and finding the man who held her captive. At least now he knew where to start, and he could picture in his mind how he would find the ship that they were on and rescue her.

He had friends in Richmond and he was sure that he could get a ship ready in no time to be ready to chase the seas for Sorrel.

Picking up his bags he went downstairs and waited for Alex, his thoughts focused on finding this Clifford Sumter who had dared to steal what was his.

Chapter Seventeen

The weather had begun to change, from bright sunny days to days of dark clouds hanging low and ever ominous.

Sorrel found that each breath she took seemed harder than the last. The air for the last two days had seemed thick with tension and the smell of an impending storm. And by all accounts it would be no minor storm, but a fierce and vengeful gale that would surely take some toll on them.

Clifford had not come to escort her above ship that day, but she was no longer locked in her cabin. Everyone aboard the ship thought her unsound, all avoiding eye contact with the young beautiful woman who was demented. No one talked to her, her husband having assured everyone at mealtimes of the danger when she was not given her own way.

Almost everyone aboard the ship thought Clifford Sumter the most kind and loving of husbands as they watched him taking a tray to his wife's room or strolling along deck with her on his arm. They all secretly agreed that it perhaps would be a kindness to himself if he would find a suitable, quiet place to board his insane wife. They all thought highly of him for taking the full responsibility for her care.

Sorrel herself, after several days on the ship, no longer cared what these people or the captain of the ship thought. It was obvious from the looks of pity that were directed toward her and also toward Clifford that they had all believed what he had told them about her. She knew that if she went to any of them with the truth they would instantly take her story as a fabrication of her sick mind and would at first chance tell the man they thought to be her husband of her wish to escape him.

She had seen much too often of late the short rein on Clifford's temper, and she had no wish to find out in which way he would punish her for speaking to someone about his being her abductor.

Pushing the door open wide, Sorrel stood in the companionway. Wiping her brow with a scented handkerchief, she started toward the deck.

Darkness seemed to envelope the world, she thought as she stood near the rail and looked out at the dark sea and even darker sky.

The crew scurried about as they had been doing since the day before. They all seemed ready for the clouds to unleash their mighty power and fury; the captain of the ship was not one to be caught unawares or unprepared.

Sorrel sighed aloud as she let her emerald eyes scan the sea spread out before her. She wished that the storm would come quickly, for she hoped that there would be no delay, and that they would rush on to Texas.

Something far in the distance caught Sorrel's eye, something lighter in color than the darkness all about her. At first she strained, thinking that she was seeing something she had conjured up, but as she kept her eyes focused ever in the same direction she soon realized that what she was seeing was not an illusion, but, in fact, a sail from another boat.

For some reason Sorrel began to feel the racing of her heart and the faster beating of her pulse. Why the sight of a boat in the far distance so enraptured her was beyond her understanding, but for some reason the feeling persisted, and when she felt a light tapping on her shoulder she jumped in surprise. Turning quickly about she looked into the face of their captain.

Looking sternly at the young woman before him the captain took hold of her arm. What was the lass about? he wondered. Was she contemplating jumping overboard? If so, he had told himself, he would put a quick stop to any such notion. "Young woman, you must step back some from the railing. My men and myself are far too busy to fish you out of the ocean if you fall overboard."

Sorrel smiled for a moment into the kindly old face, and for a second she thought that just perhaps she could tell him the circumstances of her being on board his ship, but then as quickly she realized that the reason for his concern was that he thought her unbalanced and quite capable of throwing herself over the rails of the ship.

"Where is your husband, Mrs. Sumter?" The

captain's eyes searched about looking for Clifford, so he could leave her in his care.

At the name Mrs. Sumter, Sorrel saw fire. "I am well capable of watching out for myself, sir." She spoke in the haughtiest tone that she had ever used. "And I will thank you if you will not address me by that name again." She once again turned her back on the man and looked out to sea.

The captain looked at her back for a full minute more before leaving her side. He could well see now that all that the young husband had said about the wife was true. What did she mean she did not wish to be called by her married name? Well, he thought, there was no understanding the mind of one who was not stable, and as far as he was concerned the best thing that could ever happen to this woman's husband would be for her to indeed throw herself over the railing and put a stop to the torture that she was putting him through.

For a few minutes Sorrel felt her blood boiling with her rage. Mrs. Sumter, indeed. She would like nothing more than to choke Clifford Sumter for putting her through this humiliation. But soon, as she felt the coolness of the wind, which had not blown in two days, beginning to stir against her cheek and through her hair, she began to feel a sense of peace coming over her.

The captain had not seen the sails of the ship that she had been watching and neither had anyone else aboard ship sounded the call that would tell everyone that a ship was fast approaching them. They were all too involved in the excitement that was stirring everyone aboard from the winds and the lightning that was now flashing through the dark sky.

Sorrel felt a deeper excitement beginning to grow as she realized that the other ship was indeed heading toward them and was not just another ship passing by in the distance. Of all the people aboard this ship she was the only one who knew this fact, and for some reason she felt the wish to keep her secret as long as possible.

But all too quickly this thought was swept from her as she heard the voice of the one she most hated. "You had best get out of this weather." It was a shout given from behind her, but loudly placed to be heard over the din of the noise from wind and thunder and lightning.

Sorrel's only reaction to his words was the slight turning of her head in his direction, but as quickly she turned back to the water.

"What are you about out here, anyway? The captain found me and told me of his concern that you not throw yourself overboard." Still with no answer from Sorrel he took hold of her arm, and as he did he also saw what she was looking at.

Before them was a large ship bearing down upon them with a mighty speed. "Why did you not call out and tell someone that a ship was approaching?" Clifford demanded. He shook her, not believing that she would not call out to the captain.

Calmly and with deliberate intent Sorrel spoke. "I thought that perhaps you had done your job so well of besmirching my name and that if I dared to tell someone of my discovery they would laugh me to scorn and put my words down as coming from an idiot." Her look dared him to rebuke her for her words.

All that she received, though, was the tightening of his grip upon her forearms. "Go down below to your cabin," he ground out between gritted teeth.

Sorrel was not about to budge, and with the lifting of her chin Clifford read her meaning.

"Go yourself, or I shall take you and lock you up again." Clifford's mind was frantic. From the speed with which the ship was gaining on them it was obvious that it had a purposeful intent, and to his mind only one person would chase this ship across the seas. Graylin Morgan in search of his daughter. He would have to keep her locked up. With the assurance that he had already married Sorrel and the captain's word backing him up, he was sure that he would be able to turn Graylin around. He would assure him of her safety, but as her husband he would have total say over whom she would be able to see, and she would not see Graylin Morgan until they arrived in Texas and he had the chance he needed to wed the girl. He had not thought until this moment that he would have to wed her before reaching his home, but the second he could he would talk the captain into marrying them here at sea. "Do as you're told." Thinking that it would be easier to take her himself he started to pull her toward the companionway, but he was pulled up short by the call from a lad who had just climbed above to test the strength of a mast. "Sail ho!"

Sorrel also heard and thought this to be her

reprieve. "I shall go to my cabin myself." She pulled her arms, releasing them.

For a second Clifford stood in indecision looking down at her and glancing at the men rushing to the rails and pointing toward the ship that was gaining on them with each moment.

"Go then. I shall be only a moment and shall be down to your cabin myself." He did not wish to take the time at just this moment, but he would soon have to lock her in the cabin if his suspicions about this ship were correct.

Sorrel fled the moment that her arm was released. Heading down the few steps to the companionway she slowed her steps as she rounded a corner. She knew that she could not go down to her cabin. Once she was in there Clifford would not let her be released. And for some overpowering reason she had to see what this other ship wanted.

On slow, quiet steps she turned and went back the way she had just come. Making sure that Clifford was no longer in sight she quickly made her way over to a group of crates stacked up at one end of the rail. Without a second thought she hid herself, squatting down behind the crates, making herself as small as possible.

It was not long before the excitement of voices came to her ears. She felt rather than heard the loud thumping of ship hitting on ship.

Mathew Danner stood with legs braced apart and arms akimbo as his dark blue eyes watched the ship before them. The lightning flashing all about them seemed to increase the pumping of his heart as he scanned the faces watching from the rail of the other ship.

He hoped that this time he had not approached the wrong vessel. Since leaving Richmond he had spotted two other ships and after chasing them both down and, to his mind, wasting precious time, he had not found his wife or the man who had abducted her. Mathew felt that his time was running out and the need to find Sorrel quickly was ever present in his mind.

Alex had been told that another ship had been sighted, but he had not as yet come from his cabin. Mathew waited now for the other man, the ship's captain near at hand directing his men on how best to approach the other ship.

As the ship that Mathew was on hit slightly against the other one, Mathew braced himself, ready to jump over to the other's deck as soon as the captain called over to the other ship's captain and gained permission.

Within moments their permission was forthcoming as Mathew's captain called loudly that they were friends and that they only wished some information. And when he added that he had an oversupply of coffee and sugar and that both would be given freely as a gift the older captain called in a friendly tone that his people would be more than willing to help with anything that they could.

With this Mathew jumped the small distance between the two ships before a plank could be stretched across.

Clifford stood to the side, watching all that was happening, and with a sigh of relief he realized that he must have been mistaken. If Graylin Morgan had been aboard this boat he would have been the one jumping aboard their ship, not this younger, large man with the angry set to his dark features.

"I am looking for a woman." Mathew's voice was loud and strong, carrying across the noise of both ships and the weather that was now starting to blow intensely and to bring large droplets of rain pummeling down upon their heads.

The captain who Mathew was addressing looked at him in astonishment. "I am afraid that your stopping my ship, then, has been in vain. I carry only a few passengers and no single women." The captain's voice also was loud and clear.

Mathew felt the let-down in his chest but he tried again. "I did not say that she was alone. A man is accompanying her. His name is Clifford Sumter." Mathew's eyes scanned the group of faces staring at him.

Clifford Sumter could not move as he heard the other's words and then as he saw Alex Gentry coming over the plank that had been erected he turned quickly and rushed down the companionway. He had to get to Sorrel's room and lock her door before she found out that her rescue was almost within sight. He would not let these men hired by her father find her, they would leave with the same information that he had planned to give her father.

Upon entering Sorrel's cabin Clifford's anger

reached a raging boil. Where was she? He looked in every space that she could be hiding in, but she was nowhere in the cabin. Hurrying out he ran down the hallway to his own cabin and hurriedly pulled out his pistol from his suitcase. He would not let anyone take Sorrel Morgan from him. She was his, promised since childhood, and he would let nothing in his way of getting her father's ranch.

With quick steps Clifford hurried back out to the main deck. His eyes darted quickly about the deck.

Sorrel could hear only a mass confusion as the rain beat down upon her and the thunder roared in her ears, and reluctantly she decided that it was time for her to leave this open space for a sheltered spot.

Clifford instantly saw the golden curls as she raised her head and pulled her sodden dress down as she started to the companionway. At this same instant Mathew's eyes were also pulled in her direction by some instinct.

As his blue eyes filled with the sight of her wet form he felt within him a strong mixture of love and desire mixed with a red-hot anger. If she was here then the man who had abducted her was here also. Taking a step in her direction he was brought up short by Alex's arm.

Sorrel also was drawn to look, as though an irresistible string pulled at her, in the direction that her husband was standing and, as she saw him, quick tears came to her emerald eyes. Without thinking she began to run toward him, but as quickly as Mathew had been she also was brought up short.

Mathew saw the man lay hold of his wife as he felt

his own arm being halted. With a powerful pull he got his arm free, but at the words hitting his ears he stilled.

"Have a care for the girl, Mathew," Alex called, so that only Mathew could hear. "Look at his jacket, it is bulging as though from a gun beneath his belt. He could well hurt Sorrel if what Cam Brash said about him is the truth, and we know already from what happened to both your dog and your Indian friend that he is well capable of anything."

Reason came to Mathew before he could bring harm to his wife. But the sight of her grasped tightly to the other's chest put a cold wedge in his heart. When she was safe he would give this foul blackguard his due.

Sorrel struggled within the arms that bound her, but Clifford seemed hardly aware of her futile attempts. Her gown was a sodden mess clinging to her at every move and making her even more of a prisoner in his grasp. "Let me go!" she called loudly.

Clifford did not realize that her struggle was to gain the side of her husband but thought that she had recognized Alex Gentry and now saw him as her help. "Shut your mouth or I shall shoot the man where he is standing," Clifford seethed at her until she quieted her struggling. "Now you will do as I bid you, like any good wife." He began to pull her toward the group of men beside the rail who stood waiting, the captain wanting to know why these other men were searching for Clifford Sumter's demented wife and all the crew from both ships watching for any kind of excitement.

Clifford pulled Sorrel to within only feet of the men and with an arrogant tilt to his jaw he looked first Alex and then Mathew full in the face. If he had been more observant he would have noticed the latter's angry features, but to him none of it had any meaning, only the outcome that was to suit him was of any importance. "Did I, sir, hear you right? You are looking for Sorrel Morgan?"

Alex was the first to answer. "You heard right."

Sorrel, afraid for the life of the man she loved, held her tongue but her eyes were her betrayer as they looked at that face that she had loved. It was all written in her emerald eyes, and Mathew pulled his fist in back of him to steady it and listened to Clifford, also afraid that the man might hurt the one that he loved.

"I know that you work for Mr. Morgan, so I shall tell you what you can do," Clifford started.

"And what is that?" Alex questioned as though on friendly terms.

"Why, sir, you will have to return to Mr. Morgan and tell him that his daughter is in excellent hands."

"You say, sir," Alex rejoined, playing with him as though enjoying the game.

"I certainly do. You see, you may tell Mr. Morgan that his daughter is now my wife."

The full force of his words hit at Mathew as though a brick hitting him full in the chest.

Alex felt the tension given off from the man next to him and quickly placed a hand upon his shoulder. "Is that right, sir?" He cocked a brow in the other direction, and with Clifford's affirmative nod he went on, "Then pray tell me, sir, what am I to tell the lady's other husband?" Alex now looked straight at Mathew. "This, sir, is Sorrel's husband." As soon as the words left his mouth Alex reached out and pulled Sorrel toward him and with this movement Mathew's body went into motion.

Clifford realized his mistake as he felt Sorrel being pulled from him, and then within seconds he felt the full force of the huge man's body being flung at him.

Mathew was incensed as his mind filled with the visions of Sorrel in this man's hands. His wife was not to be trifled with and he would show this bounder so, once and for all. His fists landed again and again in Clifford's face and stomach, sending him sprawling across the rain-soaked deck and at the feet of whomever stood by. Mathew went after him and again the pair rolled about the deck, Mathew ever on the attack and on the top, sending his balled fist over and over into the other's body.

Finally, though, thinking that he had finished with the job and wishing now for nothing more than to hold Sorrel in his arms, Mathew stood over the bent, crumpled form lying in a tight defensive ball and with a booming voice he spoke. "Never again lay hands to my wife. The next time I shall not be as lenient and I shall finish the job I have just started." Turning he made his way through the crowd of men who had been cheering him on and found his way to Sorrel and Alex.

Sorrel threw her body full force into Mathew's arms, her tears rolling down her cheeks as she wept over and over. "I knew that you would find me. I knew that I would not be parted from you for long!"

Tears also filled the large man's blue eyes as he bent down and placed kisses on the golden curls upon the head that he loved so much.

"You know me well, my love. For with you gone from me it was as though life had no meaning. I could not live without you at my side." He brought his mouth down to the tear-dampened one below his own and fully tasted of the joys that he had kept alive with each thought of her in her absence.

Alex left their side to allow them some moments of privacy and also to take the gun that was now plainly showing from Clifford's pants. He wanted nothing to go wrong now that they had found Sorrel Danner. He would also be assured by this good captain before he left his ship that this man would be taken the rest of the way to Texas as a prisoner for kidnapping. He turned once more and looked at the couple so enraptured with one another and he thought back to the days when he had thought himself worthy of this woman. He knew now that no other could be a fit mate for her, as no other woman but she could be a fit wife for Mathew. Mathew's tall, dark frame and Sorrel's golden form melted together in his eyes as though an artist had sculpted them. The rain swept down upon them and everyone rushed about putting everything into order.

"Never again will I let any harm befall you, my sweet," Mathew whispered as he looked into eyes that had the power to sweep away all pain and remembrance.

Sorrel fully trusted this man who was her husband,

as she had in the past, and with a small cry of love and desire she wrapped her arms about his neck as though their audience was of no importance, and pulled his adoring face toward her. "I love you, Mathew, with all that is in me. You are my support and my dreams, I care for naught but you."

Epilogue

Sorrel Morgan Danner's life had seemed to take a full turn since she had first left Texas. She was no longer the girl-woman of those days long past, she was now a complete woman.

With a small smile Sorrel turned in her chair and with gentle movements she watched her boys at their simple play. It was almost two years now since she had left the Cumberlands and had been rescued from Clifford Sumter. Her boys were now lovely, fun-loving children, taking most after their father. With a pat to the nearest one's dark curls she smiled a warning of quiet, her emerald eyes turning from the pair to the larger version of her children.

Mathew stood at the front of his church, behind the pulpit, his strong voice falling on the ears of the congregation. Graylin Morgan would be arriving this very day from Texas for a visit with his daughter and her family. He thought suddenly of his wife and let her image fill his mind, going back to the day she had first come into his life. His dark blue eyes went to the far side of the church where the Danner family pew was, and there sat his family.

Even his father, Justin, after the arrival of his bride and babies at Crescent Mist, had become a regular figure in the small wood church. He also sat in the family pew, his large chest swelling with his pride as he looked at his daughter-in-law and grandchildren. He had seemed to grow younger with the arrival of his son's family in his home. With a squeeze of the small hand lying next to him on the seat he looked at the young woman who now bore his last name. He could never have asked for a finer bride for his child—she was all that he could *ever* ask for for him.

Mathew's eyes left the pew that contained his family as he glimpsed at the front door a figure entering. With a smile he saw that Graylin Morgan had indeed arrived, and as he preached on to his congregation he watched the man approach the Danner family pew.

Sorrel's attention was upon her husband's words. "This is my commandment, that ye love one another, as I have loved you." Mathew's words filled the small building as he quoted the bold print of the book set before him resting upon the pulpit.

With the feel of a hand resting upon her shoulder Sorrel turned about and with some surprise met the smiling face of her father.

Trying not to disturb the congregation Graylin took the seat next to Sorrel, taking the twins up into his lap and kissing them fondly.

"Papa," Sorrel breathed, leaning over and kissing Graylin's cheek. "We did not expect you until later this afternoon," she whispered softly.

Graylin smiled at his only child, noticing the beauty that she seemed to abound with, her golden curls beneath a silver fur hat, tiny ringlets escaping about her face. Her delicate pink gown brought her coloring out to its fullest and Graylin could also discern that soon there would be more grandchildren for him to dangle upon his lap. Sorrel was plainly pregnant to any eye and, as her parent could quite easily see, she was far along, her gown having a definite protrusion about the middle. "My boat arrived a bit earlier than expected." he softly said, and then taking his eyes from his daughter he sat back and looked at his son-in-law.

Mathew Danner was indeed quite a man, he reflected. He could never have found a better mate for his child than the man standing before the gathered group of people. There was a strength within him that stood boldly forth, proclaiming to all that he was not bendable in his dealings and would stand firm in his beliefs. For a small moment he glimpsed the blue eyes resting upon his daughter, and in their depths, even from as far away as they were, he could feel the love that the young man had for his wife.

Turning, Graylin looked at his child, and in her eyes he glimpsed this same light of love as she looked at her husband. Here was no ordinary marriage. There was a bond here that could not be broken, a fusing together that was for all time and would withstand all obstacles. Though their past had had stormy moments, their future would be sealed by a love that few had known.

BESTSELLING ROMANCES BY JANELLE TAYLOR

SAVAGE ECSTASY (824, $3.50)
It was like lightning striking, the first time the Indian brave Gray Eagle looked into the eyes of the beautiful young settler Alisha. And from the moment he saw her, he knew that he must possess her—and make her his slave!

DEFIANT ECSTASY (931, $3.50)
When Gray Eagle returned to Fort Pierre's gates with his hundred warriors behind him, Alisha's heart skipped a beat: would Gray Eagle destroy her—or make his destiny her own?

FORBIDDEN ECSTASY (1014, $3.50)
Gray Eagle had promised Alisha his heart forever—nothing could keep him from her. But when Alisha woke to find her red-skinned lover gone, she felt abandoned and alone. Lost between two worlds, desperate and fearful of betrayal, Alisha hungered for the return of her FORBIDDEN ECSTASY.

BRAZEN ECSTASY (1133, $3.50)
When Alisha is swept down a raging river and out of her savage brave's life, Gray Eagle must rescue his love again. But Alisha has no memory of him at all. And as she fights to recall a past love, another white slave woman in their camp is fighting for Gray Eagle!

TENDER ECSTASY (1212, $3.75)
Bright Arrow is committed to kill every white he sees—until he sets his eyes on ravishing Rebecca. And fate demands that he capture her, torment her . . . and soar with her to the dizzying heights of TENDER ECSTASY!

Available wherever paperbacks are sold, or order direct from the Publisher. Send cover price plus 50¢ per copy for mailing and handling to Zebra Books, 475 Park Avenue South, New York, N.Y. 10016. DO NOT SEND CASH.

YOU WILL ALSO WANT TO
READ THESE CAPTIVATING HISTORICAL ROMANCES!

TEXAS FLAME (1013, $2.95)
by Catherine Creel
Amanda's journey west through an uncivilized haven of outlaws and Indians leads her to handsome Luke Cameron, as wild and untamed as the land itself, whose burning passion would consume her own!

RAPTURE'S RAGE (1121, $3.50)
by Bobbie Walton
Renee's dazzling looks brought her many suitors, but she only had eyes for Marshall. Though he vowed never to love a woman again—he couldn't deny his desire!

SAVAGE DESIRE (1120, $3.50)
by Constance O'Banyon
Mara knew it was fate that brought her and virile Tajarez together. But destiny would not allow them to savor the joys of love. They would only be bound by SAVAGE DESIRE.

TEXAS RAPTURE (1195, $3.50)
by Jalynn Friends
With her ripe, sensuous body and wicked green eyes, Laura Karell could only captivate Logan. How could he know that she was truly innocent? All Logan had to do was convince her of his love—and bring her the unrelenting joys of TEXAS RAPTURE.

Available wherever paperbacks are sold, or order direct from the Publisher. Send cover price plus 50¢ per copy for mailing and handling to Zebra Books, 475 Park Avenue South, New York, N.Y. 10016. DO NOT SEND CASH.